A SHAMELESS INVITATION . . .

As burning tears threatened to overflow her brimming eyes, she felt his hands on her shoulders, turning her back to face him.

"Don't—please don't. I've got to go."

Yet even as she said it, he drew her into his embrace, holding her close. And as his warm breath caressed her cheek, she twined her arms around his neck, inviting more.

"Stay with me tonight, Matt—please. Hold me tonight."

"Rena—"

"I don't want to die a spinster without ever knowing how it ought to be. Just for tonight, I want you to love me."

Her eyes were like great dark pools, drawing him in, threatening to drown him. He kicked the door shut behind him and kissed her again, damning tomorrow.

DANGEROUS

Anita Mills

A TOPAZ BOOK

TOPAZ
Published by the Penguin Group
Penguin Books USA Inc., 375 Hudson Street,
New York, New York 10014, U.S.A.
Penguin Books Ltd, 27 Wrights Lane,
London W8 5TZ, England
Penguin Books Australia Ltd, Ringwood,
Victoria, Australia
Penguin Books Canada Ltd, 10 Alcorn Avenue,
Toronto, Ontario, Canada M4V 3B2
Penguin Books (N.Z.) Ltd, 182–190 Wairau Road,
Auckland 10, New Zealand

Penguin Books Ltd, Registered Offices:
Harmondsworth, Middlesex, England

First published by Topaz, an imprint of Dutton Signet,
a division of Penguin Books USA Inc.

First Printing, September, 1996
10 9 8 7 6 5 4 3 2 1

Printed in the United States of America

To Larry,
I couldn't have done this one
without you.

Natchez on the Mississippi: May 20, 1874

Beyond the darkened gaming room, a slice of yellow light fanned out from a half-closed door. And on the other side of that door, four men sat sprawled beneath a single lantern suspended over the baize-covered table. For what seemed like an eternity there was no sound beyond the creak of the paddle wheel as it rhythmically churned through the dark river water. Finally, silver-haired Roland Fletcher sighed, then leaned forward. A large diamond on his little finger flashed in the flickering light as he pushed an assortment of chips and banknotes to the center of the table.

"I ought to call it quits," he said heavily, "but I guess I might as well see what you've got."

Beside him, a heavy-browed fellow considered his hand, then tossed it down. Reaching for the pocket watch that dangled from a thick gold fob, he flicked open the cover, then observed laconically, "Three-fifteen—time to turn in, I'd say." With that, he heaved a decidedly corpulent body from the chair and inclined his head slightly. "Good night, gentlemen. Giroux."

A derisive smile lifted the young Frenchman's perpetually petulant lips as the fat man left. "One should not play if one cannot afford to lose," he observed contemptuously. His pale eyes reflected the kerosene's yellow light as he turned his attention to the dark-haired gentleman across from him. "It is a privilege not to be taken lightly—*n'est ce pas, monsieur*?"

Matthew Morgan regarded him almost lazily for a moment, then smiled faintly. Straightening in his chair, he retrieved his wallet from beneath his perfectly tailored coat and counted out ten one-hundred-dollar banknotes as if the large sum meant nothing. "Call," he said abruptly.

Giroux's face flushed, betraying his excitement. "Ah, but you have made the grave mistake of challenging my skill with the cards, *messieurs,*" he announced smugly. "This hand—like this night—is mine, I think." Looking across the table, he grinned broadly now. "I have beaten you at your own business—*mais non,* Monsieur Morgan?"

"I said *I* was calling you, too," the gray-haired Fletcher reminded him. "I reckon I've got as big a stake in this as he does."

"Ah, but you have not the reputation," Giroux said softly, his eyes still on the elegant gentleman across from him. "You have the money, yes, but he is *Morgan*—he is the gambler."

"You going to show that hand or not?" Fletcher demanded testily.

"But of course. I have—" To prolong the moment of satisfaction, the young Frenchman held out his cards, but did not lay them down. "Ah, *messieurs*—it is so perfect, I think—so very perfect—"

"Damn you—just get on with it!" the older man snapped.

Enjoying himself enormously now, Giroux looked again to Matthew Morgan. "And you—are you in such a hurry to lose also, I wonder?" he murmured. "No, I shall make you think of what you have lost perhaps before I—" His words died on his lips as the gambler's fingers suddenly gripped his wrist, forcing his hand to the table. His whole body stiffening, Giroux's face reddened.

"Now, open those fingers real slowlike," Morgan said, his voice deceptively soft. Instead of complying, the Frenchman's hand closed around his cards, holding them so tightly they bent. The gambler sighed, then looked to Fletcher. "Since he's not going to make this easy, pry 'em loose."

The Frenchman's flush turned to a sick pallor. "*Monsieur*, this is an outrage!" he blustered when he found his voice. "I shall, of course, demand satisfaction for the insult! No one has *ever* called Philippe Giroux a cheat and lived! You will—"

"If you're honest, you'd want to show your cards," Morgan cut in curtly.

Fletcher hesitated. "Old Alexandre's not going to like this, Matt. And I don't know as I'd want the old man for an enemy—not in these parts, anyway."

Giroux seized on the notion like a drowning man hanging on to a life raft. "You'll pay for this, monsieur. When my father is done with you, you'll never—*ooowwwwww!*" he yelped as Morgan slammed his wrist hard against the edge of the table. His hand opened involuntarily, releasing the crumpled cards.

"Count 'em, Roland," Morgan ordered.

"Look, Matt, I don't—"

"How much are you down—twenty thousand?"

"Probably more than that." Sighing, Fletcher picked up the Frenchman's poker hand. As Giroux's gaze dropped to the floor, the older man looked up at Matt Morgan. "Wait a minute—there's only four here. All he's got—" He paused to lay each card down, then declared, "Two pairs—just treys and queens. All right, Philippe, where the hell's the other one?"

"On the floor," Morgan answered. Releasing Giroux's hand, he kept his eyes on the sullen Frenchman. "Well, do you want to move that foot, or do you want me to kick it out of the way?"

The young man's jaw worked visibly; then he seemed to accept the inevitable. With both of them watching him, he slowly lifted one highly polished black slipper, revealing the painted back of a card beneath it. Morgan bent down to retrieve the nine of spades, and laid it in the center of the table.

"Not exactly a thousand-dollar bet, is it, Philippe?" he murmured. "Not with Roland sitting there with those three nines you dealt him."

"How the hell did you know I had nines?" Fletcher demanded testily.

"I could see them in the lantern glass—and so could he. That's why he moved it a couple of hands back. When he couldn't beat the nines with two pair, and one of those matched the card up his sleeve, he decided to use it. Go on—show him the queen," Morgan prompted Giroux.

"But we've been playing with four queens all along," Fletcher protested. "I counted out the deck myself."

Morgan shrugged. "Sometimes four aren't enough for a cheat."

"I still don't get it. Why just hold an extra queen?"

"It's a high card, but it's not an ace—an ace draws too much attention. This way he could wait until he knew you and I didn't have one in the same suit as the one he was hiding—right, Philippe?"

"I don't know what you mean," the young man retorted. "I have nothing, *monsieur*—nothing! Go on, take your money," he growled at Fletcher.

The older man stared hard at him for a moment, then shook his head. "Maybe you'd better roll up that sleeve, and give me a look-see first. If Morgan's right, and you've been cheating, I figure you owe me a whole lot more than one pot."

Giroux's hand went to his other wrist as if he meant to unbutton the fancy frilled cuff. Then he rose suddenly, overturning the table. As the money and chips scattered over the carpet, he produced a small Colt Cloverleaf. Pointing the pocket pistol at Fletcher, he said nastily, "Now—which one of you killed the other, I wonder?"

"Don't be a fool, Philippe!" Fletcher snapped, trying to get the table off his lap. Before he could stand, the gun belched fire, and the older man clutched his bleeding shoulder. "You little French bastard," he choked out. "You'll never get—"

Half turning toward Morgan, Giroux cocked the

hammer again. As the shot went wide, he staggered backward several steps, a bewildered expression on his face. He dropped the little gun and grabbed the knife hilt protruding from his chest. He looked down, and saw the blood seeping between his fingers. Then he collapsed. By the time Morgan reached him, the light had left his pale eyes.

The gambler leaned down to retrieve his knife; then wiped it on Giroux's expensive silk coat. Sliding it back into the sheath beneath his shirtsleeve, he saw the corner of a card lying under Giroux's hand. Using the toe of his boot, he eased it into the open. It was the queen of diamonds.

"You all right?" he asked Fletcher over his shoulder.

"I'm bleeding like a stuck pig, but I'll live. Giroux?"

"Dead."

"Whoooee, but that was some lucky aim, son," the older man declared. "Another second, and he'd have plugged you, too."

"Yeah."

"You know, I've been around a long time," Fletcher went on, "but I've never seen anybody come up with a knife that fast—except maybe Jim Bowie, back when I was a kid. Where'd you learn to do that?"

"Around. I'd have gone for my gun, but the table was in the way," Morgan admitted.

Shaking his head, Fletcher stared down at Philippe's body. "Well, I'm glad the bastard's dead, but I'm afraid you've bought yourself some real trouble. Old Man Giroux won't care whether it was self-defense or not, you know. You won't get a fair trial around here."

"Yeah, I know."

"If you don't run, you'll hang."

The words were barely out of Fletcher's mouth before somebody started pounding on the outer room's door, shouting, "What's going on in there? Who's shooting?"

"Nobody!" Morgan yelled back. He looked to Roland Fletcher. "You'd better come with me."

"I can't. I can't swim, and I'm losing too much blood. Look, I owe you—when they come through that door, I'll cover your escape," the older man said quickly. "When all hell breaks loose, you get down on all fours and get going. And if I was you, I wouldn't stop anywhere before New Orleans."

"What about you?"

"I'm going to tell 'em I hit the floor and didn't see anything after Giroux shot me. Hell, everybody knows I don't carry a knife. But you go on and get out of here."

A crowd was gathering in the corridor, and the pounding and shouting grew louder, more determined. "Open up in there, or we'll break down the door!"

"If he can't find me, Alexandre Giroux'll turn on you," Morgan warned.

"I'll tell whatever lies I have to. Now, when all hell breaks loose, you just run for it. Here"—still holding his bleeding shoulder, Fletcher grabbed a wad of banknotes and held it out to Morgan—"you'd better take this. When the rest gets counted up, I'll keep your half safe for you." With his free hand, he unhooked the lantern. "They'll be breaching the outer door, and when they do, I'm throwing this out there. That ought to make 'em dance around while you're crawling past 'em, eh?"

"Looks like the best odds I'll get, anyway." Morgan stuffed the money in his pants. "Thanks."

"One—two—let's go, boys!" a loudmouth shouted. "Hit it!"

The wood splintered around the lock, and the heavy doors caved inward, sending a mass of men hurtling into the dark outer room, stumbling into the deserted tables. As they cursed, Fletcher hissed, "*Now,* boy! Get the hell out of here!"

As he said it, he reached around the half-closed door to fling the lantern across the room. "Over here!" he shouted. The glass shattered, spattering kerosene up the heavy velvet curtains, and spilling it onto the patterned carpet. Flame from the wick shot along the liquid trail with the speed of lightning. Then there was a loud *whoosh* as the drapery caught fire. Between stomping at the flames and beating burning pantlegs, the crowd disintegrated into pandemonium.

"Fire! Fire! Man the water pumps!"

"Jesus! What happened!"

"Fire! If we don't get it stopped, the boat'll burn!"

As they shouted and trampled each other frantically, Matthew Morgan crawled beneath a line of tables all the way to the corridor beyond the doorway. He'd barely gotten to his feet when he saw two men running toward him. He waved to them, yelling, "Place's on fire! Get help, or we're all going to burn up!"

They didn't have to be told twice. Unable to see much for the billowing smoke behind him, they turned and ran back toward the engine room, picking up the cry, "Fire! Fire!" Below deck, panicked people screamed in the darkness and scrambled for the stairs. By the time they fought their way up, the whole thing would be under control. But right now the commotion they were making would cover his escape.

When he reached the outer deck, it was deserted, and the river below was pitch-black beneath a cloudy, starless sky. He glanced toward the stern, trying to judge the riverboat's speed by the rhythm of the paddle wheel. He couldn't even see where the river met the bank, and once he was in the water, the boat's wake could confuse his sense of direction. Taking off his coat, he climbed onto the rail and sat there for a long moment, hoping to get a sense of where he had to go. The last thing he wanted to do was swim the Mississippi at night. The only thing worse would be swinging from the end of a hangman's rope.

"There's the bastard! He killed Giroux's boy—don't let him get away!"

They'd gotten through the smoke to the body, and he was all out of time. With one last, quick look downward into the murky, muddy river, he took a deep breath and jumped. He hit the water hard. Then the cold, wet darkness closed over him. His clothes sagged, dragging him downward. Working frantically, he shed his boots, and shot upward, gasping as he broke the river's surface. A spray of bullets hit the water a few feet in front of him, forcing him under again.

When it felt as though his lungs would burst, he came up, and forgetting everything else, he swam for his life toward Louisiana. It wasn't until he found the shallow water, stood up, then slogged his way onto the riverbank that he even thought about the occasional alligator sightings. But he was too exhausted to care as he lay down in the mud and tried to catch his breath. Finally, he forced his tired body onto its side and looked back across the river. Lights from the boat twinkled like stars in the blackness, reflecting off the water below, while wood and coal smoke mingled overhead.

Somewhere down the riverbank, something large croaked, then slithered almost silently into the water. That was enough to revive him. Still gasping, he heaved himself up. As soon as he could find somebody, he was going to get himself some clean clothes and a horse; then he was heading for Texas. But right now all he could do was walk inland, distancing himself from the Mississippi River as fast as his legs could carry him. For the first time in an otherwise lucky life, he was a wanted man.

Galveston, Texas: May 29, 1872

The sun overhead was already oppressively hot, the air damp and heavy, but to Verena Howard, the Texas port was one of the truly welcome sights of her life. After her harrowing, storm-tossed crossing from New Orleans, she understood exactly how Christopher Columbus felt when he kissed the ground on Hispanola. She had to fight an unladylike urge to run down the gangplank to the pier. Instead, she tugged the pointed hem of her jacket down at the waist, then smoothed it over her wrinkled walking skirt. She probably looked a complete fright, but right now she was beyond caring.

In the nine and a half days since she'd left home, she'd traveled through Pennsylvania, Ohio, Kentucky, Tennessee, Mississippi, and Louisiana, stopping at an assortment of dingy, dirty train stations at the most inconvenient hours to choke down the greasiest, most indigestible food she'd ever eaten. It had taken almost a week to reach New Orleans and anything truly edible. During an overnight stay there, she'd purchased a large wicker hamper and stocked it with pastries, fruit, and sandwiches, then looked forward to a pleasant cruise across the Gulf of Mexico, she recalled wryly.

And as the boat got under way, she'd sat on the deck, watching the sparkling expanse of blue-green water, smugly eating a delectable French pastry for breakfast, thinking this must surely be the best part of her journey. She hadn't had the slightest inkling then that four hours later, the sky'd be pitch-black at midday, the wind whipping the sea into a meringue of white-capped waves.

When the storm first hit, there'd been a general panic. Then as it wore on, the continuous roll of the ship sent seasick passengers and crew groping for every available washbasin. At first, she'd tried to help the frantic young mother and the two crying children sharing her cabin, but as her own nausea overwhelmed her, she'd abandoned them and crawled up to the deck, seeking air. Clinging to the railing with the storm raging around her, she'd alternated between heaving her insides up and praying for deliverance. By the time the awful sickness was over, she'd made herself a solemn promise to stay on land for the rest of her life.

Now that she dared think of it, her stomach was so empty that it hurt with hunger, making her first order of business on land a real meal. But until she debarked, she had to think of something else, she decided resolutely. Something like how foolish it had been to come to Texas.

In retrospect, she should have just written Mr. Hamer and told him to take care of everything for her. Instead, for reasons she herself didn't completely understand, she was traveling to the ends of the earth to bury a man she despised. And she wouldn't even get the chance to look him in the face, to ask him how he could abandon a wife and daughter, leaving them to depend upon parsimonious relations. Even now, she wanted to scream at him, asking why he'd disappeared, leaving no trace of his whereabouts until now. But he was dead, and now she'd probably never know the answer.

Maybe she ought to feel something, some small bit of gratitude for being remembered at the last, but she couldn't. No, a small, almost worthless Texas farm could never erase those bitter, painful years of watching her mother wait and hope for something that never happened. It had been like seeing a blooming flower slowly wither, then die—only it had taken years, not days. The doctors had called it a wasting sickness, but she'd always believe it started when her mother realized her "dearest Jack" had not only deserted his country, but his family also.

"You aren't quite as green around the gills as you were this morning," a male voice behind her observed. "Last time I saw you, you were hanging over that rail, looking like death'd be a blessing."

Startled, she half turned to look up into an arrestingly handsome face. Unlike the other men waiting, he was bareheaded, and unruly waves of coal-black hair strayed over his forehead, giving him a slightly reckless air. Below a straight nose that would have done a Roman god proud, a faintly amused smile lifted the corners of a sensuous mouth. Her mother's bitter, oft-repeated words of warning came instantly to mind.

Always remember it's the really handsome man of this world who is the most dangerous, for he has an instant advantage over a woman, and believe me, he is practiced in the art of using it. Having been cosseted and flattered by the female sex all of his life, he's learned early on to take a woman's heart lightly, worthy of little or nothing in exchange. You can never trust a handsome man.

And from the glint of the sun in his dark, almost black eyes to his easy, confident manner, this one definitely had to be dangerous. And the fact that he'd sought out the only unaccompanied female in sight certainly seemed proof of less than proper intentions.

"You have the advantage of me, sir," she said stiffly. "I'm afraid I don't recall the acquaintance."

"There isn't one—not yet, anyway," he acknowledged, his smile broadening. "But since we were both occupying the same rail this morning, I figured we had a little something in common."

"Really?" Lifting a disbelieving eyebrow, she fixed him with an icy stare. "Well, you were wrong, I'm afraid. Where I come from, no gentleman would ever accost a strange female."

Instead of backing down, he continued to regard her lazily. "Well, half right's better than all wrong, I guess."

The lout was impervious to the setdown. "I beg your pardon?" she said, almost without thinking.

"I don't claim to be a gentleman."

"So I have noted." To put a period to the unwanted conversation, she turned her attention to the dock.

"But to my way of thinking, you're a strange female, all right," he went on. "Where I come from, a woman takes a man's interest as a compliment."

"Even in the swamp, I doubt you'd find one who appreciated being described as 'green around the gills,' " she snapped.

"There aren't any swamps in Tennessee."

"Well, I'm not from Tennessee." Taking a step closer to the rail, she muttered under her breath, "I can't imagine what's taking so long."

"The boat's overloaded. When you've got Comanches, Kiowas, and Cheyennes on the warpath out west, almost everything gets shipped into Texas by water. Even people."

This time, she wasn't answering.

His gaze traveled over her, taking in the coil of rich chestnut hair, her finely sculpted profile, clear hazel eyes, faintly blushed porcelain skin. Then it dropped lower to the swell of well-rounded breasts demurely covered by the braid-trimmed basque jacket that nipped at her slender waist. When he'd first noticed her, he'd thought she was a pretty woman, and now he could see he hadn't done her justice. She was more than just pretty—she was probably the best-looking female west of the Mississippi.

With everything from her words to her manner telling him she wasn't interested in playing any flirting games, he knew he ought to back off, but she'd piqued his interest. He had the soul of a born gambler, and somewhere in the recesses of his mind, a perverse imp whispered, *The longer the odds, the bigger the payoff.*

"East coast," he guessed aloud. "Probably New York."

"No."

"Baltimore? Philadelphia? Boston?"

"Actually, it's Philadelphia," she said tersely.

She could have bit her tongue for taking the bait. Now he'd probably think that she was encouraging him, that she was just being coy. Well, it didn't matter what he thought, she reflected grimly. If she ever got off this steamer, she was heading straight for San Angelo, where she intended to settle Jack Howard's affairs as quickly as possible, and when that was done, she'd take the shortest way back to Pennsylvania.

"Philadelphia's a long way from here—a real long way for a pretty woman to travel alone," he observed. "They say Texas chews pretty women up and spits them out old and ugly. I guess that's a way of saying the menfolk out here are pretty rough on their women."

"Look, mister—"

His eye caught a stack of wooden crates stamped THOS. MCCREADY & SONS, AUSTIN, and the name seemed about as good as any. "McCready—Matthew McCready," he supplied, smiling. "But my friends call me Mac."

"All two of them?" she countered sweetly.

"Now that was uncalled for," he chided. "That was downright sassy."

"*Mister* McCready—"

"All right. I guess you're not much in the mood for funning," he conceded, sobering. "Look, I'm just as tired of this boat as you are, and I was just trying to pass a little time talking to you. I guess I'm the sassy one."

The new tack caught her by surprise. It sounded halfway like an apology. Verena cast a quick, suspicious glance upward, but the fellow's expression seemed utterly guileless, making her almost ashamed of herself. Since she'd never see him again, anyway, he couldn't possibly pose any danger to her peace of mind or to her person. She relaxed her guard.

"I'm too tired to talk sense to anyone, Mr. McCready. It seems like I've been traveling forever. I just don't feel very civil right now, I'm afraid."

"Uh-huh."

She couldn't tell if he was agreeing or disputing. "And I certainly wasn't expecting the rough crossing."

"It was kind of out of the ordinary," he allowed.

"Well, in any event, we shall be on dry land soon." There. She'd been civil enough to soothe her conscience. Feeling almost charitable now, she scanned the harbor, studying the other boats coming in. She'd had no idea anyplace named Galveston, Texas, could be this busy.

"Finishing school," he hazarded behind her.

"I beg your pardon?"

"You have that high-toned air they give girls in those places. I've seen it often enough to recognize it."

She half turned to face him again. "I'm afraid you're wrong in this case, Mr. McCready. It was the Bancroft Normal School."

"You're a teacher?" he asked incredulously.

"I was. Unfortunately," she admitted ruefully, "my first employment was in western Pennsylvania rather than in Philadelphia. It wasn't anything like I'd been led to expect—it was rather remote."

"I don't know as you're going to count Texas much of a gain—the state's got more rattlesnakes than people."

"Believe me, I don't intend to stay."

"Even so, it's not any place for a woman traveling alone. Texas is a far cry from Philadelphia."

"Yes, I've already noted a progressive decline of civilization since Cincinnati," she murmured dryly. "But I'm capable of taking care of myself, so you needn't worry for me."

"Carry a gun?" he asked bluntly.

"Of course not."

"Then you'd better get yourself one, and you'd better know how to use it."

"I'm not going that far—just to San Angelo."

"Just to San Angelo," he repeated, shaking his head.

"Yes, and as I'll just be settling my father's estate, I hardly think a gun will be necessary."

"Do you have any idea how far it is to San Angelo?" he asked curiously.

"No, but it doesn't matter, anyway. I have to get there."

"Well, it's a helluva long way from here—hell, it's further than San Antonio."

"There's no need to be vulgar about it, is there?" she countered stiffly.

"No." He took a deep breath, then exhaled it fully. "Look—I'm sorry about your father."

She looked down for a moment, then shook her head. "You don't have to be. I didn't know him very well."

"Then I guess I'm sorry for that."

"From all I've heard, I didn't miss much."

There was no mistaking the bitter edge in her voice. "But you came down, anyway," he reminded her.

"Yes."

"He left money."

"No." Annoyed again, she retorted, "As far as I know, he didn't have any. There's just a small farm near San Angelo, and I've already been told by the lawyer that it isn't worth much." She added almost defiantly, "However, I'm going to try selling it. Hopefully, the sale will cover at least part of the cost of the trip."

Out of the corner of his eye, he could see the first passengers going down the gangway, and he knew if he wanted to continue the game, he'd have to place his bet right now. "I don't know about you, but I'm downright hungry. I don't suppose you'd let me buy you a little breakfast on shore?" he asked casually.

"It wouldn't be proper." Then, realizing how ungrateful she sounded, she managed a smile. "I'm sorry, but it wouldn't."

"Galveston's pretty rough—maybe I could see you to your hotel?"

"Thank you, but no."

"Like I said, a lot can happen to a lone female out here."

She knew now that she'd not been mistaken—he was exactly what she'd suspected in the beginning, and it was high time she deterred him once and for all. "That won't be necessary, Mr. McCready. And I doubt Mr. Howard would appreciate it."

"Mr. Howard?"

"My husband," she lied. As his eyebrow quirked in disbelief, she threw herself into invention. "We would have traveled together, but I couldn't leave home." No, that sounded somewhat suspect. "Our daughter came down with the measles at the last minute, so it was agreed he'd go ahead," she added baldly. "One of us needed to be with her just then."

"Your husband. I see." Just as he was about to throw in his cards, he glanced down at her fingers. Following his gaze, she hastily plunged her left hand into a pocket in the seam of her walking skirt, but not before he'd seen there was no ring. One corner of his mouth twitched as he suppressed a smile. "Well, I'd say he's a damned lucky man. You can tell him I said so."

"I hardly think it would be appropriate." Relieved that the people in front of her were finally moving, she picked up her carpetbag. "Good day, Mr. McCready. Since I won't be seeing you again, I do hope you'll have a pleasant journey."

The stifled smile broke free and broadened. "I'm sure I will, Mrs. Howard," he murmured. "In fact, I'm looking forward to it."

As she walked down the gangplank toward solid ground, she congratulated herself on finding a perfect deterrent. Instead of a gun, she was going to purchase a wedding ring.

He stood at the rail, watching her until she disappeared into the milling crowd on shore. She was a fine-looking woman, all right, a real fine-looking woman. But she was in for a rude awakening if she thought those haughty manners were a defense against the cowboys and desperados she'd encounter in Texas. It would almost be worth the price of the ticket just to see her try. He'd been headed for the gaming hells of Helena, but he guessed it'd be just as easy to hide out in San Angelo. Maybe easier. Helena already had more than its share of hardcases and outlaws, and everybody knew it. From what he'd heard, there wasn't much of anything at San Angelo. As long as he could find himself a good poker game, he could stand a little peace and quiet.

Near San Angelo, Texas: May 29, 1874

"You hear that, Bob?" the man closest to the campfire asked nervously.

"What? That coyote?"

"You sure it's a coyote?"

"Yeah."

"There you go again, Frank," Lee Jackson complained. "Damned if you ain't seeing a Comanche behind every creosote bush. Makes me jumpy just being around you."

"That's damned near a full moon, ain't it?" Frank Beemer countered. "Hell, I don't have to be a Texan to know what that means. I tell you I don't like it when the moon's out like this."

"I just wish Gib'd get here, that's all," Charley Pierce muttered, tossing a broken twig into the fire. "We're all too damned jumpy, if you ask me."

"Yeah, but if Frank's gonna come out of his skin every time a damned coyote howls, I'd just as soon he wasn't here," Lee grumbled.

"Yeah." Bob Simmons turned to Frank Beemer.

"Look—I'm tellin' you there ain't an Injun in a hundred miles of here. Hell, we ain't but ten miles from Fort Concho!"

"I guess so," Beemer mumbled, obviously unconvinced. "I just want to get out of here with my hair on my head."

"And the gold," Lee Jackson reminded him. "I don't know about you, but I've spent damned near eight years of my life waitin' for my share of it, and I aim to get it."

"Yeah," Charley agreed. "I just wish the lyin' bastard hadn't died afore I got to him—I'd a killed him real slowlike. I'd a made him tell me what the hell he did with it. Then I'd a blown his brains out his ear."

"Yeah, well, he's already dead, and we ain't no closer to it than we were the day old Jack took off with the whole thing," Simmons reminded him.

"You think Gib's found out anything from that lawyer?" Beemer asked abruptly. "There's nothing as says he'll talk to Gib any better than to any of the rest of us."

"Gib's got his ways—and if they don't work, he's always got this," Jackson spoke up, patting his gun. "One way or another, if the old man knows anything, he'll spit it out."

"Mebbe so, but I don't like sitting out here waiting for the likes of Gib Hannah any more'n I liked letting Jack hold m'money. If I couldn't trust the major, how do I know I can trust anybody?"

"It was Gib that got wind of where Jack settled," Pierce pointed out. "He didn't have to tell any of us—

he could've just gone for the money and kept it to hisself."

"Yeah, but by the time he found Jack Howard, the bastard was already dead. You ever notice how many of us is gone now? I mean, there's Evans and Tate and Connors dying afore their time—and they ain't never found out what happened to McCormick, have they? And then the major—somebody shot 'im up and left 'im out for the coyotes to pick his bones plumb clean. I tell you I got a bad feelin', a real bad feelin', and I—" Beemer froze suddenly. "There it is again. You hear that, Bob? If that's a coyote, then where's the rest of the pack? I don't like this. No, sir, not a-tall."

"You want out, Frank?"

"You know better'n that, Bob," Beemer retorted. "I'm just sayin' something ain't on the up and up. It ain't right for a man to make it through the war, then die afore he's thirty, which is what happened to three of us—that's all I'm saying. And the major—hell, he was still in his prime, but he's dead, too. Murdered."

"Sounds like you're accusing somebody," Jackson muttered.

"No, I ain't. I'm just saying I got a bad feelin', that's all."

"Well, I wish to hell you'd keep it to yourself," Pierce grumbled. "Pretty soon you'll have us all jumpin' every time the damned coyotes howl."

"I just don't like the sound of it, that's all. Ever' time I hear it, it makes my skin crawl. Ain't you heard, Charley?—the damned Comanches can howl just like 'em!"

"Maybe it's a Tonk. You know what Tonks do to you,

Frank? They roast a man like he was a pig, and then they eat him. But I don't guess you got to worry none," Pierce gibed. "Way I hear it, Tonks don't eat no cowards."

"You ain't got no call to say that. No call at all!"

"Listen—!" Lee Jackson hissed loudly. "Horses!"

"I told you—it's goddamned Injuns!" Beemer grabbed his shotgun. "You all wasn't listen'n, but I told you!"

In the flickering yellow-orange light of the fire, Bob Simmons's face paled. "Holy Jesus!"

"Somebody's riding hell for leather—like all hell's after him! Kick out that fire, Lee—*now*!"

Even as Charley Pierce barked out the order, they heard the first volley of gunfire, and within seconds Gib Hannah was upon them. His tired horse stumbled into camp, then went to its knees, too winded to go on. He kept whipping it, trying to get it up, yelling to the other men, "Comanches! Must be a dozen of 'em! Don't let 'em stampede the horses! If they get the horses, we're done for!" Dragging his leg from beneath his downed mount's belly, he scrambled to his feet.

Frantic now, they all raced for the pickets as the small war party crested the hill. The Indians paused, silhouetted against the moonlit sky for several moments, taking stock of the panic below. Then the leader lifted his war lance, and they swooped downward, filling the night air with their war cries.

His heart pounding, Lee Jackson pulled a Henry rifle out of his saddle roll and started firing. "Mount up, men! We gotta make a run for the river! Come on!" As he swung up into his saddle, he picked a moving target, and his shot found its mark. A Comanche warrior jerked, then pitched forward over the neck of a piebald pony.

"You got 'im! All right—I'm right behind you, Corporal!" Simmons shouted.

"You're a couple of fools! You ain't seen an Injun pony go!" Pierce called out. "We got to stand 'em off—take the vinegar out of 'em!" Taking aim with his Sharps, he pulled the trigger. The buffalo gun boomed, and a whoop turned to a howl as an Indian fell from his wooden saddle. "Got one!" he shouted triumphantly. "Gib, cover me while I reload!"

It seemed like whooping Comanches were everywhere, circling the five Anglos, cutting off escape. Having nowhere to go, Jackson and Simmons dismounted and backed almost to the smouldering campfire, shielded by their horses. The other three men joined them for the desperate stand.

Pierce picked off another one; then dropped down to reload while Jackson kept a steady cover with the repeating Henry. Gib Hannah brought down a pinto, throwing its rider to the ground, and Frank Beemer killed the crawling Indian with a single shot from his old Army Colt. Standing again, Charley Pierce rested the heavy Sharps across his horse's back and took aim, sighting a heavily painted warrior. As the buffalo gun's report deafened Jackson, the .50 caliber bullet slammed into its target, lifting the Comanche clear out of his wooden saddle. At almost the same moment, Frank Beemer's body spun around, then fell forward into the coals.

Suddenly, the Indians broke off their attack and retreated out of the buffalo gun's deadly range. For what seemed like an eternity of nerves, the two sides faced each other until, finally, a pair of warriors raced downhill at breakneck speed, dropped almost to the ground to grab a fallen comrade, then sped off again. As they started back for another, Simmons drew a bead on one of them, but Gib Hannah grabbed his arm. "Save your bullets—they're carrying off their dead! They're going!"

"The damned bastards got Frank!"

"Yeah, and now there's just four of us! If they'll go, let 'em!"

Reluctantly, Bob Simmons lowered his rifle and watched as the Comanches retrieved the last of their fallen comrades. The war cries were keening death wails now, and as they disappeared over the hill, the eerie sound grew fainter. It wasn't until he could no longer hear it at all that he realized his forefinger was still tightly curled around his trigger. It took an effort to straighten it out.

Lee Jackson walked over to the smouldering fire, and leaned down. He didn't have to touch the body to know. "Frank's dead, Gib," he managed. "They plumb blew his face off. Poor bastard."

"Yeah." Coming closer, Hannah rolled the dead man over with his foot, then looked up at the others. "He never had enough guts to last, anyway."

"He lived through the war, Gib." Unable to stand the sight, Simmons kept his eyes on a stunted mesquite tree. "It don't seem right for a man to come through the war, then die like this."

"Yeah, but he was sure skeered of Injuns," Charley

Pierce observed. Settling his shoulders, he exhaled. "Well, I reckon we'd better get to burying him."

"No," Hannah said curtly.

"You can't just go off and leave him like this."

"Coyotes'll just dig him up before morning. Come on—we'd better head out."

The other three exchanged glances. Then Lee Jackson spoke up. "Hell, if the Injuns are gone, we might as well post a watch and get some sleep."

"We've got ground to cover—it's a helluva long way to Galveston."

"Galveston! What the hell's in Galveston?"

"Jack left a daughter, and she's on her way here to settle his affairs."

"But he didn't have nuthin' to settle!" Jackson protested.

"I never knew the major to say anything about having a girl," Simmons said, shaking his head.

"Well, he did, and she's coming down by way of New Orleans. And we're going to be there to welcome her to Texas," Hannah added significantly. "I figure she's coming for the gold."

"I ain't riding all the way to Galveston," Jackson grumbled. "I think we oughta wait right here."

"That's why you don't have anything, Lee," Hannah said impatiently. "You don't think."

"I don't get it."

Gib Hannah's expression was pained. "How many times have we been over Jack's place? If he'd buried a needle there, we'd have it."

"Yeah."

"There's nothing to say it's not between here and

Galveston. While he was running from us, Jack had hiding places all over Texas." Having said that, Hannah turned to the others. "If you're in this, you'll ride with me. Otherwise, you don't get your cut. Right now, there's four shares, but—"

"Four? What about Frank's?" Bob Simmons spoke up.

"What about it?"

"Well, he left a wife back in Illinois, you know. He was always writing to her."

Hannah shrugged. "She's nothing to me."

"Yeah, but—"

"Look, Bob, I don't care what you do about your quarter—or third, if that's the way it works out," Gib added, his eyes on Lee Jackson. "Way I look at it, when Frank took that bullet, he lost his share."

"All I was saying is I don't know why we got to go to Galveston if the girl's coming here," Jackson protested. "It ain't giving up my share to say it."

"And he just told you why," Pierce pointed out. "Jack left everything to the girl."

"Including our gold," Simmons reminded him.

"So the way I've got it figured," Hannah went on, "we get the girl, and we've got the money. Any more stupid questions before we hit the trail?"

"How do you know she ain't coming in at Indianola?" Pierce persisted. "Why don't we just go into 'Angelo and wait? Be a damned sight easier, you know. Hell, there's boats coming in both places all the time, so what's to say we don't miss her?"

"She wrote Hamer she was coming by Galveston the first or second so she can make it here for the probate

June tenth. I don't aim to wait until the tenth to find out what she knows."

"Hell, Gib—you ever see one of them boats? Folks is stampedin' off 'em like cattle!"

"Either you're in, or you're out, Charley."

Pierce paled, then smiled sickly. "You're funning, ain't you? I been in since the day we ambushed them Rebs, ain't I?"

"Leave 'im alone, Gib," Simmons muttered. "Ain't but four of us left nohow, and we started with ten, including the major and Billy McCormick. I reckon we all got a right to know what's goin' on, and I'd kinda like to know how we find Howard's girl myself, if you want the truth."

"She's traveling alone," Hannah snapped. "How many women you know fool enough to come out here alone? According to Hamer, she's about twenty, and her name's Verena Howard." Stopping to fumble in his pocket, he drew out a folded paper and tossed it at Bob Simmons. "Here's the letter she wrote him. Go on—read it."

"Ain't nobody can read at night, Gib."

The bigger man bent down to retrieve the paper, then returned it to his shirt pocket. "It says," he said evenly, "that she's five foot four, built slender, and she's got brown hair."

"How'd you get 'im to give you that?" Lee Jackson asked curiously.

"I told him I was a ranger."

"Jesus. He can check that out, Gib."

Hannah swung up into his saddle, then adjusted his

hat carefully before answering, "Not too much he can ask anybody in hell, is there?"

"But—"

Hannah's jaw tightened visibly. "I haven't spend eight years of my life hunting down Jack Howard for nothing, Lee." Using his knee, he turned his horse. "One way or another, I'm going to make his girl lead me to that gold," he declared grimly. "One way or another, I'm going to get it."

To conserve her dwindling dollars, Verena had walked the four blocks between Mrs. Harris's boarding house and Galveston's train station, and with each step, the carpetbag had seemed heavier and heavier. By the time she reached the ticket window, her carrying arm felt as if it had grown six inches. It was with a great deal of relief that she set the bag down and opened her purse at the ticket window.

"One passage to San Angelo, please," she told the clerk, taking out carefully folded banknotes.

"Eighteen dollars to Columbus," he said without looking up.

"Eighteen dollars just to Columbus?" Verena gasped. "Why, that's outrageous!"

"Yes'm." If he had a nickel for every time he'd heard the complaint, he'd own the railroad. "But if you're going to Columbus, you'll have to pay it."

"How much more to San Angelo? Perhaps you didn't hear me right, but I need to buy a ticket to San Angelo, which I understand is some distance past San Antonio. Columbus is this side of it, isn't it?"

"Yep, but that's as far as the train goes." Stamping her ticket, he repeated, "Eighteen dollars."

She didn't have to count her money to know she only had sixty-seven dollars left. And even with her return ticket from New Orleans to Philadelphia paid, she had a sinking feeling that unless she realized some money from her father's estate, she was going to be alone and broke in Texas. Right now, she could think of no worse place to be stranded. But she'd come this far, and she had to go on.

"I don't suppose you know how I'm supposed to get to San Angelo, do you?" she asked wearily.

"Have to take the stage at Columbus."

"For eighteen dollars, the train ought to go all the way. How much is it for the stage?"

The fellow shrugged. "Can't say—never took it. All I know is the stage line don't go that far neither. It stops 'bout twenty miles t'other side of San Antone."

It took a moment to digest that; then she declared positively, "You must be mistaken. I was given to understand that there was transportation all the way to El Paso, and I believe that's clear across this state."

"Well, there *used* to be a stage to El Paso, but it ain't running now. Injuns," he explained succinctly.

"Then just how am I supposed to get to San Angelo?" she demanded. "On horseback by myself?"

He shrugged again. "I reckon most folks try and get a ride on one of the mail wagons going across to the forts—San Angelo's right by Concho. If I was you, I'd go into Concho, then cross over the river there. Put you right in the place, what there is of it."

"I see." But she didn't. Where she came from, trains went everywhere, and it didn't seem possible that there wasn't even a stagecoach line out here. Indians didn't seem to be a sufficient explanation.

"You'll probably have to spend a few days in San Antone, though," the clerk added more kindly. "The mail don't go out but two or three times a week, and that's if the weather's good. If it ain't, it don't go that often."

"But I'd hoped to be there by Tuesday next. I have an appointment," she said desperately. "Surely—I mean, there's got to be another way."

"No'm. Mebbe you'll make it—and mebbe you won't," he observed philosophically. "Like I said, it depends on the weather—and the damned heathen Comanches. Seems like they're always stirring up something out there."

"I thought they didn't come that close to settlements."

"Humph! And why d'you think there's forts out there? Why, them Comanches has even been here, which is about as far east as a body can go. And this is a real town, which San Angelo ain't."

"You're just trying to scare a Yankee," she decided.

"No'm. Them Comanches does it for us. Why, they don't think nothing of raiding all the way down into Mexico. Like I was saying, they been right here afore the war."

"Well, that was quite some time ago," she said, reassuring herself.

"Ma'am, the U.S. government just got done building Concho, and it sure wasn't so's the Army could watch rustlers," he countered. "And like I said, San Angelo's right smack across the river there."

"Then I'd think it'd be safe."

"Well, it ain't. Them Comanches has been known to steal U.S. government horses right out of the pens—right under the soldiers' noses. You know, if I was you, I wouldn't be going out there by myself. Ain't no place for a lady, no place at all."

"Yes, well, I don't have much choice." Carefully counting out the money, she slid it under the window. "I still think this amounts to legalized robbery," she muttered.

"It ain't me as sets the fares. I just take 'em," he reminded her, wetting his thumb with spit before he deftly recounted the bills. Satisfied, he stamped her ticket and pushed it toward her. "Train'll be in any time now." Looking past her, he beckoned to the incredibly filthy fellow in line behind her. "How far you going this time, Bill?"

The man spat tobacco juice onto the stained floor, just missing Verena's foot. "Spanish Bend." As she pulled her skirt hem back, he grinned broadly, and the smell of whiskey on his breath was almost overwhelming. "Well, now, if you ain't just about the purtiest little thing this side of Nawlins, I'm a—"

"Be seven dollars, Billy," the ticket agent said, cutting him off. "You got seven dollars left?"

"Yeah, won big last night over at Dub's Place." The cowboy fumbled in a bulging pocket on his stained flannel shirt, then produced a big wad of bills. "If

Trainor wasn't expectin' me, I coulda had me a real good time, huh? I coulda got me a real fancy piece, and—"

"You're drunk, Billy," the clerk interrupted him again. "Just give me the seven dollars, then go sit alongside that wall."

"Ain't had but half a bottle," the cowboy mumbled in protest.

"Well, I'd say it was too much."

"Yeah." Bill half turned to look for Verena. "Hey, where'd that purty little thang go? I was wantin' to get acquainted," he complained loudly.

"If you don't get that seven dollars through this window, you ain't going nowhere," the clerk reminded him.

Clutching her ticket in one gloved hand and her carpetbag in the other, Verena looked for another woman, but the only one she saw was a worn-out, shapeless creature with five pinch-faced children and a dour-looking husband. Casting a quick look back at the ticket window, Verena then hastily made her way to one of the pine benches along the farthest wall, hoping the drunken cowboy wouldn't find her. She sat down, leaned back, and closed her eyes.

To satisfy her curiosity about a man she'd despised, she'd come to the end of the earth, and it was still a long way to San Angelo. If she'd had any sense, she'd have stayed home and left everything to Mr. Hamer. Instead, she was alone, nearly broke, and exposed to the attentions of the worst sort of riffraff anywhere. And just now she felt terribly vulnerable, as if she were at the mercy of all these uncouth strangers.

"Well, well—if it isn't Mrs. Howard," the oddly familiar voice said softly. "World's getting smaller all the time."

Her eyes flew open, and she sat up. "What in the world are you doing here, Mr. McCready?" she demanded irritably.

"Is that any way to greet a fellow traveler?" he countered, feigning injury.

It wasn't, but she was too out of sorts to apologize. Instead, she asked bluntly, "Where are you going?"

Undaunted by the chilly reception, he dropped his tall frame down to the bench beside her and placed his new black felt hat over his knee. "I see you found your wedding ring," he murmured.

She glanced down at the plain gold band on her left hand. "It wasn't missing."

"You weren't wearing it on the *Norfolk Star*."

"You don't miss much, do you?" she muttered sourly.

"In my business, I can't afford to."

She considered retreating behind a wall of icy silence, but she'd already discovered he was beyond discouraging. She sighed. "And just what *is* your business, Mr. McCready?"

"Poker."

Uncertain she'd heard quite right, she repeated, "Poker? But that's a game, isn't it? Is that all you do? I mean, you *surely* don't do that for a living?"

"Uh-huh."

"I can't imagine such a thing."

"Not too many things out here a man can do without getting himself dirty, and I've got a real aversion to dirt—I can't abide dirty clothes or dirty fingernails," he admitted, smiling.

Against her better judgment, she allowed herself to look at him. Aside from the devilish light in his dark eyes, he'd obviously cultivated the look if not the manners of a gentleman. Everything from the cut of his black coat and pants, the wine brocade waistcoat with its gold watch fob showing, the impeccable white shirt with the black silk tie, to his well-polished boots contributed to an impression of studied elegance. The hand resting on his knee matched the rest of him—long, tapered fingers with clean, well-buffed nails—and yet there was a decided masculinity to it. Just like his face.

"I see," she managed.

"When about all a man's got are quick hands and a steady nerve, he's either a gunfighter or a gambler," he added. "I found gambling a whole lot easier than killing."

"Yes, of course," she agreed faintly.

"And I'm usually pretty good at sizing up a man—or a woman." He looked straight into her eyes, his smile broadening. "Where *is* Mr. Howard, by the way?"

The way he said it brought up her guard. "I beg your pardon?"

"Your husband," he reminded her. "I don't see the lucky fellow."

"I fail to see that it's any of your business, Mr. McCready," she responded stiffly.

"The way I've got it figured, he's your defense against importunity."

"I don't know what you mean by that, but I can assure you—"

"Importunity?" His smile spread into an outright grin, enhancing his handsomeness. "It's annoyance—troublesome persistence."

"I *know* what the word means," she snapped, "and you convey it perfectly."

"Well, *is* there a Mr. Howard? Or am I right about that ring?"

"Of course, there's a Mr. Howard, sir," she retorted. As one of his eyebrows lifted, she felt compelled to defend the lie. "Look, my hands swell sometimes when I travel, that's all, so I keep my wedding ring in my purse. And—and because I was late arriving, he went on ahead to confer with Papa's lawyer in San Angelo. He wanted to make sure that at least one of us would be present for the probate hearing. He left a message for me at Mrs. Harris's boarding house, if you must persist in prying."

He knew she was lying, but he couldn't blame her, not out here. Nor could he resist needling her a little. "You know, if I were Howard, I sure as hell wouldn't go off and leave my wife alone in a place like this. I'd be worried about her safety."

"Well, you aren't." Feeling utterly foolish for responding at all, she took a deep breath and exhaled it fully. "So you needn't concern yourself, Mr. McCready."

"I was just thinking maybe you'd be better off sharing a seat with somebody you know." He nodded toward where the man called Bill had joined a raucous bunch of cowboys. They were loud, profane, and obviously drunk. "At least I had a bath this morning."

"So you're going to San Antonio."

"Uh-huh."

"I might have known."

"The way I look at it, we're both strangers to Texas, and we both could use a little company on the trip."

"We're both strangers to each other," she declared flatly. "And, speaking quite frankly, I prefer to leave it that way. I'm not the sort of woman who dallies behind her husband's back, Mr. McCready. Now, if you'll excuse me—"

"You know, you're a lot like some of those shiny red apples—real pretty to look at, but downright sour on the inside," he complained.

"I'm not a fool," she shot back. "You obviously saw a woman alone, and you tried to take advantage of the situation."

"I was sort of hoping the advantage would be mutual," he said, rising. "I thought maybe we could help each other out, but I guess not."

"I assure you I am not the weak, defenseless creature you think I am. I don't need the sort of help you are offering."

Towering over her, he looked down for a moment, his dark eyes mocking her. "Drunk cowboys don't look for wedding rings. I'd keep that in mind, if I were you."

"Good day, Mr. McCready."

He put his black felt hat on with one hand, then tipped it back slightly, exposing a fringe of black hair. "Well, if you change your mind, I'll be at the back of the car—I always like to see what's going on in front of me."

As he walked toward the platform outside, she was both relieved and annoyed. Yet as her mind repeated his words, she was momentarily intrigued by them. *I thought maybe we could help each other out. . . .* Now that she actually thought about it, they seemed more than a little odd to her. No, she was being ridiculous, trying to see something that wasn't there. What he'd really wanted was pretty obvious.

"Train's coming!" the clerk called out. "Passengers outside!"

She grabbed her carpetbag and headed for the waiting passenger car. As she crossed the station's threshold onto the platform, another large splat of tobacco juice just missed her foot. Looking up, she realized she was facing the group McCready had pointed out, and they all had the look of starving men drooling over a big beefsteak. She was wearing at least three layers of clothing, but as their eyes raked over her, she felt downright naked.

"Whooeee, Billy, would you look at that! If that little filly ain't a sight for m'eyes, I don't know what is!" one of them declared loudly. For emphasis, he punched the cowboy she'd seen at the ticket counter. "Hey, little lady, what're you doing out here all alone?" he asked, coming closer. When she didn't answer, he moved in front of her, blocking her way. "Whatsa matter, honey—cat got your purty little tongue? Wanna have some of this?" He waved a half-empty whiskey bottle under her nose. "I'd give ya some fer a little kissin'."

"No, thank you." Her heart pounding, she spoke with a calmness she didn't feel. "Please, if you'll stand aside, I've got to find my husband. He—he's already aboard."

The man guffawed, then turned back to the others. "You hear that? She even talks purty!"

"Hey, you wait your turn, Hank. It was me that saw her first!" Billy said, pushing him out of the way. "I reckon I got first claim. Ain't that right, little lady?" He reached a dirty paw out, touching the collar of her waistcoat. "What'd you say? How about you'n me gettin' a room, huh? Wanna see my money? I got money—real money."

"Trainor won't like it if you're late, Billy," another cowboy reminded him.

"Hell, he can damned sure wait. I got m'eye on—"

As Verena backed away, the bigger man grabbed him, shoving him aside, and Billy swung on him. Taking advantage of the ensuing skirmish, Verena gripped her carpetbag with both hands and ducked past both of them. Behind her, the others brayed like a bunch of donkeys.

Unnerved now, she thrust the bag at the porter and grabbed the railing, pulling herself up the steps without the customary help. Pressing a dime quickly into the Negro's hand, she yanked open the door to the passenger compartment, then froze in dismay.

The car was not only packed, but most of the men crowded in the aisle looked as rough as those outside. As the stench of hot, sweaty bodies assaulted her nose, the drunks who'd just accosted her came up behind her. Catching her arm, the burly one breathed whiskey over her shoulder.

"Ain't no need fer you to go getting uppity with Big Al Thompson, girlie," he said thickly. "Mebbe if I was to tell you I got fifty dollars in my pocket, mebbe you could be real nice to me, huh?"

"You're drunk, mister," she told him coldly.

As she jerked away from him, the train lurched into motion, and she stumbled, almost falling. Frightened, she pushed her way through the mass of smelly bodies, enduring pinches and leers in a desperate attempt to reach the back of the car. Behind her, the big cowboy was gaining on her, shouting obscenities at everybody in his path.

She spied McCready in the last seat, and pushing a fat fellow out of the way, she lunged for the gambler. As he looked up, she stumbled over his outstretched leg, then threw herself into the seat between him and the window.

"I've changed my mind," she gasped.

"I had a notion you might," he murmured, moving his booted foot to make room for her. "I kept a seat open, just in case."

"Thank you," she mumbled, keeping her head down.

Out of the corner of his eye, he saw the cowboy, and sighed. "You know, you'd have made this a whole lot easier on both of us if you'd come with me in the first place."

"Just don't let him find me."

"The hairy Lothario?"

"It's not funny. You don't see him, do you?"

"Uh-huh." He turned slightly to face the aisle. "It's all right—just stay back out of the way and don't say anything."

She didn't need to be told twice. Grasping his left

arm, she shrank behind his shoulder and tried to slide down in the seat. She was too late.

The drunken cowpuncher reeled, then reached across the gambler to grab her. His big, beefy hand caught her by her hair, and he tried to jerk her to her feet, but she held on to McCready. "Enough of this," he growled. "Ain't no fancy bit going to—" His words froze on his lips, and he suddenly looked almost sober. His grip on her went slack, and his leer changed to an almost blank bewilderment. Finally, he found his voice.

"Who th' hell're you—?"

"Her husband."

As the import of that hit him, the boozy flush faded from Thompson's face. He looked to Verena. "That right? You belong to him?"

"Yes," she managed.

Her gaze dropped, and she saw the gun in the gambler's hand. It was cocked and aimed at Al Thompson's breastbone, and McCready's finger was crooked around the trigger, tensed and ready.

"Either turn her loose or say your prayers," the gambler said evenly. For emphasis, he jabbed the gun barrel into the cowboy's gut. "Which is it?"

"I didn't mean nothin', I swear it, mister. I just thought—"

"I'd be real careful what I said right now," McCready warned him. "She's got a temper."

Sweat pouring from his forehead, Thompson took a step backward, his hands out, palms up. "Hey now—I ain't got no hard feelin's," he protested. "I didn't know—I didn't. I thought she was all by herself, I swear."

"That's not good enough," the gambler responded softly.

The big man passed his tongue over dry lips. "I didn't mean nothin'—honest."

"You still owe my wife an apology."

"I'm sorry, ma'am—right sorry," Thompson said hastily. "Didn't know—"

"Keep going."

"Listen, I—" The cowboy's temper started to flare, then cooled the instant he felt the gun touch his belly again. He swallowed hard. "Look, I ain't got nothin' more to say. I done said I was sorry! What more d'you want outta me?"

"Repentance."

"Jesus." Groping for words, Thompson tried again. "Well, it damned sure won't happen again, ma'am—I swear it," he promised.

"Louder. I don't think she can hear you."

Casting an almost desperate glance at Verena, the cowboy cleared his throat, then raised his voice. "It ain't going to happen again, I said. I just thought you was—"

"Careful now, you don't want to get her dander up," McCready reminded him. Inclining his head slightly toward Verena, he murmured wryly, "It's a little short on eloquence, but I think it's about as good as you're going to get. But if you're satisfied, I'll let him go. Otherwise, I'll pull the trigger, and then we'll be getting off at the next stop to buy clean clothes."

It seemed as if half the occupants of the car were turned around, watching them. Acutely embarrassed now, she wanted to hide, but there was no escape from the smirks and knowing smiles. "Please—I just don't want any trouble," she said wearily. "Just tell him to go away somewhere and stay there."

"Well, it looks you're lucky this time, cowboy. You heard her—go on."

Thompson didn't have to be told twice. Heedless of the packed aisle behind him, he backed his way into the crush and disappeared from sight. At the far end of the coach, his friends could be heard ridiculing him, and then a drunken fight broke out. Finally, another group of ruffians started cracking heads with gun barrels until Thompson's bunch settled down.

McCready waited until it was over to carefully ease the Colt's hammer down. Rotating the cylinder until the hammer rested on an empty chamber, he returned the revolver to its holster. Beside him, Verena Howard gave an audible sigh of relief.

"Thank you," she whispered, removing her hand from his arm. Looking down the aisle, she shook her head. "What awful, vile people—they're utterly uncivilized."

"No. They just don't get into town very often, and when they do, they make up for it by raising a whole lot of hell. The West's full of cowboys just like 'em."

Still trying to regain her composure, she swallowed. "I must say you were rather calm about it."

"I was expecting it. It was bound to happen."

"I beg your pardon?"

"Out here, anytime you throw a woman between fifteen and fifty, especially a pretty one, in front of a bunch of drunks, the odds are at least seven to one that's there's going to be trouble. This isn't Philadelphia, you know—there's a whole different set of rules for surviving."

"Now, wait just a minute—*surely* you don't think that I—that I *encouraged* the lout!"

"Rule Number One," he went on, cutting her off, "you'd better avoid anybody who smells like whiskey and cow chips at the same time—anything in a petticoat's going to give him ideas your mama never mentioned. He'll have the mating instincts of a bull buffalo at the first whiff of that perfume you're wearing."

"Mister McCready, I hardly think this is appropriate. I can assure you—"

"I'm not done yet. Rule Number Two, if you're going to travel alone, you need more than a wedding ring on your finger. Fellas like Thompson stop looking about eight or nine inches south of your chin. When the train pulls in to the station for lunch, you'd better get yourself a hatpin four or five inches long. Believe me, it'll do you a whole lot more good than that withering look."

"I have a hatpin," she retorted. "I just couldn't get to it."

"Even better, get a gun and learn how to use it. Nothing like about forty grains of lead in the gut to cool a man right down."

"I thought you didn't believe in killing."

"You don't listen very well, do you? I just said gambling was easier."

"Well, I'm sure I couldn't kill anybody, no matter what the circumstance."

"Don't tell me I've saddled myself with a Quaker," he murmured, looking heavenward.

"No, of course not."

"Good. The Quakers' views on Comanches aren't exactly appreciated down here—in fact, you could say they're downright unpopular."

"Well, I do think we've behaved abominably to the Indians."

"In Texas, you'd better keep that to yourself. Now, where was I?"

"I don't have the least notion, nor do I care."

"It was Rule Number Three," he decided, "and that's to never ever walk into a bunch of drunks. For one thing, a man doesn't think clearly when he's drunk, and he does a lot of things he wouldn't do sober. For another, he doesn't hear anything he doesn't want to, and 'No' sounds like an invitation."

"Are you *quite* through?" she demanded angrily. "For the last time—" Suddenly noticing that the man in front had turned around to look at her, she glowered until he retreated, then she lowered her voice. "Listen, I don't care what you think, Mr. McCready," she whispered furiously, "but I'm going to tell you again that I did absolutely nothing to encourage that oaf—and if you think otherwise, he's not the only peabrain on this train." Her piece said, she deliberately turned her attention to her window.

"I'll say one thing—what you lack in sense, you make up for in spirit."

"If that's your notion of a compliment, you can keep it to yourself," she snapped, refusing to look at him.

"Look, I'm just trying to keep you from getting yourself hurt and me killed." Reaching out, he possessed her hand with warm, surprisingly strong fingers.

"If it's all the same to you, I'd rather not spend the honeymoon defending your honor." Feeling her body tense beside his, he leaned closer to whisper low, "So which is it—are we calling ourselves the Howards or are we the McCreadys?"

She could feel her whole face go hot, but to her chagrin, she knew he had her cornered. If she created a scene and tried to crawl over him to the aisle, she'd be jumping from the frying pan into the fire. Infuriated by his altogether smug self-assurance, she forgot her earlier gratitude entirely. As his warm breath sent shivers down her spine, her free hand loosened the drawstring on her purse. Forcing what she hoped was a dazzling smile, she jabbed her hatpin into his thigh.

Recoiling at the sudden pain, he looked down in disbelief at the pearl-headed pin, then up at her. "What the devil was that for?"

"You ought to be pleased," she murmured. "That was your Rule Number Two, I believe, wasn't it?" An almost unholy light danced in her hazel eyes as she added sweetly, "Sometimes one's advice comes back to haunt one, doesn't it?"

He met her gaze reproachfully for a long moment, then his face broke into a rueful grin. "On second thought, maybe you'd better forget the rest of that one."

"You mean your recommendation that I purchase a gun?" she asked, feigning innocence.

"Yeah. I think my Army Colt's probably enough for both of us." He rubbed his thigh, trying to take the sting out of it. "You sure don't stay thankful very long, do you?"

"Well, if you'd spared the lecture and kept your

hands to yourself, I'm sure I could have maintained a state of charity considerably longer. But once you cross the bounds of propriety, to my way of thinking, you don't really seem much different from that cowboy."

"Now that was downright cruel."

"Perhaps, but you deserved it."

"Before you stabbed me, I was just about to make you a little proposition."

"So I gathered—and I didn't want to hear it."

"Look—" Taking care to remove the hatpin from her hand first, he moved closer. As she stiffened, he murmured low, for her ear alone, "Don't say anything until you hear me out, will you? Just listen for once. Then if you're still determined to go on by yourself, I'll get off at the next stop."

The images of Big Al Thompson and his friend Billy flitted through her mind momentarily, and the prospect of facing them alone was utterly daunting. Reluctantly, she held her tongue just long enough to hear the first part of his suggestion.

"If we travel together, you've got a better chance of getting to San Angelo in one piece. As my wife—" Before he could finish the thought, she cut him off.

"Mr. McCready—"

"If you pretend to be my wife, you get the protection of a husband," he pointed out.

"And just what do you expect to get in return? I'm not quite as green as you think, sir."

"Shhhh. Listen, all I'm asking for is the appearance of respectability, nothing more. And that wedding ring is a whole lot more convincing when you've got a husband to go with it."

"Yes, but—"

"Look, there's two kinds of women in this world, and believe me, I can tell the difference. As hard as it is to say it, and as hard as it is for you to believe it, I'm not going to cross the line with you."

"Then why would you want to do this?" she countered suspiciously. "We don't even know each other. It doesn't make any sense."

"I've got my reasons, and they don't have anything to do with you. Think it over. The deal's all yours, if you want to take it." With that, he eased back into his own seat, then handed her her hatpin. "You'd better keep this handy," he told her.

"Believe me, I will."

Abruptly, he stood up and stepped into the crowded aisle. "I'll be back."

Alarmed, she couldn't help asking, "Where are you going?" Then, as the obvious occurred to her, she turned beet red. "That's all right—I don't need to know."

"I see a game going," he answered anyway. "And like I said, poker's my trade."

"Oh—yes, of course."

Still, as he disappeared from sight, she felt uneasy. Forcing her attention to the window, she studied the green countryside with foreboding. She shouldn't have come, she knew that now. But she had. And right now all she had was a brief, baffling acquaintance with a handsome gambler to sustain her all the way to San Angelo. She sat there for a long time, wondering about why he'd followed her. A platonic concern for her safety just didn't seem reasonable. No, he was hiding something, she was certain of it. Closing her eyes, she heard her mother's words ringing in her ears again.

You can never trust a handsome man.

When he finally came back, he dropped down beside her, murmuring, "Like taking candy from a baby." When she looked up, startled, he grinned. "Looks like your friend Billy's paying for our honeymoon trip," he added, tossing a wad of crumpled banknotes into her lap. "Ought to be just about a hundred dollars there."

A hundred dollars. It was enough to answer her prayers. But she couldn't keep any of it. She forced herself to hand the money back to him.

"I can't take your winnings, Mr. McCready."

"Why not? The way I figure it, you've got a stake in that. Billy and Big Al went out of their way to make amends to me." His gaze met hers, and his expression sobered. "You've made up your mind."

"Yes."

She didn't have to tell him—he could see the answer in her eyes. He sighed. "All right, but I can't get off until we're past Spanish Bend. Otherwise, our cowboy friends might get suspicious."

"Thank you."

Leaning back, he placed his hat on his head, then slid it forward to shade his eyes. "You might want to get a nap in," he murmured. "After Eagle Lake, you'll be sitting up with that hatpin in your hand."

"Eagle Lake?"

"It's the first stop after Spanish Bend."

Discreetly fanning her damp legs with her petticoat, Verena silently envied McCready. Seemingly oblivious to the noise and the miserably hot, stifling air within the passenger car, he slept like a baby, while she kept shifting her position, trying to find any comfort at all in her cramped seat.

The door opened behind her, and a man lurched past her, leaving a steamy cloud of strong odor to follow him. The circles of sweat under the arms of his filthy shirt almost met the one on the back of it. The thought crossed her mind that if those dingy stations where the train stopped for food had bathhouses behind them, the journey would be considerably more bearable. But, she had to concede, those needing the service the most would probably be the least likely to make use of it. Apparently when they crossed the Texas border, men stopped washing and changing their clothes. The only exception she'd seen so far had been Mac McCready.

Ironically, that was another thing she was beginning to resent about the man. While she wilted like a dying flower, there wasn't even a trickle of sweat coming from beneath that hat brim. Despite a few creases in his coat and trousers, he looked nearly as elegant as he had when he'd boarded, as if he could step down from the railroad coach and go directly on with his business. It just wasn't fair.

In fact, there wasn't anything about him that was fair. By some misplaced grace of God or inheritance, he'd been given all of the obvious advantages. The face and form of one of those Greek statues. That thick, slightly waving black hair and those dark, dark eyes. Looks, grace, intellect, and even a disarming amount of charm in one human package. Not to mention the veneer of a gentleman. But by his own admission, he wasn't a gentleman—he was a gambler. He earned his living by preying on the folly of his fellow man.

And she didn't doubt that he preyed on women. His manner was too engaging, too easy. Just looking at him she could see her father. It didn't matter that Jack Howard's hair had been lighter, his eyes hazel like hers, or even that he'd been considerably shorter than McCready. When it came to questionable character, both men were probably cut from the same cloth. Dangerous men. The kind only a fool would trust. Well, she wasn't a fool—her mother had seen to that.

While he slept, she'd mulled it over in her mind a dozen times and more, trying to figure out why he'd decided to follow her. And no matter what her mirror told her, she was fairly certain his attempt at acquaintance went beyond her looks. A man like that didn't put himself out unless he wanted something, she reasoned. In his case, he could have found a dozen pretty females ready, eager even, to fall under the spell of those dark, dark eyes. No, there was something else.

I was sort of hoping the advantage would be mutual. . . . I thought maybe we could help each other out. . . .

That was the puzzle. While she still thought his intention was seduction, she wasn't entirely sure. *If it's all the same to you, I'd rather not spend the honeymoon defending your honor. . . . So which is it—are we calling ourselves the Howards or the McCreadys. . . ?*

Then there was the other side of the coin. *All I'm asking for is the appearance of respectability, nothing more. . . . Look, there's two kinds of women in this world, and believe me, I can tell the difference. . . . I'm not going to cross the line with you. . . .* No, it didn't make any sense.

If he hadn't chosen cards for a living, he'd probably have made an accomplished actor. He was most likely toying with her, playing upon her fear of men like Thompson. That had to be it. It just had to.

At least the fighting and most of the cursing had died down. Some of the cowboys had left at the meal stop, while others had either made themselves sick or drunk themselves into a stupor. But the heat and the mingling odors of cigar smoke, tobacco juice, vomit, and sweat were unbearable.

She eyed an open space in the aisle, wishing she dared get up and ease her aching limbs and relieve the uncomfortable fullness in her nether parts. But McCready's long legs were stretched out, effectively making her small corner a prison, bounded by him on one side and a window that wouldn't open on the other.

And there he sat, his head leaned back, his hat pushed forward, dead to the world.

She had to stand up, to move around, to pull her itchy, damp petticoat away from her legs. And whether she wanted to or not, she had to visit the lavatory. Leaning forward, she tried to push his feet toward the aisle. They wouldn't budge. It was as though those boots of his were anchored beneath the seat in front of him.

"Mr. McCready," she tried softly. He didn't miss a breath. "Mr. McCready." Nothing. Sitting on the edge of her seat, she considered using the hatpin again, then discarded the notion. Instead, she decided to discreetly shake his shoulder. Reaching out, she grasped his coat-sleeve and gave it a tug. That was a near-fatal mistake.

As he jerked away, one of his hands pushed his hat back, while the other dropped beneath his coat. In less than an instant, she was staring down the barrel of his gun. For an awful moment, her heart paused. There was nothing sleepy about his eyes or his manner now.

"What the hell—? Oh, it's you," he muttered, lowering the weapon.

"Well, I'm glad you noticed before you shot me," she managed shakily.

"A man gets jumpy in a strange place," he mumbled.

She could almost feel the color coming back into her face. "How on earth did you do that?"

"What?" Then he saw that her eyes were still on the Colt. "Oh, *that*."

"I thought it came out of nowhere."

"No—it was under my coat. It's too hard to draw sitting down." He raised his hip, straightening his leg, and slid the gun into its holster. "What the devil did you think you were doing, anyway?"

"I was trying to wake you so I could get out."

"Next time, just say so."

"I did—twice. But maybe you were snoring so loudly that you couldn't hear me."

"I don't snore—or if I do, you're the first woman to notice it."

"And I'm sure there have been many," she said sweetly. "*Now* will you let me out, or do I have to resort to my hatpin?"

"If I thought Howard existed, I'd feel sorry for him," he said, rising. Stepping out to let her by, he asked, "Want me to walk you back to the water closet?"

"No, of course not."

"Suit yourself." He waited until she'd taken several steps, then reminded her, "Better hold up your skirt and petticoat—there'll be a lot of spit on the floor."

"And I thought you were a gentleman," she muttered.

"When you get back, I'm going to take a good look at your ears."

She stopped and half turned to look back at him. "My ears?"

"Uh-huh. My mama always used to say lying would make a body's ears grow."

"Really?" She couldn't help smiling. "Then I guess that explains why I have small ones, doesn't it?"

The floor of the passenger compartment was so filthy that the sawdust spread over the tobacco spittle lay in clumps. She paused, trying to decide whether to use both hands to hold her clothes out of it or to risk just one so she could use the other to hold her nose.

Saving her dress won out just barely. Disgusted, she eased her way the length of the car, sidestepping snoring drunks hanging into the narrow passageway.

One fellow roused enough to grab her skirt before she could get past him. He looked up, a silly grin on his face. "Nobod-nobody tole me they got angelsh on trainsh."

His seat companion managed to get both bloodshot eyes open. "Not an angel," he pronounced solemnly. "Ish a girl."

Across the aisle, the Bill fellow sat up for a look, then shook his head. "Better leggo of 'er—shesh got a hushband."

Pulling her dress free, she kept going. Behind her, the cowboy was explaining, "Mc-Cready'sh wife. Woulda kilt Al fer 'er. Bad man, McCready."

"Ain't never heard of 'im."

"Big Al'll tell yuh."

Just as she finally reached the narrow door, the porter stopped her. "Privy's closed, ma'am—coming into the station."

"But it can't be—it just can't be!"

"It's the law, ma'am."

Gritting her teeth, she hurried back through the gauntlet, then stumbled over McCready's feet into her seat. "Trouble?" he asked.

"No," she lied.

"You know, if you don't watch out, you're going to die with elephant ears."

"We're coming into a station."

"Oh. Well, I guess that explains it." Reaching into his waistcoat pocket, he took out his watch and looked at it. "Five-forty-three. I guess we must be eating here." Putting it away, he added, "I don't know about you, but I'm pretty hungry myself. I could sure use one of those thick Texas steaks right now."

"I suppose it's too much to hope that this is Eagle Lake, isn't it?"

"Not until tomorrow morning. But we've got to change trains at Harrisburg sometime before nightfall. Here—I've got a copy of the timetable," he said, offering her the folded sheet.

"It doesn't list anything at five-forty-three," she noted peevishly. "And I don't remember coming through Richmond."

"Looks like we're running late."

The train crawled to a creaky stop. Verena glanced out the window, then stared. There wasn't any sign of a town. As far as she could see, there were only cattle. Hundreds and hundreds of them. Exasperated, she sat back.

"Something the matter?"

"Yes, Mr. McCready, there is," she responded wearily. "It looks like your steak is still alive."

"Huh?"

"There isn't any station out here. All there are are cows as far as I can see."

"Maybe it's on the other side."

"Cattle on the tracks, folks!" the conductor announced, coming down the aisle. "Soon's they're cleared off, we'll be pulling in to eat. Twenty minutes!"

"I beg your pardon, sir," she said, motioning for his attention. "Are you saying we won't be there for another twenty minutes?"

"No, ma'am, we's there. But there ain't but twenty minutes to spare for eatin', if'n we's to make Harrisburg t'night."

The news didn't seem to faze McCready, but she was already too miserable to sit still. "Excuse me," she murmured to him, "but I've got to get out again." Climbing over his feet, she managed to stand up. Squaring her shoulders for another walk down to the front of the car, she gathered up her skirt with both hands and got about twenty feet before the trainman stopped her. Not meeting her eyes, he said low, "Privy's closed, ma'am."

"But we aren't anywhere," she said desperately.

"Sorry, ma'am, but we're stopped."

There was nothing to do but go back. Taking her seat again, she tried not to think about her discomfort. Beside her, the gambler murmured, "I understand that since time is so short, there'll be someone coming on to take supper orders."

"I don't care about that—I'm getting off this train if I have to climb over a cow to do it," she told him through clenched teeth.

"Need to go that bad, huh?"

Under other circumstances, she would have taken offense, but just now she was beyond that. "Yes," she admitted baldly.

"All right, let's go."

"Now?"

"Yeah. The way I figure it, if somebody can get on, we can get off."

Swinging into the aisle, he wrenched the back door open and held it for her. Stepping past the sign that said

NO EXIT, she found herself on a narrow platform, facing another car. On one side, two cowboys on horses were shouting and waving big hats, herding the animals away. On the other, there was nothing but flat grassland and several small buildings. Certainly nothing she would call a town.

McCready jumped down, landing on a bare patch of ground, and reached up to her. "Come on, I've got you."

Once down, he grasped her elbow and struck out for what looked to be a house. Instead of going in, he guided her around back, then pointed to a lopsided, bare-board outhouse.

"Want me to wait for you?"

"I can't just go in there—it belongs to somebody."

He looked at her for a moment, then shrugged. "You can suit yourself, I guess, but once that car unloads, everything else's going to be full."

He had a point. She looked both ways, then ducked inside, pulling the door shut after her. It was dark, hot, and smelled as if it hadn't been limed in years. Unable to see anything, she opened the door a crack to let in a slice of light and immediately wished she hadn't. The seat was a rough, warped board with two holes cut in it. In front of it, bugs crawled over a box filled with dried corncobs. She needed at least three hands—two for her clothes and one for her nose, but unfortunately humans didn't come equipped that way. Removing her embroidered lawn hanky from her purse, she started dusting off the seat.

When she came out, the gambler was nowhere in sight. But now that she could breathe again, she smelled the ominous odor of rancid grease burning, and it was coming from the house. In the yard that had been deserted five minutes ago, passengers milled, waiting to get inside. If her stomach hadn't growled, she'd have been inclined to get back on the train and forgo supper entirely.

Before she could get in line, McCready came out with what looked like a rag wrapped around something. He was frowning.

"You don't have any relations down here, do you?"

"No, of course not. Why?"

"I'll tell you when we get back to our seats," he said, taking her arm. "Come on, I've got supper."

"In that rag?"

"Yeah."

He was walking fast, making it difficult to keep up. "The train's not leaving for twenty minutes," she reminded him. "I'd rather eat out here where it's cooler."

"I wouldn't."

Instead of going to the front of their car, he climbed over the rail where they'd come out, then gave her a hand up. Inside, the car was deserted except for the conductor and porter, who were eating in separate seats at the other end, and several cowboys too drunk to get off.

McCready all but put her in her seat, then sat down to open the cloth. "Here," he said, handing her a rolled tortilla. "As near as I could tell, they didn't have much else."

"You must have been first in line," she decided.

"No."

"Mr. McCready, are you hiding something?" she asked curiously.

"Funny, but I was about to ask you the same thing."

"What?"

"There's a couple of hard cases in there looking for you."

"*What?* There can't be—I don't know anybody in this entire state," she declared positively. "Nobody but Mr. Hamer even knows I'm coming."

"Hamer?"

"The lawyer. He was appointed by the judge to handle my father's estate, but I'd hardly call that an acquaintance. I've never met him."

"They aren't lawyers—I'll go bail on that."

"There must be a mistake."

"I don't know. But while you were taking your time in the privy, they were meeting everybody coming off the train, asking if anybody'd seen a Verena Howard—a *Miss* Verena Howard, that is. Seems like they're some long-lost relatives of yours."

"They can't be—I don't have any. At least none that I know of, anyway," she amended. "After my father deserted us, I don't know what he did."

"They're older than you are."

"How odd."

"Yeah, like I said, these are a couple of hardcases."

"I'm afraid I don't know what that is."

"Ugly customers."

"That doesn't help much either."

"Real rough looking. I don't know—maybe they're Texas Rangers. All I know is that they were expecting to find you on this train. They were looking for a single woman traveling alone and bound for San Angelo."

She eyed him suspiciously. "You're just saying this, aren't you? This is some part of your scheme, isn't it? For some reason, you're wanting to accompany me, but for the life of me, I can't see why."

"Actually, I may be leaving this train before Eagle Pass."

She digested that for a moment, then asked suddenly, You're in some sort of trouble, aren't you?"

"They weren't asking about me," he countered. "Not unless they expect me to be disguised as a young woman, slender and in her early twenties, going across Texas all by herself. No, it's you they're after."

"I don't believe you."

"Uh-oh. Speak of the devil, there's one of 'em right now," he said low.

"What?"

"Keep your head down—better yet cover your face with my shoulder."

"I beg your pardon?"

"Just do it." Before she could refuse, he reached out and drew her left hand to his opposite arm, exposing the band on her finger. "Don't look up," he murmured, almost under his breath. "Here he comes."

"This is ridiculous," she whispered. "I feel like a complete fool."

"Just let me do the talking."

With considerable skepticism, she turned her body, buried her head in his coat, and clasped his shoulder. "If I find out this is some sort of ruse—"

"Use your ears instead of your mouth," he whispered

against her hair. "It's all right, Bess, honey," he said aloud, his Southern accent suddenly heavy. "I guess those tortillas were too much for that queasy stomach. You just hold on until we get to Austin, and things'll get a whole lot bettah, I promise yuh."

"What—?"

Feeling her stiffen, he held her more tightly and went on, "It's the baby, that's all—and yuh got a delicate constitution. I should have left yuh back in Little Rock with Mama. Now yuh just stay real still, honey, and it'll pass."

"She sick, mister?"

"First baby," she heard McCready answer proudly. Under her ear, his voice resounded as if it came from the inside of a barrel. "Been real sick with it—real sick. Right now, it don't look like that tortilla she ate is gonna stay down." Reaching around her with his right arm, he held out his hand. "Name's McCready—Tom McCready, but folks call me Mac. And this here's m'wife, Elizabeth McCready."

"Mac. Ma'am." He didn't return the introduction. "Can't say as I can see much of her."

"Ever' time she sits up, she pukes," McCready explained. "I just got the last mess cleaned up."

The stranger's eyes narrowed. "You a Reb?"

"Yep—and mighty proud of it. Hell Brigade, Third Arkansas. And you?"

"I was a Yankee." There was a pause. Then, "I was on the winning side."

"Yeah, I know," McCready murmured dryly.

"Don't suppose you chanced to see a girl on this

train?" the fellow asked casually. "She'd be traveling alone."

"Not too many women on this run. There was one that got on this side of Galveston, but she had some kids with her."

"No, this one's young—looks about twenty, maybe a little older."

The gambler furrowed his brow, then shook his head. "Not that I remember, anyway, but with taking care of Bess here, I might not've noticed. I'm right sorry."

The stranger expelled a deep breath. "Yeah, so am I."

"Friend of your'n?"

"My sister. She's coming from back East alone."

"And she's lost?"

"Yeah. We missed meeting her in Galveston, and now it looks like she's plumb disappeared. I figured maybe she'd be on this train."

"Maybe she's in one of the other cars," McCready offered helpfully.

"Ain't nobody seen her. We already asked damned near everybody."

"Tell yuh what—yuh give me your name and direction, and if Bess or I happen to see her when we change lines at Harrisburg, I'll wire yuh."

The stranger didn't take the bait. Instead, he said, "Her name's Howard—Verena Howard. It's real unusual, the kind if you heard it, you'd remember—the Verena, I mean."

"Well, we'll sure be on the lookout for her," McCready promised. "I'd hate to have my sister out here fending for herself. No tellin' what kind of riffraff she'd be running into—there's Yankees damned near everywhere now."

The man's jaw tensed and his hand dropped to the six-shooter strapped to his thigh. Then he caught himself. Forcing a smile, he said tightly, "Guess we'll ride on to San Antone and look for her there. Guess she coulda gone by stage or something."

"That's what I'd do—look for her in San Antonio, I mean."

"Where'd you say you were going?"

"Austin. At Columbus, we'll be headed for Austin. We got people there." McCready shifted Verena slightly, murmuring, "Feeling any better, Bess, honey?"

"I can't breathe," she choked out.

"It's all that throwing up yuh been doing," he assured her.

"Well, I guess I'll be going," the stranger said. "She didn't just go up in smoke, that's for sure."

"Wouldn't think so, anyway," McCready murmured. "Sure hope yuh find her before anything bad happens."

"Oh, we'll find her, all right—one way or another, we'll find her."

Verena couldn't see, but she could hear the jangle of the man's spurs fading as he walked away. Yet the gambler's arm still held her so close that his heartbeat kept its rhythm beneath her ear.

"All right," he said finally, releasing her, "you can sit up now. But he just got off, so I wouldn't be looking outside yet."

"I think you've given me a crick in my neck," she muttered.

Leaning back in her seat, she furtively glanced toward the window, hoping to catch a glimpse of the man. But he had his back to her, and all she could see was a big felt hat, a plaid flannel shirt, and a pair of short, decidedly bowed legs above badly worn boots. He walked with a limp.

"Recognize him?"

Caught, she turned guiltily toward the gambler. "No, of course not. I don't know who he is, but I can assure you he isn't my brother."

"Maybe he's from the wrong side of the blanket?"

"My father didn't leave home until '61—until the war started."

"Well, I didn't see much resemblance, but you never know."

"*I* know. My father was taller—and exceptionally handsome." *Like you,* something in her mind whispered. But she didn't repeat it. Instead, a small smile teased the corners of her mouth. "But I will give you one thing, Mr. McCready."

"Yeah?"

"You're quite the accomplished liar. If your mother'd been right, your ears ought to be dangling down to your ankles by now."

"I got rid of him for you, didn't I?"

"I hope so, anyway. But where on earth did you come up with Bess? I've never liked that name—ever. It sounds as if it ought to belong to a fat old woman."

"It's my mother's."

"Oh. Well, then I suppose you're entitled to feel a certain attachment to it," she conceded.

"I do."

"I'm sorry," she said, sighing. "I shouldn't be so blunt, I expect."

"Actually, she always admired honesty. But talking about Bess McCready won't explain what that cowboy wanted," he murmured, returning to the subject at hand. "You're sure you don't know?"

"If I did, don't you think I would have told you?"

"No."

"Well, I don't, anyway."

"Somebody knew you were coming down."

"Just Mr. Hamer, and I hardly think he would have instructed a couple of ruffians to meet me the instant I set foot in Texas."

"What do you know about him?"

"Mr. Hamer? Nothing really, but I gather from his letter that he's an entirely respectable attorney."

"There isn't any such thing."

"Well, in any event, he writes like an old man, and I don't know as he was even acquainted with my father at all. According to the papers he sent me, he was appointed by the county to handle what little there is of an estate. And I gather from what he wrote that my father didn't really leave enough to bother with—just a little farm with a three-room house on it. It could've gone to probate without my even appearing in court."

"Which brings me to another point—if that's the case, why bother coming down?"

"Right now, I wish I hadn't—I truly wish I hadn't. It's been an expense, and a near nightmare." Taking a deep breath, she looked out the window again. Exhaling, she turned back to McCready. "I guess I just wanted to see what Jack Howard did with his life after he deserted us. I guess I'm just looking for a reason why he did that." She looked up at him. "That sounds rather foolish, doesn't it? To spend money that I'll probably never even recover just coming down here, I mean."

"No."

"I don't suppose there can be two Verena Howards, can there?" she asked, sighing again.

"Probably not. As your friend pointed out, Verena's not exactly common."

"No. I only knew one other, anyway—and she was the aunt I was named for. Verena Summers was her name."

"Well, it's got me beat," he admitted. Leaning back, he unwrapped the tortillas again. "Here, you'd better get something on your stomach before we leave out."

The grease had already congealed on them. "I couldn't—I just couldn't. They didn't even smell good when they were cooking."

Taking out his watch, he flicked the case open, then decided, "All right, we've still got about eight minutes. You wait here, and I'll fight the crowd to see what else they've got."

"You didn't look while you were there?"

"No. When I heard 'em asking about you, I just grabbed these off the counter when the cook wasn't looking."

"You didn't even pay for them?" she asked incredulously. "You stole food?"

"I threw down a quarter." His gaze dropped to the greasy rag and the offending tortillas. "Even free, they wouldn't be much of a bargain." Rolling up the rag, he stood up and dropped his right arm, sliding the narrow knife from beneath his sleeve. “Here, this’ll work even better than a hatpin.”

She looked first at the knife, then back to the food in his hand. “I’ve changed my mind, Mr. McCready—I’ll eat those.”

“You want my gun? I guess I could leave it with you.”

“No.” Her gaze went to his face for a moment. “I don’t want you to go anywhere right now.”

Favoring her with a look of long suffering, he sighed, then dropped back into his seat. “You know you’re damned hard to please, don’t you? If there were a school where females just learned the art of contrariness, you’d have graduated from it with high marks,” he complained. “And the same way about lying.”

“I haven’t lied to you, Mr. McCready,” she protested.

“No?”

“Well, not really, anyway.”

“*Is* there a Mr. Howard?”

“I’m sure there must be—somewhere. I mean, Howard is a fairly common name, after all.”

“But you don’t really have a husband.”

“No.”

“What about the rest of it?”

“The rest of what? Really, sir, but—”

“What else are you lying about?” he cut in curtly.

“Nothing. And I wouldn’t have claimed to be married, but I was hoping to avoid unwanted attention,” she explained defensively.

“Like that fellow that just left?” he gibed.

“Like *you,* Mr. McCready—and like those awful

cowboys." Daring to meet the skeptical look in those dark eyes, she declared evenly, "Everything else I've told you is the truth."

"That's pretty hard to swallow, you know."

"And what about you?" she countered. "Let's turn the table, Mr. McCready. What's sauce for the goose is sauce for the gander, isn't it? All right, then—why are you making my business your business? What are you hiding from me?"

"Nothing much," he lied.

"*Is* there a Mrs. McCready?"

"Lots of 'em."

"I beg your pardon?"

"My father had four brothers, all of whom married and produced mostly sons. And those sons—"

"You can spare me the litany," she cut in. "I was asking about you."

"No." Leaning back, he regarded her lazily for a moment, then asked, "Why? Were you thinking of applying for the position?"

"No, of course not!" she snapped.

"Anything else bothering you? About me, I mean."

"I'm not a prying person, Mr. McCready."

"Oh, I don't know—that struck me as a pretty personal question."

"You asked it of me first, didn't you? What difference did it make to you?"

"None, I guess. But a man sees a pretty female traveling all by herself, and—"

"And he gets notions," she said, finishing his sentence for him.

"I'd rather call it curiosity, Miss Howard."

"And I'd rather call it what it is."

"All right, then have it your way. Here"—handing her a cold tortilla, he added—"you'd better eat and enjoy the company while you've got it."

"What's that supposed to mean?"

"I get off at Eagle Lake, in case you've forgotten."

It was a dispiriting thought, one she didn't want to deal with just now. But no matter what, she wasn't going to ask him to stay with her, she told herself. She wasn't about to give him any power he could use against her. Instead, she took a small bite out of the fried tortilla. It was soggy with grease, but it was food for an empty stomach.

"She wasn't there, Gib! I'm telling you she wasn't there!" Lee Jackson all but shouted at Hannah. "You tell 'im, Charley—tell 'im there wasn't any sign of the Howard girl!"

"Gib, we looked the length of the whole damned train," Pierce explained patiently. "She wasn't on it."

"Hell, we even watched 'em get off to eat, and when we didn't see her, Charley got on to look for her!" Jackson went on angrily. "I'm telling you there wasn't no lone female there. There wasn't but a couple of women on the whole danged thing! Doncha think we'd a told you if we'd found her?"

"Maybe he's kinda thinking you were wanting to keep her to yourselves," Bob Simmons spoke up. "Maybe he's thinking you could be planning to split it two ways instead of four."

"Is that what you think, Bob? That we'd cheat you?" Pierce demanded. "If that was the case, why the hell would we come back at all? Why wouldn't we just grab 'er and run?"

"I wasn't meaning *I* thought it, Charley—I was saying maybe that's what Gib was thinking," Simmons said soothingly. "Hell, we've been in the saddle night and day now, and it ain't easy to think straight like that. We're all downright jumpy."

"Been like looking for the needle in the haystack," Jackson muttered. "I knowed we oughta waited in San Angelo—said so even."

"She's got to be on that train," Gib reasoned. "She was on the *Norfolk Star*'s passenger list coming into Galveston. And she sure as hell didn't hire herself a buggy to travel halfway across Texas in."

"Looks like she's vamoosed," Jackson declared.

"The word is vanished, Lee,"

"Huh?"

"It looks like she's *vanished*."

"Hell, I ain't got book learning like you, Gib," Jackson countered sarcastically. "But I've sure as hell got eyes! And there's nothing wrong with Charley's neither!"

"All right, all right." Gib Hannah ran his fingers through his hair, then rubbed the stubble on his face. "Look, there's no sense in quarreling amongst ourselves. We missed her, that's all. But we know she got off that steamer, and we know she stayed overnight at the Harris house—I saw the register myself. And according to the Harris woman, she asked for an early call to breakfast so she'd have time to make the train," he recounted. "Damn."

"Maybe we shoulda waited until the agent got back to ask 'im," Pierce offered.

"There wasn't time. Train'd been gone nigh to an

hour by then, and the window was already shut down," Simmons reminded him. "Hell, it wasn't opening again until four o'clock, and by then, it'd a been too damn late to catch up at all."

"Something must've happened, and she didn't get on the nine-fifteen—that's got to be it, Gib," Jackson insisted. "Ain't no other way of explaining it."

"You said the Harris woman told you the Howard girl was real pretty—maybe something happened to her. I mean, there's a lot of rough customers in a place like Indianola."

"It was a short walk in broad daylight," Hannah snapped. "Somebody would've seen something, and the whole place would've known it."

Lee Jackson sighed. "All right, then, Gib—we ain't got no brains between us—that's what you're saying, ain't it?"

"Yeah, Gib," Charley said, "if you're so damned smart, then you tell us where in the hell she is."

"She's on the train."

"And I suppose that makes the both of us blind," Lee muttered. "Well, since you got all the brains and two good eyes, why don't you find 'er?"

"Look, it doesn't do much good to fight among ourselves, does it?" Hannah said tiredly. "All right, you looked over the passengers, and—"

"And saw nobody as could be Verena Howard," Charley Pierce finished for him. "There wasn't any women but a farmer's wife with a passel of kids hanging on 'er and—"

"And what?"

"The only halfway young one had a husband with her."

"Did you get a good look at her?"

Pierce shook his head. "Couldn't. The poor little thing was so sick she couldn't hold her head up, and her husband was having a time of taking care of her. She's having a baby, he said."

"Maybe she got off before we caught up," Simmons ventured slowly. "Maybe she got fed up with the company."

"And went where?"

"I dunno."

"No, she's on that train," Hannah declared positively.

"Well, if she is, she's passing herself off as a cowboy and doin' a damned good job of it," Jackson muttered. "Ain't nothin' but cowpunchers and Mexicans on the whole damned thing."

"She wouldn't have any reason to disguise herself," Bob Simmons pointed out.

"Unless she knows about the gold."

The other three looked at Gib Hannah. Then Charley Pierce found his voice again. "How the hell would she know that? You said the Hamer fellow didn't even know."

"Jack left everything to her. Everything," Gib repeated for emphasis. "It's not impossible that he might have written to her before he died. Or that he could have left something to be mailed to her afterward."

"But I'm telling you there wasn't no—"

"Charley, did you get a good look at the husband?" Hannah asked suddenly.

"Yeah." Pierce sucked in his breath, then let it go.

"He was a real good-looking Reb from Arkansas. Fought with something called the Hell Brigade, he said. Got black hair—brown eyes, I think—real nice clothes, too. Looked like he could be a lawyer or something."

"Or a sharp. Anything else?"

"He was sitting down, so I couldn't say for sure how tall he was, but he looked like maybe he was a little taller than you, Gib."

"What about the wife?"

"Hard to tell. Like I said, I couldn't see her face, but she looked pretty well-dressed to me." Charley's forehead furrowed as he tried to remember. "She was sick, real sick, Gib. And he called her Bess. Yeah, that's about all, I'd say. Oh, yeah, she had a wedding ring. Guess that lets her out, don't it?"

"Maybe. Maybe not."

"I think mebbe we oughta go back to San Angelo and wait," Lee Jackson murmured. "Make a whole lot more sense. She'll be showing up for probate, anyway."

"We already know what you think," Hannah snapped. "No, I still think she's somewhere on that train, and I aim to find out for sure."

"How you going to do that, Gib?"

"The way the train's running, having to stop every few miles to clear the tracks, we'll keep up with it. Every time the passengers get off to eat, I figure there'll be one of us there watching."

"Yeah, but—"

"And if she knows, sooner or later she's going to make a mistake that'll give her away."

"It'll be dark when they change at Harrisburg. Can't see much in the dark, Gib," Bob pointed out.

"To make the stage connection for San Antonio, she'll be going on to Columbus. What're the stops after Harrisburg?"

Unfolding the timetable, Bob Simmons smoothed it with his hand, then read the list aloud. When he was finished, Gib Hannah nodded. "All right, I figure we ought to catch up somewhere past Harrisburg. After that—"

"Ain't they gonna wonder how come the same strangers is showing up everywhere?"

"They won't question a Ranger."

"But we ain't—"

"I've still got this," Hannah said, cutting Jackson off again. Reaching into his coat pocket, he took out the state police badge and polished it on his sleeve. "The further west a man gets, the more everybody trusts a Texas Ranger."

"I didn't know the Rangers was using badges, Gib," Charley mumbled. "I didn't think they was gettin' anything but pay and ammunition."

"Some of 'em buy their own," Jackson pointed out.

Hannah nodded. "This one was going to cost me two dollars, but I wasn't about to pay any Mexican for it," he declared flatly. "I never liked the notion of Negroes and Mexicans enforcing the law, anyway."

"You killed 'im to get his badge?" Simmons asked incredulously. "You killed a state policeman, Gib?"

"I killed a Mexican. I don't figure that counted."

"Hell, there ain't any state police no more, Bob," Pierce reminded him. "Way I heard it, everybody hated 'em, so the governor finally had to do away with 'em and bring back the Rangers. All there is down here now is a few Rangers—and a bunch of county sheriffs," he added.

"For once, you've got it right." Hannah took another look at the badge, then slipped it back into his pocket. "I guess you could say this Yankee made himself a Ranger," he said, smiling. "And there've been some times when that's come in real handy."

She'd been asleep, her head pressed against the window, when the train stopped so abruptly that she pitched forward. She would have hit the empty seat in front of her if McCready hadn't caught her.

"What—what on earth?" she managed, coming awake. "What was *that*?"

"We stopped again."

"Yes, I know. That much was pretty obvious. But why?"

Opening the door behind them, the conductor stood beneath the NO EXIT sign to announce, "Trouble on the track, folks! Crew'll be coming out from Eagle Lake to fix it!"

"How long will that take?" somebody called out.

"Can't tell—rail's broke!" he shouted back.

To Verena, it seemed like the final straw. After numerous unscheduled stops for cows on the tracks, they were now stranded just before supper. Leaning forward, she rested her head on the seat back, too tired to even cry. Every bone in her body ached with fatigue, and there just wasn't any end to it. She'd been traveling forever, and she was nowhere.

"How far to Eagle Lake?" she heard McCready ask.

" 'Bout four miles," the trainman answered.

"I could've walked from Galveston to Columbus by now," she muttered under her breath. "And the worst of it is that once I get there, I won't even be halfway to San Antonio. I'm beginning to feel as though Pennsylvania is a world away." Taking in the rough assortment of remaining passengers, she sighed. "Texas might as well be another country."

"You're not exactly seeing the best it has to offer," McCready murmured. "But at least the worst of the bunch got off at the last stop."

"I wish I could believe you."

"Have I lied to you yet?" he asked lightly.

"Have you ever told the truth?" she shot back.

He looked injured. "I could've left you to your long-lost relations, you know, but I didn't."

"Quite frankly, I'm still wondering why you didn't," she admitted.

McCready looked up at the conductor. "I don't suppose there's any chance of getting a ride into Eagle Lake instead of waiting for the track to be repaired, is there?"

The trainman glanced over at Verena. "The missus sick again?"

Before she could deny it, McCready laid a warning hand on her shoulder and nodded. "I expect it's the heat. I'm afraid if she doesn't get some fresh air, she's going to faint."

"You could walk her around outside."

"That won't help for long. She'll just be coming back in, and now that we're not moving, the heat's going to get considerably worse. And with the lavatory closed—"

"They'll be sending a wagon out with the repair crew, but—" The man's gaze shifted to take in the rest of the car. Already a number of passengers were grumbling among themselves, and as the temperature rose inside, tempers were sure to flare. "Well, there's just not room in a wagon for everybody as'll want to be going," he finished lamely.

"Right now, I'd pay just to get her somewhere where she can lie down for a while." Reaching into his coat pocket, McCready found the wad of bills. Pulling it out, he peeled off ten dollars. "Don't suppose you could make some sort of arrangement to accommodate her, do you?" he asked casually.

Eyeing the money, the conductor considered a moment, then allowed, "Well, I could see about it, anyway."

"You do that," McCready murmured, handing the banknote to him. "I've got another one exactly like it if you succeed."

As Verena looked on in disbelief, the trainman discreetly folded the money and stuffed it into his watch pocket. Barely waiting until the man had backed out of the car, she turned on McCready.

"I've never fainted in my life," she declared. "Never. And that was nothing but bribery, plain and simple."

"Uh-huh."

"Do you always throw your money away like this?"

"Would you rather sit here and stew in your own

sweat?" he countered, obviously unrepentant. "In fifteen minutes, it'll be like sitting in an oven."

"What about everyone else? How's it going to look when we just get up and leave, and they cannot?"

"If they get hot enough, they'll figure out something."

"That sounds terribly selfish, Mr. McCready. And don't think for one moment that I don't know you're just using me for an excuse to escape the heat yourself," she told him severely.

"My mama always said, 'Take care of yourself, son, and let God worry about the rest,' " he murmured. " 'Course she was talking about behaving myself at the time, but I've since found a lot of other uses for the advice."

"So I've noticed."

Looking out the window, she could see the undulating waves of heat rising above the grassy prairie. Along the horizon, small hills boasted stands of timber that beckoned invitingly. But in this heat, they were too far away for anyone on foot, she noted wearily. And with silk stockings, elastic garters, knee-length drawers, a chemise, a corset cover, and a starched petticoat beneath her dress, she felt more than halfway to a heat stroke already. If she had to be grateful for anything right now, she guessed it'd have to be her decision not to wear the corset.

"How long do *you* think it will take to repair the track?" she asked abruptly.

"I'm a gambler, not a railroader," he reminded her.

"Well, you must have an opinion. You seem to have one on everything else, anyway."

"You know, this heat's making you downright cranky," he complained. As her color heightened, he relented. "But if I had to place a bet on it, I'd say several hours at the least."

"I'd give almost anything for a bath and a decent meal," she muttered under her breath. "I feel like a wet dishrag before it's been hung out to dry."

"You can probably have both—for a price."

"Yes, well, I can't afford any luxuries right now. I'm determined to hoard what money I have left."

"I tried to give you part of my winnings," he reminded her.

"I don't want to be beholden to anyone, Mr. McCready. All I want is— Well, it's too late for that, anyway. He's dead, and I should've stayed home." Turning her body away, she leaned her head against the warm window glass and closed her eyes. "I'm all right," she said, as much to convince herself as him. "I'll survive."

"We all do, one way or another."

He felt as tired as she looked, but rather than give in to his fatigue, he heaved himself up from his seat, and stood to stamp the numbness from his legs. His toes tingled painfully in the heavy-soled boots. To get his blood circulating, he walked the length of the car and then back, several times.

"Game, mister?"

He turned around, spotting a terribly young, obviously green cowboy. And for a moment, he was tempted. No, he hadn't sunk to fleecing innocents—not yet, anyway. Not when the kid already looked pretty desperate. He shook his head.

"It's too hot."

"I figger a man's gotta do something to take his mind off his misery," the boy responded. "You're a gambler, aincha? Afore they got off, Al and Billy was sayin' as you're a real sharp, mister."

"How much have you got?"

"It don't matter—I got enough."

"How much?"

"I got money left," the kid insisted. "I ain't lost all of it."

"Then you'd better hang on to it."

As he turned away, he heard the telltale click of a gun hammer being cocked, and the hairs on the back of his neck prickled. His first instinct was to go for the Army Colt, but if the kid's gun discharged wildly, everybody around him was at risk. Besides, killing the young fool would be a stupid thing to do—all it'd get him would be closer scrutiny from the law than he could stand. He'd have to gamble that the kid wouldn't shoot him in the back.

"Ain't nobody says my money ain't good enough," the boy said evenly.

Instead of responding, Matt took a deliberate step away.

"You're yellow-bellied, mister," the kid said.

He still didn't answer.

"Better put that gun away, son—there's no telling who you might hit," a cowboy behind the boy said.

"Ain't nobody walks away from John Harper and lives," was the kid's response. He raised the gun and aimed it at the gambler's back.

"You better start praying, mister."

As everyone held a collective breath, Matt kept walking.

The sudden and total silence drawing her reluctant attention, Verena sat up and looked down the aisle to where McCready stood. For a moment, she was merely curious. Then she saw that everyone around him seemed to be frozen in position. Standing up for a better view, she caught a glimpse of the boy holding the gun. It was aimed at Mac McCready.

Alarmed, she stepped into the aisle, and cried, "Don't shoot!" to draw the gunman's attention. As all eyes turned to her, she squeezed hers shut, held her breath, and pitched forward as if she'd fainted. The instant her body hit the floor, the smells of tobacco juice, dirt, and sawdust assaulted her nose. She had to fight the urge to gag from the nasty stuff. And she was getting it all over her dress.

Startled, the kid lurched from his seat for a look. "What the hell—?"

Taking advantage of his confusion, McCready swung around, ducked his head, and charged, throwing his shoulder into the boy's chest, knocking him backward. As the kid stumbled, the gun fired, and the bullet pinged against the tin ceiling of the car. The older cowboy took quick advantage of the boy's confusion by whacking his head with the butt of an old six-shooter before he could get up. At the sound of the thud, the kid's body crumpled, and the gun dropped harmlessly to the floor.

"Don't teach youngsters no manners nowadays, do they?" the older man observed as he returned his own gun to its holster.

Surprised by the sudden turn of events, Matt pushed his way through the gapers crowding into the aisle, then dropped to his knees beside Verena. Lifting her head, he cradled her against his knees while calling out, "Stand back—give her air! She's fainted!" Even as he said it, he could feel her tense. Leaning over to shield her from the eyes of the curious, he spoke low for her ears alone. "Don't move yet, and thanks."

"My dress—it's ruined," she wailed.

"I'll buy you a brand-new one."

"You can't."

With one arm holding her halfway onto his bended knee, he slipped his other one around her and quickly undid the top buttons of her bodice. When he slid his fingers under the cloth, her whole body went rigid.

"No!" she gasped, catching his hand.

"Shhhh. It'll look better if I loosen your corset," he murmured against her ear.

"I'm not wearing one," she gritted out. "And if you touch me again, I'll scream."

"What sort of husband would I be if I didn't?" he countered. Looking back over his shoulder, he announced, "I've got to get her outside—she can't breathe."

The conductor burst through the NO EXIT door, demanding, "What's the commotion in here? Who discharged the firearm?" Then he saw the woman on the floor and thought the worst. "My God—what happened?"

"She fainted afore the kid could shoot her husband," somebody answered.

"Better look t' his missus. Tom done took keer o' the

boy fer ye. Whupped his haid with the back end of a six-shooter, he did. Be nightfall afore that kid comes to."

"She's all right, isn't she?" the trainman asked Matt hastily. "She's not injured?"

"She's plumb overhet," another passenger answered. "Plumb overhet. Ain't no s'prise she done swooned plumb out."

"Hell ain't no hotter'n this, I'll be bound," someone else declared.

"If it is, I ain't going," his companion added.

"If I can just get her someplace where she can rest, she'll be all right, I think," Matt said, looking up at the conductor. "But I've got to get her out of here. And she's got to have water."

Feeling as though they were all blaming him for the heat, the poor trainman raised his hands for silence. "I'm doing all I can, folks," he tried to reassure them. "I knowed she was sick, so I've done sent for an ambulance to take her in to Mrs. Goode's. Wagon ought to be here anytime now, bringing the work crew with it."

"It ain't doin' no good a-comin'," a burly fellow insisted. "His missus could be daid afore it gets here. Like Jake was sayin', she's plumb overhet."

"Overheated," Verena gasped, correcting him.

"What I said, ain't it?"

Apparently, someone else took the request for water to heart, because just as she was about to sit up, he emptied a full canteen over her head, soaking her hair. Sputtering and choking, she fought the hands that held her down.

"Danged if she ain't havin' a fit!"

"Now, dearest, you just lie real still, and everything will be all right," McCready said soothingly. Afraid she was going to expose the ruse, he moved his hand to cover her mouth and nose with his palm. Looking up again, he announced, "She's hot—feels like she's running a fever." Thoroughly bedraggled and embarrassed, she closed her eyes to hide.

"*Told* you—woman's het up—had a dadblamed heat stroke!" the burly man insisted triumphantly.

At the other end of the car, a group of men were hammering and pounding furiously, cursing all the while. Then there was a shout of victory.

"We done got it! Here, Tad, gimmee a hand with this!"

Almost immediately, there was a traveling ripple of expletives as the flat slab of metal was passed head over head until it reached the men hovering over Verena. Somebody set it on the floor next to her.

"Come on, boys, let's get 'er on it and carry 'er outside fer air."

Verena's eyes flew open as somebody grabbed her feet and shoulders. Looking up, she saw McCready stand back, his expression of concern marred by the tic of a suppressed smile, and she realized the scoundrel was laughing inside.

"I can walk—really," she protested as they shifted her onto something hard. "Please, I don't need—"

Instead of listening, they pushed her down, stuffed her petticoat and skirt underneath her, then hoisted her up. Afraid of changing the balance, she couldn't even turn over and really hold on. It was all she could do to stare at the moving ceiling and pray silently. Grasping the sides of the door, she endured a frightening descent from the car to the ground. When she dared to look up, a crowd of strange men, most of them in dire need of a bath and a shave, ringed her, studying her as if she were a sideshow exhibit.

"I'm quite all right," she managed shakily, again trying to sit up.

"No, y'ain't. Ya better stay right where y' is," one of them said, pushing her back down again.

She twisted her head, trying to see McCready, but there was no sign of the miscreant. "Where's—where's my—my husband?" she managed to choke out.

"Raisin' a mite o' hell with the danged railroad," the big fellow answered. "Ain't no wagon here yet, and if'n it don't come right soon, I reckon we'll be a-carryin' yuh aller way t' Eagle Lake."

Unnerved by the thought, she insisted, "I need to speak with Mr. McCready—*now,* if you please."

"Eh, Mac, th' missus wants ye!" he called out loudly.

When the gambler bent over her solicitously, she caught his lapels in her hands, pulling him down almost head to head with her until she was looking through her wet hair into those dark eyes of his. "Don't—you—dare—leave—me," she told him through tightly clenched teeth. "And—and if you so much as *think* about laughing—"

Her words died as his lips brushed hers, and she could feel her cheeks go hot. If it hadn't been for the public disgrace of it, she would have slapped him. When he pulled away, he murmured, "Believe me, I'm trying not to." But there was an unholy look in those eyes. The corners of his mouth twitched as he added,

"You have to admit though that it's a pretty inspired use of a lavatory door."

"Wagon's coming!" a cowboy shouted.

"Ambulance is here," the trainman announced loudly. "Soon's it's unloaded, you can put her in it for the ride back to Sheriff Goode's house."

Despite the awful tightening in his gut, Matt managed to speak casually, observing, "I thought we were taking her into town—into Eagle Lake, that is."

"Ain't no town at Eagle Lake!" the cowboy roared. "Ain't no lake, and no eagles neither! Leastwise, none that I ever seen, anyways."

Matt pulled the timetable out of his pocket to reassure himself. "But it's a scheduled stop, isn't it?"

"Yep, but there ain't nothin' there."

The trainman tried to clarify the matter. "Now, I wouldn't say there's nothing there," he said judiciously. His eyes met Matt's for a moment. "It's the Goode Ranch mostly. Lot of ranches around here, in fact. But the road to Columbus cuts right through the Goode spread, so a lot of cowboys that work around these parts get off there. If they didn't, they'd be wastin' money going all the way to Columbus, then turnin' around and comin' back by horse."

"I suppose this means there's no hotel—and no bath to be had, either," McCready murmured.

"I reckon Mrs. Goode'd take care of it, if you was to ask 'er. She and the sheriff is real accommodatin' folks."

He didn't move a muscle, but the irony wasn't lost on Matt. After being on the run all the way from Natchez, he'd managed to deliver himself right into the clutches of a damned sheriff. All he could do was console himself with the notion that it'd be pretty hard to recognize the immaculate, fastidious Matthew Morgan in Mac McCready. And nobody would be expecting him to be traveling with an ailing wife. He'd just have to lie low and wait until Columbus to leave her. Until then, she'd be his excuse for avoiding Goode whenever possible.

"Looks like the crew's unloaded," the trainman announced. "Be careful puttin' her on the wagon." Before the conveyance was mobbed, he called out, "Mr. McCready's going with his missus! Wagon'll be back for everybody else as soon as it can make the trip around!"

"I'd like to sit up," Verena protested through the gambler's fingers.

The trainman looked at her, then at the lavatory door, wondering how he could explain to his superiors if it came up missing. "Reckon it ain't going to harm anything if the mister's with you," he decided. "That way you boys can be putting this privy door back up while you're waitin'."

"Thank you," she murmured, pushing McCready's hand away.

She stood up and shook out the folds of her ruined skirt, then started to climb onto the wagon. But the gambler caught her from behind and swung her up into his arms. "You know, you're a damned sight heavier than you look, my dear."

"Nobody could accuse you of an excess of chivalry," she muttered. "If I didn't consider myself a lady, I'd be tempted to snatch you baldheaded, I hope you know."

"Do you really want rid of me?" he whispered into her bedraggled hair.

"Just as soon as you give me ten dollars for this dress," she answered fervently.

Dumping her into the back of the wagon, he climbed onto the seat and grasped the reins. Flicking the ends over the rumps of the two mules, he called out, "Yee-haw!" One of the animals moved, dragging the other with it.

"Don't you need to ask the direction?" Verena muttered, righting herself behind him.

"I figure if I give 'em their heads, they'll go home." Leaning back on the hard board seat, he admitted, "I was hoping for a chance to talk this over before we get there."

Grasping his shoulder for balance, she climbed up beside him. "I don't care how it looks—I'm *not* bouncing around back there."

"What I started to say was I've been thinking, and—" Seeing her eyebrows lift behind the hair plastered over her forehead, he decided to soften her up a little before he broached his proposition. "That was one brave thing you did back there—you know that, don't you?"

"Well, I couldn't let that boy shoot you." Then, realizing that sounded as if she had an interest in him, she added, "Actually, I couldn't have let him shoot *anyone*. But I guess that almost evens us up, doesn't it? I mean, you got rid of my so-called brother, and I kept you from being shot. Now I have absolutely no reason to be beholden to you." Looking down at the tobacco juice stains on her dress, she grimaced. "Truth to tell, I think I've gotten the worst of the acquaintance. So far, nobody's poured water on you, and your clothing is still wholly presentable."

"I said I'd take care of that—and I meant it. It doesn't look like there's anyplace to buy anything you'd wear around here, but as soon as we get to Columbus—"

"But you aren't going to Columbus," she reminded him sweetly. "You're getting off here, as I recall."

"Like I said, I was just thinking about that, and I was kind of figuring that I owed you now."

"I'll just take the money, thank you."

"Yeah, well, maybe you'd better hear me out first. Right now, everybody on that train thinks I'm your husband. Once I take off alone across the prairie for Austin, you're going to get a lot of skeptical looks from those folks. Some will probably think you've been abandoned by a real rounder, but others. . ." He let his voice trail off while she considered the possibilities, then he nodded. "Uh-huh. It's not a very pretty notion, is it? And once some of those thick-skulled cowboys get that in their heads, who's going to fend them off for you? It'll be worse than that train station in Indianola. No, the way I look at it, I'm stuck with you until Columbus. Either that, or we both get off here."

"No, Mr. McCready—it is *I* who's stuck with *you,*" she declared wearily. "And as you already know, I've got to go on. No matter how anybody looks at or acts toward me, I've still got to get to San Angelo." Raising her eyes heavenward, she sighed heavily. "If I believed in reincarnation, I'd be wondering what I ever did in my last life to deserve this."

"Look, am I really that hard to take for a few hours

more? If everything goes right, we'll be parting company at Columbus tonight, anyway."

"Yes, Mr. McCready, you are. Never in all of my twenty-two years have I *ever* encountered anyone quite like you. Despite my rather pointed discouragement, you have managed to insinuate yourself into my life for some unfathomable but probably utterly nefarious reason. And absolutely nothing I can say or do seems to put an end to it. Furthermore," she added pointedly, "*nothing* has gone right since you first laid eyes on me."

"You didn't have to pretend to faint back there," he reminded her.

"Believe me, I am already regretting that," she muttered. "Now I have ruined a perfectly good traveling dress, and even worse than that, I smell as if I have been chewing tobacco and spitting it all over myself."

"For at least the fourth or fifth time, I said I'd buy you a new dress."

"You cannot. As you have already noted, there's no place to buy one," she retorted. "And it is extremely unlikely that you could find one already made, anyway. Although I think it highly questionable that a man of your obvious experience wouldn't know this, it is dress *lengths* that are bought. No, I shall just have to purchase the cloth and findings and make a new one for myself. Whenever I have time to do it, that is. So I will take your money in restitution and try to get along with the two I have left."

"Hire a seamstress to make you one."

"In the middle of nowhere? Yes, Mr. McCready, I shall do that," she countered tiredly. "Look, I'm finished talking about it, so just give me the ten dollars, and we will be totally even."

"That's another thing I was meaning to mention."

"What?"

"You can't go around calling your husband Mr. McCready, you know."

"Well, I intend to."

"Oh, it sounds all right when you are referring to me to someone else, I suppose," he conceded. "But when you are talking *to* me, you'd better call me by a name."

"Nothing that comes to mind would be suitable."

"My friends call me Mac," he lied.

"That's a little too informal. Surely you have a given name?"

"Yes." Taking a deep breath, he considered whether to invent one, or whether to use his own. "All right," he answered finally, "it's Matthew, but I'd rather you used Mac."

"Matthew," she repeated, mulling it over. "There's nothing wrong with Matthew," she decided. "All right—when speaking face-to-face, I shall use that."

He was already regretting that small bit of truth. He should have said Tom or Bill or Henry, or something like that. If it wasn't already, the name Matthew Morgan would soon be on posters in every sheriff's office between Florida and New Mexico. Old Alexandre Giroux would see to that. And Matthew McCready sounded too damned close to Matthew Morgan for comfort. But he'd done it. Once he parted company with her, he wouldn't make the mistake again, he promised himself.

"And you'd better not call yourself Verena," he said

aloud. "You never know when you might encounter your brothers."

"I told you—I don't have any brothers."

"You take my meaning."

"Well, I won't be Bess. I don't care if it's your mother's name or not, you know. I just don't happen to like it for myself."

"It's more than a little possible those two railroad men overheard me say it."

"Mr. McCready—"

"Mac."

"Matthew." Rearranging her disgusting skirt, she reflected that he actually had a point. "All right, but at least make it Elizabeth."

"Elizabeth McCready. It does have a certain sound to it," he admitted. "Well, then that's settled."

"Until Columbus." She looked up, studying his handsome profile for a moment. "You don't care a button about what happens to me, do you? We're doing this for you and not for my reputation at all."

"I was trying to protect you, that's all."

"You're a dangerous man, Mr. McCready, but not for the reason I first thought," she decided. "When you first latched on to me like a barnacle, I suspected you had designs on my person. And while you may have, I think you've got something else to hide."

"The first instinct is always the best," he murmured. "You're a lovely, lovely lass, Mrs. McCready."

"If you can look at me now and still say that, I *know* you're pretty adept at lying," she responded dryly.

"You know, if you'd soften that tongue, you wouldn't be a spinster."

"I'm sure there are worse things, Mr. McCready. And if my tongue delivers me from marriage to most of the men I've known, it's been a blessing to me," she stated flatly.

"Somebody soured you on the institution."

"That is none of your concern."

"The bounder led you astray and abandoned you," he hazarded.

"Don't be absurd."

"He chose someone else."

"No."

"He already had a wife."

"No."

"He wouldn't convert to Catholicism for you."

"I'm not a Catholic, Mr. McCready."

"Where I come from, something's wrong with a fine-looking woman if she's not married by the time she's sixteen or seventeen."

"And I wasn't born in the backwoods of Tennessee either." Fixing him with a withering look, she declared, "This is just your way of turning the tables, isn't it? You're afraid I'm going to ask you something you don't want to answer."

"How's that?"

"Why do you need to pretend you have a wife?" Before he could say anything, she hit him with the other one. "Just what are you running from, Mr. McCready?"

"Most everybody coming to Texas is running from something, Verena. Even you."

"We were speaking of you. For all I know, you could be a thief—or even a murderer."

"No to both counts. So for now, I guess you'll just have to trust me."

"Well, I don't."

"Who was he?"

Startled by the suddenness of the question, she blinked. "Who was who?" she asked cautiously.

"Who soured you so young, Verena?"

He had no right to expect an answer, and she didn't have to give one. But she took a deep breath, then let go of it slowly. "My father," she admitted.

"Your father?"

"Yes. He was handsome and charming and quick-witted around women, but behind that facade he was cunning, cruel, and heartless. He never came home from the war, Mr. McCready."

"War takes a terrible toll on a man."

"Oh, he survived it, all right," she said bitterly. "Some months before it was over, he deserted his country, then vanished. He deserted Mama. And he deserted me."

"I'm sorry."

She met his eyes again. "I don't want your pity. I watched my mother slowly die inside—she was a dead woman living those last few years. And when she finally left this earth, I promised myself I'd never let anyone give me that kind of pain. And if that means I go to my grave a spinster, then so be it."

There was dead silence between them for a long moment, then he looked away. "Well, you've made a tough hill for any man to climb," he said soberly.

"My father was a dangerous man, Mr. McCready—handsome and seductive. Just like you."

He looked up at that. "I may have done a lot of things that I'm not exactly proud of, but whether you want to believe it or not, I've never run out on anyone. Call it curiosity or call it folly, but I've always played the hand to the end."

"I expect there are dozens of women who could tell a different tale."

"Maybe they could, but they won't. Like I told you, there's two kinds of women in this world, and I can tell the difference. So I always went for the bad ones. That way, they didn't expect anything, and I didn't disappoint them. When it was over, it was over, with no regrets on either side."

She didn't have any answer to that, none that would prick his conscience, anyway. If he really believed that, then he'd just never looked back to see the women crying behind him.

Verena was so hungry her stomach hurt, and making matters even worse, the smell of fried chicken completely permeated the air, almost haunting her, driving everything else from her mind. Somewhere at the other end of the ranch house, her fellow passengers were probably gorging themselves on that chicken and everything else.

Closing her eyes, she could envision the mashed potatoes, the cream gravy, the early beans, the biscuits. . . . No, she told herself severely, she'd just have to wait until somebody brought her supper. At least she was cleaner than when she arrived, she reminded herself.

As soon as McCready had lifted her down from the wagon, Mrs. Goode was there, hovering over her solicitously, insisting she get out of her clothes, wash up a bit, and lie down to conserve her strength in the heat. As Verena balefully watched McCready wander off to, no doubt, enjoy himself, she was taken by the arm, guided to this small bedroom, and left with two pitchers of warm water and a big chunk of homemade soap. Mrs. Goode then left her alone, promising to send her "a mite to eat later."

So Verena had stripped down to her chemise and drawers, then washed the sweat and dirt from every place she could reach. Finally, she soaped her hair and rinsed it as well as she could. Before she was finished, a young Mexican girl had darted in to snatch up her soiled dress, and disappeared without a word, leaving her no choice but to remain in her room. With nothing else to do, she'd lain down on the lumpy, totally unsatisfactory bed and stared at the cracks in the plastered ceiling, tantalized by the mouthwatering aroma of that fried chicken.

While she waited, she listened as numerous wagonloads of rowdy railroad passengers were brought in. Judging by the noisy cursing and loud behavior, it sounded as if they'd congregated right outside her window. Then the dinner bell rang, and somebody shouted, "Come and get it—food's on the table! Everybody as gets in line gets served, but where you eat it is your business! Just get the vittles and keep movin' on through, 'cause there ain't room to be sitting down in the house!"

It wasn't until everything had pretty much quieted down that another girl, this one a thin, tired-looking blonde of maybe fourteen or fifteen years, appeared at Verena's door, tray in hand. Placing it on a table near the bed, she'd started to leave when Verena looked down in dismay. There was only a scant bowl of brown liquid and one slice of unbuttered bread.

"Excuse me," she said, stopping the girl, "but you

must have forgotton the rest of it—I mean, there's been some sort of mistake."

"Huh?"

"This cannot be my dinner," she declared positively.

"Yes'm, it shore is."

"Then I need to speak to Mrs. Goode."

"She cain't come, she told me to tell y'all real perlite like. But what with nearly a hunnerd passengers and ever'body on the repair crew, her hands is plumb full." Smiling now, the girl added proudly, "Me 'n' Juana 'n' the missus, we done fried up nigh t' thirty hens, while's Betsy and Angela wuz a-peelin' a bushel and a half o' potatoes."

"Oh, I see," Verena said with relief. "This is just the first course. You made soup to go with dinner."

"No'm. That there's broth Juana had left from bilin' the beef bones. She wuz a-gonna make some gravy with it, but there wuzn't enuff beef t' go 'round, so they's ettin' th' hens instead." Seeing that the visitor wasn't at all pleased, she took several steps backward before explaining, "Bein's y'all wuz sick and in a del-lycut sit-u-a-tion, th' missus allowed as how too much on your stummick'd make y'all a whole lot worse off."

"But I'm already so hungry I could cry," Verena protested.

"Oh, Ah reckon she'll let y'all have somethin' t'night, if'n y'all wuz to keep that down yuh."

"Tonight!"

"Yes'm." Taking advantage of Verena's obvious consternation, the girl made a hasty exit.

"Wait a minute—where's my dress?"

Either the girl didn't hear, or she was deliberately ignoring her. It was all some sort of hideous mistake. By the time the sun went down, Verena wouldn't even be here. She'd be in Columbus, parting company from Matthew McCready. Coming off the bed, she ran to the door, shouting, "Will somebody please fetch my dress? I've got to talk to someone!"

With the exception of an elderly Mexican walking toward her, the corridor was empty. As he caught sight of her standing there in her thin lawn chemise, his face broke into a toothless grin. Unnerved, she retreated enough to close the door and slide the bolt, locking it.

The room was airless, stifling. Moving to the window, she could see the train's passengers everywhere—leaning against tree trunks, sitting on the grass, on bare dirt, perched on the porch railing even—and every one of them had a plate of food. The Mexican girl who'd taken her dress was circulating among them with a pitcher, filling cups.

Dispirited, Verena went back to sit on the edge of the bed. The springs under the mattress creaked ominously and the whole side dipped downward. Tearing off a piece of the bread, she dipped it into the broth, and then carried it to her mouth, telling herself it was better than nothing. Just barely. Beneath a film of grease, the liquid was salty and heavily flavored with onions. It certainly wasn't anything she'd feed a guest in *any* condition.

Some time later, there was a soft rap on the door. Thinking it must be the girl finally returning her dress, she hastily threw the bolt and opened the door. She'd been wrong again—it was Matthew McCready with a big carpetbag in one hand and what looked to be a rolled-up napkin in the other.

"You'll have to come back later," she said, quickly getting behind the door to close it. She was too late. His foot was in the way.

Seemingly impervious to her embarrassment, he walked right into the room, leaving her standing there, gaping. As she watched in disbelief, he put something down on the chair's seat, dropped his bag, then shrugged out of his coat and hung it over the chair's back. Crossing her arms over her breasts, she elbowed the door shut. Then her temper exploded.

"Just what do you think you're doing in here?" she demanded furiously. "In case you didn't notice, I'm not dressed!"

"Shhhh—they'll think we're quarreling."

"I don't care what they think, Mr. McCready. Get out of my room this instant!" Looking about her for a weapon, she saw nothing useful. "Did you hear me? I'm telling you to get out!" He was loosening the thin black silk tie at his neck. Shocked, she took a couple of steps toward the window to call for help, but the realization that there was no telling just who or what might come to her aid stopped her. As a precaution against the Al Thompsons of the world, she lowered her voice. "Answer my question—just what *do* you think you're going to do in here, anyway?"

He looked over at her, an unholy gleam in those nearly black eyes. A smile lurked at the corners of his mouth as he answered, "Make myself comfortable."

"Before I let you lay so much as a finger on me, I'll bring this whole house down on you. If I have to, I'll scream until Sheriff Goode comes in here himself." When McCready didn't seem impressed, she licked her dry lips and threatened, "I'll tell him you're a wanted man—that you're trying to ravish me—that—"

"I brought you some fried chicken," he murmured.

"You're not listening to me! I'm not dressed, and you cannot be here! It's indecent!" Then it dawned on her what he'd just said. "You brought me some supper?" she asked cautiously.

"There's three pieces of chicken in that napkin." Grinning now, his gaze slid over her lazily. "I never did understand what it is in a woman that makes her think she's naked when she's still got everything covered."

"If you had any shred of decency, you'd know," she retorted. "Where is it?"

"My decency or the food?"

"The food."

"I put it on the chair seat. Come on over and get it." As he was answering, his hands undid the top button of his shirt.

For a moment, she just gaped, then she found her voice. "I may be hungry, Mr. McCready, but I'm not *that* hungry," she declared coldly.

"Suit yourself. If you don't want it, I guess I'll probably eat it sometime before I turn in. After the feed she just put on, I doubt if the Goode woman's going to cook another full meal today."

"Well, you're not turning in here, whatever that means."

He considered the bed, then her. "In spite of what I said about you being heavy, you don't look like you'd take up much room. Tell you what—you just take that

hat pin to bed with you, and if I roll over onto your side, you can jab me with it."

Taken aback, she choked out, "*What?* Surely you don't think—well, you can just rid yourself of that notion right now! This is *my* room, Mr. McCready! And I don't know what you think you're going to do, but I'm not about to go along with it." Spying an old iron poker in the corner behind the empty potbellied stove, she edged toward it. Out of the corner of her eye, she could see him remove his shirt. "For the last time—*will* you get out?"

"Not until I wash up."

"You can wash up outside. Surely they have a water pump somewhere out there. Then you can go sleep off whatever you've been drinking under one of those trees until we leave."

"It was lemonade. I don't think the sheriff wanted to give an already short-tempered bunch of men anything stronger."

"I don't care what it was," she snapped. "Believe me, I cannot wait until nightfall to reach Columbus." Snatching the poker, she swung around. Rather than heading for the door, he had his hand on the water pitcher. As she lifted her weapon, he raised an eyebrow.

"You know, before you go to swinging that thing, maybe I'd better tell you it's going to be tomorrow sometime before they get the rail fixed. The damned thing's buckled."

"*What?*" she fairly screeched.

"You know, for an educated female, you repeat yourself a lot."

Do you mean to tell me that after what I can only

consider an utterly miserable ride on the train—that—that we're *stranded* in this godforsaken place?"

"Uh-huh. Looks like part of the rail buckled because of the heat, or at least that's what one of the crew told Goode. If they can't get it straightened out, they'll be sending back to Harrisburg for another one. So, my darling Bess, I guess we'll just have to make the best of it."

"Ohhhh no, we don't. There's no way on God's green earth that I'm going to share this room with you, Mr. McCready." Brandishing the poker with both hands now, she said evenly, "Now—for the last time, are you getting out—or do I have to divide your thick skull with this?"

Before she knew what he meant to do, his hand caught her arm, forcing it down. Leaning into her, he was so close she could feel the warmth of his breath on her face. "You know, if your mama was anything like you, I can see why the old man left her." As her eyes widened, he nodded. "Now, let's get a few things straight right now, Miss Verena. First, I'm just as tired and just as cranky as you are. Second—second, seducing a shrew is just about the last thing on my mind. Third—"

Her chin came up. "There's no need to be rude or crude, Mr. McCready."

"Third, you can raise the roof if you want to, but you'd better think about it first. When it gets dark around here, every nook and cranny on the place is going to be filled with disgruntled passengers—they're already talking about putting thirty to forty men on that porch out front. And right now, you've got just about everybody's sympathy except mine. But if you let the cat out of the bag that we're not man and wife, you're going to find yourself out on your ear and facing those men all by yourself." His piece said, he released her hand. "Still want to hit me with that?" he gibed.

"Yes. But I won't." Dispirited by almost everything, she let the poker slip from her hand. "I guess you can sleep on the floor." Turning away, she leaned her head against the wall. "I'm nothing like my mother, Mr. McCready."

He'd dealt from the bottom of the deck, and he knew it. Coming up behind her, he felt almost helpless. "Look, there's no need to cry, Verena," he said, sighing. "I shouldn't have said that. I didn't know either of them."

"I'm not crying, Mr. McCready," she responded tiredly. "I never cry. I watched Mama shed enough tears to last both of us a lifetime." Savoring the coolness of the plaster against her temple, she closed her eyes. "I'm just weary, hot, hungry, and alone. I don't belong here, and I don't know why I've come. Maybe to spit on his grave—I don't know."

His own anger gone, he laid his hand on her shoulder. "You want to close the book. It's like that for me, you know. I hate to throw down my hand before that last card's turned over." Turning her around to face him, he smoothed her damp chestnut hair back from her forehead with the palm of his hand. "When you hit a run of bad luck, Rena, you just keep playing and hoping tomorrow's going to be better. And eventually it is."

"Is it?"

"Yes."

She was too pretty, too vulnerable for him to resist. Before he realized what he was doing, he found himself bending his head to hers, tasting the salt on her lips. When she didn't resist, his arms slid around her shoulders, holding her so close, he could feel the warmth of her body through the thin cotton chemise.

For a moment, she yielded to his kiss, savoring the heady strangeness of it. Then the shock of his bare arms and shoulders touching hers caught up with her. Stiffening, she brought her hands up between them, pushing him away.

She looked more shocked than angry. Stepping back, he ran his fingers through his hair before he managed, "I'm sorry, Rena—I didn't intend to do that."

Her eyes still wide, she stared into his face. "Papa used to call me Rena," she whispered, swallowing the lump in her throat. "He was the only one—ever. To Mama, I was always Verena."

The spell totally broken now, he exhaled heavily. "You'd better eat before you faint. Then after I get cleaned up, maybe we can walk around—maybe look the place over before it gets dark. There's no sense in being cooped up in here."

"I can't go anywhere in my underclothes, Mr. McCready."

"Oh—yeah. Well, at least I think I can fix that."

"I don't see how."

"I guess it's my fault it's gone." Before she could lose her temper again, he went on to explain, "Since there's nowhere to replace your dress out here, the sheriff's wife offered to try cleaning the worst of it with a little fuller's earth and baking soda water.

Knowing how upset you are over ruining your clothes, I didn't think anybody could do much more harm to it, anyway, so I told her to go ahead and see if she could improve the looks a little."

There was no figuring him out. Every time she thought she had assessed him right, he did something wholly unexpected. "You're having it *cleaned*?" she asked incredulously.

"I know it's not going to look like you'd want, but it ought to be a damned sight better than it was. But in case it isn't, the last crew back tonight is supposed to be bringing your bag in." Passing his palm over the stubble on his face, he added ruefully, "You're not the only one inconvenienced by this, you know. I figured by nightfall I'd be bathed and shaved and looking to scare up a good game of poker in Columbus. Now I'm going to be spending the night cooped up in here with you glowering at me, thinking as soon as you let that guard of yours down, I'll be expecting to take liberties with you. Well, I won't."

"If you get up off that floor, I'll scream loud enough to wake the dead," she warned him. "I won't care what anybody thinks of me."

"I'll cut you for the bed," he offered.

"You'll do what?"

Leaning over, he retrieved a worn pack of cards from his coat pocket. While she watched, fascinated, he shuffled them expertly, then held out the whole deck in his palm. "Go ahead—pick one."

"You want me to take a card? Just any card?"

"Uh-huh."

Curious now, she reached out and pulled one from the middle of the stack, then turned it over. "It's a five."

With his left hand, he slid one out and held it up. "Jack of Spades. Well, my darling Elizabeth," he announced blithely, "it looks like the bed is mine."

"Now that's not fair! I've never gambled on anything in my life, and you know it!"

"You just did—and you lost."

"I don't even play cards," she protested. "We never had any in the house."

"They go up in value, starting with the deuce and winding up with the ace. Two, three, four, five, six, seven—"

"I can count, Mr. McCready," she snapped.

"Eight, nine, ten, Jack, Queen, King, and ace," he went on. "My knave of spades is higher than your five, and in a cut, the higher card wins. I'll take the bed, and you can have the covers on the floor."

"I don't suppose we could try that again?" she asked hopefully. "If I'm going to gamble, I ought to at least know what I'm doing."

"It's based on luck, not knowledge."

"Then I should have known better," she muttered. "I don't have any luck."

A loud knock interrupted them, then a voice called through the door, "Missus Muh-Cray-dee, I done got y'all's gown."

It was Matthew who opened the door. The thin blond girl looked up, taking in his bare chest, and her whole face broke into a smile. "Y'all's the mister?" she asked, simpering.

"Uh-huh." Turning to Verena, he murmured, "I believe your dress has arrived, my dear."

The girl's gaze shifted to her, and the smile faded abruptly. "It ain't all out, but it's near as Juana could get it." Her eyes raked Verena from head to toe. "Guess y'all ain't been missin' it none, huh?" she added knowingly, nodding toward the wrinkled quilt on the bed.

"I hardly think so," Verena responded, coloring. Then, thinking perhaps that that didn't sound quite right, she added, "He just got here." No, that sounded even worse. "And it's broad daylight." Mortified now, she gritted out, "Just leave it on the bed, and I'll pay for the cleaning as soon as my things arrive. I'm afraid I left my purse on the train."

"I'll take care of it, my dear," Matthew said, digging into his pocket. Taking out a silver dollar, he flipped it to the girl, who caught it saucily, then promptly hustled herself out of the room. As he closed the door behind her, he looked across the narrow area to Verena, and as one eyebrow went up, one corner of his mouth curved downward. "If you think it's got to be in the dark, you sure don't know much about seduction, do you?"

Her face beet red now, she retorted, "No, of course not—nor do I care to learn."

"I know."

The way he said it didn't sound quite right to her ears. "What's that supposed to mean?"

"When I first laid eyes on you, I figured you were a plum ripe for picking." Cocking his head slightly, he sobered. "On closer inspection, you've turned out to be downright green."

"And sour?" she asked sweetly.

"No—just green. And," he added, sighing, "I've never been a man to pluck the green ones." Going back to the chair, he picked up the napkin and held it out to her. "While I wash up, you go ahead and eat. Then we'll get out and about while there's still a little daylight. Go on—it'll give you something to do besides watch me take my clothes off."

"I beg your pardon?"

"I'm going to wash up."

"Not while I'm in here, you aren't—and I don't intend to leave."

"Suit yourself." Leaning over, he unfastened the hasp on his bag, opened it, and took out a folded shirt. Holding the garment up, he shook it out, surveying the wrinkles with resignation. "If Jean-Louis could see this, he'd probably cry over it."

"Jean-Louis?" she repeated, momentarily diverted.

"My tailor."

"You've got a tailor," she muttered. "And I suppose you've got a diamond stickpin, too."

"Jean-Louis uses only the finest French cambric and sews as fine a seam as a Parisian modiste—makes the best shirts in New Orleans. There's an art to shirtmaking, you know. And no, I don't have a diamond stickpin—not anymore, anyway."

"I hope you lost it gambling." Seeing his hands move to his waist, she demanded, "What are you doing?"

"Fixing to wash up."

"Oh—no, you're not."

"Well, I'm sure as hell not putting clean clothes over a stinking body," he countered. "You don't have to watch, if you don't want to. Just turn that chair around, and you won't see a damned thing. Give me five minutes, and I'll be cleaned up and all my offending parts will be covered enough to suit you."

"Right now, everything about you is offensive, Mr. McCready," she said with feeling. "You have no decency, no morals, and moreover you—"

As he unbuttoned the first button on his pants, the scathing words died on her lips. Averting her eyes, she stumbled over her own feet in her haste to turn the chair around. Picking up the food, she then sank down, facing a rough-plastered wall. Not daring to look up, she untied the napkin.

"By the time you get that eaten, I'll be about done," he promised her.

He'd brought her three pieces of golden crusty chicken—two thighs and an odd-shaped, unfamiliar piece. As she looked at it, she was too hungry to resist. Venting her anger on it, she tored into a thigh with her teeth.

"When you get to the pully-bone, don't break it."

"The what?" she managed with her mouth full.

"The funny-looking one. When you've got all the meat off the bone, you hold one end and somebody else takes the other, then you both pull until it breaks. Whoever winds up with the longer part gets good luck."

"Well, I—" She looked sideways, and the way the light angled into the mirror, she could see Matthew McCready. He didn't have a stitch on anywhere.

When her sentence abruptly ended, he swung around, affording her her first complete view of the male animal. "Something the matter?"

Mortified, she ducked her head. "No—nothing—

nothing at all. I don't know what I was going to say. It—it wasn't anything important, anyway."

It was then that he noticed the mirror above the small dressing table. "Why, Miss Verena, you ought to be ashamed of yourself," he murmured.

"If I'd wanted to see you, I wouldn't be sneaking peeks at your reflection, Mr. McCready," she countered acidly. "I would have simply turned around and stared you up one side and down the other. But I didn't—and I won't. In fact—" She stood up, and taking care to keep her back to him, she edged toward the bed, where she snatched her gown, then pulled it over her head. "I don't know where I'll go, but as soon as I find the comb Mrs. Goode lent me, I'm leaving. I don't care what anybody thinks—I'm not spending another minute in here!"

The comb sailed over her head and landed on the bed. Grabbing it, she fairly dived for the door. As her hand closed around the knob, she heard him ask, "Aren't you forgetting something?"

She looked down to where the bodice of her dress gaped open. "Oh." Her face red-hot, she hastily fastened the small buttons.

"That, too—but I was meaning these."

She wasn't about to turn around. "What are they?" she snapped.

"Your shoes. Unless you want to tickle your feet with splinters, you'd better wear 'em. Here." He sent them sliding across the floor.

Bending down, she scooped her black high-tops into her arm, then wrenched the door open and plunged through it. Stopping in the small, narrow hall, she put the comb between her teeth, balanced herself against the wall, and forced first one foot, then the other into her shoes. As she bent down to tighten the laces, she could hear voices carrying around the corner, and she froze.

"Gib ain't gonna like it, but that Howard woman ain't nowhere."

"Yeah. I knowed she wasn't on that train."

"If I didn't have a stake in this, Lee, I'd be going home and leavin' him to figger it out."

"You think the sheriff suspects anything's up?"

"Naw. I told him what I told 'em at the last place—I said I was just a-following the railroad, hopin' to find her. He told me less'n there was a warrant or something, there wasn't much he could do exceptin' watch for her."

"What're you gonna tell Gib?"

"Same thing you are—there still ain't no Howard woman on that train. Hell, except'n' the sick one and the one with a passel of kids, there ain't no women between fifteen and forty on it."

"Well, I don't care what he says—I ain't goin' around askin' no more. He can start doin' some of his dirty work hisself."

"You quit, and he'll cut you out. Sure as anything, he'll cut you out."

"I don't like messin' up a woman, Charley. And that's what it's going to come to, I know it. Way I look at it, once he's done with 'er, he ain't letting 'er go. It'll be just like it was with that damned lawyer. Coyotes'll be diggin' up her bones."

Having already heard more than enough, and afraid

of encountering them, Verena crept on her hands and knees back to her room. It wasn't until she could feel the doorknob that she dared stand up, and when she did, she all but dived through the door.

"It sure didn't take you long to miss me," McCready murmured sardonically.

"Don't say anything—don't say anything at all." Still holding the doorknob, she leaned her head against the door and listened. But there was nothing more to hear. Finally, deciding they must've gone the other way, she let go.

She was obviously pale and shaken. Curious now, he came up behind her. "What's the matter?"

She gulped air. "There were two men out there—they were hunting for me."

"Did you get a look at them?"

"No, of course not. If I had, I don't think I'd be here right now."

"Your long-lost brothers again?"

"I wish you'd quit saying that," she snapped. "I don't *have* any brothers, long-lost or otherwise."

"All right, then. Were they the same ones from the train station?"

"I didn't see the ones at the train station," she reminded him, "but they must surely be. Judging from what I overheard, one of them told Sheriff Goode I was his sister, anyway."

"I don't suppose they happened to say why they'd want to lie about you, did they?"

"You don't believe me."

"Of course, I believe you. For some unknown reason, two fellows claiming to be relations of yours are scouring East Texas for you. Makes sense to me, I guess, if that's the story you want to stick to."

"There's no reason on earth why anyone would want me," she declared behind him.

"Besides the obvious, which, if they got to know you, might not be nearly so obvious to them," he murmured, retrieving his gun from its holster. Easing past her, he held it close to his side as he nudged the door open. While she held her breath, he kicked the door wider, then sprang into the narrow hallway with the gun cocked, ready to fire. The area was deserted. She followed close behind him.

"Where were they?"

"Down that way—just around the corner."

"Yeah, well, it looks like they took off," he said, lowering the Colt. "I suppose you want me to go looking for them, don't you?"

"You can't go anywhere like that."

"You didn't give me time to get my pants on. But I am covered, in case you didn't notice."

He had his half-buttoned shirt on, and it came well below his hips, but his legs and feet were bare. He ought to look ridiculous, but he didn't. He was too tall, too broad shouldered, too dangerously handsome. Looking into those dark, nearly black eyes, she found herself almost speechless.

"I've still got to shave and get the rest of my clothes on," he went on smoothly, "but I'll be ready to go out by the time you finish tying your laces and fixing your hair. Maybe if we take a look around, we can find out just what it is they're up to. I'd like to get another look at 'em, anyway."

"I don't want to take a chance on meeting them."

"Why not?"

"I don't frighten easily, Mr. McCready, but I think somebody named Gib wants to kill me." As his eyebrows went up, she nodded. "The exact words I overhead were 'Once he's done with 'er, he ain't letting 'er go.' "

"You've read too many dime novels, my dear," he declared.

"*Will* you listen to me?" she demanded furiously. "He also said the coyotes would be digging me up just like they did some lawyer. That is exactly what I heard out there."

As he looked at her, his eyes narrowed for a moment as he reconsidered. There was no mistaking her fear. He took a deep breath and exhaled it before he decided, "All right. But first you'd better fess up."

"Fess up?"

"Tell me what it is they're after."

"But I have no idea! No idea at all, Mr. McCready, I swear it! I don't even *know* anyone down here. And I assure you that there's absolutely nothing in my life that could be of interest to anyone. Except for one miserable term of teaching in western Pennsylvania, I haven't even been out of Philadelphia until this trip. No, they've got me confused for someone else—that's got to be what's happened. It just has to."

"Like the man said back on the train, Verena's not exactly a common name," he reminded her. "And with Howard, it'd be pretty hard to mistake."

"Nobody even knows I'm coming except Mr. Hamer—and you."

"Somebody does."

"Well, I can't think of any reason they'd even care if they did know. I'm going to report this to Sheriff Goode," she decided.

"I don't think I'd do that."

"Why not?"

"Well, for one thing, what are you going to tell him? You yourself admitted this doesn't make any sense."

"And just what would *you* do in my shoes?" she countered sarcastically. "Wait until you were murdered in your bed?"

It was a long moment before he answered, and when he did, he surprised her. "Let me finish dressing and shaving, and then we'll go out and walk around. If we're lucky, maybe we'll get a good look at 'em while they're not expecting it. Right now, you've got some advantages."

"Such as?"

"They don't know what you look like, and they're looking for Verena Howard, not Elizabeth McCready. And you've got me—until Columbus."

Somehow that didn't seem like much comfort.

After a casual search of the ranch house and the immediate area around it yielded no trace of her mysterious pursuers, Matt and Verena joined the other passengers beneath the darkening sky to eat a late repast of cold beef sandwiches, homemade pickles, and dried apricots, all washed down with the sheriff's own potent, well-aged cider. Mellowed with food and drink, everyone finally gathered by an old oak tree to hear an old fiddler play lively reels and to watch the ranch's hired girls dance with enthusiastic, albeit, inebriated cowhands.

Sitting on the ground hugging her knees, Verena closed her eyes and thought longingly of a home so far away it might as well have been a foreign country. That it was a narrow rowhouse jammed between others just like it didn't matter anymore. It might be plain and ordinary, but it was safe and familiar. Unlike Texas.

Against her will, her mind kept going over that strange conversation she'd overheard, trying to make sense of why two complete strangers were looking for her, of why somebody called Gib would want to harm her. She didn't even know anybody in Texas, except Matthew McCready, and she couldn't claim to really know him. Nor did she have much of anything anybody would want. Everything she owned could be had for fifty dollars. No, that wasn't quite true, she supposed. There was her father's farm. But by the tone of Mr. Hamer's letter, it wasn't worth much either. He hadn't even actually encouraged her to make the trip to claim it, saying if she preferred, he'd try to make the sale for her. After taxes, probate fees, and the expense of advertising it, she might clear a few hundred dollars, or it might be even less.

And somehow that seemed to fit what she knew of her father. In forty-six years, he'd managed to squander nearly everything that came his way—his family, his education, his reputation. A handsome man with an eye for the ladies, he'd been murdered, apparently leaving behind nobody to weep for him, not even her. No, least of all her.

And now this. It was preposterous—and frightening. For two cents, she'd turn around and go home. But if these men were determined enough to find her that they'd search every rail stop for her, what was there to say they wouldn't try to look her up in Philadelphia? At least in Philadelphia there were places to hide, she reminded herself. Out here she stuck out like the proverbial sore thumb. Out here she had no one.

Beside her, Matthew McCready leaned up against a stump, watching, sipping cider. As the warm night breeze ruffled his hair, his thoughts turned to the decadent elegance of New Orleans, to thick carpets and baize-covered tables, to high-stakes games played under glittering chandeliers. To those fancy salons where light-skinned octoroon girls presided like princesses over a court of wealthy, paying swains. To the stately brick mansions guarded by wrought-iron fences and ornate, locked gates. A heady world for a Tennessee boy with nothing to recommend him but a handsome face, a good memory, and a talent for games of chance. Until the night he'd killed Philippe Giroux, he'd enjoyed an extraordinary run of luck. Now he was just on the run.

If he'd had any sense, he'd have stuck to his original plan and headed straight for Helena. Instead, he'd gotten himself sidetracked into what should have been an amorous little adventure with the lovely Verena Howard. And the irony of that wasn't lost on him. There'd been plenty of adventure, more than he'd bargained for, but without so much as a dash of romance to go with it. And his second notion of using her to cover his tracks wasn't panning out either. Instead of drawing less attention as a married man, he'd attached himself to a girl with some pretty dangerous enemies. The way things were going, he'd be damned lucky if she didn't turn to Goode for help. She wasn't the kind to lie to the sheriff, and when she told the truth, they'd both be facing a lot of unpleasant questions. No matter how he answered, he'd be suspected of something.

No, he ought to cut his losses and run, he reflected soberly. It wasn't the gentlemanly thing to do, but then he wasn't a gentleman. If he could just get her out of Eagle Lake without any more trouble, he could still part company with her at Columbus. Then, if she went to a lawman, he'd be out of it. To be on the safe side, he'd make sure she thought he was on his way to Austin, but just as soon as he put her on the stagecoach bound for San Antonio, he'd buy himself a horse and strike out alone for Helena.

With almost everybody there either hiding from the law or running from an unsavory past, it wasn't a place where anybody'd be asking him any questions. From what he'd heard about it, a nosy man didn't last long in Helena, and when he turned up dead, nobody knew anything about it. Even in death, there was a certain anonymity there, and the town cemetery was said to have more than its share of desperados buried under colorful ephithets instead of Christian names. While he hadn't been there to see it, he didn't doubt the stories.

Yeah, that's where he'd go, all right, but it wasn't anyplace he wanted to stay. It was just a place to get lost for a while, he told himself. Just a place where he'd change his name again, grow a beard to change his looks, and lay low long enough to be forgotten. A lawless, rough-and-tumble, wide-open town, where laundresses were said to practice another, less respectable profession, where men in dirty flannel shirts and bandanas indulged their vices. To fit in there, he'd be giving up his baths and his fancy clothes, and about the only things he'd be keeping were his knife, his Army Colt, and his silk underwear—and the latter only because it couldn't be seen.

There was a certain irony in going to Helena, too. While he'd grown up a dirt farmer's boy in Tennessee, he'd left home at sixteen, determined to give himself a better, easier life. It had taken him years to acquire the polish and style that got him into high-stakes games in

New Orleans' fancier establishments. No, he didn't want to go back to dirty, dingy saloons, where all a man could smell was sawdust, cheap tobacco, cheaper whiskey, and rank sweat. And he didn't want to grow that beard.

Forcing his thoughts from his bleak prospects, he considered Verena. On the one hand, she was as prim and proper as the schoolteacher she claimed to be. On the other, she had to be hiding something. Something more valuable than the nearly worthless farm she was coming to claim. And yet she'd been so concerned about her expenditures, about getting him to pay for her ruined dress. As if she couldn't afford another. But somebody—no, make that at least *two* somebodies—wanted whatever it was that she did or didn't have. And it had nothing to do with her being a fine-looking girl; he'd go bail on that. So that made her either the innocent victim of some sort of coincidence—or a damned good liar.

He had to admit it had him intrigued. Yeah, if she were lying, she was a convincing enough actress to earn her living on the stage. The way she told of her teaching disappointment in backwater Pennsylvania was pretty damned believable. So what did she have that total strangers wanted so badly they'd talk of killing her for it? The thought crossed his mind that maybe she was a runaway heiress. Then he discarded that. She didn't behave like somebody used to having money. He knew that much. He'd worked too hard to learn that act himself.

Well, it didn't matter, anyway. He couldn't afford to get himself tangled up with her. He had enough trouble of his own, and it would only take one mistake to get that noose around his neck. If he got caught now, Alexandre Giroux would intimidate or bribe whoever it took to make sure he was hanged. And to folks who didn't realize the old man's power, the fact that Matthew Morgan ran made him guilty. No, he had to keep going. He had to hide in Helena, a place where everybody was on the run.

"You're certainly quiet," Verena said finally.

"Huh?"

"You haven't said ten words in ten minutes."

"You know, I was just thinking the same thing about you," he countered, recovering.

"Oh?"

"Yeah. I was thinking this is the most peace and quiet you've given me since we met."

"It wasn't I who forced the acquaintance," she reminded him stiffly.

Out of the corner of his eye, he noticed a stranger watching her speculatively. It was probably one of the ranch hands, but he wasn't about to take any chances right now. Grabbing at a low-hanging branch, he pulled himself up, then turned to lean over her.

"I don't suppose you know that fellow over there either, do you?" he said low.

"Who?"

"No, don't look yet. Wait until I'm between you and him, then you can just sneak a peek over my shoulder." As he spoke, he grasped her hand to pull her up. "You dance, don't you?"

"Not very well—why?"

" 'Cause that's just what we're getting ready to do."

"*What?* Oh, I couldn't—I just couldn't—not in front of everybody, anyway. Really, I can just barely waltz—nothing else, I assure you. In fact, I'm not even very—"

"Shhhhh."

"But if you think he's looking for me—" she tried desperately.

"Ever hear of hiding in plain sight?" he whispered, his head bent within inches of hers. "Right now, you're just dancing to a little fiddle music with your husband." Seeing that she drew back, he explained, "Look, you can't run like a scared rabbit without giving yourself away."

"I don't see why not."

"Trust me." As he said it, he slid his hand around her waist. "Put a smile on that face, your hand on my shoulder, and follow me." When she didn't move, he added, "An adoring look or two wouldn't hurt anything either. What you need to do now is play your role to the hilt."

"I'm not an actress, Mr. McCready," she retorted.

"Oh, I don't know—you did a damned good job of fainting. And it's Mac, in case you've forgotten again."

"Matthew," she reminded him. Smiling sweetly, she added, "And if I didn't have to, I wouldn't trust you as far as the corner of that house, so don't go getting any notions otherwise."

"Is that any way to talk to your beloved?" he chided, leading her into the small open area. While clasping her hand with his left, he placed his right one against her back, then held her so close she could feel his breath against her skin. "Think of this as your bridal trip. Pretend there's nobody else in the world but you and me."

"I feel as if I've descended into the pits of hell," she muttered. "And I don't know what he's playing, but it's *not* a waltz."

"It doesn't matter—just do the opposite of what I do. I go forward, you go back."

"And when you go left, I suppose I go right?"

"Tell me one thing," he murmured, easing her around to the music, "were you born contrary, or is it just something you've cultivated?"

"Do you really expect me to smile?" she countered. As his arm tightened around her, forcing her almost cheek to cheek with him, she demanded, "Just what do you think you're doing?"

"Dancing, but it's not easy."

"I tried to warn you—you can't say I didn't."

"All right. If all you can do is waltz, then I guess it'll have to be a waltz."

He stopped and dropped his arm from her back. Still holding her hand, he led her toward the fiddler. Reaching into his coat pocket, he fished out a bright, shiny dollar, and flipped it at the man. The musician nimbly caught it, then grinned.

"Slowest damned waltz you've got," Matt told him. "For the prettiest lady this side of the Atlantic Ocean—my wife."

"Yessirree, suh!"

"That was a whole dollar," she protested.

"Frugal, too," Matt added, straight-faced. "Ready, my dear?" Before she could pull away, he rubbed his cheek against hers, murmuring into her ear, "Try not to look like I'm getting ready to strangle you, will you?"

This time, when he maneuvered her into the dance area, everybody cleared away, leaving them alone. As his arm encircled her waist, a huzzah went up from the crowd. She could feel her whole body go hot as the blood rushed to her face. Thoroughly embarrassed, she all but buried her head in his shoulder and held on.

"Now *that's* more like it," he said softly.

The music was slow, and Matthew McCready's arm was steady, but she was too self-conscious to give any fluidity to her steps. She felt stiff, almost wooden, and his next words did nothing to dispel the feeling.

"You'd never shine in a New Orleans ballroom."

"I never aspired to."

"Maybe if you hummed the music to yourself, you'd get the rhythm," he suggested hopefully.

"I have no musicality whatsoever," she gritted out.

"You've got to have some—everybody does."

"None. My piano teacher wouldn't even take Mama's money, saying any expectation of my having any rhythm or of my hearing the difference between the notes was wishful thinking of the highest degree."

"You can't sing either? I thought that was a required accomplishment for a lady."

"Nothing recognizable. Please—now that we've established I can't sing *or* dance, can we sit down?"

"Not until I get my dollar's worth."

"You're making fools of both of us—I hope you know that."

"You're the one who told me you could waltz," he reminded her.

"You cut me off before I could say 'not very well at all,' " she shot back.

"You know, I'm beginning to think everything about you is a sham."

"Because I can't dance? That's just about the most ridiculous thing I've ever heard."

"Because nothing you've ever told me seems to be the truth. For all I know you aren't even Verena Howard."

"What? Oh, now that's too much! *Everything* I've said is the truth, whether you choose to believe it or not. Which is a great deal more than can be said for you, Matthew McCready!"

"Smile, Rena."

"What?"

"He's still looking at you."

"Why should I care? I've already made myself look like a clumsy idiot, anyway."

"Do you know him?"

"Which one?"

"The one smoking a cheroot—over by that tree."

Forcing her most dazzling smile, she dared to look as McCready took her into a wide circle. "I've never seen him before in my life," she declared flatly. "Ever."

"Maybe he's smitten by your looks."

"He's probably thinking I'm making a spectacle of myself," she retorted.

"Keep smiling."

"My face hurts from trying."

By some act of divine mercy, the fiddler either didn't want to play more than two verses, or perhaps he decided to spare her, but the music stopped. To complete her mortification, Matthew McCready gave her one last turn, then caught her in his arms and brushed his lips against hers in a public kiss. And there was nothing she could do about it without making matters worse.

"You are a miserable example of humanity—you know that, don't you?" she said under her breath.

"Unless you want to try convincing Sheriff Goode that two strange men are following you, claiming to be related to you, and threatening your life for no apparent reason, you'd better hang on to me until you reach Columbus safely. Right now, I'm all you've got."

"I didn't give you permission to kiss me, and you know it."

"I figured I'd better show 'em I didn't marry you for your dancing." As her face darkened ominously, he caught her hand again. "Now, now—none of that. You'd better keeping smiling, dearest, at least until we get to our room."

"My room, you mean."

"Anybody ever tell you the Lord hates a sore loser?" he murmured, pulling her back through the crowd.

"Find that for me in the Bible, will you?"

The fiddle had started up again, and couples were filling the clearing, while a number of cowboys began tapping in time, their spurs jingling with the music. In the renewed enthusiasm, nobody seemed to notice as she and Matthew McCready walked away. Passing the stranger by the tree, Matt nodded. The man stared at Verena for a brief moment, then lifted his hat. He was of medium height, well-built, blond, and quite handsome. She guessed him to be somewhere in his early to mid-thirties.

"Evening, mister. Ma'am."

"Good evening," she responded politely.

It wasn't until they were almost in the house that Matthew murmured, "Any idea now?"

"No. He couldn't be one of those two you saw earlier, could he? The ones at the waystation, I mean. Or did you get a good look at both of them?"

"He wasn't one of them."

"Well, he didn't sound like either of the ones I overheard in the hall, either," she said, sighing.

"Then I guess we'll just have to assume you've gotten yourself an admirer, won't we?"

"I don't find that amusing, Mr. McCready. Right now, I don't want any admirer. All I want is to get to San Angelo, take care of my father's affairs, and get home again safely. After this, I won't even mind going back to teaching."

"You might want to take another look," he murmured. "While I'm not much of a judge of what a woman'd want in a man, I'd say he's pretty good-looking."

"I didn't notice."

"The hell you didn't."

"I'd rather you didn't swear, Mr. McCready."

"He was sure giving you the once-over," he pointed out, leaning past her to open the door to her room.

"I said I didn't know him," she declared firmly.

Finding the kerosene lantern in the semidarkness, she removed the chimney and trimmed the wick by feel. Behind her, McCready struck a match on the wall, then cupped his fingers to shelter the flame. The yellow flame beneath his face, coupled with the odor of burning sulfur, gave him an almost evil aspect. She held the lamp while he lighted it. As soon as the soaked wick caught, sending flickering shadows up the wall, he shook the match out, then turned back to shut the door. Replacing the curved glass chimney, she set the lamp on the small bedside table.

"Actually, I'm still trying to figure you out," he admitted. "I've never met another female quite like you."

She spun around at that. "I'm afraid I've already heard that before, Mr. McCready—from Mr. Wendall. And I assure you that I'm no more gullible now than then."

For a moment, he was at a loss, then he understood. "Oh, you thought that I— Well, I wasn't. In fact, I'd be a fool to pull anything on you, and you ought to know it." Moving to the chair, he loosened his tie and pulled it off. "In case you've forgotten, neither of us can afford any kind of ruckus right now." While he talked, he shrugged out of his coat and hung it over the chair back, taking care to smooth the shoulders. "And I don't know about you, but I'm figuring to get a good night's sleep myself."

"I probably won't sleep a wink with you in here," she told him with feeling. "Even with you on the floor, the arrangement is positively indecent."

"Unn-uhhh. I get the bed. You lost the cut, as I recall," he murmured, opening the window. "So you'd better fold that quilt before you put it down there."

"What do you think you're doing?" she demanded, betraying her alarm. "Have you lost your mind?"

"It's too damned hot in here."

"I don't care!" she snapped. "What if somebody tried to climb in through that window?"

A faintly sardonic smile played at the corners of his mouth as he turned back to her. "Oh, I'm a pretty light sleeper, Rena. The way I figure it, he'd have to come in right over you, and when that happens, I'll hear you screech. I'll be sleeping with my Colt handy, so I'll be ready for him. But if I were you, I wouldn't be worrying my pretty little head over anybody coming in the window—I'd be a lot more concerned about that," he added, nodding significantly.

"About what?"

"That trail of big red ants down there. I don't know as I'd want to bed down with 'em."

"Where? I don't see any—" She stopped. Cutting across the floor, headed toward the inner wall was an army of the creatures. "My word—"

"Yeah. Kinda reminds me of those Indian torture stories."

"What Indian torture stories?" she asked hollowly.

"I don't guess they talk much about Indians in Philadelphia, do they?" he responded, enjoying himself immensely now.

"No, of course not."

"Well, they've been known to stake their enemies on ant hills and smear 'em with a little honey. Not much left of 'em when the ants get done, I'm told."

"I don't believe you."

"But maybe these are grease-eating ants," he allowed. "I guess you'll be finding out."

"I guess I will." Walking to the bed, she pulled off

the quilt and shook it out. "I may be green, but I'm not stupid, Mr. McCready."

As she folded the bedcovering in half, he sobered. "Whether you believe me or not, you'll be eaten up before morning. Here—"

"Here what?" she snapped.

Sighing, he unbuckled his gun belt and untied the holster thong at his thigh. "Go on—take it."

"For what? Surely you don't expect me to believe I'm supposed to *shoot* those things?" she demanded incredulously. "Don't you think you've just about carried this far enough?"

"It's got five bullets loaded. All you've got to do is pull back the hammer to cock it, take aim, then pull the trigger. Those forty-five slugs will blow a big hole in just about anything. You can put it under your pillow."

"You're taking the floor," she managed with relief.

"No, I'm offering to share the bed. You take whichever side you want, and you put that gun where you can get to it. Then if I roll over onto your side, you can use it. Believe me, a dose of lead in the gut'll stop anybody." Seeing that she stared at it in horror, he offered, "I'll even show you how to shoot it, if that'll make you feel any better."

"No." She eyed the floor with misgiving, then went to the chair. Still holding the quilt, she removed his coat and tie from the straight back and gave them a toss toward the bed. "Since you aren't going to be a gentleman, I guess I'll take this chair instead of the floor."

"You can't sleep like that."

"I've slept sitting up most of the way from Philadelphia," she reminded him wearily. "I can't see where one more night will make much difference."

"I don't shame easily, Verena."

Turning her back on him, she arranged the quilt so that it provided a measure of padding to the ladder back. It wasn't very satisfactory, she noted with asperity, but she was going to have to make do with it. Plopping herself down on it, she tried to arrange her skirt around her legs. At the creak of rusty springs, she looked up.

The mattress dipped down dangerously where he sat. "Bed's kind of rickety, but I guess it'll be all right once I get myself situated." Already halfway to the floor, he leaned down to pull off his boots, then sat back to take off his vest. Reaching across the bed to the other side of the feather mattress, he eased his body into it, then lay down. The side came up as he propped his feet on the footboard. He looked over, grinning at her.

Goaded, she gritted out, "*Now* what's so funny?"

"You."

"Well, I wish you wouldn't stare. I don't need to be reminded that I look a fright."

His grin faded. "Actually, I wasn't thinking that at all. I was thinking my mother would have liked you. In fact, you remind me a little of her." Abruptly changing the subject, he said, "You know it's damned hot in here—if I were you, I'd get out of that dress and skinny down to my chemise and drawers."

"But you aren't me."

"Suit yourself."

Rolling onto his side, he reached out and turned

down the lantern wick. The flickering flame shrank to a small orange bead, then went out, casting the room into near darkness. An acrid wisp of dying smoke rose above the glass chimney, momentarily lingering in the warm night air.

She heard the springs creak again, and then the rustle of clothing. "What are you doing?" she demanded nervously.

"I'm not cold-natured like you, so I'm taking my pants off." He could almost hear her choke. "I've still got my drawers on," he added to reassure her. "I'm still decent enough for you to change your mind."

"For the last time, Mr. McCready—if you were decent, you wouldn't be here," she shot back.

"Morning's going to come early, Verena, so if I were you, I'd try to get some sleep. You'll want to be in real fine fettle when it comes time to part with me in Columbus."

"I can scarcely wait."

He didn't answer. Instead, he rolled to face the wall, and the feather mattress sagged in the middle while the sides of it came up, enveloping him like a lumpy, padded hammock.

She sat as still as stone for quite some time, until she heard his breathing finally even out, and she knew he slept. Easing her tired, aching body from the chair, she crept toward the open window and peered out into the moonlit night. The music had ended now, and the yard and porch were strewn with people bedded down end to end for the night. But over by the tree, there was a small glow of red, fading and brightening as the man stood there, sihouetted against the moon, puffing on another cheroot, looking her way. More than a little unnerved, she closed the window as silently as possible.

Returning to her chair, she sat down in the airless room, listening to McCready breathe. And her indignation grew with the realization that he was all but dead to the world, sleeping like a baby. The selfish lout was utterly oblivious to her suffering. Suddenly, she stiffened, aware of footsteps stopping just outside the window. Her heart in her throat, she held her breath and waited while the stranger from the tree looked inside. Finally, he tossed the little cigar away, then moved on.

"Mr. McCready—" she whispered.

Nothing.

"Matthew!" This time, she said it a little louder.

There wasn't even a break in his breathing. He was too sound asleep to hear her.

"Matthew!" she tried again.

Instead of actually rousing, he turned over, murmured something unintelligible, then resumed the same even rhythm. So much for his assertion that he was a light sleeper.

Hot, tired, miserable, and more than a little frightened, she rose to tiptoe closer to the bed. A thin slice of moonlight slanted past the roof of the porch, casting a narrow ribbon of illumination across Matthew McCready's face. With his eyes closed and the clean angles of his face softened with sleep, he didn't look nearly as dangerous now. And if she lay down, keeping to the other side, he wouldn't even know it.

Moonlight glinted off the metal and polished walnut grip of the Army Colt where it hung from the bedpost above his head. For several seconds, she hesitated, then she carefully eased the gun out of its holster. Holding her breath, she crept to the other side of the bed and slid it under the pillow.

"Some help you'd be," she whispered. "I don't think a herd of wild horses could waken you."

When he didn't move, she very gingerly sat down on the edge of the bed. The whole thing seemed to sigh as she loosened the laces on her shoes and wriggled her feet free. Casting one last surreptitious glance over her shoulder, she eased the top half of her body down, and then she pulled her legs up.

Before her feet even touched the featherbed, the rusty springs suddenly gave way. Wood cracked like a rifle shot, and the whole bedstead shuddered, then caved inward, folding her and Matthew McCready together in the mattress. As broken boards skidded across the floor, the featherbed landed with a heavy thud, sending a cloud of choking dust into the air.

He came awake with a jolt. "What the devil—?"

Panicked, she struggled to right herself, but she and McCready were tangled together in the bedclothes. He managed to roll over her, imprisoning her beneath his body, while she clawed and scratched to get free.

'Let me go!" she cried frantically. Feeling the cold steel of the gunbarrel under her back, she reached behind her, getting her fingers on it. Bringing it up, she had her arm raised, ready to strike his skull with it, when she heard the pounding and shouting. Somebody threw his weight against the door, shattering the frame, then five or six men burst through it, with Mrs. Goode right behind them.

"What on earth—?" the woman gasped. "What happened?"

"Plain as the nose on his face, ain't it?" the burly man from the train declared. Pulling McCready off her, he shook his fist in the gambler's face. "Yuh, suh, are a damned annymule! A-forcin' yourself on the missus in her dellycut condishun!" he shouted belligerently.

As the man's beefy fist connected with McCready's eye, Verena screamed, "No!" Scrambling to her feet, she tried to grab the big fellow's arm. "You don't understand! It isn't his fault!" He shook her off as if she were no more than a pesky gnat, then hit Matthew again. "I ain't amin' to mess 'im up much," he assured her gruffly. "Just enough to teach 'im a lesson."

Thoroughly awake now, McCready butted the bigger man in his gut. An *Ooof!* escaped, but as the man staggered backward, knocking over the bedside table, breaking the unlit lamp, several half-inebriated fellows piled on, eager to join the fight. With the rest of her furniture breaking around her, poor Mrs. Goode ran to the door shouting for her husband, while everybody else punched and cursed and rolled on the floor in the semidarkness.

Totally humiliated, yet unable to escape past the sheriff's wife, Verena sank to the floor with her head in her hands. When morning came, she didn't know how she could face any of them, least of all Matthew McCready.

"How badly does it hurt?" she asked, breaking the seemingly interminable silence between them.

Instead of answering, he slid his hat back from his face and regarded her balefully through the narrow, swollen slit that was his left eye.

She sighed and looked out the train window. They were about twenty minutes out of Eagle Lake, and while the number of passengers had thinned down considerably, and most of those were sleeping off the effects of the sheriff's strong cider, a few in the front of the car were singing loudly, drowning out most conversation.

Not that it mattered. Matthew McCready was just sitting there, his expression inscrutable. Straightening her tired shoulders against the train seat, she dropped her gaze to her hands. The false wedding band seemed to mock her now, but until she reached Columbus, she didn't dare take it off.

Casting another surreptitious glance at McCready, she felt more than a little guilty for the beating he'd taken. That eye was as puffy and discolored as any she'd ever seen, and the lower jaw bore a dark bruise where he'd taken a hard blow. Whether from discomfort or resentment, he was obviously in no mood to talk.

"You know, I did tell you I was sorry," she said finally, keeping her voice low. "But I'm not wholly to blame. It *was* your idea to share, wasn't it? Obviously you had no more notion it was going to collapse like that than I did."

No response.

"Can't you at least say something?"

"Yeah." As he spoke, his jaw ached. "I may be dangerous, but you're just plain trouble."

"If you hadn't fought back—"

The eyebrow over the black eye lifted, causing him to wince.

"Well, then, if you hadn't tried to fight *all* of them, maybe I could have tried to explain—" Yet even as she said it, she could feel her face flush with remembered embarassment, and she knew there wouldn't have been any acceptable explanation.

First there'd been the fight. Then, once it'd been broken up by the sheriff, and McCready's attackers hauled out to cool off, things had only gotten worse. The two Negro boys and the hired girl sent in to nail boards over the broken frame had kept rolling their eyes and giggling. If she lived to be a hundred, she'd never forget the impudent way the girl had stood there, her hands on her hips, scolding her and McCready, "Y'all oughter be ashamed o'yersels—a-going at it right where folks cud hear yah." Then there'd been Mrs.

Goode. Returning to survey the damage to the room, she'd simply handed Verena a kettle of water and a tin of salve, then left, but it was apparent that she wasn't amused at all. As a goodwill gesture, McCready had given her forty dollars to replace the broken furniture.

But this morning's breakfast had been unbearable. By then, everybody who'd not actually witnessed the debacle had heard of it. The kindest comment was a whispered, "They must be newlyweds," but almost everything else was either a furtive glance or an outright snicker. McCready hadn't said anything then, either, but she knew he heard the snide comments also.

She was still too mortified to get up and walk around. She hadn't even drunk her morning coffee for fear she'd have to use the privy before she got to Columbus. No, once she got off this train, she hoped she never saw any of her fellow passengers again. No, that wasn't entirely true, she realized. Without McCready, she'd be utterly, completely alone.

"You're miserable, aren't you?" she asked, trying again.

"I'll be all right." Shifting in his seat, he tried to stretch his cramped legs. "You know, if I'd had any sense, I'd have bought myself a horse in Galveston and left you to fend for yourself—that's what I should have done."

"I didn't ask you to come."

" 'What fools these mortals be,' " he murmured sardonically.

"Shakespeare's *A Midsummer Night's Dream,*" she said, trying to smile.

"Not one of my favorites, but at least the thought's

appropriate," he admitted. "You know, when I first laid eyes on you, I was actually fool enough to foresee a very different diversion." His mouth twisted wryly. "If you had shared the notion, we could've had a real nice trip in spite of all this."

"Well, it wasn't a very flattering notion—not of my character, anyway."

"When a man looks at a pretty woman, the last thing on his mind is her character—unless there's a lack of it. No," he said, straightening in his seat, "I should've folded that hand at the outset."

"What are you going to do now?" she dared to ask.

"At Columbus? Get off this accursed train."

"Besides that, I mean."

"Well, for a start, I aim to get myself a tub of good hot water and some soap strong enough to wash the sweat off. Then I'll be looking for a poker game and some real Tennessee mash."

"Tennessee what?"

"Mash. Good sipping whiskey—the kind that goes down smooth, then kicks like hell later." He touched his sore jaw gingerly, then nodded. "Right now, I could drink the whole bottle by myself."

"But then you'd be drunk."

"That's the idea, anyway."

"You'll be paying the piper afterward."

"One way or another, we all pay the piper, Rena." He leaned his head back, closed his eyes, and pulled his hat down over his forehead. "Even you."

"Are you still intending to go to Austin?" she asked, changing the subject.

"Yeah," he lied, "there ought to be some high-stakes games in a state capital. Why?"

"Well, I guess if that's all you want out of life, then that's what you ought to do." She studied what she could see of his face for a moment, then admitted, "You know, you surprised me last night."

"How's that?"

"Well, given the expensive clothes you wear, I more or less had you figured for a—"

"Fancy man," he cut in curtly, pushing back the hat and opening his eyes again. "You might as well go ahead and say it. Sparing my feelings hasn't stopped you yet."

"Well, not that—at least not precisely. Having seen the way you went for your gun, I knew you weren't exactly what you look. I was just meaning I never took you for a brawler. You seem so neat, so . . ." She paused, groping for the right word. "So fastidious about your person," she finished finally.

"I am. I hate dirt and sweat," he declared flatly. "But growing up with a couple of older brothers, I learned to hold my own."

"I always wanted a brother," she admitted wistfully.

"It got pretty rough sometimes. Whenever there was any dispute, Pa threw us outside and made us settle it between ourselves. Being the littlest, I had to bite, butt, kick, and gouge, or I'd never have gotten my share of anything."

"How awful," she murmured.

"Oh, I don't know—I guess we finally came to terms with each other. Hell, I *know* we did. By the time I was ten or so, we'd pretty much closed ranks against the rest of the world. Whenever we got to go to school, nobody gave us any trouble."

"Well, if it's any comfort at all right now, I think you gave better than you got last night. In fact, I know you did. While I was salving you up, Mrs. Goode was sewing up some of the others."

It was hard figuring her out. Yesterday she'd been eager to get rid of him, and now that it was about to happen, she seemed determined to coax conversation out of him, as if she didn't want him to leave her. If he were in a better mood, maybe he'd be up to understanding her, but he wasn't. All his brief acquaintance with her had got him was trouble, and he didn't need any more of that.

"Don't you ever get tired of gambling?" she asked suddenly. "Don't you ever want to do something worthwhile?"

"Is this your way of asking me to stick around?"

She shook her head. "I can take care of myself. I've been alone ever since Mama died."

"You'll be all right." But even as he said it, he didn't believe it.

"You're really determined to go to Austin, anyway."

It was a statement, not the question he'd already answered. And the resignation in it pricked what was left of his conscience. He tried to smile, but his mouth hurt too much, so he just nodded. "Yeah." Looking down with his one good eye, he saw her twisting the ring on her finger. "You know, you could just go back to Galveston and write that lawyer, telling him you've changed your mind." Raising up just enough to wrench a sore rib, he reached into his coat pocket and took out the thick roll of banknotes. "You yourself said your father's place wasn't worth much," he reminded her, counting out two hundred dollars. "Here—go home and forget it." As she stared in disbelief, he added another fifty dollars to it. "That ought to get you there with plenty to spare."

It took her a moment to regain her speech. "Are you offering to *buy* my farm, Mr. McCready?" she asked incredulously.

Until she said it, the thought hadn't crossed his mind. Yet now that she'd planted the notion, he mulled it over, considering the possibilities. No, he didn't want anything to do with any farm. But he didn't really want to go to Helena, either, and he sure as hell wasn't going to Austin, no matter what he'd told her. While he'd place a bet that Jack Howard's farm wasn't anything more than a little dirt patch in the middle of nowhere, there was something to be said for that. It'd be a place to hide out, a place where nobody would expect to find Matthew Morgan.

Suddenly, in his mind's eye he could see his mother, worn-out and old before her time, as faded as her shapeless flour sack dress, and his father standing beside her, his weathered skin as tough as boiled leather from too many years of backbreaking labor. No, he couldn't even pretend to be a farmer. He'd rather die nameless in Helena than plant crops anywhere. It had just been a fleeting, utterly stupid notion.

"No," he managed, his voice harsh, "you just take the money and go back where you came from. There's enough there for a pretty dress and a whole lot more.

Fix yourself up nice and go hunting for a husband to take care of you."

"I don't need anybody to take care of me."

"Well, you sure as hell don't belong out here, Rena. Eking out a living on dirt takes a heavy toll on a woman, especially on a pretty one like you. A couple of years, and nobody back East will even recognize you."

"I wasn't intending to stay—I don't know how many times I've said it, but I'm not staying."

"You can think that, but maybe you won't have the money to go home. Unless I miss my guess, what you came with is about gone—or it will be by the time you get to San Angelo. You know, it could take a year, maybe longer, to sell a farm down here. Look at what we've come through—damned near all cattle ranches. This is Texas, and everything gets bigger and rougher down here," he argued.

"I'm sure I can manage. I can price the place low, you know. All I have to have is enough to get home on."

"Yeah, and while you're waiting for a buyer, who's going to help you out? It sure as hell won't be me, if that's what you were angling at. I walked behind my last plow a long time ago—a real long time ago."

The money in his hand was terribly tempting. Two hundred and fifty dollars was well over a year's wages without the room and board. More than enough to get her back to Philadelphia. Even enough to give her the luxury of choosing rather than just taking any teaching position. And it obviously didn't mean nearly as much to him. It was as though every fiber of her body cried out, telling her to take it and go home.

"No," she said finally. "It wouldn't be right—you don't owe it to me, and I can't accept all that money. Just give me ten dollars for my dress, and we'll be more than even."

"Take the rest of it, and I won't have to worry about you. I'll just be thinking it's a good riddance."

"In a couple of hours, maybe even less, you're going to be rid of me, anyway," she reminded him, her eyes still on the money. Drawing upon her last bulwark of resolve, she declared more definitely, "I have to go on, Mr. McCready—my father's will comes up for probate, and I promised Mr. Hamer I'd be there."

Studying the determined set of her face, he felt goaded. She was too damned obstinate to make sense. Unless . . . No, he could think of only one reason why after all that had happened to her, she was still hell-bent on getting to San Angelo. If there wasn't something more to it than she'd told him, she'd have taken his money and hied herself back East with it. His good eye narrowed to match the half-closed one.

"Then you're a damned liar, Verena."

She blinked blankly at the sudden, unexpected attack. For a moment, she just stared. "And just what do you mean by that?" she demanded when she found her voice.

"You don't want my money because you've got something better waiting at San Angelo. That's why you've got those hardcases chasing you. There's some reason why you're so all-fired eager to claim a supposedly worthless piece of ground over there. I don't know what it is, but it's something real important to you."

"I don't know what you're getting at, but I don't like

the inference," she told him stiffly. "As far as I know, all my father left me is one hundred and sixty acres of land about eight miles out of San Angelo. But even if there *were* something else, I don't see where it would be any business of yours, anyway."

"When you hide behind a man, he's got a right to know if there's going to be somebody shooting at him because of you."

"Nobody's shot at you yet," she retorted.

"No, the way I've got it figured now, you know what they want, and you've been playing me for a damned fool," he went on. "While you've been acting like Miss Innocent, all you've wanted is somebody to throw 'em off. That's it—admit it."

"Ohhhh, now that's just rich, it is!" she hissed at him furiously. "May I remind you yet again that it was *you* who followed me—not the other way around! Ever since I first laid eyes on you, I've wished you in Purgatory at the least!"

"Now *that,* my dear, is a barefaced lie. As I recall, it was you turning to me just yesterday, claiming you'd overheard—"

"It wasn't a claim—it was a fact," she snapped, cutting him off.

"Keep your voice down, will you?" Rising slightly in his seat, he looked the length of the car to make sure no one had heard her. "Apparently, that caterwauling drowned you out," he decided, leaning back. "I guess you'd have to shout loud enough to wake the dead before anybody'd notice."

"Nobody got any sleep last night," she reminded him. "And whether you choose to believe me or not,

Mr. McCready, I not only do not have the least notion who those men were, but I also don't have so much as an inkling of why they are following me," she declared, returning to the matter at hand. "I cannot fathom what they want with me."

"Do I really look that gullible to you?"

Seething, she opened her mouth, then shut it until she got control of her temper. "Right now, you look positively stupid. And for your information, there's nothing even remotely suspect about my motives," she said, biting off each word precisely. "Papa only had fifteen dollars and ninety-two cents in the bank when he died. There isn't any money—none."

"You're still expecting me to swallow that tale about your wanting to know why he left your mother, I suppose."

"I don't care whether you swallow it or not. It's still the God's truth. And maybe when I go through his papers, I will at least understand what he was thinking."

"This lawyer you're supposedly meeting could've mailed everything to you," he countered. "You yourself said he offered to handle the sale."

"But I need to *see* the place—can't you understand that? I want to see the place, and then, maybe then, I'll know why he chose to live in such a place rather than come home from the war. Before he deserted, he was a hero, Mr. McCready—a *hero*."

"You're a damned good actress, I'll give you that."

"And you, sir, are beneath contempt," she retorted. "Just because you are in pain, you are determined to take your ill-humor out on me." Grasping the empty seat in front of her, she pulled herself up and tried to step over his outstretched legs. "You don't need to say good-bye in Columbus, Mr. McCready," she said icily. "I shall consider it already done."

The effect of her speech was lost when the car braked suddenly, causing her to trip over his feet. She stumbled backward and fell into his lap. He groaned as he caught her.

"Watch out," he muttered, "I've got a sore rib there."

"Believe me, I'd rather be anywhere else," she said, crawling back into her seat. "I feel as if I've descended into the pits of Hades right now. It's already stifling in here, and we're stopped again."

Halfway down the aisle, the conductor leaned over a passenger to peer out a window. Straightening, he announced loudly, "Looks like sheep this time, folks! Whole danged bunch of 'em on the tracks! Got a couple of Mexicans a-trying to herd 'em off." He added, "Reckon that'd about put us on the Brassfield place."

It was the last straw for Verena. She was hot, she'd had no sleep, and she was in the middle of a quarrel with the only person she knew in this godforsaken place. Columbus, Texas, was a myth, something beyond reach. Fighting back tears of frustration, she swallowed, then whispered, more to herself than to Matt, "If I were superstitious, I'd think I've been cursed by an evil spirit."

The huskiness in her voice moved him where her anger hadn't. And he realized he'd been goading her as much for her rejection of his money as for anything else. If she'd taken it, his conscience would have been clear. But she hadn't, and now he'd be wondering if she even got to San Angelo, or if she'd fallen into the hands of her pursuers somewhere between there and Columbus.

He had no business getting involved, he argued with himself. He was a fugitive from the law, and he had to take care of his own skin first. But she was a woman alone, and God only knew what those two fellows wanted with her. All he knew for sure was that she'd been shaken by what she'd heard at Eagle Lake. And while he hated to admit it, he knew he couldn't just abandon her. He had to at least get her on that stage bound for San Angelo. Then she could be someone else's problem. He could wash his hands of her. Maybe. Or maybe not.

For a moment, he actually considered taking her with him, then he caught himself. Helena, Texas, wasn't a fit place for an Eastern-bred schoolteacher. It wasn't even a fit place for him. No, he'd be asking for more trouble than he already had if he showed up there with the lovely Verena in tow. Somebody'd be sure to take a shine to her, he'd be trying to defend her honor, and then there'd be hell to pay.

What he ought to do, he realized, was to see that she got past San Antonio, that she got onto the military-contracted mail wagon bound for Fort Concho. But then he'd have to board the stagecoach with her at Columbus. That could be pretty damned tricky, particularly if those two were meeting the train there. All he needed was for something to happen that'd bring him to the attention of the law, and he'd be headed back to a hangman's rope.

A shotgun blast tore through his thoughts, jolting him back to reality. He looked down the aisle to where a cowboy had blown a hole in one of the windows, shouting that he wasn't "waitin' for no goddamned, stinkin' sheep!" Somebody behind him, apparently awakened by a shower of broken glass, rose up cursing. As the cowboy swung around, another gunshot rang out, this time from the victim's forty-five, and the cowboy slumped forward. The shotgun butt struck the floor hard, discharging a second load, spraying the car's ceiling with buckshot, and everybody around ducked for cover.

Beside Matt, Verena gasped, "Did you see that? He just shot that man!"

"Yeah." In that moment, he made up his mind. He wasn't about to stick around for any investigation. If the cowboy died, there'd be rangers and railroad detectives crawling all over the place at Columbus. Taking advantage of the confusion, he said tersely, "Come on—it's too damned dangerous in here." He stood up, caught the shelf above his head, and swung out into the aisle. "Let's go."

"What?"

"We're getting out before all hell breaks loose." Before she could argue with him, he grasped her arm and pulled her into the aisle. "Hurry up."

Almost before he got the words out, a dozen guns were drawn as men jumped to take sides in the fracas. White as a sheet despite the heat, the conductor dropped to the floor and crawled in between two empty seats.

Verena hesitated. "But—"

"I'm going," Matt told her. *"Now."* Making good on

the threat, he wrenched open the back exit. His eyes met hers. "Are you coming or not?"

She cast an almost frantic look over her shoulder as another shot rang out, then she hastened past him onto the small back platform. As the door closed behind her, she felt an immense relief. At least she was safe from stray bullets out here. But Matthew McCready's next words stunned her.

"Come on—we've got to get off while we can."

"*Off!*" she choked out. "Off where?"

"Here. Let's go."

"Oh, but I—but there's nothing here!" she protested.

As a shriek cut through the air, the train jerked into motion, throwing her against the iron rail. Matt eased down onto the small step, then turned back to her.

"I'll go first, but when I yell to jump, you jump! Otherwise, I can't catch you!" he shouted over the noise.

"I can't get off this train!" she protested. "I don't—"

Either he didn't hear her, or the sound had drowned her out. Holding on to the small iron railing, he swung out, then dropped to the ground as the engine picked up steam. Running alongside, he yelled, "Now, Rena—jump!"

She looked down at the gravel, seeing the ties moving faster. Hanging on with one hand, she leaned out toward McCready's outstretched arms. He grabbed her other hand, pulling her, then caught her by the waist as she fell. They rolled down the incline, away from the heavy wheels. She could feel the gravel and taste the dirt as McCready's body pinned her down.

Feeling her struggle, he heaved himself up to sit while he caught his breath. The last car was now some five or six hundred yards down the track and picking up speed.

"You aren't hurt, are you?" he asked her.

She looked down to where her dress and petticoat were hiked up, exposing her drawers from mid-thigh downward. "Just my dignity," she managed. Sitting up, she worked her skirt back down to her ankles before she noted the disappearing train. If she'd been the weepy sort, she would have cried, but she wasn't—not yet, anyway. Instead, she gave a sigh of resignation.

"Everything I brought with me is in my carpetbag."

"When we get to Colombus, I'll pick it up at the depot. If the train gets there before we do, the porter will leave it there."

Her gaze took in the flock of sheep moving at a right angle to the now-deserted track, and her spirits sank further. Beyond the animals and the two shepherds, there didn't seem to be anything. No road. No house. Nothing. Just a few hills, some grasslands, and a ridge of trees.

"You know, if I'd had any idea you meant to jump off that train, I would have gotten down on the floor instead," Verena told Matt with feeling. "I just thought you were putting a steel door between us and the shooting."

"I had to get off—and so did you."

"I'd like to hear one good reason why," she said with asperity. "Now we're out here without so much as a toothbrush, and we *still* don't know how to get to Columbus."

"I can give you two good ones."

"Well?"

"To start with, right after that train pulls in, there'll be lawmen all over the place, and everybody in that car will be giving a statement on the shooting."

"I don't have anything to hide, Mr. McCready."

"Maybe, maybe not. But be that as it may, it'll take a day or two for a ranger or a railroad detective to get everything sorted out. That's plenty of time for your friends to show up, and unless they're idiots, they'll have everything added up by then. Do you want to be there when that happens?"

"They're not my friends. How many times do I have to tell you that I don't know them?"

"Until I believe you."

"Well, I'm not saying it again." She dared to look up at him. "You know, if anybody who knew you before saw you now, he probably wouldn't recognize you. I don't think I've ever seen a worse-looking eye on anyone."

"Nobody's looking for me."

"Well, somebody must be—you didn't jump from a moving train on my account, Mr. McCready. You jumped because you didn't want to face the authorities. And there's no sense in denying it, because I won't believe you."

"You're too damned suspicious, Rena."

"*I'm* too suspicious? What about you?"

"You didn't see me running from Sheriff Goode, did you?"

"I don't know where you would have run."

"I didn't have two fellows looking for me," he countered.

"Well, I can't account for that."

"I know."

"I suppose it'd be too much to expect you to know where we are," she observed tiredly.

"The Brassfield place."

"Yes, well, there doesn't seem to be much to it." Turning toward him, she sighed again. "You know, that conductor didn't seem particularly sure, as I recall. I think he said we *should* just about be to the Brassfield place."

"I figure those sheep had to come from somewhere."

"Well, I don't see any place," she countered.

"Oh, I expect we'll have to walk a ways," he conceded. "I don't suppose you happen to speak Spanish, do you?"

"I can read the classics in Latin or French, and I can recognize a smattering of Greek, but Spanish wasn't offered as a subject at the Bancroft Normal School. Why?"

"Because I can count every Spanish word I know on both hands, and a lot of 'em aren't polite enough to use."

"I beg your pardon?"

"You heard me the first time. And there's a Mexican kid headed this way."

Sure enough, one of the shepherds had noticed them, and he was running across the grass toward them, waving a greeting. As he got closer, she could see a friendly, gap-toothed grin. Matt stood up and brushed off his coat and pants with his hands, then reached down for her.

"Turn around, and I'll see if I can make you presentable," he offered.

"It's hopeless—utterly hopeless," she muttered, surveying the damage. "I think I've even torn a piece or two." A heavy sigh escaped her. "And without my bag, I don't even have the other skirt."

"I'll find you something."

"I thought we'd already established the impossibility of that yesterday."

"Just leave it to me." He started toward the boy, his hands outstretched.

"*Donde es* the Brassfields?" he tried hopefully.

"*Sí . . . sí . . .*"

"Are you quite certain you said that right?" Verena asked behind him.

"*Donde esta* Columbus?"

"*Sí . . . sí . . .*" the boy responded again, bobbing his head.

"The Brassfields or Columbus?"

"*Sí . . . sí . . .*"

"I wouldn't be surprised if this is the wrong place," she said under her breath.

"You want to try it?"

"No."

"All right, then be patient. *El rancho—Donde esta el rancho?*"

That brought forth a spate of rapid Spanish he couldn't begin to understand. "*Donde?* Uh—*where* is the Brassfield place?" he shouted.

"If he couldn't understand you the first time, I don't think yelling is going to help," she pointed out. Stepping around Matt, she approached the boy. "Brassfield's?"

"*Sí.*"

"This is Brassfield's?"

"Sí."

"I got that much out of him," Matt muttered.

"Yes, but I'm going to get the direction." Making a big circle around herself with her hand, she asked, "Brassfield's?"

"Sí?"

"The house?"

"*Casa,*" Matt supplied. "*Casa* is house—I know that, anyway."

"The *casa*—where is the *casa*? Over there?" she asked, pointing to her left.

"Sí."

"I don't think you're getting anywhere, if you want my opinion."

Ignoring him, she pointed to her right. *"Casa?"*

The kid shook his head. Coming to stand beside her, he sighted a line directly left of her, then nodded. "Brass-field *casa,*" he said succinctly. Holding out his own hand, he turned in a full circle. *"Rancho."*

"We're on the ranch itself," she decided. "And the house is somewhere over there."

"That's what I asked him, you know."

"No, you asked where the ranch is."

"Why don't you ask him how far it is?" he suggested. "Let's see you do that."

"No. I can already tell it's a long way."

"Gracias, mi amigo." Retrieving a quarter from his pocket, Matt tossed it to the boy. "*Por—?*"

"Eduardo."

"*Por* Eduardo."

Eduardo gestured toward the other shepherd. "Pablo."

"Eduardo and Pablo." Digging in his pocket again, Matt couldn't find another quarter. "You don't have two bits on you, do you?" he asked Verena.

"No, but I've got two dimes and a nickel."

"Well, give it to him."

"I hope you know that was for my lunch," she muttered, fishing through her purse. "Here."

"Thanks." Taking the coins, he held them out. "*Por* Pablo."

The money was a qualified success. After considerable debate over whether it was better to have twenty-five cents in one piece or three, the matter was finally settled. The cherubic-faced Pablo, apparently the younger of the two, wound up with the quarter. Waving, he indicated they were to follow him.

Taking Verena's arm, Matt leaned close enough to murmur, "When we get there, let me do the talking."

"Then you'd better hope they speak English."

"With a name like Brassfield, I'll lay money on it." He stopped long enough to look down at her through his good eye. "Look, it's hot, you're tired, and we're apparently in for a long walk. Instead of arguing about everything, let's just call a truce until we get to San Antonio."

Her heart almost paused, then relief washed over her. He'd said San Antonio, not Columbus. Hiding an unexpected surge of elation, she fell into step beside him. He was going to San Antonio with her. She wasn't alone.

The large woman shaded her face against the sun, and even then she squinted. As she made out the two people with Pablo, her eyes widened with astonishment.

"Lord a Mercy! Pa! Pa, you gotta c'm'ere! Pablo's bringin' us some comp'ny!"

Her husband, a tall, thin fellow with a bald head, came outside wearing nothing but a pair of flannel drawers. "Here now, Sarie—there ain't no need t'be wakin' the dead, is thar?"

"Lookee up yonder," she said, pointing. "It's comp'ny, I'm tellin' you! And one of 'em's a woman." Turning to him, her gaze took in his lack of clothes. "Now, Pa, you ain't hardly presentable," she complained. "You'd better be a-gettin' yer pants on before they get here."

"Must be a hundred 'n' ten in there, Sarie." Taking another look at the three figures walking across the open ground, he muttered, "Wonder where they's a comin' from."

"It don't matter—they's a-comin' here, I'm a-tellin'

ya." Tugging her soiled apron down over her ample stomach while she patted her wild hair into place, she tried not to appear too eager. "How'd I look?"

"It don't matter. They ain't a'goin' nowheres," he declared. "They ain't got no horses."

"If you don't put on your britches, you ain't eatin' with the comp'ny," she threatened him.

"Well, I kinda got a hankerin' to hear what they's doin' out year first—I ain't so dadblamed lonesome that I got no sense."

Stepping back over the dusty threshold, he reached behind the door to retrieve a double-barreled shotgun. As Pablo and the strangers drew closer, he lifted it, sighting them. His finger curled around one trigger.

"Hold it right thar!" he yelled.

Alarmed, his wife pushed the barrel down. "Don't mind him!" she shouted. "We ain't got comp'ny offen enough fer him to remember the manners his ma taught 'im! Y'all come on in, ya hear?" Over her shoulder, she told her husband, "Seth Brassfield, put on your pants—now! You ain't a-drivin' off the only folks t' come this way in nigh on to a year!"

Verena surveyed the place with disbelief. It made the Goode house look like a palace. As she hesitated, Matthew took her arm.

"They're just farm folk, that's all," he reassured her.

"This isn't a ranch—it's a hovel." To her horror, the woman was coming off the weathered board porch. "Matthew, I don't think—"

"Howdy!" Holding out a work-roughened hand, Sarah Brassfield grinned broadly, betraying a missing front tooth. "I'm Sarie—and Seth's inside a-fixin' hisself up for ya. I reckon you'll be a-stayin' fer supper, huh?" she added eagerly. Her eyes took in Verena's torn dress and Matthew's bruised face, and her grin faded. "Mercy me! Y'all's been in an accident?"

Matthew and Verena answered at the same time. "No," she replied. "Yes," he said.

For a moment, the woman was taken aback, then she let out a heavy breath. "Now one of you's gotta be confused a mite, huh? Was it an accident or not?"

"Uh—yes, sort of," Verena decided, looking to McCready. "Uh—?"

"We fell off the train," he announced baldly.

"Huh?"

"Being from back East, Rena hadn't seen a flock of sheep," he explained.

"I thought you was a-talkin' mighty funnylike," the woman admitted, nodding. "I knowed you warn't from around here." She looked Verena over again, then clucked sympathetically. "Rena, eh? That's a right purty name, ain't it?"

Realizing that McCready was nudging her, Verena managed, "Thank you."

"How come you to fall offen the train?"

"While we were stopped to clear the sheep off the track, I took Rena outside to watch. Unfortunately, when we started up again, she lost her balance and fell off. I jumped down to save her. By the time we got back up the hill, we couldn't catch up."

"By the looks of it, you musta landed on your head, mister. That's a right ugly eye—you musta hit somethin' mighty hard goin' down that hill. I reckon Seth'll bring you some o' that salve he makes up from sheep oil t' put 'round it. Heals up real good, it does—if'n ya don't get it in yer eyeball."

"Thanks."

"As fer the missus, ain't no wonder she fell off—more's the wonder she's a-walkin', what with them fancy shoes on her feet," Sarah declared. "God didn't make women to stand on them heels. If He'd a-wanted 'em to, He'd a-made us with our toes a-pointed down so's we couldn't walk no other way, but He didn't." She looked down at her homemade slippers. "I ain't about t' war anything if it don't feel good, I ken tell ya. And I ain't about t' spend an hour a-lacin' anythin' up neither."

"Where I come from, these shoes are rather plain," Verena told her. "In fact, they were just about the most serviceable pair I could buy."

"Well, I ain't bought no shoes in a whiles," the woman conceded. "Don't need 'em. When I go t' the pens, I just war Seth's old boots." Looking her company over again, she sighed. "I'm gonna git out m' needle fer that dress before that rip gets any bigger. But I don't know as I kin do much for them fancy duds on the mister."

"Oh, that's all right—really, there's no need. I'm sure we won't be staying long enough for that. Later, when there's time, I can sew it up myself."

The woman's face fell. "Oh, but you just hav' to! Why, where else would you be a-goin' tonight? There ain't another body fer miles!"

"The Brassfields. I—uh—guess the boy didn't understand us."

"You're thar."

"I beg your pardon?"

"That's where you are. Your a-standin' on it." Smiling again, the woman nodded. "Reckon I fergot m'manners in the excitement, huh? I'm Sarie—Sarah Brassfield, that is." Turning back to the house, she noted with satisfaction that her husband had managed to pull on a shirt and pants. "And that's Mistuh Brassfield—Seth to y'all."

"Oh."

"Uh-huh. And that boy whut brung y'all in, that was Pablo. His ma had two of 'em afore she up and died, a-leavin' 'em to that no-count man o' hern. An' he walked in heah one day last winter sayin' if we was to want 'em, they was ours, 'cuz he didn't want to take keer of 'em no more. I told Pa—Seth, that is—why, two of 'em'd almost make one man, ya know, and with them we could get us some more sheep."

"We're up ta two hunnerd fifty head now," her husband interjected proudly. "Come next year, we'll be a-dublin' that."

"We got mor'n any two hundred fifty now, Pa. Yer fergittin' th' ones Eddie found yesterday, ain'tcha? Them you'd given up fer dead." Reaching out, she beckoned to the boy. "Come here, youngun." As the boy stepped forward, she ruffled his dark hair affectionately. "You're a good little feller, ain'tcha? Yes, ya is."

"The father just gave his children to you?" Verena said incredulously.

"Yep. But I ain't mindin't it none. Me'n Pa, we always wanted kids. None of ourn lived long enough ta grow. Diptheria," she explained succinctly. "There was three of 'em—took 'em all. But," she added, recovering, "these are good boys—real good boys. Pa's started learnin' em to talk like white folk, but it ain't took yet. No so ya'd know it, anyways." Turning again to Matthew, she asked hopefully, "Y'all kin stay fer supper, cain't ya?"

"Uh, we're not very far from Columbus, are we?" Verena spoke up.

" 'Bout eight mile if a crow was to fly it."

"We could be there tonight, Matthew."

"But you ain't crows," Sarah pointed out. "If'n y'all wus t' stay here t'night, I reckon either Seth or one of the boys'd getcha into Columbus tomorry—eh, Seth?"

"Road's bad," he grumbled. "And the wagon ain't much good neither." He looked to his wife, and he could see the longing for company in her eyes. "Guess I could work on that wheel after the sun goes down a mite," he allowed. "And s'pose I could spare Eddie fer the day tomorry, if'n he was t' make it back a-fore dark." Turning his face to Matthew, he explained, "Don't want the boy tuh be out with the rattlers and painters at night."

Seeing that Verena looked puzzled, Sarah Brassfield translated, "The snakes an' the cuggars."

"Cuggars?"

"You don't have cougars in Pennsylvania?" Matt murmured.

"Oh, cougars."

"We got 'em real fiercelike at times," Seth said. "Now the rattlers, the onliest time they ain't out is winter. Come fifty degrees, and they's a-gone underground until it warms up. But now as it's gittin' hot, you cain't walk fifty feet without you seein' one of 'em—mebbe more'n that. Sleep underground in the day and come out after dark, when the ground's warm, but the sun ain't out."

"Now, Pa, you'll be a-skeerin' the lady. It ain't that bad in daylight, cuz they ain't a-likin' this heat neither. It's night when you gotta be a-lookin' out fer 'em—and then it ain't like you cain't hear 'em. They buzz real good a-fore they hit you."

"Ain't that whut I was just a-sayin', Sarie?" Seth complained. "If'n you wants tuh be safe about it, a-fore you go a-stickin' yer hand unner or behind anything, you'd sure as hell better be a-looking first. Them rattlers gets unner things fer shade."

"I'll be sure to look," Verena promised. "Everywhere."

"See as you does. T'uther week, they wus one in the outhouse. I wus just a-closin' the door when I heerd it. Been takin' m'shotgun in with me ever since," the older man declared. "A body cain't be too keerful."

"Oh, it ain't that bad," Sarah Brassfield insisted. "Onliest things we really worry over is keepin' the sheep and the dawgs close by after dark." Catching herself, she shook her head. "Lord a-mercy, but where's my manners? Here I been runnin' on, and I ain't even let you innerduce yerselves, let alone took you inside and outta this heat."

"Hotter'n hell inside," Seth muttered. "But you sure are welcome—you and the missus."

Matthew offered his hand. "Name's McCready—Matt McCready—and this is my wife, Elizabeth."

For a moment, the woman's gaze went to Verena. "Thought you wus callin' 'er Rena."

"Elizabeth Corrina."

"She don't look Mexican," Seth protested.

"Her mother was a hopeless romantic, I'm afraid. She read quite a lot of poetry."

"Eh?"

"Herrick," Matt explained.

"He means she wus a Herrick," Sarah declared, putting an end to the matter. "Her name wus Lizzie Herrick a-fore she was married—ain't that right, honey?" she asked Verena.

Rather than try to straighten the woman out, Verena agreed. "Yes."

"Good. Now that we got that settled, you come on in and cool off a mite while Pablo fetches water from the pump." Turning to the boy, she spoke softly in Spanish. As he hurried around the corner of the house, she smiled. "I told 'im if'n he wus real good he'd be the one a-drivin' y'all into Columbus in the mornin'."

Filing past the beaming woman, Matt and Verena found themselves inside a large, dim room. Seth moved a sleeping dog with his foot, then directed Verena to a rickety rocking chair with a cushioned seat. Unaccustomed to the change in light, she was about to sit down when the cushion came to life, clawing, spitting, and hissing.

"Danged cats is ever'where," Seth muttered as she jumped back. "Sarie named that one Cider, cuz it's full o' vinegar. Then thar's Punkin, 'Lasses, an' 'Tack fer the rest of 'em. Don't know why she's gotta name 'em, cuz they don't come when a body calls 'em, enyway." Turning to Matt, he cautioned, "Now, if'n you steps on Molly, she's a biter."

"I usually get along with dogs," Matt murmured.

"She ain't a dawg. Bird and Rufus is the dawgs—Molly's a sow. Heat makes 'er a mite tetchy."

"There's a live pig in here?" Verena asked faintly.

"Pigs is cleaner'n dawgs if'n you let 'em be."

Afraid Verena would say something more on the subject, Matt admitted, "We raised pigs when I was a kid."

"An' I'll bet you ate 'em, didn't you?"

"Or sold them."

"We ain't eatin' Molly. Be like a-killin' a member of the fam'ly. But you been a-walkin' quite a ways," Seth said, recalling his best manners. "Go on—make yourself t'home while Sarie's wringin' a hen's neck so's you kin eat afterwhile. I reckon I better have a look-see at the privy a-fore you use it."

"Yes, please do," Verena murmured. Waiting until he had left, she looked around the room and winced openly. "We can't stay here, Matthew," she whispered. "We just can't. I'm not eating or sleeping with a pig at my feet."

"I don't know anywhere else to go, do you?" he countered. "If you can come up with something better, you tell me, will you?"

"I think I'd rather walk to Columbus." As she said it, a huge black-and-white sow emerged from the shadows, snorted in her direction, and then lumbered over to the rocker, settling in front of it, obviously daring anyone to sit there. "Is that thing dangerous?" Verena asked nervously.

"She's a biter," he reminded her.

"I can't believe anyone would keep a pig for a pet."

"Not in the house, anyway. But if you ever got a close look at a little piglet, you'd find they're real cuddly, and after you've handled 'em a little, they follow you around like a dog."

She eyed Molly skeptically. "Cuddly's the last word I'd use. I don't think I've ever seen one up close before."

"Not even in western Pennsylvania?"

"Oh, I saw the pens, but I didn't particularly care to look at the animals. I always figured I wouldn't want to eat the meat if I did." Gingerly skirting around the pig, she found another chair, dusted it off, and sat down. "I cannot fathom why anyone would want to live like this," she said tiredly.

"This place, or anywhere in Texas?"

"Both."

Walking over to the small window, he lifted a faded calico curtain to look outside. Sarah Brassfield was moving stealthily among about fifteen or twenty gangly chickens, until she found the fattest one. Her hand shot out, snatching it. As he watched her, she wrapped her apron around the squawking bird, then took it around the corner.

"It's not just here, Rena," he said, letting the curtain drop. "I used to ask my pa why anybody'd want to live on a farm."

"Did he answer you?"

"No. But looking back, I think some folks are born wanting to own land, to sink their roots down somewhere. They put all their dreams into having some little piece of ground. Sometimes they make a living on it, and sometimes they just keep trying until they either go bust or die on it." He lifted the curtain again, but this time when he stared out, his mind saw bare Tennessee dirt, an old gnarled tree, and a weathered barn. "For me, it was like quicksand," he found himself saying slowly. "I didn't want to be sucked under and suffocated by a few acres of land."

"Is that what happened to your father?"

"He didn't see it like I did. As far as I know, he's still alive, still trying."

"You don't hear from him?"

"I haven't heard from anybody back in Tennessee for a couple of years. I guess they're all right, or somebody'd be writing me." He swung around to face her. "I guess that probably makes me sound pretty hard."

"Yes."

"Your father never wrote you," he reminded her.

"My mother wasn't quicksand, Mr. McCready. She gave him no reason to leave."

"So it's back to Mr. McCready again, is it?"

"There's nobody around right now."

"You keep that distance, don't you? That way you don't put your trust in anybody."

"I don't know what you're talking about."

"I'm a gambler, Rena. I make my living by looking for signs of what somebody else is thinking." Moving away from the window, he picked up a photograph of a woman standing behind a man in a chair, both of them young and ill-at-ease. While it didn't look much like them now, he'd be willing to bet money he was looking at his hosts. "When I get into a game, I'm like a bird of prey, circling, waiting for something weak to make a mistake."

"Like you were doing when you accosted me on the steamer?"

"When I saw you on the boat, I was looking for a little diversion, and you were pretty enough to pique my interest. I didn't know you had liabilities of your own. I figured I'd make a few sparks fly, then move on. I didn't know we were going to be on the run together, or I'd have done this differently."

"I'm not 'on the run,' as you call it. Not exactly, anyway," she amended truthfully.

"No? Well, you've sure as hell got somebody chasing you, and I seem to remember you weren't all that eager to get caught," he reminded her. "I didn't see you going around that corner at Goode's for a closer look when you had the chance."

"I didn't know what they wanted, and I still don't."

"But you know it isn't anything good."

"Obviously. As nearly as I could tell, somebody named Gil intends to kill me."

"Then you're on the run, Rena."

"I didn't want to jump off that train, Matthew—you all but pulled me off it." Her gaze swept the room before returning to him. "This isn't exactly my notion of a place to stay. By now all the other passengers are in Columbus, already registered at a decent hotel."

"No, they're all telling different versions of that shooting to some lawman."

"At least they'll be getting a decent bed tonight." A sudden, embarrassing thought hit her, and it must've been written on her face. "Uh—"

"Yeah, it looks like we're stuck together for one more night—unless you want to share the floor with Molly. But after last night, I'm so damned tired you could be the best-looking dance hall girl in the world, and it wouldn't matter. I don't want anything but a night's sleep."

"And you think you'll get it here?" she asked incredulously.

"Look—come morning, we'll move on. By the time we get to Columbus, everything will have calmed down, and the train'll be making its run back to Galveston. Then—"

"With my clothes on it. Matthew, I can't go meet Papa's lawyer like this. Look at me—just look at this dress! It's got stains and holes all over it! I don't even have a toothbrush—or a comb!"

"Actually, you don't look half bad." Seeing her color rise, he hastened to reassure her. "They won't take your bag back. It's only ticketed to Columbus."

"But I won't be there to get it!"

"I told you I'd collect it, didn't I?"

"Don't you think somebody's going to ask just why we departed in such haste, not to mention in the middle of nowhere?"

A faint smile formed at the corners of his mouth, then twisted slightly. "I was figuring on blaming that on you."

"*Me?*" she choked out.

"Yeah. You were already high-strung from lack of sleep, and between the shooting, the heat, and the delay, you were on the verge of a breakdown. I figured if I didn't get you out of there, you'd work yourself into another fainting spell, and in your delicate condition—"

"Well, you can figure again," she cut in, interrupting him. "I'm not flighty, I have never swooned, and I refuse to pretend a mental breakdown to suit your story. And if you ever tell anyone again that I'm in a delicate condition, I'll shoot you and plead self-defense!"

"Hold your voice down, will you?"

"No, if you want to make something up, use yourself! If you can stand the scrutiny, that is. I'm not a gambler at all, but if I were, I'd bet everything I had that you're hiding something terrible, Matthew McCready—if that's even your name."

"Rena—"

"Well—? Are you really Matthew McCready?" she demanded. "Are you really even from Tennessee? Or is everything about you just made up from whole cloth?"

"Why would you say that?" he countered, evading the questions. "Why would I want to lie to you?"

"I don't know, but you do. Because it's you who's on the run from the law. That's why you didn't stay on the train—it didn't have anything to do with me. Can't you just tell the truth for once?"

"What difference does it make? Once I get you to San Antonio, I'm moving on, anyway. We're just strangers thrown together for a little while, that's all."

"Yes, but for this little while, I'd like to think I could trust you."

"Nobody can trust anybody, Rena. We all adjust the truth to suit our purposes. Even you." Before she could refute it, he pointed out, "If man told the truth all the time, there wouldn't even be a human race. Most of the time, a woman wouldn't want to know what's on a man's mind."

"And that's probably the closest thing you've said to fact since I met you."

Carefully setting the picture back on a shelf, he exhaled fully before turning to her. "What do you think you want to know about me?"

"Who *are* you?"

He couldn't risk the whole truth. He couldn't put that much trust in anyone's hands, least of all in a woman who wasn't all that truthful herself, but he had to tell her something she could believe, something that wouldn't get him into trouble if she went to the law.

"My name's Matthew James McCready, and I was born in Tennessee in the spring of '46."

"Where in Tennessee?"

He shrugged. "Pretty much nowhere."

"Every place is somewhere."

"Well, it might as well be nowhere," he said defensively. "It's just a little dry hollow my Grandpa called Pigeon Creek. Sort of like Eagle Lake, I guess—no pigeons and no creek." Looking at her through his swollen eye, he forced another smile. "You sure you want to know all this?"

"Yes."

"So what else do you think I'm lying about? Go on—I'm listening."

"You told that man you were in a Hell Brigade from Arkansas, and if you were born in 1846, you were barely twenty when the Rebellion ended."

"Whoa now—you've got that part wrong. It wasn't a rebellion—it was a *war* the damned Yankees waged on us."

"But you didn't fight in it, whatever you want to call it."

"The hell I didn't. I was fifteen when I ran away to

join up. I said I was almost eighteen, which I admit was a damned stupid thing to do, but I wanted to serve in the Army of Tennessee with my brothers. I wanted to do my share for the Cause before they won it without me," he remembered, his voice betraying bitterness. "Yeah, I went, all right. I had good eyes and steady hands, so they made me a sharpshooter. I probably picked off close to two hundred Yankees before it was over." His mouth flattened into a straight line. "Yeah, I went for the wrong reasons, and I came out without even a scar to show for it. It was my brothers who didn't make it."

"They were killed?"

He nodded. "All three of us ended up in Bragg's army—Drew, Wayne, and me. Drew fell at Chickamauga, Wayne two months later at Chattanooga. You know what they say—it's the good that die young. I'm still here to tell about it."

"I see. Well, at least your mother didn't lose all her sons. At least she still had you when it was over."

"I never went home, Rena. I figured if I did, I'd never get away again. I figured since the Almighty let me live, He didn't mean to hold me prisoner on a little piece of land I hated."

"What about your parents—your mother—? Didn't you care that you were all she had left?"

"Oh, I write her from time to time, but I don't think anybody misses me anymore. She wrote back once, telling me my sister Maggie married the Logan boy after the war, that he was helping out on the place. I figure he'll get it someday, which'll be good, because he'll want it."

"Yes, but—"

"Ma understood. I just wasn't cut out to be a farmer, and if I'd gone home the last son, there'd been no escaping it. I couldn't do it." His gaze dropped to his hands, to his carefully pared nails, and the corners of his mouth turned down. "I didn't want to be poor for the rest of my life."

Listening to him, she could almost feel sorry for him. On the outside, he looked as though he had everything—looks, confidence, the clothing of a gentleman—but underneath that handsome exterior, he had nothing to anchor his life to. No family. No roots.

"But you could have comforted her, and she could have comforted you."

The way she said it made him feel like a damned fool. He didn't even know why he'd betrayed as much as he had. Every bit of information he'd given her beyond the McCready name would probably be coming back to haunt him.

"Don't," he responded, his voice suddenly harsh. "I didn't want to be a damned farmer, and by God, I'm not. You want to feel sorry for somebody, Verena Howard, you feel sorry for yourself."

At first, the vehemence in his voice stunned her, then she understood. "I wasn't feeling sorry for you, not at all, Mr. McCready," she said quietly. "I was sympathizing with your mother, because I know what it's like to be left. I know how it feels to be abandoned by someone who's supposed to love you."

"Yeah, you felt so bad, you came running down here. He's dead, and he's still got a hold on your mind, doesn't he?"

"I just want to understand, Matthew. My father was

an officer with the Pennsylvania Regulars—an *officer,* Matthew. He was *Major* John Howard, and he deserted. It wasn't just me and Mama he left, either," she said evenly. "It was everybody—his men, his state, and his country. He just rode off into thin air, and nobody knew what happened to him until I got the letter from the attorney in San Angelo."

"Into thin air?"

"Yes. For a long time, he was listed as unaccounted for, and I watched my mother wait and hope and pray that he'd somehow be found alive. Finally, when she was sick and reduced to penury, she was forced to apply for an army widow's pension. After a military investigation, the war department determined that he'd deserted. And I think that was the blow that killed her."

"They could've made a mistake."

"Not in this case. There wasn't even much of a battle the day he disappeared. 'A minor skirmish with a Confederate supply guard,' the report called it. After that, he and several of his men just vanished. He wasn't on any prisoner of war list. There wasn't a body or anything. He was just gone."

"Maybe he couldn't take any more of it. War changes a man, Rena."

"Enough to make a man turn his back on everybody he was supposed to love?" she countered bitterly.

"I don't know. A lot of Yankees deserted—and so did some of ours. Some were just too green, two raw to handle what they saw."

Fixing her gaze on the flock of sheep beyond the window, she swallowed, then went on, her voice low. "No, he just left us for something or somebody else. I don't think there was any constancy on his side from the beginning of their marriage. But no matter how indiscreet he was, Mama pretended not to know. She always wanted to believe he loved her. But I guess he didn't."

It was his turn to feel sorry. "Look," he said gently, "you may not like what you find."

"I know."

"My earlier offer still stands. You can still take the money and go home."

"I can't."

"A couple of hundred dollars doesn't mean anything to me, Rena. Money comes and goes easy with me."

"If I were to take your money, I'd expect myself to do something to earn it, and I couldn't. I could never repay you," she said simply.

"I wasn't asking for anything—not even the obvious."

"I know."

Noting the set of her shoulders, he realized it would be useless to insist. While he still wasn't prepared to admit everything she'd told him since they met was the truth, he could at least recognize principle when he saw it. And in the jaded world he knew, that alone made her a rare creature.

"I know you don't believe me when I say I don't know anyone out here," she said quietly. "I know you can't understand why I'd want to come all this way for next to nothing. You probably still think I'm hiding something."

"What if I asked you what you asked me?"

"I suppose turnabout would be fair. All right,"

she decided. "I was born Verena Mary Howard in Philadelphia on the Fourth of July, eighteen hundred and fifty-one."

"On Independence Day?"

"Before you make any connection between my temperament and fireworks, I can tell you it won't be original. There's nothing you could say on the subject that I haven't already heard."

"Well, there is a certain volatility, but all that aside, go on. You're just a hair shy of twenty-three," he prompted.

"And any comments about spinsterhood won't be appreciated either," she declared flatly. "If I wanted a husband, I'm sure I could get myself one. Now, where was I?"

"An almost twenty-three-year-old spinster, I believe. From Pennsylvania."

"Yes, and right now I'd swear on a stack of Bibles that if God will just let me get home in one piece, I'll never leave again."

"No kin?"

"What?"

"No relations?"

"No one I'd want to claim. Mama and Papa are both dead, and I was an only child. And my grandparents are gone, too. No, there's just Mama's brother, Elliot, and I don't feel particularly charitable toward him. He used to give us ten dollars the first of every month, and every time it came with a sermon. And when I graduated from Bancroft, he gave me a grudging reference for a teaching position, saying he knew of no *major* defect in my character, which I suppose was something," she conceded. "But I can never forgive him letting Mama work as a seamstress while he lived in a grand house filled with servants who had more than she did."

"Now there ain't no need fer ya to sit in that chair," Seth Brassfield declared, coming into the room. "Molly!" he said sharply. The pig gave him a sullen look, then moved to a corner. Turning to Matthew, the older man announced, "It ain't Saturday, but Sarie's a-bilin' water if'n y'all want ta warsh yerselfs. Said fer the missus to go fust so's she gits the clean water."

It took a moment for Verena to understand. Rising, she looked to Matthew and hesitated. "Go ahead," he told her, "it's been awhile, but it won't be the first time I've been second in the bathwater. Or even third, for that matter."

"What?"

"I get your bathwater when you're done."

"When I'm done? But surely—"

Seth nodded. "If'n the water's not too dirty, I reckon Sarie'll wash yer dress when both a'you is done."

"Oh, but—"

" 'Sall right," he said, "she's got a flour sack you kin put on while she's a-mending and a-drying it."

As Verena put her hand on the door, Matt warned her, "You may have to watch out for leftover feathers in the tub."

"Naw," Seth assured her, "Sarie plucked the chicken in the dishpan."

Her body turned away from Matthew McCready's, Verena stared at the rising moon framed in the window. Her mother must surely be turning over in her grave right now, she thought, but she hadn't really had any choice in the matter. As it was, Sarah Brassfield had given her and Matthew the bed the boys usually shared, sending them up into the loft with their blankets. Not that anyone needed blankets on a night like this.

It was too hot for sleep, but McCready didn't seem to know it. After a huge meal of chicken and dumplings, beans, potatoes, baked yams, and hot biscuits, followed by an enormous cobbler made from dried peaches, he and Seth had played checkers and swapped God only knew what lies over a bottle of elderberry wine. While they were apparently enjoying themselves, she and Sarah had finished mending and ironing the clothes she and the gambler had all but ruined in their jump from the moving train.

For once, she'd fared better than he had. Sarah's flour-sack gown had been huge, so much so that she'd had to tie it in with a rope, but poor Matthew'd been forced to make do with one of Seth's old shirts, badly stretched between buttons, and a pair of heavy twill "overalls" that were apparently designed to be worn over other clothing, but which barely went around McCready without anything under them.

As his wife, Verena had the dubious honor of washing his shirt and his drawers and hanging them up to dry beside hers on Sarah's laundry line. His pants she'd merely had to spot clean with a rag and soap. But the upshot of it all was that she'd had her head bent over her borrowed needle and thread while he'd drank and played. But in the end, there'd been a certain satisfaction in showing him that even while out of her own element, she wasn't useless. Of course, with nine tenths of Seth Brassfield's elderberry wine gone, McCready would have been happy no matter what she'd done, she reflected wryly.

As fastidious as he seemed to be, he'd made a point of not holding himself above the Brassfields. In fact, he'd scarce paused in his conversation when Molly had reared her ugly snout above the edge of the dinner table for a closer look at his plate. To prevent a like occurrence, Verena had headed the animal off with a good-sized biscuit dropped quietly on the floor. But Seth Brassfield had put an end to the pig's begging with a simple, "Get down, girl," at which Molly ambled over to the other side of the room, grunting her discontent.

She found herself smiling in the darkness, remembering the sound of Seth and Matthew singing a mongrelized version of "Bringing in the Sheaves" when three quarters of the way into the wine bottle. Only

Brassfield had belted it out as "Brangin' in the sheep, brangin' in the sheep," while McCready's rich baritone kept to the right lyrics until he forgot the rest of the lines.

She'd looked across at Sarah then, catching the older woman's glistening eyes. "Been awhile since we was t'church," Sarah'd allowed in a husky voice. "That man o' yours, he sings right purty, don't he? D'you reckon they'd mind if'n we was t' join 'em?" And once said, no amount of demurring would dissuade the woman, who'd insisted, "The good Lord above, it's the spee-rit He's a takin' notice of." In the end, there'd been no help for it—she'd had to stand behind Matthew, her hand on his shoulder, mouthing the words to "Take Me Home, Sweet Chariot," praying that he couldn't hear her.

She closed her eyes, remembering the solid feel of that shoulder, the warm glow of the yellow flame coming from the tin kerosene lamp reflecting off his clean, shining black hair, the almost velvet sound of his voice resonating through the room. And the way he'd reached up, covering her hand on his shoulder with his fingers, had only seemed to magnify the moment. For a time, she'd forgotten what he was, what a hoax they were pulling on the Brassfields. She'd even forgotten the danger lurking in the man beneath her hand.

Later, when they were back in their chairs, finishing the last stitches while the boys heated the iron outside, Sarah had leaned over to whisper, "You got yerself a fine figger of a man, Rena—a fine figger of a man. If'n 'twarn't fer that black eye o' his, he'd be enough ta make this old heart thump, I kin tell ya. But it'll be gone in a coupla days, so's I wouldn't be a-worryin' none."

Her eyes misting over, she added, "Makes me remember what it was like when Seth and me was younguns like y'all." Touching her grizzled hair with a work-roughened hand, she'd recalled wistfully, "I was real purty oncet—oh, not anythin' near as purty as you, but—"

"And you still are," Verena'd hastened to assure her, hoping to avert the subject from herself.

"You think so?"

"Yes."

"Well, I don't guess it matters none, 'ceptin' Seth thinks so, huh?"

"No."

" 'Sarie,' he used t' say to me, 'you got eyes like them stars up thar, bright as them demons thuh fancy ladies is a-wearing,' " she recalled.

"Demons?" Verena repeated. "Uh—"

"You know—like they's a-wearin' on thar fingers."

"Oh—diamonds."

"Uh-huh. Me, I never was one t' want one of 'em, you unnerstan'," the woman confided. "How 'bout you?"

"Me?" Verena glanced down at her hand, seeing the gold band she'd bought herself. "No."

"He's a fine figger of a man, all right—and he's got hisself a good woman," Sarah pronounced solemnly. "That's the way it's spozed t' be, you know. 'S long as you got each other, you got all you need."

"Yes, of course." Squirming uncomfortably in her seat, Verena tried valiantly to find something else to talk about. "Is it always this hot down here?" she asked quickly.

"Oh, thar's hotter times a-coming, honey. This ain't nothin' fer Texas, I kin tell you."

That was a daunting thought. Shifting slightly in the bed, Verena stealthily pulled the damp nightgown up enough to let the night air touch her legs. She was exhausted beyond bearing, and yet the heat made it impossible to sleep. No, McCready's soft, even breathing behind her gave the lie to that thought. Maybe if she'd had half a bottle of wine, she wouldn't be noticing the heat either, but she hadn't. If she didn't doze off soon, the circles under her eyes would be as black as Matthew's shiner.

If she'd been alone, she'd have slept in her chemise, but she wasn't. Besides, it was all ironed and folded on the chest, ready for tomorrow. No, she'd have to endure the big, voluminous gown swamping her legs like a collapsed tent.

She'd had no sleep to speak of for more than two days, and her mind wouldn't even hold a complete thought now. Opening her eyes again, she looked at the window, wondering if it opened. Easing her feet down to the floor, she sat up, then crept on tiptoe to look at it. It ought to come up—it was rope hung. She pushed upward on it, and it moved, rasping wood against wood. But as she started to take her hand off, she could feel the weight coming back down. It'd have to be propped open. Turning around, she almost tripped over one of McCready's boots. Lifting the window again, she shoved the boot sideways into the gap, affording about four inches of fresh air.

Barely back in bed again, she heard the ominous buzz, then felt the prick of a mosquito bite. Smashing it in the act, she started to turn over, then heard another one. And another. It was as if they'd swarmed outside the window just waiting for the feast.

There was the smack of hand against skin, a muttered, "Damn," and she knew Matthew McCready's blissful sleep had ended. She lay still, not moving a muscle, as he sat up.

"What the hell—?" Another loud smack. "Damn," he grumbled sleepily, "some damned fool's opened the window." Heaving his body up, he padded over and tried to close it. A string of expletives cut through the night air when he found his boot. Retrieving it, he slammed the window shut, then walked around to her side of the bed. "Did you do this?" he demanded.

She played dead while another mosquito found dinner on her neck. She even managed to keep her eyes closed when he found a match and struck it to light the kerosene lamp on the table. She could hear him come back, but she was totally unprepared for the whack on her backside. She sat up, snapping furiously, "What was that for?"

"I was killing a damned mosquito you let in," he muttered. "Get up," he ordered. "They're everywhere." Carrying the lamp, he examined the room, looking for something, anything he could use as a swatter. When he turned around, she'd burrowed under the sheet. He grasped the bottom of it, snatching it off the bed. "You let 'em in, you kill 'em," he told her curtly. "I'll be damned if I'm going to spend another night like the last one, Rena. You get up and start swatting."

In the yellow light, his blackened eye looked greenish and disfigured, giving him an evil aspect. And when she didn't move, he lunged for her, ready to pull her out of the bed. Before he could catch her, she dived out the other side, then backed away.

"Lord a mercy! What—?" Before Sarah Brassfield got out the question, she could hear the answer. "Skeeters! Pa! Eddie! Fetch the swatter—*muy pronto*! They's a-takin' over!"

Seth Brassfield lurched through the door, obviously bewildered by the sudden commotion. One of the insects buzzed him, and he began jumping and waving. "Sarie, what fool's left the dad-blamed winder open?"

"It don't matter—they's everwhar! Eddie! Pollo!"

The two boys came skinnying down the ladder from the loft, falling over each other. The bigger boy, naked except for some sort of breechclout, charged into the room waving a yellowed newspaper, flailing at the circling mosquitos.

"Not that one!" Sarah wailed. "I was a-gonna order me some o' that linnyment in thar!"

"If you don't kill them critters, you'll need tonic fer your blood instaid," Seth declared, taking the paper from the boy. "Get the alminnik," he ordered, swatting at a wall. "And shut the danged door a'fore they's all over the house!"

McCready had pulled off his borrowed shirt and was snapping it like a towel, trying to bring an errant mosquito down. Instead, he caught Verena's arm.

Incensed, she turned around and slapped his shoulder hard.

"Missed it," she announced sweetly.

His hand flattened her nose. "I got him for you." Before she could retaliate, he showed her the dead insect on the heel of his palm. "One down, ninety-nine to go."

Behind her, Seth was muttering something about Texas mosquitoes being big enough to carry a man off, while Sarah was trying to hush him up, whispering, "Now, Pa, they ain't from down here, you know. How was they t' know you gotta have nettin' if'n you want t' open the winder?"

It took about ten or fifteen minutes to kill most of the insects. By then, the Brassfields were wide awake. Surveying the bedclothes on the floor, Seth stood with both hands on the waist of his red flannel drawers, allowing as how he had "nuther bottle o' elderburry wine, if any of you wants ta share it. Reckon ahm gonna need a mite if'n ahm gonna get any sleep—my nerves ain't what they used to be."

Adjourning to the other room, the older man filled a large tin cupful for each person, including the two boys, and they all sat around the table sipping his wine. After he sent the boys back to bed, he refilled the rest of the cups. By the time she'd emptied the second one, Verena was having trouble keeping her eyes open. Exhausted beyond bearing, she sat with her head propped in her hands, trying to follow Seth's conversation, but it wasn't any use. Her head dropped to rest on the table.

Sarah leaned over to murmur, "He's tellin' you ta use the pot—he kilt a rattler 'tween here and the outhouse after y'all went to bed."

The next thing Verena knew, McCready had his arm under her shoulder, lifting her up. "Come on—night's half over," he told her as she sagged against him. She felt her feet leave the floor and her body fold over his shoulder, but she was beyond caring. Tomorrow she might raise a ruckus, but not now.

"Close the door after yourselves!" Seth called out. "I'm all et up already!"

McCready kicked the door shut, then dropped Verena on the bed, where she just lay there, looking up at him.

"Never had any wine before, have you?"

"So tired," she mumbled. "Tired and hot."

"You know, if you were a dance hall girl, you'd just be getting started."

"Huh?"

Verena's chestnut hair spread over a pillow like a tangled mass of shimmering silk. And Sarah Brassfield's calico nightgown was so big that it slipped off a bare shoulder, revealing the soft curve of an almost alabaster breast. For a moment, Matthew felt his mouth go dry with desire. Then he looked away.

"Get on your side," he said, his voice thick.

"Too tired . . . to move."

"You know, you're too damned hard on a man."

"No." Instead of rolling over, she fumbled with the buttons at her neck. "It's hot . . . so hot . . . I can't breathe."

"What else have you got to wear?"

She tried to sit up, but her head spun. "I could sleep standing," she whispered. "So tired."

"Yeah."

"Thirsty."

"You've had enough."

"Water."

He touched her forehead. It was moist, her hair damp at the temples. He couldn't blame her for thinking she was hot. He felt like he was in a damned oven. He stood there, thinking he'd got himself into a real pickle, and it wasn't over yet. Now the only thing he needed to completely ruin what was left of the night would be for her to get sick from drinking too much wine. She already had that clammy skin.

"All right." He walked across the room to pour a little tepid water into a cup. "If you're going to throw up, hang over the bed," he said over his shoulder.

"I'm not," she managed, closing her eyes. "I'm too sleepy." She swallowed. "It's hot . . . so hot."

"Yeah, I know."

Carrying the water back to her, he sat down beside her. "You'll have to sit up."

"Can't. Dizzy."

"You can't get sick on me, Rena. I'm as tired as you are. Here"—balancing the cup with one hand, he pulled her up with the other—"don't drink too much."

She took a sip, then pushed back her hair. "Sorry . . . about the window," she managed. "I just couldn't breathe."

"If you'd ever spent a summer in New Orleans, you'd have known better, but you haven't," he murmured to console her. "There—and here apparently, you don't open a window without hanging mosquito netting around the bed first. But it's done, and it's over. Now we've just got to get a little sleep."

"I feel—" She swallowed again. "I feel like I'm in an oven, Matt."

"Yeah. Drink up," he said. Rising again, he went back to the washstand and poured more water, this time into the basin. Wetting a cloth, he carried it back. Leaning over her, he wiped her sweaty face. "If you think you're going to be sick, tell me."

"No."

"It's that damned gown," he muttered under his breath. "You're bundled up as if it were winter in the Rockies. Isn't there anything cooler you can wear?"

"My chemise." This time, she took a gulp of the water, and between it and the face washing, she felt better. "But it's clean."

"Where is it?"

"On the chest."

"I'll get it."

When he returned with the folded garment, he circled the bed, coming up behind her. "Come on—let's get this on you."

She was dizzy, and she had a notion she was drunk, but she wasn't totally lost to all propriety. "No." She felt his hand reach around her neck for the top button, and she caught it with both of hers. "Don't."

"I'll blow out the lamp," he offered. "I won't see anything." Easing onto the bed behind her, he caught her arm, pulling away one of her hands, then he shook off the other. His fingers found the second button and slid the buttonhole over it. He could feel her whole body stiffen. "Easy now—I'm not wanting anything but sleep. Way I figure it, about the only way that's going to happen is if you get cool enough to sleep yourself."

"I can do the rest," she whispered.

"All right." Keeping his promise, he turned away to turn down the wick. The yellow flame rose narrowly, then dropped to a tiny blue ball before going out. The wick glowed red as a thin, acrid band of smoke escaped through the glass chimney. "How's that? Feel better now?"

"No. It's not dark enough."

"I can do a lot of things, Rena, but I can't put out the moon." When she didn't move, he sighed. "If you think can get into the chemise by yourself, I'll keep my back turned."

It didn't matter, she told herself wearily. She was alone in the room with him, and once she went to sleep, she'd be pretty much defenseless, anyway. Finishing the buttons, she worked Sarah's gown down from her shoulders, then she shook out the clean chemise and pulled it over her head so the bottom hung down enough to cover her breasts. Thrusting her arms through the armholes, she wriggled the cloth down to her hips. With an effort, she stood up to push the gown down with one hand and tug the hem of the chemise with the other. Trying to step out of the nightgown, she stumbled dizzily, slipped, and fell backward into bed.

"You sure you're all right?" Matt asked her.

"Just barely."

He turned around then and rolled her onto her side, where she lay, facing away from him. Easing his own aching body down into the feather mattress, he heard the buzz of another mosquito. Exhaling his resignation, he crawled to the bottom of the bed, retrieved the sheet, and pulled it up to cover both of them. The mosquito, he decided, was welcome to what it could find.

Lying there, he stared up at the ceiling, trying not to think of the woman beside him. It was a losing effort. She was a beauty, but no more beautiful than some of the other women he'd had, just in a different way. It was that damned vulnerability, he supposed. The women he usually encountered were hard, almost brittle by comparison. They knew how to play the game, but she didn't. No, by her own admission, she was a twenty-two—almost twenty-three—year-old-spinster schoolteacher, and her only armor seemed to be an inbred distrust of men like him.

If he had any sense, he'd put her on that stage at Columbus and wash his hands of her. But from the beginning, nothing he'd done where she was concerned made much sense. Oh, there'd been the possibility of seduction, and the notion that he could use her to cover his own tracks. Neither of which had panned out, he reminded himself. At all.

But for all her sharp words, she was an innocent when it came to dealing with men, particularly the sort she was likely to encounter between here and San Angelo. It'd be like abandoning a babe teetering above a pit of rattlesnakes. But he had to do it. Eventually, anyway. He had to think of his own neck. He couldn't afford to get in any deeper with Verena Howard.

His thoughts stalled, jarred by the realization that her shoulders were shaking. Well, he couldn't blame her for crying, not when he considered everything that had happened to her so far. Telling himself he was doing it so he could finally get some sleep, he rolled onto his side behind her, and reached his arm around her body.

"Hey, everything's going to be all right, Rena," he whispered into her soft hair. Rubbing his chin against her crown, he drew her closer, protectively curving his body to hers. "Come on—don't cry. Another couple of days or so you'll be in San Angelo taking care of your business. Then before the month's out, you'll be on your way back to Philadelphia." His hand brushed against her breast, sending a current of awareness through his body. Pulling it away as though it had been burned, he opted for the safety of smoothing her hair instead. "Rena, I'm beyond bearing anything more," he said softly. "Don't break down on me now." Her shoulders shook harder. "Hey, come on—"

"B-but I'm not crying!" she burst out finally. "I can't help it—it's just funny! I've been humiliated and mortified half a dozen times in less days, and yet when I look back on it, it's funny!"

"You're *laughing*?" he managed incredulously.

"I can't help it!"

"I don't understand this—I don't."

"No, don't you see? For as long as I can remember, everything was about being prim and proper—even the schoolteaching. No, *especially* the teaching—and look what's happened to me!"

"You had too much wine, that's all," he murmured. "Come morning, you'll be a real sourpuss."

"Is that what you think I am—a sourpuss?"

"No. But you're going to be." Feeling a very real sense of relief, he brushed her damp hair back from her temples with his fingertips. "You're going to have one hell of a headache."

"I don't care, Matthew. I don't care." She rolled onto her back to look up at him. "I'm not what I thought I was."

Her eyes were luminous in the faint moonlight, and her lips were moist, parted. And the chemise was so thin he could feel the heat of her body. She was almost asking him to take advantage of her. No, it was the damned wine, fooling his mind into thinking she was like every other woman he knew, that he could taste and take, and it wouldn't make any difference, but he knew better. She was a ball and chain waiting to snap around his leg, and she didn't even know it.

"What you are is drunk, Rena."

"Oh."

"Yeah. A body oughtn't to drink when he's as tired as you are."

"What about you?"

"I'm used to it. I can handle straight whiskey."

"I never had anything stronger than coffee before."

"I know."

"You think I'm silly, don't you?"

"No. I think you're damned pretty—and drunk. And if you don't turn over, you're just asking for something you don't want. When your hangover wore off, you'd be expecting me to make it right, and I'm not the staying kind, Rena."

"No, you're a gambler," she said solemnly.

"It's not a winning hand. Even a fool would fold it." Dropping his hand from her hair to her shoulder, he pushed until she turned over onto her side of the bed. "Now, go on—get some sleep."

"Good night, Matthew McCready," she murmured as he tucked the sheet beneath her chin.

"Good night, Rena."

This time, it was he who lay awake. He was losing his edge, there was no doubt about it. There'd been a time, and it wasn't all that long ago, when conscience wouldn't have played much of a part in anything he did. But tonight, he probably could have had Verena Howard, and he'd backed off, knowing it would have been too hard to face her tomorrow.

"Get on, Jake! Go, Crow!" Eduardo yelled.

The blacksnake whip cracked above the backs of two mules, one a rusty brown, the other black, both of whom had seen better days. Jake was short, with wide, bowed-out ribs and spindly legs, while Crow was tall and as sleek as the blue-black raven for which he'd apparently been named.

As the rickety wagon struck a weathered tree stump, Verena held her head and moaned. She was hungover, all right, and Sarah Brassfield's strong coffee had only made her as green as the clumps of grass by the outhouse. And Seth Brassfield's offer of a "heer o' thuh dawg" had been rejected with the revulsion of one experiencing the painful effects of already having imbibed too much.

Matt felt a real sympathy for her. If he lived to one hundred, he'd never forget his own experience when as a raw fifteen-year-old he'd tried to drown the memory of a man's head exploding by downing more than a pint of Tennessee whiskey by himself. The next morning, he'd had to crawl to roll call, and every blast of the damned bugle felt like it was going off between his ears. It'd made him a teetotaler for a long time.

"You want to try lying down?" he asked her.

"I feel as if I could die."

"It'll get better."

"I can't even open my eyes."

"It was that second cup last night," he murmured. "Mrs. Brassfield sent a blanket you could roll up and use for a pillow."

"No." Wincing, she looked at Eduardo's back. "We haven't missed a hole or a bump yet," she muttered.

"Road's pretty bad," Matt agreed.

The whip cracked again, sending a shudder through her. "How much farther to Columbus?" she asked dully.

"I figure we've gone a couple of miles."

"That's not what I asked."

"If you were a bird, I'd guess about six miles. On this road, I wouldn't even try to estimate it."

"I'll never drink anything fermented again—not as long as I live," she declared flatly.

"It'll get better."

"You keep saying that, but I don't see any sign of it. You should have stopped me, you know. You knew this was going to happen, didn't you?"

"I thought maybe you were too tired to sleep, and the wine would help."

"It wasn't worth this morning."

With an effort, she turned her head sideways to look at him. His black hair was still wet from where he'd stuck his head under the Brassfields' pump. Maybe she should have tried it. Instead, she'd held on to the chest with one hand while trying to drag a comb through hair that seemed to be as sore as her head.

The eyebrow over his good eye lifted. "Surely, I don't look that bad."

"No. The swelling's gone down a little, and it's not quite as dark a purple," she decided. "Can you see any better out of it?"

"Some."

What she really wanted to know, she was afraid to ask. As bad as she'd felt when she woke up, she could still wonder how she came to be in her chemise instead of Sarah's big, cumbersome gown. She distinctly remembered sitting at the table, drinking Seth Brassfield's elderberry wine in the nightgown. Beyond that, her recollection was downright hazy. But waking up in bed with Matthew McCready's backside against hers and her chemise pulled up to her knees gave rise to thoughts she was afraid to put into words.

Wetting her parched lips with her tongue, she allowed cautiously, "I don't remember much about it—about last night, I mean. At least, not after the mosquitoes, anyway."

He knew what she wanted to know, but he was curious as to how she was going to get around to it. "Yeah. Well, I don't remember much before they hit."

"You were sound asleep."

"You know, that's the second ruckus you created in two nights," he reminded her. "If the train's gone on by the time we get to Columbus, I'm getting a room to myself."

As hot as it was, her cheeks felt hotter. "I was

warned about coyotes, cougars, and rattlesnakes, but nobody said *anything* about mosquitoes the size of—of bumblebees!" The instant her voice rose, she regretted it. The pounding in her head was unbearable. When it finally subsided, she managed, "Yes, I think that would be wise—separate rooms, I mean."

"I thought maybe we could claim to be brother and sister until I put you on the mail wagon. After that, you'll have an armed escort, so you won't have to worry about getting to San Angelo." Studying her fine profile, he couldn't resist making her squirm a little. "Yeah, you wouldn't want a repeat of last night," he added wickedly.

"No, of course not." Now she was worried. Casting a quick look at Eduardo's back, she hesitated. "Uh—"

"I wouldn't worry about the kid, if that's what you're thinking. As far as I can tell, he's been shouting the only English he knows at those mules. And if he's learning to speak it like Brassfield, he won't understand you, anyway."

"Yes, I suppose you're right." Dropping her gaze to her hands, she considered for a moment, then ventured, "I guess I *was* pretty silly last night."

"I wouldn't exactly call it silly," he murmured noncomittally.

She'd just have to try another angle. "Well, I suppose a woman who has drunk too much must be rather disgusting." When he didn't respond, she managed a furtive side glance. "Well?"

After the collapsed bed and the mosquito horde, she deserved to fret before he let her off the hook. "Well, I don't know. . . ." He let his voice trail off.

"I suppose you were too drunk to notice yourself," she suggested hopefully.

"There are some things a man remembers no matter how much he's drunk."

"Like what?"

"Like the way chestnut hair spreads across a pillow. Like the way a woman's lips part when she's inviting a man to kiss her. Like the way her skin glows in lamplight. The way fire reflects in hazel eyes—"

Mortified, she closed her eyes and swallowed. "You don't need to go any further, Mr. McCready. Please."

"It was Matt last night," he reminded her.

"You, sir, are no gentleman," she whispered.

"I thought we established that on the *Norfolk Star*, Rena."

"But I thought we were friends, and you—you—"

"Took advantage of you?"

"Yes."

"I suppose now you want me to make an honest woman out of you," he said, sighing.

"Certainly *not*!" The pain shot through her head, mocking her now. "I wouldn't marry a dishonest man if he were the last one left on earth." Twisting the ring on her finger, she shook her head miserably. "I just can't believe that two cups of wine would make me do something like that. I can't believe I'd let you kiss me, that I'd—" No, she couldn't even put that thought into words.

"A person's real character doesn't change with drink, Rena."

That was an even worse thought. As hot tears stung her eyes, she swallowed again, this time to force the lump in her throat down. Her mother's warning echoed loudly in her ears.

Always remember it's the really handsome man of this world who is the most dangerous, for he has an instant advantage over a woman, and believe me, he is practiced in the art of using it. Having been cosseted and flattered by the female sex all of his life, he's learned early on to take a woman's heart lightly, worthy of little or nothing in exchange. You can never trust a handsome man.

But she didn't even have the excuse of succumbing to his blandishments or even false promises. No, she'd had two cups of elderberry wine, then thrown herself at him with an apparent lack of any persuasion whatsoever. And she didn't even remember any of it.

"What you must think me," she choked out.

One look at her stricken face told him he'd carried the joke too far. "Actually, I think you're quite a lady."

"I think we'd better part company in Columbus—I don't think I want to face you any longer than I have to."

"You didn't hear me, did you? I said I think you're quite a lady, Verena Mary Howard," he said softly. "I probably owe my life to your prompt thinking on the other side of Eagle Lake."

"There's no need to flatter me now, I assure you."

Now he had to retrieve the situation. "Oh, I see," he said as if it had just dawned on him. "You thought that you and I—that we—"

"There's no need to say it."

"Well, it didn't happen."

"But you just said—"

"I know." His mouth turned down in a wry, twisted

smile. "Let's just say that was a lot of wishful thinking on my part."

"Ohhhhh—of all—"

"Well, you didn't want it to be true, did you?"

"No!"

"I had you going for a while, didn't I? Made you even forget that pain in your head."

Torn between immeasurable relief and boundless fury, she took a deep breath and held it, counting for calm. Thinking she'd mastered herself, she let it out. "You know, I'd like to believe you, but all you do is tell one lie after another."

"I'd swear on a stack of Bibles I didn't touch you, if it'd make you feel any better."

"I woke up in my chemise, Mr. McCready." Giving that a chance to sink in, she paused, then declared flatly, "I went to bed in that awful calico tent of Mrs. Brassfield's."

"Is that what's bothering you?"

"Yes."

"You kept saying you were too hot to go to sleep, so I fetched your chemise, turned off the lamp, and faced the other way while you changed into it."

"And all the rest of it—all those other things you said?"

"I told you—wishful thinking." The corners of his mouth lifted into an outright smile, making him look almost boyish. "Believe me, if anything had happened, I wouldn't be wanting a room alone tonight. I'd be doing my damnedest to get a repeat performance."

"Do you know how low you are?" she demanded.

"I suppose you're going to tell me."

"My head hurts as if it could burst—and if it did, it would be a relief, Matthew McCready. You sat there and watched me drink that stuff, knowing what was going to happen, and you didn't even warn me. And then you tell me I behaved with wanton *abandon* last night, and—"

"With what?"

"You know perfectly well what I mean. Anyway, for your own *perverse* enjoyment, you let me believe that I was no better than a . . . a cheap tart, knowing full well that it would . . . would . . ."

"Mortally wound you?" he supplied.

"I don't know what I was going to say," she snapped, "but whatever it was, it would have blistered your ears."

"Okay, I'm sorry. But if you believed it, you didn't have a very high opinion of me or my morals either."

"I wasn't aware you had any."

"Now that was uncalled for. For two days and nights, I've nursemaided you, fending off over-amorous cowboys and imposters, going without sleep, getting myself beaten up, and you don't have so much as one ounce of gratitude for any of it. Go on, admit that, will you?"

She couldn't refute it—it was all true. She regarded him tiredly for a moment. "All right," she said finally, "but I didn't ask you to do any of those things for me, did I?"

His eyebrow lifted again. "Not even at Goode's?"

"Well, maybe then," she conceded. "Look, all I know is if I don't get some relief from this headache, I might as well die. And you've just been sitting there laughing at me, and you know it. You don't know how bad I feel, or if you do, you just don't care."

"Yeah, I do," he admitted, soberly. "First time it happened to me, it was Tennessee whiskey, and I couldn't see straight for two days. I'll bet it was a year before I took another drink, and even then I was mighty cautious about how much I had."

"I can't even hold my head up."

"Lean against me," he offered. "I'll hold it up for you."

"I wouldn't even—"

At that moment, the wagon hit another stump, almost bouncing her out of her seat. As her aching head snapped forward, sending acute pain through her eyeballs, Matthew caught her, pulling her against him, steadying her head with his shoulder. Beyond fighting any more, she leaned into him and held on with both arms. It was disgraceful behavior, but she was beyond caring about appearances right now. And whether she wanted to admit it or not, there was comfort in being held.

The wagon jolted, this time to a halt, and the boy driver shouted something in Spanish. Coming awake suddenly, Verena straightened up and looked around. What she saw first was a river.

"Where are we?"

"About to cross the Colorado," Matt murmured. "Columbus is right over there. As soon as the ferry deposits us on the other side, we'll get a couple of rooms. Then while you sleep off the last of that hangover, I'll go pick up our bags."

"Oh."

"Feel any better?"

She sat still for a moment, then decided, "My neck's half-broken, and my head still feels like it's been kicked between my eyes."

"That hour-and-a-half sleep didn't help any?"

As she turned her head, her neck popped audibly. "I don't know—I'm still too tired to tell."

"We'll get you a real bed and some peace and quiet," he promised. "Come tomorrow, you'll be all right."

"That's the ferry?" she asked suddenly, momentarily forgetting her pain.

"Yeah. It's not much, is it?"

"It's medieval, that's what it is."

As ferries went, this one was a small boat, piloted by one man, whose source of power was a frayed rope over a windlass with a block and tackle. Coming back across to pick them up, the whole apparatus creaked and groaned until the boat came to rest by bumping against the small pier.

"It's probably the same boat Stephen Austin came across the Colorado in. This is kind of the cradle of Texas, you know. Right over there, the first three hundred settlers branched out to homestead this area back in the twenties," he said, pointing to some big oaks on the other side.

"Really?"

"Yeah."

"You've been here before?"

"Once. It was right after the war, when I was looking for someplace that wasn't overrun by Yankees. But Texas wasn't much different from the rest of the

South—and what the carpetbaggers weren't running, the Indians were raiding. So I went to New Orleans, where things didn't seem to change as much. It'd been overrun by the Spanish, the French, and us before, and instead of knuckling under, it just absorbed 'em. I figured maybe it'd swallow up the Yankees like everybody else. And it more or less did. New Orleans," he declared flatly, "will always be New Orleans."

"So you stayed there until now."

"Yeah. Well, more or less, anyway. Sometimes I rode the riverboats up to Natchez and Vicksburg, plying my trade."

"Playing cards, you mean."

"Same thing. Once a man decides to make his living at something, it's not much of a game anymore. It becomes like everything else, pretty much work. For a man to make it into the big games, he's got to have the right clothes, the right manners, the right connections—and once he gets there, he's got to be damned good at counting his cards, or he's broke." He looked across the river again, then shook his head. "There's nothing much worse than a broke gambler, Rena. He's got to have a stake, or he can't play. And every time he sits down at a table, he's got to have the nerve to risk losing it, or he doesn't win. It's a hell of a life."

"I don't understand why anyone would want to live like that."

"There's nothing like winning—no whiskey, no woman, nothing can make a man feel the way he does when he's winning. When a man gambles at poker, he's pitting his skill and nerve against everybody at the table."

"And luck."

"And luck. But you can help luck along a little."

"I suppose that means you cheat?"

"No. I bluff, Rena, and I'm damned good at it."

"Take two trips to take the wagon, mister!" the ferryman called out. "Dollar apiece! Extra for the wagon!"

"A dollar for each of us to ride that?" Verena asked incredulously. "Just across the river?"

"Ain't no other way across," he declared smugly, " 'less you're wanting to swim it."

"No, of course not." More than a little daunted by the cost, she started to loosen the drawstrings on her purse.

"I'll take care of it," Matt assured her. "Put that away—you'll need your money for the stagecoach fare."

"No, it wouldn't be right. I'm not in desperate straits." *Yet,* her mind added silently. "I just think it's somewhat extortionate, that's all." To be fair, she knew she ought to offer to pay half of the two dollars for Eduardo and the wagon also, but she simply couldn't afford the added expense. "You know," she said suddenly, "it doesn't seem particularly logical to pay for something we aren't going to need in Columbus, does it? I mean, we *could* walk from the boat dock into town, I'd think."

"What about your head?"

"It will probably hurt less walking than riding. At least I don't expect to hit every single rut and bump on foot."

"All right."

Jumping down from the board seat, Matt reached into his coat for his money. He peeled off a ten-dollar banknote and handed it to the astonished boy. "Here—*por Eduardo*."

The kid stared until Matt repeated himself. Then he took the money, turned it over a couple of times as if he still didn't believe it, and finally slipped it between his foot and the sole of his sandal. As soon as Verena climbed down, he cracked the whip over the backs of the mismatched mules and made a wide circle with the wagon, turning it into its own tracks. It rattled out of sight in a cloud of dust to the sounds of "Get on, Jake! Go, Crow!"

"Don't you think that was a little excessive?" Verena managed between coughs. "Ten dollars is more than two weeks of teaching wages."

Matt shrugged. "Everybody needs a stake." Taking her elbow, he turned her toward the ferry. "Looks like the boat's waiting on us."

At water's edge, she eyed the ferryboat dubiously. "Are you sure this is safe?"

"You watched it come across, didn't you?"

The river water appeared red and muddy. "How deep is it right here?" she wanted to know.

"Two tickets," Matt told the boatman, handing over two silver dollars.

"Hit don't matter," the fellow said, answering Verena's question. "Hit ain't like we was meanin' to walk across her."

Once on board, Verena stood in the middle, holding on to one of the windlass support posts, while the man cranked the handle, tightening the rope. Slowly, amid a great many creaks and moans, the ferry pulled away from the river's edge, leaving a wide, shallow wake of white-tipped red water. Beneath her feet, she could feel the current trying to push the boat sideways.

On the other side, brick-red dirt met the water under the weathered pier. She kept her eyes focused on it throughout the crossing.

"What makes the ground so red?" she asked.

"The same clay that colors the river. There's a lot of red clay between here and East Georgia."

"I don't think we've got any of that around Philadelphia."

"Probably not. But down here bands of it stretch up into the Indian reservations above the Canadian River and across the desert all the way through New Mexico Territory."

"And things grow in it?"

"Where there's water. Enough to run cattle, anyway."

"I wonder if it's like this at San Angelo," she murmured.

"San Angela," the boatman corrected her. "Ain't San Angelo—it's San Angela."

"I have a letter postmarked 'San Angelo,' " she told him definitely.

"That's the U.S. government for you, ain't it? Mr. DeWitt names his place San Angela for his wife's sister, a nun named Angela, and they go and change it on him, 'cause somebody thinks it don't sound right. Like it makes a damned difference to 'em. Be like me namin' a place Pig, and them deciding Hog sounds better."

"Is the ground red there?"

"Don't know. Never been, far as I remember. Used to be called Over the River 'til Mr. DeWitt named it," he added. "Ain't nothin' to speak of there, from what I hear—just some *jacals* and a few shanties—and a place called Veck's."

"I don't believe jackals are native to America," Verena murmured.

"Ain't the Indians that live in 'em," he declared flatly. "Mostly Mexicans and a few white folks."

She decided not to pursue the matter. Obviously he wasn't referring to wild dogs in Africa or Asia. And there wasn't enough time to enlighten him before they landed. Seeing the bank looming, she braced herself. The ferry hit the posts and shuddered, sending a pain shooting up her neck to her head. For an awful moment, she thought she was going to disgrace herself by vomiting. The boatman was securing the rope, but it felt like the boat was still moving.

"That wasn't too bad, was it?" Matthew said low. Then he noticed she was pea-green. "Lean over the side and let go," he advised.

"I'm all right," she managed through clenched teeth. Very gingerly, she turned loose of the post and walked over the board plank laid between the ferry and the dock. "Whew," she said as the nausea passed.

"You all right?"

"Yes." Turning her attention to the deep-rutted red road, she squared her shoulders resolutely. "As soon as I get my bag, I'm going to take a bath, and then I'm going to bed and sleep until I wake up, even if it takes an extra day."

"I thought we'd get checked in, maybe find someplace to eat, and then I'd find out what happened with the train." Taking her arm again, he began to walk. As soon as they were out of the boatman's hearing, he leaned closer, keeping his voice low as he said, "If it's still around, we're still the McCreadys. If it's left, I still think you ought to call yourself something besides Verena Howard, just to be on the safe side."

"I can't think right now."

"You don't like Lizzie or Bessie."

"No."

"What was your mother's name?"

"Mary Veronica—and I don't much care for that, either."

"Caroline?"

"Too Southern."

"Juliette? Now there's a Yankee name, if there ever was one."

"No."

"How about Harriet?—for the Stowe woman," he suggested.

"No."

"You don't look much like a Martha."

"Good."

"Catherine? Charlotte? Anne? Margaret?" When she didn't respond, he sighed. "All right, then—what are you going to name your children?"

She looked up at that. "Since I've pretty much decided on spinsterhood, I haven't given the matter any thought at all," she responded dryly.

"Any dolls?"

"Two—Amy and Louise."

"There you go."

"Mama named Louise, and I can't say I liked it. And when I think of Amy, I think of some frail little creature."

"I've got a sister Maggie," he offered.

She took a deep breath, then let it out. "I'll come up with something when I register."

"Don't you think I ought to know it first?"

"What about you? Who are you going to claim to be this time?" she countered.

"Any ideas?"

"How about Ralph? Or Heywood? Or maybe Orson?"

"Heywood?"

"My great-uncle—Uncle Elliott's father."

"No. I'd rather have something with a little more dash to it."

"George? Henry? Frank? John?"

"Do I really look like a Henry to you?" he asked, feigning injury.

"No more than I look like a Lizzie," she responded sweetly.

"All right—what do I look like?"

"Right now? Maybe an Al—not an Albert—an Al."

"Al?"

"Well, quite frankly, right now you look like a brawler." In spite of the godawful headache, she found herself suppressing a smile. "I suppose you think of yourself as a Stephen?"

"He was a weak king."

She was lost for a moment, then she recovered. "Mathilda's rival?"

"Yeah."

"How about Richard the Lionhearted? He wasn't wholly admirable, but nobody seemed to notice it at the time—except maybe Leopold of Austria and the

Saracens. And his brother John, of course, who was even worse."

"Richard." He mulled that over, then nodded. "All right, that takes care of me, I guess. But Berengaria sounds a tad old-fashioned, don't you think?"

"You didn't learn that at a gaming table," she said. "And I suspect you didn't learn it on a farm in Tennessee either."

"No. Actually, when I got to New Orleans, I was pretty much just a backwoods bumpkin with nothing but good looks to recommend me."

"And your conceit."

"Yeah. When I looked around, I could see the big houses, the fancy carriages, the fast horses—"

"And the fancy women," she threw in. "I'm sure there must have been a lot of them."

"And the fancy women. Anyway, I knew if I ever wanted to run with the set, I'd have to look, sound, and act like I belonged. I emptied my pockets, went down to the docks, and found myself a poker game. The next day, I took my winnings, looked up a tailor, bought a subscription to a library, and started practicing the gentleman act." He paused to look down at her. "I'm a lot of things, Rena, but I'm not a quitter. Two years after I stepped off that riverboat, I was dancing with a society belle at a ball in one of those big houses."

"And you supported it all by gambling," she murmured.

"Yeah."

"I don't believe you. If you were that lucky, you wouldn't be down here walking into a little Texas town."

"Yeah, well, Lady Luck took a night off. But we're off the subject, and you know it. We're Richard and Eleanor who?"

"Eleanor?"

"Eleanor of Aquitaine was a strong woman, Rena. Surely you'll admit that."

"Yes, but—"

"How about Herrick?"

"Corinna Goes A-Maying?"

"You taught English, didn't you?"

"And history—and just about everything else. It was an eight-grade, one-room school, with nineteen pupils between the ages of six and twenty."

"Twenty?"

"Twenty. He dropped out of school at twelve, but after I was introduced at a town meeting, he immediately declared an intent to finish his education. Unfortunately, he was hoping to give rather than receive lessons."

"Smitten?"

"And too stupid to understand the word 'no' until I finally had to throw the ash bucket over his head."

"Live coals?"

"Yes. And then I resigned before I could be discharged."

"Everything the Almighty gives carries a price."

"Who said that?" she asked curiously.

"Me. And by the way, we're there, so you'd better make up your mind. Surely you can be Richard Herrick's sister Eleanor for one night, can't you?"

"It says Columbus House, Richard. We can't stay here."

"It's a hotel. It says right there 'Hotel.' "

"Yes, but it's the Columbus House, and I'm not staying here. Sarah Brassfield said she and Seth came to town last winter to get custody of the boys, and this is where they stayed."

"I don't follow."

Grasping his arm, she leaned close to his ear to murmur low, "Bedbugs."

"Bedbugs!"

"It really did me a lot of good to whisper it," she grumbled. "But, yes. Sarah said she and Seth didn't sleep a wink the whole night, so I'm not staying here. Richard Herrick can go ahead and register, if he wants to, but Eleanor's going down the street to a boarding house."

Turning loose of him, she gathered up her mended skirt and started walking. For a moment, he stood there, torn between the board hanging beneath the hotel sign that read BEST STEAKS WEST OF THE GULF OF MEXICO and Verena Howard. "Damned woman," he muttered under his breath, "you're more trouble than you're worth." Then he went after her.

"All right, mister, put your hands above your head, and turn around real slowlike."

Matthew froze as a figure stepped behind him from the dark alley. As his hand instinctively dropped for the Colt, he felt the gun muzzle against his neck.

"Go for it, and I'll blow your head plumb off," a low voice said.

He gingerly lifted his hands while considering the possibility of using the knife. But with the cold steel touching his skin, he decided against it. Right now, any sudden movement could buy him that ticket to hell.

His assailant reached around him to lift the Colt from its holster, then threw it halfway across the deserted street. "Where is it?" he demanded tersely.

"Where's what?"

"The money."

Still hoping to slide his knife from beneath his sleeve, Matthew stalled. "What money?"

"Now don't you go acting stupid with me, Herrick. I

know you got a whole lot of money on you. I saw you win it."

"Oh, *that* money."

"Yeah—where is it?"

"In my pocket," Matt said, lowering his hand as if he were reaching for it.

"No, you don't—I ain't a fool as was born yesterday," the voice growled. "You just keep those hands reachin' for the sky, then come around nice and easy." For emphasis, he cocked the gun.

At the sound of the click, Matthew knew he'd been had. He turned around slowly. Moonlight reflected in a stranger's pale, glittering eyes, revealing a grim, determined face. He considered his chances, and decided with the hammer back like that, even if the knife hit home, the gun would fire.

"Just tell me which pocket, then hold real still while I get the money."

"Look, friend—"

"I ain't got no time for games, Herrick—which pocket?"

At least he had a chance to keep some of his money. "The right one," Matt answered finally.

The man reached out with his left hand, patting the coat pocket, then delving into it. Pulling out a sizeable wad of bills, he held it up to the moonlight.

"I'd sure appreciate it if you left me a little stake out of that," Matt murmured.

"I'm not a fool," the fellow said curtly. He crammed the money under his shirt, then quickly searched the other coat pocket, finding the neatly folded banknotes. "This all of it?"

"Yeah."

To make sure, the robber's fingers probed Matt's vest and pant pockets, finding and removing three silver dollars and several quarters. Then he jerked on the watch fob, pulling it loose.

"I always hankered for a good gold watch," he said, stuffing it and the change into his trousers. "All right, turn around and start walking down that alley."

The words held a warning, telling Matt that he was about to be shot in the back, that his assailant didn't intend to leave any witness. And there wasn't another soul about to help him. The hairs prickled on his neck.

"Get going."

The man didn't know he still had a knife, and that was his one chance. Sucking in his breath, Matt took a step, dropped his right hand, then dived into the shadows as the bullet struck an adobe wall above him. As the gunman cocked his pistol again, Matt let the knife fly. The second bullet went through his coat sleeve, missing his arm by less than an inch. Unarmed now, Matt rolled behind some barrels, then came up into a crouch, ready to run for his life.

The alley was ominously silent. After several seconds, he took a cautious peek. Holding a barrel top, ready to duck again, Matt inched up for a better look. There wasn't a sign of anyone anywhere. All he could see was the glint of moonlight on steel. His knife and gun lay in plain view on the dusty street.

It was a trick. It had to be. As soon as he exposed himself, he'd be a goner. Sinking back behind the barrels, he waited.

Then he heard running footsteps, and somebody shouted, "Anybody back there? Who's shooting?"

It was a kid, maybe sixteen or seventeen years old, looking down the alley toward him. Matthew pulled himself up and dusted off his coat before walking out.

"You all right, mister?" the kid asked.

"Yeah." Bending over, Matt picked up his knife, turning it over in the moonlight. The blade was dark and wet. "Yeah, I'm all right."

"What happened? I was coming around the corner when I heard the shots."

If he said he'd been robbed, he'd be facing a sheriff or marshal, maybe even a ranger, and he didn't want that. "Nothing, kid," he answered. "I didn't see anything either. I guess it must've been a drunk trying to shoot up the place."

"That your knife?"

"Yeah. When he fired into the alley, I threw it." Before the boy could get a better look, he slid the bloody knife under his sleeve into its sheath. With the kid following him, he picked up the Colt. "Gun must've fallen out when I hit the ground."

"Why didn't you use it?"

"I was running for cover."

Clearly disappointed by the answer, the kid declared, "If it was me, I'd a used it—I'd a kilt myself a cowboy."

Matt eyed him for a moment, then told him, "And if he'd had a friend, you'd have been dead." Jamming the gun into the holster, he started walking toward the boarding house. To his irritation, the boy fell in beside him. "Look, kid—"

"You got that holster tied down like a gunslinger, mister."

"Yeah."

"You ain't Clay Allison, are you?"

"No."

"But you're a gunfighter, ain'tcha?"

"No."

"Them's fancy clothes you got on."

"Look—"

"I think you're a gunslinger."

"No."

"Ever kilt anybody?"

"Yeah. In the war." Matt stopped. "Anything else you want to stick your nose into before I go inside?"

"How'd you get the shiner?"

"My bed collapsed." He started up the stairs to the wide porch. "See you around, kid."

"You sure you're all right, mister?"

"Yeah."

But he wasn't. He was tired, sore, and broke. Flat busted. The damned robber hadn't left him a penny. And come morning, he'd have to ask Verena Howard to pay for both rooms with money she couldn't spare. Intending to get a good night's sleep, he'd left the poker game early with between three and four hundred dollars in his pockets, and now he couldn't even buy himself a cup of coffee, let alone breakfast.

Now he was stuck here in Columbus until he could get himself a stake. He'd have to earn himself twenty or thirty dollars, then look for a game. Without a stake, he couldn't even play.

Inside the house, he walked down the narrow hall to

climb the stairs to his room. He felt stupid. And angry. Only a fool would take a shortcut through backyards and alleys with a wad of money in his pocket. But he'd been damned tired.

The stairboards squeaked under his feet as he mused on his predicament. He was going to have to do an honest day's work for wages, he reflected, resigning himself to it. It wouldn't be the first time he'd found himself broke, and it probably wouldn't be the last. Easy to come by, easy to lose—that's what he'd told Verena, anyway. Only he hadn't lost like this in a long time. And the way he lost it made him feel like a greenhorn fool.

He let himself into his room, closed the door, and loosened his tie. Taking off his coat, he draped it over the single chair, then started unbuttoning his shirt. When he got to the right wristband, he could see the bloodstain where the knife had touched the snowy lawn. At least he'd gotten something for his money. While he hadn't killed the damned robber, he'd stuck him pretty good.

With that consolation, he sat down on the edge of the bed and reached for the nearly full bottle he'd had the proprietor get for him. Pouring himself a good shot of Tennessee mash whiskey, he downed it, then lay down, propping his boots on the footboard. That was another thing he couldn't pay for. But at least he could drown his troubles in it.

God, but he didn't want to face Verena. Now he wouldn't be going on to San Antonio with her, and he felt a surprising pang of regret. Yeah, in the space of a couple of days in her company, he'd come to admire her for a lot more than her looks. He'd grown to like that good mind, that quick, sharp wit, and he was going to miss those little skirmishes with her. Alone and with little or no money, she'd resisted the temptation to take the easy way, to use her beauty for gain, and instead had retreated behind that tongue of hers, relying on it to hold a besieging world at bay.

But Pennsylvania was a far cry from Texas, and an armor of words was damned near useless when it came to dealing with the woman-hungry Big Als on a wild, brutal frontier. And it sure as hell wouldn't count for anything with those hardcases hunting her. If they'd had a full brain between them, they'd have already caught her. And fools like that were bound to wise up eventually, probably sooner than later with him out of their way. A lone woman wouldn't be any match for them.

Damn. He couldn't let her go on without him. He'd been kidding himself when he'd thought he'd just get off at Columbus and disappear. And he'd even been kidding himself when he was planning to put her on that mail wagon a few miles on the other side of San Antonio. He didn't know when it had happened, but at some time, somewhere in the back of his mind, he'd realized he had to get her to San Angelo. Everything since then had just been his own struggle against the inevitable.

Until now. Until the Almighty had intervened. Now it was out of his hands. Now he didn't have any way to get her there. But he had to. All he needed was a stake, the means to right the crazy tilt his world had just taken.

Maybe he could raise a stake. Sell something. But

even as he felt the surge of possibility, some inner voice reined in the notion. With the exception of his coat, he didn't have anything he could part with, and it wasn't likely anybody'd pay much for something that had a bullet hole in the sleeve. Well, there were his shirts, but while he'd paid a lot for them, they wouldn't be worth much out here. The same with his boots. And he sure as hell wasn't about to give up his gun. Not in a place like Columbus, Texas. That just left the knife. But he was damned good with it, and the element of surprise it afforded had saved his life a number of times. Like tonight.

That left only Verena. But as he closed his eyes, he could see her digging in that drawstring purse for twenty-five cents. He could almost hear her indignant howl when he dared to ask her for twenty-five dollars. It'd be damned hard to talk her into risking what little she had on the outcome of a poker game. And if he lost, she'd be stranded, unable to get herself to San Angelo. Unable to get back to Philadelphia. And along about then, she'd never forgive him. No, he couldn't do that to her.

"You fool—you stupid fool!" Gib Hannah ranted, pacing the clear area by the campfire. "You were supposed to kill the bastard! It was supposed to look like a robbery, but you were told to kill him!" Walking up behind Bob Simmons, he planted a boot in the man's back. "I ought to kick you into the fire and watch you burn."

"He threw a knife at me, Gib! Here—take a look at this, if you ain't wanting to believe me. Danged if he didn't about take my arm off," Simmons declared, showing the blood-soaked rag he'd tied around his right shoulder. "He cut me deep, Gib. But I winged him—I know it. I saw him hit the ground."

"But you didn't kill him. When I told you to kill him, I meant it."

"You don't even know if it's the right girl," Charley Pierce pointed out. "Maybe she is, maybe she ain't."

"Well, I aim to find out," Hannah snapped. "But I wanted rid of McCready first."

"He's calling hisself Herrick now," Lee Jackson noted.

"Way I got it figured out, they ain't got nothing to do with the Howard gal. Notice how he wears that gun all strapped down? Ain't too many as does that, is there? No," Charley answered himself. "And that's my point. First he's calling hisself Mac McCready, now it's Richard Herrick, ain't it? Well, to me, it's plumb plain he's hiding from somebody, and it ain't us! I think he's running from the law, and she's probably just his fancy woman running with 'im."

"Makes sense to me," Lee agreed. "If'n she don't know we're looking for her, why'd she be running, changing her name?"

"That's because none of you've got enough brains or gumption to figure anything out," Gib muttered. "If she didn't know before you two got onto the train, she knew it then."

"Not if she ain't the Howard woman."

"I'm saying she is."

"Then what's he doing with her?" Lee asked.

"I don't know."

"It's like I told you," Charley persisted. "They're on the run, and it ain't from us."

"You should've snatched her when you had the chance," Hannah grumbled.

"I don't know when we'd have done it, Gib," Lee reasoned. "Ain't been no time when he ain't been with her. Besides, if you wanted to do it so bad, you had your own chance back at the Goode ranch. But all you did was stand under a damned tree with a damned cheroot in your mouth, waiting for us to do it for you."

"I don't know who made you the boss, anyways," Bob muttered.

"What did you say?" Gib asked, his voice deceptively soft now.

"You want to hear it out loud? All right—I'm getting damned sick and tired of being pushed around by you. Seein's as we all got a share in the money, we ought to have a share in the say. I ain't helping get the girl, less'n I know what you're gonna do to her. I ain't killin'—"

His words died at the touch of Hannah's gun against his head, and his ears never heard the explosion. He pitched forward, reaching out by reflex, and his legs twitched, and then he was still.

An acrid trail of gunsmoke wafted skyward in silence as Gib Hannah looked from Charley to Lee. A faint, almost derisive smile curved the corners of his mouth. "Anybody else got any problem with how I run things?"

It was a moment before either of them spoke. Pierce found his voice first. "Hey, I ain't complainin'—long as I get my share, it's all right with me."

"I just don't cotton to killin' no girl, that's all," Jackson said, his eyes on Bob Simmons's corpse.

"Lost your nerve, Lee?" Gib asked, sneering.

"Fór God's sake, he was at Gettysburg, Gib! Lay off him—he just don't think it's right to kill Jack's girl, that's all he's saying. He ain't got no problem followin' you with anything else—that's right, Lee, ain't it?"

"Just say you won't kill her."

"Aren't you forgetting that it was Jack who double-crossed all of us? As long as you get your third, why do you care?"

"He up and left her while she was little, Gib. It ain't her fault. Look, what's to say she even knows about the gold?"

"What's to say she doesn't?" Hannah countered.

"I don't know."

"Doesn't it seem damned funny she's traveling with a fancy man like McCready? Doesn't it seem damned funny they got off the train and walked in?"

"Yeah," Charley conceded. "But what if it ain't even her?"

"I'm saying she's got something to hide, and she's hiding it from us." Hannah blew the last vestige of smoke from the gun barrel, then looked Lee Jackson in the eye. "Play the game right, Lee," he said silkily, "and you've got a third of that gold. Play it wrong, and Charley and I'll be dividing the whole thing between us." When Jackson said nothing, he prompted him. "Well? Which way do you want it?"

"I ain't afraid of you, Gib," Lee lied. "But I aim to collect my share, so I guess I'm in."

Hannah shoved the gun into its holster. "I thought

you were, but I wanted to be sure." As Pierce exhaled his relief, he added, "So while I'm gone, you two are going to take care of this mess. By morning, he'll be stinking."

"What're you gonna do now?" Jackson asked cautiously.

"Ride in and look around for myself. Maybe tell the sheriff Richard Herrick is a wanted man."

"You gotta have a warrant for that," Charley reminded him.

Gib shrugged. "He won't question a ranger. All I've got to do is say the warrant's coming. I don't know—I haven't made up my mind yet. All I know for sure is I'm getting rid of McCready or Herrick, or whatever he calls himself."

"And then what?"

A slow smile formed on Hannah's lips. "You know, she's a real pretty girl," he said softly. "It just might be time to do a little courting." He smiled at them, then mounted and rode off.

"Man's more dangerous than a damned rattler," Lee muttered after Gib left. "And I ain't staying around to get bit."

"Yeah."

"Cold-blooded."

"Yeah."

"He ain't dividin' it no three ways neither, Charlie. He's gonna pick us off one at a time."

"Maybe."

"Kinda makes a body wonder what happened to Evans and Tate and Connor, don't it? Ever' one of 'em dead afore his time, and it wouldn't surprise me none if it was Gib as helped 'em along."

"Yeah." Pierce looked down, seeing Simmons's blood making a pool in the red clay dirt. "Jesus."

"I'm gonna go get that girl myself," Lee decided suddenly. "I'm gonna find out if she's Jack's girl, and then I'm gonna tell her we ain't greedy—all's we want is our share. She can have Bob's third, and you and me get the rest. Be enough to make her comfortable for the rest of her life. She can take it and go back wherever she came from."

"You're cutting Gib out?"

"Damned right. Otherwise I ain't seein' none of it." Lee eyed Pierce soberly. "You surely ain't stickin' with him after this, are you?"

"No." Charley exhaled heavily. "I used to look up to him, you know. Now I know he ain't nothing but a killer. That's all he is, Lee—a damned killer. That gold's made him greedy. Hell, he ain't gonna be satisfied less'n he gets all of it!"

"Yeah, wouldn't surprise me none if he had something to do with the others—damned funny they're all dead—Evans, Tate, Connors, Frank, Major Howard, too."

"It was Comanches that got Frank. And the major was dead 'fore Gib got wind of where he was," Charley reminded him. "If he'd a-knowed, he would've done run off with everything."

"Yeah, but they was all gone afore their time, wasn't they? And you know what? Ain't nobody seen McCormick in a long time. Way I figure it,

McCormick's gone, too, and they just ain't found the body. Gib probably took care of him, too."

"Either that or he gave up on getting the money."

"He's dead," Lee declared. "A man don't disappear off the face of the earth like that and be alive."

"Howard did," Charley reminded him.

"Yeah, but he had the money. I was talking about the others now. And you know, the last time anybody saw Pete McCormick, he was with Gib, wasn't he? Don't seem too healthy to hang around him does it?" Lee fell silent for a long moment, then looked up. "So—which is it? You staying with Gib?"

"No. I reckon I'd rather split it two ways and get to keep my share of it."

"Three ways—if she leads us to it, she gets Bob's share. Only fair, ain't it?"

"Yeah. But Gib's got a head start on us, and I sure as hell don't aim to cross him to his face. He sees us in town, he's gonna know. We gotta be mighty careful, Lee."

"If I know him, he'll look the town over first, take his time planning his move. I'm aiming to go in the back way, get into the boarding house, and get the girl."

"How?"

"Knock on her door, and when she answers, you throw your coat over her head and cover her mouth. When it's clear, we carry her down the back stairs."

"What if they ain't got any? Back stairs, I mean."

"It's a boarding house, ain't it?" Lee countered. "While Gib's laying his plans, we'll be getting her out of town."

"What about the gambler?" Charley asked suddenly.

"If Bob winged him like he said, Herrick, or whatever he's calling hisself, ain't gonna put up much of a fight. And if she ain't the Howard girl, we'll turn her loose and high-tail it. She can go back to her fancy man. All I care about is findin' the gold."

"Gib'll find us—if we get the girl first, he'll be after us."

"But we ain't headin' for San Angelo. Not yet, anyways. No, we're headin' back across the Colorado. Don't you see, Charley? He'll be expectin' us to go to Angelo, but we go the other way. Maybe hide out in Austin for a while, until he gives up. Then Miss Verena and you and me find where Jack hid it, divide it up, and split up, so's he ain't got one trail to follow. Me—I'm headin' for Cali-forn-eye-aye with mine. I aim to get myself lost where it's warm."

"I hope to God it ain't hell," Charley muttered. "Way I figure it, Gib ain't a man to give up. Afore you take youself off anywheres, we'd better kill 'im."

Lee Jackson paused to consider the notion, then nodded. "All right. Then we'll get the girl, come back here, and wait to ambush the bastard. I reckon he's got it coming for what he did to Bob."

"If it's her, we're taking her to Austin with us?"

"I'm gonna be straight with her."

"What if she don't want anything to do with it? What if she wants it all for herself?"

"I'm gonna tell her if she runs into Gib, she won't be gettin' any of it."

"I guess that makes sense," Charley decided. Looking toward Simmons's corpse, he sighed. "Gib had no call to kill 'im like that—no call at all."

"No."

"Ain't nothin' but red clay around here—mighty hard for diggin' in it."

"We got no time to bury him, and the damned coyotes'll be diggin' him up, anyways. No, if we're gonna do it, it's got to be now."

Moving away from the campfire, Charley found Bob Simmons's greasy felt hat. Carrying it back to the body, he carefully placed it over the bloody hair. Then he stood back. "Gib done you wrong, Bob—real wrong—but me and Lee's gonna make him pay for it."

It was too hot to sleep, and after her experience at the Brassfield place, Verena wasn't about to try prying open a window. Instead, she'd forgone her high-necked lawn nightgown, deciding to wear her chemise and drawers. When even that had proven too miserable, she'd discarded the drawers, leaving only the round-necked sleeveless chemise, then lain in that scandalous state of undress on top of the bedcovers. That hadn't helped much either.

Giving up, she'd finally poured water from the pitcher into the veined crockery bowl and carried it to the table by the bed. There she wet a cloth, wiped it over her already damp skin, and then lay down again, this time with the wet, folded rag covering her forehead.

Loud cantina music, drunken curses, and high-pitched, feminine squeals, punctuated by an occasional gunshot, carried upward, breaching the thinly plastered clapboard walls. Texas might have its share of fine, upstanding, God-fearing citizens, she reflected wearily, but so far she hadn't seen many of them. All she'd encountered so far had been rowdy, uncouth, and unkempt, with the exception of the Brassfields, whose kindnesses had been endearing enough to overcome their shortcomings. And McCready. But he wasn't a Texan, she reminded herself.

With his handsome looks and that highly polished veneer of gentility, he seemed almost as out of place here as she was. He was a hard man to figure out for a number of reasons. He dressed more than well—while she wasn't an authority on masculine clothing, she could recognize expensive tailoring when she saw it, and everything he wore fit that tall, well-proportioned frame of his perfectly.

While everybody else wilted around him, he managed to remain neat, clean, and unruffled. When she'd first laid eyes on him, she'd thought him vain about those extraordinary good looks, but on closer acquaintance, she could see now that it was his things more than his face that he cared about. The clothes, the manners, the educated speech—they were the outward trappings that told him he'd risen above a humble beginning.

Despite her first assessment of him, she found herself actually liking him. And even more than that, she was *intrigued* by him. He earned his living playing a game, and he was apparently quite successful at it. For all his polished manners, there was a certain air of danger about him. When she'd dived over him with Big Al Thompson in pursuit, he'd drawn that gun so smoothly and so fast, neither she nor Thompson had expected it. She'd overheard the whispers of her fellow passengers speculating that he was a gunfighter. Something about the way he wore his holster. All he himself had said on the subject was that he had "fast hands."

She closed her eyes, recalling how scandalously close she'd been to him, sharing a bed with him even. Yet for all that he'd flirted earlier, he hadn't made so much as one untoward move in those two nights. No, she'd lain beside him, listening to his soft, even breathing, feeling oddly safe and secure with him between her and the door.

It would be so easy to fall under his spell. So easy to forget that he had to be hiding something. So easy to forget just how dangerous a man like that could be if she let her guard down, if she dared to imagine he could care for her. Men like Matt McCready, no matter how fascinating, were the stuff of heartbreak, not dreams. They didn't really love women. They left them. She knew, because her mother had had the misfortune to love Jack Howard and had paid for it dearly.

Still . . . For the briefest moment, she allowed herself to imagine what it would be like if Matt crossed that line, if he kissed her, if he whispered sweet words. . . . No, it was utter, total folly to even let herself wonder about that.

Was that her door rattling? Startled from her sinful thoughts, she lay very still, holding her breath, listening. There it was again. Someone was in the hall, turning the knob on her door.

Fright tightened her throat and chest, making her heart pound almost painfully beneath her ribs. No, she couldn't give in to it. Swinging her feet off the side of the bed, she touched the floor gingerly, then reached for the heavy kerosene lamp. Rather than light it, she carried it stealthily to the door, where she whispered, "Matt—is that you?"

There was no answer, no sound at all. And yet she could almost feel the presence of someone out there. She stood there uncertainly, wondering if she ought to scream for help. Tiptoeing carefully to the window, she bent at an angle, trying to look down the outside of the building. From what she could see, every light was out, which meant everyone was probably asleep. Moving back to the door, she waited for some time, staring at the knob in the shadowy, moonlit room.

"What do you want?" she managed to whisper.

Nothing. Her mind had been playing tricks, making her imagine she'd heard something. It was like when she was a child, when every tree branch, every rattle of a windowpane had sent her shivering beneath her covers. The only way she'd ever conquered those unreasoning fears had been to face them, to look out that window, to show herself there was a reasonable explanation for every sound.

Holding the unlit lamp in one hand, she grasped the key in the doorknob in the other, releasing the lock mechanism. The knob jerked beneath her hand, and the door pushed inward, shoving her back. Gasping, she swung the lamp with all the strength she had as someone came through the door.

"Owww! What the—?"

A callused hand shot out, wrenching the lamp from her, twisting her wrist and arm. His hand suffocated her scream.

"I got her—throw the coat over her, and let's go."

Frightened, she fought back desperately, kicking and

flailing as somebody tried to cover her head. Her attacker, trying to maneuver the coat one-handed, eased the hand over her mouth without turning loose. It allowed her to open her mouth just enough to sink her teeth into the fleshy web between his thumb and fingers. As she tasted salt and dirt and blood, he let out a howl.

"Dammit, you gotta help me, Lee! Jesus!"

There were two of them, and her only hope lay in making enough of a ruckus to rouse somebody, anybody. Kicking behind her, she managed to knock a chair over. Heavy wool enveloped her, choking her with the smells of sweat, smoke, and grease.

"I got her!"

This time, she found an arm. Her teeth closed over cloth as she bit down hard. This time, the other man got her from behind, forcing her jaws open.

"Now we ain't gonna hurt you," somebody assured her in a low voice.

"Gonna help you," his companion asserted. "All you gotta do is come along real peaceablelike—savvy?"

She recognized one voice from the Goode ranch, and her blood ran cold. But the first man bent close enough to whisper. "If you don't come with me and Lee, Gib's gonna find you, and then you'll be real dead. We ain't gonna hurt you," he repeated. "All we want is what we got coming—you can even keep your share." Apparently satisfied by her silence, he guided her toward the open door. "That's better. I ain't one to hurt a woman."

"Well, you keep a good hold on her," his friend insisted. "A real good hold."

"I said I got her."

"Then let's get the hell outta here."

She waited until she judged she was in the doorway itself, then she fought in earnest, making them force her through it. Her foot hit the frame, and one of her captors stumbled against it.

"Owww!"

"Woman's a wildcat—a damned wildcat!"

She couldn't see anything, but she felt his grasp loosen. Jerking free, she plunged into the hall, screaming, "Help! Help! I'm being attacked!" As the coat slipped from her face, the other man caught her by the arm. She twisted and turned, clawing at his face, trying to reach his eyes. "Help! *Matt!*"

He'd been asleep when he'd heard the first thumps, but Verena's frantic cries brought him to his feet. Groping for the holster he'd hung over the bedpost, Matt found the Colt, then he ran into the hall, his thumb on the hammer. As he cleared his door, the hanging lantern on the hall wall afforded enough light for him to see two men wrestling Verena, trying to drag her toward the back stairs. Afraid of hitting her, he fired the first shot over them.

Both men dropped down and scrambled on their hands and knees for the steps. As Verena leaned against the wall, catching her breath, Matt looked into the dark, narrow stairwell. When he turned back, he saw her standing there, shaking. Her chemise was torn, hanging from one shoulder, affording him a darned good look at a bare breast. And at the end of the hall, a boarder's door opened.

"It's all right, Rena," he managed, turning her in to

his arm, shielding her nakedness from view. "You're all right, sweetheart."

"What's going on here?" a groggy voice asked.

"Somebody had the wrong room," Matt answered smoothly. "Everything's all right. I guess he must've been drunk, that's all."

"Thought I heard a gunshot," the man mumbled.

"Yeah. He scared my sister, and when she screamed, I took a shot at him."

"Oh." As if that explained everything, the man backed into his room and closed his door.

"Come on—let's get you inside before anybody else comes out," Matt whispered, holding her against him as he maneuvered her into his room. Kicking his door shut, he stood there for a moment, just holding her, his arms around her shaking shoulders. "What happened?" he asked finally.

"I feel foolish . . . so foolish," she whispered against his chest. "It was stupid . . . just plain stupid."

His arms tightened protectively. "It's all right, Rena. I've got you, and I don't think they'll be coming back—not for a while, anyway."

She leaned into him, savoring the solid warmth of his body, the strong, masculine feel of him. "I'm so glad you heard me," she managed, swallowing.

"From what I saw, it looked like you were giving a damned good accounting of yourself."

"It was stupid," she said again. "I should've never opened the door." Taking a deep breath for calm, she let it escape slowly. "I couldn't sleep, Matt. I was just lying there, thinking how miserably hot it was, when . . . when I thought I heard something. It must've been my key rattling in the lock when they tried to open the door." Gulping air again, she went on, explaining, "I thought maybe it was you, that you'd just gotten in or something. I thought maybe you were mistakenly trying to let yourself into the wrong room. Or maybe somebody else couldn't see the number in the dark."

"I was asleep in the right one."

"Well, I didn't know what time it was." She paused for another breath. "Anyway, I asked if it was you, and nobody answered. So I waited awhile, wondering if maybe I'd just imagined it. Finally, rather than sit up the rest of the night like a silly coward, I decided I'd take a look."

"Go on."

Self-conscious now, she would have stepped back, but she was acutely aware of the torn cloth between them, of the fact that she had almost nothing on. She could feel the heat creep into her face with the realization that he had to know she wasn't even wearing her drawers.

"Uh—"

"Everything all right in there, Mr. Herrick?" a male voice called through the door.

"Yeah. Who is it?"

"Holmstead."

The proprietor. "Yeah, everything's all right," Matt assured him. "It was just a drunk trying to get into my sister's room by mistake. When she couldn't discourage him, I fired a shot over his head. I'll pay for the damage in the morning." As he said it, he remembered he was too broke to pay for anything, including his room. Come morning, a different hell was going to break loose.

"She all right?" Holmstead wanted to know. "There's a lamp broken out here, and kerosene's spilled."

"Yeah, I think she tried to hit him over the head with it. He was a little hard to convince, I guess."

"But you're sure she's all right?"

"As soon as I get her calmed down, she'll be going back to her bed."

"I'm real sorry this happened, mister. Bad as things are in town, me and the missus try to run a respectable place. We don't aim to allow no molesting of females here." There was a pause, and when Matt didn't respond, the fellow decided, "Well, if she don't need anything, guess I'll put another lamp in her room and go back to bed."

"Yeah."

While he waited for the man's shuffling steps to fade, Matthew rubbed Verena's upper back. Deciding they were alone again, he returned to the matter at hand. "Did you get any kind of look at either of them? Would you know them again if you saw them?"

"No, but I recognized a voice."

"That's a start, anyway."

"It was one of those I'd heard at the Goode ranch. I heard him in the hall there."

"What about the other one?"

"No. He sounded different."

"That'd make three," he mused. "All right—did you hear anything else, anything we could go on?"

She hesitated, wondering if she ought to tell him, then nodded. "It didn't make any sense, Matt. But they kept saying they weren't going to hurt me—that they were going to help me, that I could have my share of whatever it is they think I've got."

It had to be money, by the sound of it. For a moment, he wondered again if she was playing straight with him, or if she was just using him.

She hesitated again, then added, "Something else was odd—and frightening. They mentioned a Gib again, just like at Goode's. One of them said, 'If you don't come with me and Lee, Gib's gonna find you, and then you'll be real dead.' "

"But no last name? You didn't hear Gib's last name?"

"No, it was more like they thought I ought to know it. But I don't. I don't know any of them." Daring to look up at him, she took another deep breath. "I'm scared—truly scared," she admitted. "Matt, I've got to report this to the sheriff before somebody hurts or kills me."

He couldn't risk that, and he knew it. If she made a report and there was an investigation, he'd have to run out on her, and right now he couldn't do that either. He shook his head. "You can't give him anything to go on yet, Rena. You can't describe anybody to him, and you can't give him any real motive for this. Without some kind of proof, he's liable to think you're imagining things."

"But you saw those men—you know I'm not lying."

"But I didn't get a good look at either of them." Releasing her reluctantly, he stepped back. "Look, I believe you, but even if you tell a lawman everything you know, it's not going to make a whole lot of sense to him, is it?"

"Well, I can't just wait for another attempt on

my life," she retorted. "You know, the next time you might not be around to save me. I may not know why, but I can tell you with certainty that these men are desperate."

"Yeah, but there's something missing. It's got to be something else besides the obvious."

"I swear to God, Matt—I don't have anything anybody would want."

"Besides the obvious."

"Well, that wasn't what they were looking for. I'm telling you they've mistaken me for somebody else."

"Maybe."

"You don't really believe me."

"Of course I do," he lied. "But it's not me you've got to convince, is it?"

"I really think I ought to talk to the sheriff, Matt. At least he might notice something once I make him aware of this—maybe someone acting suspicious even."

He looked pained. "You're going to tell him that for reasons totally unknown, three or more complete strangers are chasing an impoverished Philadelphia schoolteacher all over East Texas, threatening to kill her. Doesn't make much sense, does it?"

"Well, I hope I can put it more convincingly than that."

"But that's what it boils down to, isn't it? No, I think you're going to have to give him at least some proof if you expect him to help you."

"But I don't know anything else to tell him! I just don't! But you saw them," she recalled suddenly. "Even if you can't identify them, you saw what happened, Matt. It's not just me saying it." When he didn't respond, she looked up. "Or is it?"

"You're not going to convince anyone without more evidence than this, Rena. You don't know what they look like, and you don't know what they want. All you can say is that someone tried to abduct you."

"Two someones," she corrected him. "And I've got to convince somebody before they kill me." Betraying her exasperation, she declared, "You know, no matter what you say, I can tell you don't believe me—it shows in your face."

"A body'd have to think about this long and hard to make any sense out of it. I don't know whether it's something you're not telling me—" He could see her stiffen, but he went on, adding, "Well, you've got to admit there's something missing somewhere. I don't know—maybe you just aren't remembering it, Rena. Or maybe you're looking right at it and don't know it."

"See? That's exactly what I meant. Somehow I'm responsible for my own abduction."

"No, I didn't mean that."

The bright moon outside cast a slice of light that fanned out from the window, making her chestnut hair seem darker, catching it in a net of silver. His gaze dropped lower to her luminous eyes, then to the pale sheen of ivory skin, the torn shoulder of her chemise, the rhythmic rise and fall of a breast barely concealed by the slender hand covering it. For a moment, he forgot everything beyond her exquisite beauty.

"Well, just what do you mean?" she persisted.

Jerked back to reality by the edge in her voice, he tried to recover his thoughts, but couldn't.

His manner had changed, building an almost palpable tension within the small room. And what she saw in his eyes was both exhilarating and a little bit frightening. Taking a step backward, she tried to tell herself she was overwrought, that she was just imagining that look.

"Is something the matter?" she dared to ask him.

"No." His mouth was so dry he could hardly speak. "It's just not time to look up the sheriff—not yet, anyway."

She hesitated uncertainly. "Well, I suppose he wouldn't want to be awakened in the middle of the night," she conceded. His gaze made her acutely aware of how she must look. "I . . . uh . . . I'd better get back to bed," she decided.

"Yeah. I reckon we both need some sleep."

"Yes—well, I'm going to put my chair against my door, so if you hear it fall . . . I mean . . . well, you will come running, won't you?"

He could tell she was still more than a little scared, and she had a right to be, he told himself. "Tell you what," he decided suddenly, "I'm going to pour you a drink of some real Tennessee sipping whiskey, and you're going to sit in that chair over there until you settle down some. Get a little good Tennessee mash in you, and you'll sleep a whole lot better."

"Oh, but I don't think—"

"Trust me, Rena." Reaching out, he lifted her chin with his knuckle. The moonlight reflected in her eyes like stars against a dark sky. No, he couldn't think things like that, not now, not at a time like this. "I want you to stay in here tonight."

"Oh, but I—"

"Wait a minute, now—before you go getting your back up like a spitting cat, you've got to listen."

"But—"

"Once I get you settled down, I'm taking your room. That way, if those two come back, they'll be dealing with me." As she stared up at him, he felt as if he could drown in those eyes of hers. "Trust me, Rena," he said softly. "I won't let anybody hurt you," he added, dropping his hand.

She'd thought he intended to kiss her, and when he didn't, her relief was tempered by a sense of disappointment. "I see. Well, I'll need my nightgown. I'll have to go back to get my nightgown."

"I'll bring it over before I go to bed." Moving away, he took the bottle from the bedside table, pulled the cork with his teeth, and poured her three good fingers of whiskey into a crockery cup. Carrying it back to her, he thrust it into her hands. "Here."

She gazed down at the liquid. In the semidarkness, it looked almost black against the white cup. "I don't know if I should try this," she said doubtfully. "I've just now recovered from Mr. Brassfield's elderberry wine. I don't think I want to feel like that again. Ever."

"That was wine—this is whiskey. It's the wine that makes you think your head's been shot out of a cannon, not whiskey. Go on," he urged her, "try it."

She took the barest sip, then screwed up her face as she swallowed it. "Ugh."

"It gets better," he promised. "Just take a little at a time and let it go down easy. Don't try to drink it down all at once."

"I couldn't if I wanted to." Seeing that he clearly expected her to keep trying, she managed another, bigger taste of it. The stuff was like a trail of fire between her throat and her stomach.

"That's better. You're getting the hang of it now."

"You don't have to do this—change rooms, I mean. I won't be stupid enough to open the door twice, I can assure you."

"It'll give you more peace of mind this way. Now, where's your nightgown?"

He was too near, the room too small, the whiskey too hot going down to do much for her peace of mind, but she couldn't say that. "In . . . in my carpetbag, I think," she managed to answer. "I'd meant to get it out, but the room was so hot . . ." Somehow the notion of his rummaging through her things, of his touching her underclothes, seemed terribly indecent. "Maybe I'd better get it myself."

He had to escape, to tear his thoughts away from her. "No, you just stay put. I'll be back in a minute with it. Then I'll pack up what I need for morning and get out of your way. All you'll have to do is lock the door, put on your nightgown, and crawl into bed. Once you get that whiskey down, you'll sleep like a baby," he promised. "Word of a Mor—" He caught himself before he got it out. "Word of a McCready."

"I don't know . . ." she murmured, eyeing the cup doubtfully.

"I do. There's not enough in there to hurt you."

As the door closed behind him, she felt uneasy, even vulnerable. Chiding herself for being a silly creature, she drank again. Now the heat of his whiskey was diffusing through her body. No, as long as she had Matthew McCready with her, she was safe. Another sip went down, warming her clear to her toes. She was in his room, and they wouldn't come back to look for her here. She didn't have to worry about anything right now.

Drinking absently now, she mulled him over in her mind. He wasn't nearly as dangerous as she'd once thought, she decided. When that dark hair of his was rumpled, when those brown eyes were sleepy in the morning, the way they'd been at Seth and Sarah's, he looked like a big, overgrown boy waking up. It wasn't until he was shaved and dressed that he turned into the shrewd, sophisticated gambler. Her mother had been wrong, she mused. Not all handsome men were dangerous.

With all that kerosene on the floor, he had to be careful where he struck the match. Groping his way around the bed, he felt on the floor for her carpetbag until he found it. He ought to just take the whole damned thing to her. Then she'd have what she needed, and he wouldn't be running his hands through frilly drawers and corset covers.

The prim, yet practical Miss Verena Mary Howard. When he'd seen her standing on that steamboat deck, he'd thought her the prettiest girl on this side of the Mississippi, and nothing he'd seen since had changed his opinion. It was a pity he hadn't met her in New Orleans. He could have dressed her up in the finest silk taffetas and brocades, the best Belgian laces and silk slippers. In his mind, he could see her turned out like the most exquisite belle in the state of Louisiana. But she wasn't that kind of girl. She wasn't the kind a man could love and leave. She was the quicksand kind—the respectable sort who had a man caught before he knew it. The kind a man wanted to settle down with after he'd finished sowing his oats elsewhere.

But he was flat broke and on the run. And a helluva long way from wanting to settle down anywhere. His fingers felt the soft cloth, the tucks and lace on what had to be a real fancy pair of drawers. Yeah, those were legs, all right. Stuffing them back into the carpetbag, he mused wryly that he wasn't half as dangerous as she was. Yeah, when it came right down to it, it was respectable women like Verena Howard who held all the right cards. And while he was a gambler when it came to long odds, he wasn't ready to play the permanent game. Not for a long time.

Pulling the carpetbag up, he felt it lighten, and he realized he hadn't closed it. Leaning down, he swept the floor with his hands, scooping up her clothes. As he straightened up, he could smell the faint scent of lavender on them, and the fragrance was more powerful than the heavy perfumes that designing women in his past had used to saturate everything from their corset covers to their love letters. He stood there for a moment, savoring the soft, clean smell of the lavender, then he shoved everything into the bag, this time closing it.

By the time he returned to his room, she was leaning back in the chair, resting her head against the wall. Her empty cup was beside her foot. Her eyes opened when he set her carpetbag on the floor.

"I spilled everything out of it, so it's all kind of

jumbled up in there," he admitted. "But come morning, you'll be able to get a better idea whether I missed anything or not."

"Yes."

"I guess I could've looked harder, but I didn't want to light a match while I could still smell kerosene," he managed diffidently, trying to smile. "I didn't think Holmstead would want me to burn the place down." He was too close to her again, almost like a moth to the flame, and she didn't even know it. "You're awful quiet," he chided.

"You were right about the whiskey, Matt. I think I got used to it."

"Are you feeling all right?"

"Like I don't have any feet."

"Like you don't have any feet?" he repeated, perplexed.

"That's what I said, wasn't it?"

"I wasn't sure."

"There's just me up here—I'm floating around up here in my head."

"You're dizzy?"

She regarded him owlishly. "No." Lifting the cup languidly, she waved it. "But I'll take a little more."

She wasn't drunk. The full power of the liquor couldn't have hit her yet, but she was obviously beginning to feel some of it. "If I give you any more, you'll hate me in the morning. Right now, you've had just enough to make you sleepy."

"I don't want to go to bed."

"What do you want to do?"

"Just to sit here and be happy," she answered

solemnly. "I never got to be happy, you know. Never. Or not since Papa left, anyway."

"Rena, if I didn't know better, I'd swear you were drunk."

Leaning forward, she rested her chin on her hand. "It's hard to watch when somebody's love turns to hate, McCready," she mused slowly. "It's hard to watch dreams disappear. You have dreams, don't you?"

"Yeah."

"Well, I don't—not anymore, anyway. I'm never going to know why he left, McCready. I'm just going to go back to Philadelphia and be a teacher until I die."

"There are worse things, you know."

"No, I don't know. I don't know anything except that I'm never going to live. I'll probably wind up just like Mama, only I won't even know what I've missed. I'll just teach other people's children until I die. That's all I'll do, McCready."

He looked at the cup, calculating how much he'd given her. About three good shots, and it had been too much. "You'd better go to bed," he said gently, reaching to help her up.

She got to her feet, but she swayed unsteadily. The torn shoulder of her gown slipped, and his breath caught almost painfully in his chest.

"God, Rena—" It didn't even sound like his own voice.

"I don't want to be like that, but I can't help myself."

She took another faltering step before he caught her, and then she was in his arms. His hand slid down her back, smoothing her chemise over her otherwise naked body, and while some small voice in his mind told him he'd be sorry in the morning, the enticing fragrance of sweet lavender, the warm musk of damp skin flooded his senses.

"You're beautiful," he murmured thickly.

Time seemed to stand still as he bent his head, his breath caressing her skin warmly, his mouth brushing hers. As her lips parted slightly, his arm tightened around her shoulders, holding her close. She could feel the heat rise in her body everywhere it touched his. Ignoring every warning her mother'd ever given her, she twined her arms around his neck and returned his kiss.

Matt McCready's strong masculine body against hers was far more potent than his whiskey. His hands moved ceaselessly over her back, over her hips, molding her to him, tracing fire over her skin as if there were no cloth there. She was hot, breathless, and drowning as his tongue teased, then possessed her mouth. No dream, no thought could ever have prepared her for the powerful, heady, giddy feeling overwhelming her now.

She'll swallow you up like quicksand. The warning reverberated through his mind, but he was beyond listening. All he knew was that her woman's body was as hot, as eager as his. Tonight he wanted to drown in it, even if he had to pay the piper tomorrow.

Tearing his mouth away from hers, he traced breathless kisses along her jaw to her ear. Then as she twisted her head, he found the soft hollow of her throat. A low moan welled deep within her, rising under his lips, asking him for more.

It was as though every inch of her body was alive to his touch and, yet, while it was his hands, his mouth, his body pulling her into the maelstrom of her own desire, she felt the power of answering his demand for more. There was no yesterday and no tomorrow. Only now.

The nipples of her breasts were taut, pressed against his chest. While one hand gathered her chemise upward toward her hips, he found the shoulder with the other, slipping his fingers beneath it, working it down over her arm. Still kissing her hot, damp skin, he backed her toward the bed. Bending his head lower, he found the button of her bare nipple with his tongue. Gasping, she cradled his head, and her hands worked ceaselessly, opening and closing, caressing his thick hair.

Desire raged, pounding his blood through his body like a drumbeat, echoing in his brain, tautening his manhood. Every fiber of his being felt it. He was going to find ecstasy within her or die. His hand moved upward, over her satin-smooth thigh to her hip, feeling her flesh quiver beneath his touch. It was *now*, his body told him.

He eased her against the bed, bending her over it. Her leg touched the siderail, then she fell backward into the depths of the thick feather mattress. Her eyes flew open with the suddenness of her fall, and she saw Matthew McCready unbuttoning his bulging pants above her bare thighs. The awful realization of what she was doing hit her like cold water.

One moment she was lying there nearly naked, her hair spilled over his pillow, her exquisite body promising him heaven. Then her eyes widened in horror, and she was rolling away, scrambling for the other side of the bed as if Lucifer himself were after her. As her feet hit the floor, she pulled the top of the chemise up and pushed the hem down at the same time, trying to cover herself. And while her breasts heaved as she gulped for breath, her beet-red face told him she was mortified beyond words.

Struggling between his raging desire and the realization that she'd come to her senses, his mind fought for control over his rebellious body. He wanted to say something, anything, but there was nothing. If she hadn't stopped him, he would have taken advantage of her, then repented come morning. Combing his disordered hair with his fingers, he knew he had to make amends somehow.

"Look, Rena . . . I . . . God, I'm sorry . . . I didn't mean . . ."

She swallowed. "Don't say anything—please."

Wincing, he waited for the accusing torrent to hit him.

Instead, she turned the invective inward. In her mind, she'd played the part of a shameless, utterly wanton hussy. Beneath her educated and respectable facade, she'd discovered a sinful, lustful creature. She couldn't face him, not now. Not ever again. Hot tears burned her eyes, then spilled over as she closed them. Her arms crossed over her breasts, her hands clenched, pressing herself to stop her shaking, she almost couldn't put her shame into words.

"Dear Lord, what you must think me," she choked out.

"Don't, Rena—"

"But whatever it is, it cannot be worse than what I feel."

He could see her throat move as she swallowed again. "Look, it's not—" Hell, he wasn't making it any better. "Things just got out of hand," he managed.

"Go ahead, say it. I'm no better than a harlot. That's what you're thinking, isn't it?"

Her reaction cut worse than if she'd shouted or cursed at him. The last vestiges of his desire gone, he wanted to reach out, to hold her again. "It's all right, Rena," he said softly. "You're not a harlot—don't even think anything like that." When she didn't move, he took a cautious step closer. "I should've known better."

"You do not know—you cannot know—" The tears spilled over onto her cheeks. "It was me," she cried. "I was liking everything until . . . until—"

"So was I, but it's over. Nothing happened."

She started to turn away, and he was afraid she meant to run, that he'd never get another chance to make things right with her. Reaching out, he touched her arm, turning her back. His other hand stroked her hair lightly, smoothing it back from her temples. Looking up now, she stood as still as if she'd turned to stone beneath his touch.

"Please don't," she whispered.

She felt cold to the core now. As brittle as if she could shatter like glass under his gaze. He couldn't let her go like that. His arms slid around her, holding her unyielding body closer, and in that moment, he wanted to curse the way women were raised. That it was Eve's sin, not Adam's. Pressing her head against his shoulder, he fixed his gaze on the long shadow of the bedpost climbing the wall.

"Listen, you were supposed to like it," he said gently. "The only things wrong about it were the man, the place, and the reason. If I hadn't given you the whiskey, it wouldn't have happened."

"You're just saying that to make me feel better," she said, her voice muffled.

"No. I might lie about a few things, but that's not one of them." Leaning back slightly for a better look at her, he lifted her chin. "You're a pretty girl, Rena—a damned pretty girl. The kind a man wants to come home to. But I'm a rambler, and I'm not fool enough to think I could be anything else."

"No."

"So let's just put this behind us. Lay the blame on me and the Tennessee mash and go on. I won't let this happen again, I promise."

It was all she could do to nod.

Dropping his hand, he bent to pick up the empty cup. "Go on—get to bed. Otherwise, you won't want to get up when morning comes."

"Yes, we have to catch the stage, don't we?"

He couldn't bring himself to tell her that he wouldn't be going, that he was too broke to buy breakfast, let alone a ticket to San Antonio. "Yeah, well, we'll see about that in the morning. Right now, you need your sleep."

The awful thought that maybe what had happened had ruined everything, that maybe no matter what he'd said, he was disgusted with her, crossed her mind.

"Matt, you're going to be here, aren't you? You aren't going anywhere, are you?"

There was no mistaking the anxiety in her voice. "Yeah, I'll be here. I'm not going anywhere, Rena." Walking to where he'd laid his gun and holster, he picked them up, then decided, "I'd better leave these with you."

"What about you?"

"I'm taking my knife."

"I couldn't shoot anybody, Matt."

"Somebody comes through that door without knocking, you'd damn well better try. Just pull back the hammer, and it's cocked. Then all you've got to do is point it at his belly and pull the trigger." Laying the gun down, he reached for the doorknob. "Good night, Rena."

As he opened the door, he could've sworn he heard her say softly, "I've never even kissed anybody before," but he couldn't be sure. And he ached for her all over again.

No, he'd escaped that quicksand once already, and he ought to be damned grateful she'd come to her senses. He wouldn't want to see himself in her eyes in the morning, not after he'd bedded her. Maybe he was getting soft, but he didn't want it to happen like that. He didn't want her to feel sorry or cheated. He didn't want to feel like he had to marry her.

As the door to her room swung inward, he stepped on something hard. And looking down, he caught the glint of metal on the frayed carpet runner. A brass button. It could have fallen off anybody—or she could've pulled it off in the struggle. Leaning down, he picked it up and held it beneath the hall lantern. Yeah, he'd seen hundreds of those on battlefields, on Union Army coats. It didn't mean much—a lot of men had kept those coats.

Once inside, his gaze swept the room, placing everything in case he had to fight his way out of it. Laying the knife on the nearby table, he sat on the edge of the bed, then looked down. Verena's draw-string purse.

There was something almost sacrosanct, untouchable about a lady's purse, and he felt a pang of guilt for opening it, for counting her dwindling money. Fifty-nine dollars. Not enough to get her home. But enough for a stake.

She came awake slowly, first aware of her aching head, then of her churning stomach. Rolling over, she looked into the semidarkness of the moonlit room. It wasn't morning yet. Swinging her legs off the bed, she sat up. The room spun and the floor tilted. Lurching for the chamberpot, she barely managed to hold McCready's whiskey down until she reached it, then everything came up. She retched until there was nothing left but dry heaves, and it was finally over.

She'd been so sick her whole body was clammy, and her nightgown felt like a wet sheet clinging to her. Her nausea gone, she peeled the gown off and moved slowly to the washbasin, holding her head to stop the terrible pounding in it.

Whiskey was better than wine, McCready had said. Well, it wasn't. In her case, it was far worse, and it had left her what her father used to call skunked. She remembered the word well, having heard him quarrel with her mother over it while Verena had hidden under her bedcovers, afraid to come out.

She poured water from the pitcher into the pan and sopped the washrag in it. Dragging the wet, dripping cloth over her face, she tried to tell herself she felt better. As the air cooled her forehead, she wiped the perspiration from her skin. Then she tossed the rag into the basin, leaving it until morning.

The warm night air felt almost good touching her skin. Yes, now that she'd purged herself of that awful whiskey and washed herself, she did feel a whole lot better.

The gleam of McCready's gun caught her eye, and for a moment she stared at it. Then the painful memories flooded her aching mind, and she was sure she could never face him again. But if he went with her as far as San Antonio, she would have to—somehow she'd just have to.

Dear God, what a fool she'd made of herself. Letting him hold her like that, shamelessly kissing him all the while. Lewd, wanton, reckless couldn't even describe her behavior. And yet as she closed her eyes, reliving those moments, she couldn't deny she'd wanted everything he did to her, and if some small shred of decency hadn't prevailed, she would have let him do anything he wanted in those heady, sinful moments.

No, she couldn't think about that—not now, anyway. Maybe in a few days, but not now. Maybe when she was in San Angelo, and he'd gone on to wherever he finally decided to go. Right now, she felt too foolish, too sinful to dwell on what could have happened. No, when she saw him next, probably the best thing to do was pretend it hadn't happened.

Her carpetbag was on the floor. Picking it up, she

carried it to the bed and opened it. Everything was a jumble, not the way she'd left it. Sighing, she pulled all of her things out, sorted them, and found her clean chemise. It still smelled of Sarah Brassfield's strong lye soap. And it was the same with her drawers.

Pulling both garments on, she went to the window. She'd been mistaken when she first awakened. Instead of being the middle of the night, it was the crack of dawn, and already there was a faint pink haze pushing back the dark sky. In a few hours, she and McCready would be buying tickets and boarding the stagecoach bound for San Antonio. And the thought of being cooped up again, of bouncing along some rutted road, made her head hurt even more. It'd be like riding in that wagon after too much of Seth Brassfield's wine all over again.

She hoped it didn't cost too much. She'd spent at least eight dollars in three days, and at that rate, she was going to find herself alone and without funds by the time she reached San Angelo. And if Mr. Hamer couldn't find a buyer quickly . . . well, she dreaded the thought. He had to. He just had to. Even if it meant taking a loss. Even if it meant she only got enough to pay her way back to Philadelphia.

Mentally reviewing her expenses, she worried that maybe it'd been more than eight dollars since she'd boarded the train in Galveston. It couldn't be much more, but that wasn't much consolation. No, she'd better count her money. The wicked thought that she should have taken the wad of bills Matthew McCready had offered earlier crept across her mind. No, that wouldn't have been proper.

As if sharing a room alone with him for two nights

had been. But it was the being beholden to him that bothered her. She couldn't have paid the debt off, not on her teacher's wages, and there wasn't any guarantee that her father's farm would bring in enough to cover her own expenses, let alone pay off McCready.

She ought to have fifty-eight or fifty-nine dollars. Unsure now, she looked for her purse. Then another, more terrifying fear assailed her. What if while she'd been kissing McCready like the worst sort of hussy, someone had filched her purse? As nearly as she could remember, she'd left the door open, all but inviting someone to take it.

Maybe when he'd brought her bag, he'd brought it over also. No, there was his gun, her carpetbag, her torn chemise. But no purse. Unless it was in her rented room, it was gone.

Forgetting her aching head, forgetting her embarrassment even, she dressed quickly and took a cautious look into the hall. The lantern had burned out, leaving it dark, but she could tell it was deserted. She went back for his gun, then eased into the hall, creeping along the wall to the next door down, where she tapped lightly.

"Matthew?" she whispered.

No answer. He probably couldn't hear her, and yet she didn't want to rouse the boarding house. She rapped louder. Nothing. So much for his being a light sleeper. Her hand closed over the doorknob, turning it. He hadn't even bothered to lock himself in after what had happened. Trying not to waken him, she opened the door gingerly, ready to spring back, then peered inside.

The bed was empty. And so was the room. He wasn't

there. Panicked now, she hurried to the bed, dropped to her knees and felt along the edge, hoping against hope that her purse had fallen underneath. Her fingers found the drawstring, and she felt a surge of relief as she pulled the knitted bag out.

Tearing it open, she carried it to the window, thinking to count her money by the early light. Her comb and Mr. Hamer's letter were there, as was her coin purse, but her stash of folded banknotes was gone. Her blood ran cold in her veins as she turned the purse upside down, shaking it over the bed. A lone dime fell out.

They'd come back, and she'd been robbed. No, if that were the case, McCready would have put up a fight, and she would surely have heard something. He was gone, and she just wasn't facing the painfully obvious. He'd left her. Worse yet, he'd taken her money with him.

Her head was pounding, keeping rhythm with her thudding heart. Sinking down on the straight-backed chair, she tried to calm herself, to think this awful turn of events out. Without her money, she couldn't survive. She couldn't pay Mr. Holmstead's bill, she couldn't buy her stage ticket to San Antonio, let alone ride the mail wagon to San Angelo, and she couldn't even afford to eat. All the coins left in her purse probably wouldn't add up to a dollar.

In her mind's eye, she could see Matthew McCready's handsome face, that engaging smile, and she could almost curse herself for being so gullible. She'd trusted a dangerous man, and it had cost her dearly. Oh, what a fool he must have thought her.

Then reason reasserted itself. If he'd wanted to rob her, he'd had a dozen opportunities before now. Besides, he had plenty of his own money, so much that he'd even offered some of it to her. No, he had no reason to steal such a small sum from her, she wanted to believe that. But where was he? Where was her fifty-nine dollars?

This time, she looked around the room, seeking some degree of reassurance. There wasn't any sign of a struggle. His coat was gone. But his valise was in the other bedchamber, and as fastidious as he was about his person, he wouldn't have left that. Besides, he didn't even have a horse. So where on earth could he have gone at this early hour of the morning?

The answer wasn't an entirely welcome one. There were only three things to be had at any hour in Texas, she'd overheard a cowboy say on the train: whores, whiskey, and a poker game. While she didn't really know him that well, she'd almost bet he'd found the latter, and while she was sitting here stewing in her own worry, he was in some gaming hell thoroughly enjoying himself. But that still didn't explain her empty purse.

Rising, she went to the window and peered out over the street below. It was quiet, deserted except for several horses tied to a hitching post half a block away. In the pale, rosy light, she could make out the sign over a door there. It said SALOON in large letters, then below it read ANY GAME YOU WANT TO PLAY. In less than five minutes, she'd gone from fright to anger, relief to annoyance, then back to anger. To suit his own ends, he'd gone off to play, leaving her and her money in danger. Either that or he'd taken her banknotes with him.

Turning around, she saw the gun she'd laid on the table, and she made up her mind. Returning to the other bedchamber, she put on her shoes, then picked up his gunbelt and buckled it around her waist. It slid down until it hung at an angle over one hip. She had to look ridiculous, but she was beyond caring. She couldn't go outside alone with no protection at all, not after what had almost happened earlier. As long as Gib and his friends were out there, she had to be careful.

Once she'd crept down the stairs, taking care not to waken the other guests, she let herself out, then walked purposefully toward the saloon. The early morning air was almost cool on her hot face, but it did nothing to soothe her anger.

Outside the saloon, the boardwalk creaked under her feet. She paused, then stood on tiptoe to look over the louvered door. As her eyes took in the place, noting the number of rough-looking men, she almost lost her nerve. And then she saw him.

He was sitting near the back of the room, directly under a tin lantern, his head bare, his coat off, his shirt-sleeves rolled up almost to his elbows. As she watched, he took a sip of what looked to be whiskey, and lazily regarded his cards. When he leaned forward, he pushed a handful of crumpled bills to the center of the table. She'd seen more than enough. Forgetting the drunks, she drew the heavy Colt revolver, cocked it, and stalked inside, her fury showing on her face.

"A fine bodyguard you turned out to be," she snapped when she reached him. "I could have been carried off, and you wouldn't even have known it. And you probably wouldn't have cared, either." Before he could answer, she gestured with the gun, pointing to the pile of money on the table. "Is any of that mine?" she demanded.

"What the hell—?" One of the other players looked to McCready. "Who the hell's she?" he demanded.

Matt allowed himself one glance at her, and what he saw was one hell of an angry woman. Standing ramrod straight, she faced him across the table like an avenging goddess ready to swoop down and kill. "My sister," he answered baldly.

"You let her carry a gun like that?" another one wanted to know.

Ignoring them, she kept her eyes on McCready. "My money's missing, Matthew—where is it?"

He didn't look up. "I believe I've placed my bet, gentlemen—either raise me or call me."

Her gaze dropped to the pile of money on the table. "Just how much of that belongs to me?" she repeated awfully.

He didn't answer that either.

"Now wait a minute," the first fellow protested, "you ain't playing with stolen money, are you?"

"Not anymore," Matthew murmured. "I figure I've been on mine for the last two hours."

She couldn't believe her ears. He was all but admitting it! Holding the gun steady with both hands, she pointed it at him. "Hand it over—I want my fifty-nine dollars *now*." When he didn't move, she waved the revolver, sending the other three men ducking. "You haven't gone deaf, have you? I'm taking my share of that back now."

"Hey now, little lady—" one of them said, raising his head to eye level with the table. "It ain't his to give, lessen he wins. We got bets out."

"I don't care about your silly game! I want my money!"

"You're a damned nuisance—you know that, don't you?" Matt told her. Turning his attention back to his cards, he said softly, "Well, gentlemen, anybody care to call me?"

"I'd sure like to know what you have in that hand," a burly man muttered, considering his own cards uncomfortably. "Damn."

"If you want to know, you'll have to call," Matt reminded him.

"All right." The fellow pushed two stacks of silver dollars out. "I'm seeing your twenty, and raising you ten."

"Not me," the man on his left decided, "I'm out."

"Yeah," a third player agreed. "I ain't got enough to throw m'money away on. I'm in too deep already."

Never having been fainthearted, Matthew leaned back lazily for a moment, then casually straightened up to push everything he had left to the center of the table. "I'm covering you and raising you another fifty."

"What?" Verena gasped. "Matthew, you can't—not with my money!"

One of those who'd already dropped out looked across the table. "Danged if it ain't gonna cost you to call 'im, Bill. You got that kind of hand?"

She could see her whole future on that table, and they were talking like it didn't matter. "Listen to me, all of you! Some of that's mine, and I didn't give anybody leave to play a . . . a . . . stupid game with it!"

Her words fell on deaf ears. Everyone was looking expectantly at Bill, waiting to see what he did. Bill flushed as his temper flared. "Damn you, Mister Herrick! You can see I ain't got that kind of money! If you was a gentleman, you'd at least give me table stakes!"

Matt shrugged. "But I'm not—so it's either pay or fold."

"This ain't fair!" Turning to the others, Bill pleaded his case. "You see what he's doing, don't you? He knows I ain't got the money, so he's bettin' high! It's cheatin' to play like that, ain't it?"

"He don't have to give you table stakes," one of them countered. "Be right nice if he did, but he don't have to."

Muttering something about a "damned tinhorn gambler" under his breath, Bill angrily threw down his cards and lurched to his feet. As he walked away, he was still complaining he'd been cheated by the "no-count sonofabitch."

The youngest one at the table turned over the disgruntled bettor's hand. "Jeez, did you see that? Three of a kind—aces!"

"So what you got there, mister?" one fellow asked, looking to Matt. "It must be pretty danged good if you was willin' to take a chance with that kind of money." He started to reach for the winning hand.

"Unn-uhhh—you have to pay to see, gentlemen," Matt murmured, raking in the pot.

"Better'n three aces?" the fellow persisted.

"I won, didn't I?"

"Yeah, but I'd kinda like to see what beat 'em."

"Only if you want to lay down eighty dollars."

"Eighty dollars!"

Unperturbed, Matt nodded. "There were three raises, I believe—twenty, ten, and fifty. Makes eighty, doesn't it, gentlemen?" he asked as he smoothed and folded the banknotes together. Stuffing the wad into his coat pocket, he started to rise. "Come on, I'll buy you breakfast, Rena." Seeing that she was gaping in disbelief, he settled the black felt hat on his head and smiled. "Bedbugs or not, I have it on good authority that the Columbus House has the best steak and eggs in town."

The loser had stopped at the door, then swung back to face Matt with his revolver drawn. "No, I ain't lettin' nobody cheat me!" he spat out, coming back. "You knew I couldn't call a bet like that—that's why you did it, ain't it? You couldn't beat me fair and square! Well, let me tell you something about Bill Hoskins, mister! I kill cheaters!"

"Now calm down, Bill—it ain't worth hangin' for," one of the others cautioned him.

"Turn over his cards." His eyes on Matt, Bill declared, "If they ain't better than mine, I'm killin' the bastard." To prove his point, he waved the gun menacingly as he moved closer. "Go on—let's take a look at 'em."

Verena held her breath as the younger man reached out for Matt's closed hand. One by one, he turned each card over. "Four of clubs. Six of diamonds. Two of clubs. Ten of spades. Ten of clubs." He looked up, announcing soberly, "Hell, he ain't got but a pair of tens."

McCready didn't move a muscle as Bill cocked his revolver, but the click of the hammer being pulled back told Verena if she wanted to keep her money, it was up to her. With no time to aim, she raised McCready's Colt and pulled the trigger. The report was deafening. Glass shattered, and a flame shot from the broken lantern, following a trail of kerosene to the floor. The four men dived for cover, then fought under the table for Bill's gun. It discharged, sending a bullet upward, blasting a hole in the wood, burning the green-felt cover.

"Fire!" she shouted. "The place is on fire!"

"What the hell's going on here?" a fat man demanded from a back door. The black, billowing kerosene smoke gave him a fair notion. "Water! Damn you—all of you! Get off that floor and fight the fire!" Grabbing the nearest bottle, he tried to douse the licking flames. As the alcohol caught in a *whoosh*, he dropped the bottle and ran for the bucket.

Crawling out on all fours, McCready was the first to emerge from the smoke. Without looking back, he grabbed Verena's arm and headed for the swinging doors. As he pushed her through them, she twisted her head to see the other two men dragging poor Bill from beneath the table by his feet.

Once outside, she took a deep breath of fresh air. "Your gun—I dropped it," she gasped.

"I got it." Taking her elbow, Matt hurried her along the walk. "You're not much of a shot, but I sure as hell admire your thinking," he told her. "That was a damned close call. I was afraid if I threw Betsy, you'd get in the way."

"Betsy?"

"My knife."

"You named your knife for some woman?" she asked incredulously.

"Nobody in particular," he assured her, slowing down. "But it's the female of a species that's usually the deadliest, so it seemed fairly appropriate. Anyway, you probably saved my life."

"I was trying to save my money," she retorted. "You stole my money, Matthew McCready—you took it without even asking."

"If I'd asked, would you have loaned it?"

"Of course not!" she snapped. "That was all I had between me and starvation—and you just took it!"

"I rest my case."

"I beg your pardon?"

"Were you just born contrary, or did something god-awful happen to make you this way?"

"Ohhhh no, you don't—you're not going to turn the tables on me, Matthew. I have every right to be angry, and you know it. I didn't steal from you, you know. It was the other way around."

He came to a dead stop in the street. Reaching into his coat pocket, he took out the large wad of bills. The sky was lightening, the rosiness fading to blue. Licking his thumb, he began counting his winnings out. "Two hundred thirty . . . two thirty-one . . . two thirty-two . . . two thirty-three. Not bad for a couple of hours' work, is it?"

She stared at it. "There's two hundred and thirty-three dollars there?"

"Uh-huh." Recounting, he separated it. "Here—you can owe me the fifty cents."

"What?"

"There's a hundred and seventeen dollars there. I figure that's your share. A half share of the winnings isn't a bad return on your investment, is it?"

"Well, it ought to be one hundred forty-six."

One black eyebrow shot up. "How's that?"

"You started out with my fifty-nine dollars, didn't you?"

"More or less."

"All right, then—if you give that back, there's still a hundred and seventy-four left, isn't there?"

"I don't have a pen and paper."

"I don't need one. I'll just take half the winnings, which ought to be—" She paused to figure the amount in her head. "Eighty-seven dollars. You owe me eighty-seven dollars more than the fifty-nine, McCready. And since you've already given me the one seventeen, I figure I've still got twenty-nine more coming."

He looked at her for a long moment, then carefully counted off a ten and a twenty. "All right—now you're ahead one dollar."

"Thank you."

"You're a hard woman, Verena. Otherwise you'd have figured you owe me for bluffing that one out back there. There's a lot more to poker than cards, you know."

"How much is your life worth?" she countered, refolding the bills. "More than twenty-nine dollars?" she asked sweetly.

It was a hard point to dispute. "Yeah."

"You had no right to take it, you know," she added. "No right at all. What if he'd had fifty dollars more?"

"He didn't."

"Well then, is he right? Did you cheat him because you knew he didn't have the money to bet?"

"He could have borrowed it if he felt strong enough about his hand—I did."

"But what if he had?" she persisted. "What were you going to do then?"

"You don't understand the game."

"Well, if you always win, why did you need my fifty-nine dollars? Answer that one, will you?"

"I was robbed." Lifting his arm, he showed her the bullet hole in his sleeve. "Look at that—he ruined a damned good coat."

"You were robbed," she echoed faintly.

"Yeah, coming back last night. I guess he saw me win and headed me off."

"Why didn't you say something earlier, when—" She could feel the hateful heat creeping into her cheeks. "When we were in your room," she managed.

"I sort of had other things on my mind at the time," he said softly. He could almost watch the guilt parade across her face. "Like saving your life," he added, letting her off the hook. "And I believe I'll take that thirty dollars back, now that I think of it."

"You're forgetting the train," she reminded him. "And come to think of *that*, there's at least another ten dollars you owe me for my dress."

"Damn, but you drive a hard bargain, Verena."

But he was smiling, and the warmth in his eyes was enough to send a shiver down her spine. As the memory of his kiss flooded through her, she had to look away. She couldn't let him know just how well she remembered that.

"Yes, well, you know what they say about money and friendship, don't you?"

"I can't think of it."

"That borrowing ruins it—the friendship, I mean."

"What about the notion that a man ought to give a friend the shirt off his back?" he shot back.

"I'm not a man. I'm a schoolteacher who can barely

make ends meet in the best of times. And it's still a long way to San Angelo and back to Philadelphia, even on a hundred and forty-six dollars." Keeping her eyes averted still, she started down the street again. At the corner, she crossed the street diagonally.

He caught up quickly. "Columbus House is over there," he pointed out.

"I know, but in case there are others awaiting the stagecoach, I'm going to be at the window when the ticket office opens."

"It isn't six o'clock yet!"

"I don't eat steak for breakfast anyway. In fact, this morning, I couldn't eat a morsel. My head hurts, and I've already been sick once." Stopping momentarily, she eyed him balefully. "You lied about the whiskey, you know. It was even worse than the wine."

"Oh, so that's what really ails you."

"No. It was finding you'd left without so much as a word, taking my last fifty-nine dollars with you. You didn't even care if somebody carried me off while you were gone. You know, I thought you'd abandoned me."

His eyebrow arched again. "I'd be a damned fool to go off without my gun or my clothes."

"I was afraid, Matthew."

In the morning light, her hazel eyes were heavily flecked with gold, making him wonder why he hadn't noticed their incredible beauty before now. Just looking into them almost took his breath away, giving him thoughts he couldn't afford. He had to look away to keep his heart from racing.

"I said I'd get you to San Antonio, Rena," he said finally. "I had to do it the only way I knew how."

The Menger House in San Antonio was a welcome relief from the rigors Verena had endured since landing at Galveston in what now seemed like an age ago. The town itself was old and decidedly Spanish, with beautiful old homes set amid shaded gardens, and the Menger seemed to be pretty much in the middle of it, set across a plaza from the famous Alamo.

It was a nice hotel, the sort one would expect to find in a civilized place, with a lovely courtyard, fountains, roses, magnolias, and dark-leaved oleander as big as trees. The sweet fragrances intermingled, permeating the air, creating a heady perfume. The place was so peaceful, so serene, she reflected languidly. She didn't even want to get out of the rose-scented bathwater to dress for dinner. She'd found an oasis of loveliness in the middle of the most uncomfortable journey of her life.

A light tap sounded on her door. Then a maid called out in heavily accented English, "Miss Herrick? The *señor,* your brother, he send you something. Miss Herrick, you still in there?"

"Yes—uh—*uno momento*—uh, just a minute!" Verena answered, forcing her weary body out of the bathtub. Hastily wrapping a huge white towel around her wet body, she hobbled to the door, turned the lock, and cracked it open. "What is it?"

"For you—he say give it to hees *señorita* seester." Smiling, the girl held out a large box, then gestured to the narrow opening. "You take—no?"

"Uh, yes—yes, of course." Stepping behind the door, Verena opened it wider. "Just put it on the bed, please. Uh—*gracias,* is it?'

"Sí."

Still smiling, the maid carried the box over and laid it atop the fringed cotton coverlet. "He say he hope you like it," she said, slipping out past Verena.

What on earth—? Quickly relocking the door, Verena turned her attention to the box on the bed. It was tied with knotted string, but she managed to slip it over the corners, then pull it off. Lifting the lid, she looked down in disbelief. It was a dress. Matthew McCready had bought her a dress.

As she lifted it out of the box, a piece of paper dropped to the floor. It was a green taffeta dress, exquisitely embroidered with black and gold thread. Taking care not to spot it with bathwater, she held it up, then looked into the mirror. It had a wide, deep neckline, short full sleeves, a fitted bodice, and a skirt that was narrow in front, and gathered to a fullness in the back. It was fancy enough to wear to an opera. Definitely too fancy for a spinster schoolteacher. And far too revealing. No, she couldn't wear it. She wouldn't dare wear it.

Laying the gown on the bed, she bent to pick up the paper, unfolded it, and read, "It more or less matches your eyes, so I bought it for you. Wear it tonight, and I'll take you out for the best dinner to be had in San Antone. I thought that as modest as you are, you might want to put the mantilla around your shoulders rather than your head." Then, on the back side, he'd added, "If it doesn't fit, there's a woman who can alter it between now and when you leave in the morning."

When you leave in the morning. It was a lowering thought. This was the last time she'd probably ever see Matthew McCready. At eight o'clock tomorrow morning, she'd be going on to San Angelo, and he'd be going somewhere else. In spite of yesterday's anger over the money, she was going to miss him. She was going to be alone again.

No, it was more than that. She was really going to miss *him*. It was silly, and she knew it, but he was the first man she'd ever truly liked since her father had left for the war. As exasperating, even as infuriating as Matthew McCready was, he was also fascinating. Dangerously so.

It seemed as if every time she was with him now, she couldn't help remembering what it had felt like when he'd kissed her, when he'd held her that night in Columbus. She couldn't even look at him without shamelessly wondering what would have happened if she hadn't come to her senses. She would have sinned, she knew that much.

It had changed things between them, there was no

doubt about that. Beneath the usual banter, the smart barbs, there was something else, an awareness that wouldn't go away. And judging by the way she sometimes caught him looking at her, he felt it also. So it was just as well that he wasn't coming with her, she told herself. Otherwise, she was in danger of succumbing to his considerable charm, then regretting it later. And she didn't want that.

No, she'd set herself on course to be a spinster for life, one of those women who never knew what it was like to love a man. And she'd done it deliberately, swearing to herself that she wouldn't let anybody cause her the pain her father had given her mother. No woman in her right mind would want anything like that. Whoever it was who'd said it was better to have loved and lost than never to have loved at all hadn't known her mother.

She couldn't wear that dress. She'd be showing far too much skin for a decent woman. But it was the sort of gift one could expect from a man like McCready, she supposed. He probably didn't really know any decent women. Being a gambler, he probably met more cantina girls than any other kind. The good women of this world didn't go to the places he frequented.

No, that wasn't what he'd said. She distinctly remembered his telling her that he'd been to those fancy New Orleans balls, that he'd danced with aristocratic belles. It had been some sort of victory for him. In his mind, it had proven he was more than a Tennessee farm boy.

She looked at the dress again, wondering if any New Orleans belle would be brave enough to wear it. Then the black lace spilling out of the box caught her eye.

The mantilla he'd mentioned. She could wear it around her shoulders, he'd said.

Intrigued, she dried herself quickly, then slipped into clean drawers. At least she'd brought her corset for the court hearing, so she wouldn't be entirely indecent. Threading her arms through the shoulder straps, she pulled the undergarment around her, straightening the stays beneath her breasts, and pulled the laces to tighten the elastic between them. The effect was an eye-popping bosom. But if she wore the dress at all, she'd have to wear the corset. Otherwise, if she wore her chemise, the shoulders of it would show, and the effect would be ludicrous.

Shaking out the dress, she noted that there was a crinoline of sorts sewn into the waist. The crisp taffeta swished as she pulled it over her head, jerked it down over her hips, and straightened the bodice. Small, concealed hooks went down the front, she discovered. As she worked upward from her waist, the material tautened, hugging her bosom. It wasn't until she was done that she dared to look into the mirror.

The effect was breathtaking. Between the sheen of the taffeta and the gleam of the gold, she fairly shimmered. And green was her color, there was no doubt about that. But the dress was daring, showing not only the pale, creamy shoulders, but also more than a hint of the crevice between her breasts. And the corset beneath made them look rounder, fuller than usual. Almost sinfully so.

She stood there, torn between tearing it off and putting on one of the two dresses he'd already seen, or wearing it, brazening it out as if she were one of those fancy New Orleans belles. She hesitated. No, that would be like making a silk purse from a sow's ear. She didn't have any necklace or anything else to break that expanse of skin.

Studying herself, she lifted her still-damp hair off her neck, holding it up. She had a good neck. And she had nice shoulders. Funny, but she'd never really noticed that before. But then she'd never had a dress anything like this before. Ever. Standing there, she allowed herself to imagine what he'd think when he saw her.

He was waiting in the lobby when she came down. At the top of the stairs, she paused, suddenly self-conscious. She must surely look naked. Adjusting the black lace mantilla about her bare shoulders, she took a deep breath, then descended slowly.

He looked up, and for once in his life, he betrayed his thoughts in his face. She was beautiful, far more beautiful than any of the painted ladies of his acquaintance. As his eyes took in her knotted hair, her pale skin, her slender, almost statuesque figure, and the exquisite green gown, his mouth was too dry for words. The taffeta swished seductively with each step. A slow, decidedly appreciative smile formed on his lips.

She negotiated the final stairstep carefully, trying not to show more than the toes of her old, black high-top shoes. As her eyes met his, she fought the urge to wipe her damp palms on her skirt. She forced an answering smile.

"You look—" He was almost at a loss for words. "You look magnificent, Rena," he said softly.

"For a moment, I thought you were going to say cold," she murmured.

"Believe me, cold was the last thing that would've come to mind," he assured her.

"I feel positively indecent." Aware that several gentlemen were staring her way, she fought the urge to flee back up the stairs. "Matthew—"

"That dress makes your eyes look almost green."

"I'm sorry, I forgot to thank you for it, didn't I?" she managed.

"You don't like it?"

"Oh, no— That is, yes, of course I like it, but I cannot imagine how you came to find it."

"I was trying to replace the one you ruined on the train. The fellow at the desk sent me to a place called Felicia's, where I found it would take a week to make up anything," he explained. "We had a little language problem, and she thought I was leaving because I didn't like the quality of her work, and—well, the long and short of it is, she brought out that dress to show me what she could do. I gather she'd made it for somebody else, but I didn't realize it then. I told her I'd take it."

"You bought somebody else's dress?"

"Yeah. At first, *Señora* Felicia wasn't having any of it, but I just kept peeling off dollar bills until she gave in."

"How much did it cost?"

"Didn't your mama teach you not to ask the price of gifts?" he countered.

"Well, it was more than the ten dollars I asked for, wasn't it?"

"Yeah."

"Quite a lot?"

"Some. Come on," he said, offering her his arm. "I'm starving for a decent meal."

"How much is some?" she persisted. "You're making me feel guilty for wearing it."

"I wanted to buy it, Rena."

"But why?"

"I don't know. Probably because it'll be like you said—you'll sell the farm and go home to Pennsylvania to teach. I don't figure you'll have much chance of buying yourself something like this. You'll spend your life being practical."

"Yes, but—"

"A woman ought to have something pretty every now and then," he said, cutting her off. As a doorman held the door, Matt stood aside to let her go first. "If you don't mind too much, I thought we'd maybe walk along the river first."

"I thought you were starving."

"I am, but I sort of wanted to show you off first," he admitted. "Besides, while you were taking your nap, I got out and walked around some. There's some pretty places in San Antonio." He stopped to offer his arm again. "The evening's young, Rena. I thought maybe we'd look around a little, eat supper, then I'd get you back here early enough that you'd get a good night's rest before you leave tomorrow."

His arm felt strong, steady beneath her hand. But this was the last time they'd be walking like this, talking like this. She felt a pang of panic at the thought.

"I imagine there are card games in San Angelo, Matt." Even as she said it, she felt incredibly bold.

"Yeah."

There wasn't much encouragement in one word. "What are you really going to do?" she asked suddenly.

"I don't know."

That was about as noncommital an answer as she could get. "Oh."

"I'm not the kind of man that sticks around, Rena," he said abruptly. "I'm not what you need."

"I wasn't asking for me, Matt. I was just asking."

"I was just telling. You sell that farm and get yourself back to Pennsylvania where you belong."

"I intend to. If I don't encounter those men again, I'll be on the first mail wagon back after the place is sold."

"I've been thinking about that. You know, they could've had you mistaken for somebody else. Maybe they just got the wrong name."

"Isn't that what I've been telling you all along?" she countered. "The notion that I have anything anybody would want is downright ludicrous."

"Except the obvious."

"I hardly think anybody named Gib would want to kill me for that."

"Doesn't seem like it, anyway."

He'd been struggling with himself ever since he'd arrived in San Antonio, telling himself that she'd be all right, and he wanted to believe it. He could feel better that way. And right now he didn't need any encumberances. Right now he couldn't afford any. And neither could she. The last thing on earth she needed was to fall for somebody like him.

"It's a pretty river, Matt."

"Yeah."

"It has so many bends and curves, and it just

flashes like gold in the sunlight, silver in the shadows, doesn't it?"

"Yeah." Stopping in the shade of a tree, he looked across the water. "It's slow and sleepy, kind of like the town." When he turned to her, the shadows of the leaves were playing on her face, while the lowering sun caught the gold in her chestnut hair. And she was looking at him with those pretty hazel eyes. For a moment, he forgot who he was, and where he was going. Reaching out, he brushed back an errant strand of hair with his fingertips. "God, Rena—" He caught himself. "No," he said almost forcefully. "I can't go—I just can't."

"I know."

"Men and women don't make very good friends, you know."

"Why not?"

"Because they're men and women. It always turns into something else. Then when that's over, there isn't anything left. I like you, Rena. I'd kind of like to keep it that way."

"I didn't know I was throwing myself at you. I certainly didn't think I was, anyway."

"You aren't. I'm just trying to explain things to you, that's all."

"Like why you bought this dress?"

"I don't know why I bought the dress—honest to God, I don't. I guess I just wanted you to have something nice, maybe something to remember me by."

"Matt—"

"What?"

"I don't know many men. I never did. But I just want you to know that despite all the barbs and hateful things I've said, I appreciate everything you've done for me. I'd like to think maybe we're different, that maybe we'll stay friendly somehow. Maybe someday you'll get to Philadelphia."

"Philadelphia's a big place, Rena."

"I live—" No, that wasn't going to help. When she got back, she was going to have to find another place to stay. "Well, I don't guess it matters, does it?"

"No. I probably won't get there, anyway."

"No, of course not."

"Ready to eat?"

"Are you?"

"Yeah. There's a real nice place not too far from the Menger. Fellow at the desk says the food's good, so I thought we'd try it out. I'm still wanting to buy you that steak."

"All right."

The walk back was a quiet one, with neither of them saying much. Finally, when she couldn't stand it any longer, she blurted out, "Why can't you come with me?"

All the glib words of his life disappeared, and for once he decided to tell her the truth. "You guessed right in the beginning." He tried to smile and couldn't. "I've got to lay low." Not daring to look into those eyes again, he studied a pretty Spanish house on the other side of the street. "I'm a wanted man, Rena." When he couldn't help himself, he met her sober gaze. "So now you know. I guess you can run screaming for the law."

"I think I've known all along," she said quietly.

"Well?"

"Well what?"

"Do you still feel like eating with me?"

Her hand tightened on his arm as she looked up at him. "I don't want to know what you're wanted for, Matt. No matter what it is, I still believe you're a good man. I wouldn't be standing here without you."

"Well, at least that makes us even." He took a deep breath, then exhaled it fully. "I guess I'm ready for that steak."

"So am I."

The eating establishment was small, but there were white linen cloths and individual oil lamps on every table. All the business was conducted in Spanish. Finally, after much gesturing and haggling in a combination of pigden English and pigden Spanish, an order was arrived at. As the server left, Matt leaned back against the whitewashed adobe wall.

"I guess only God knows what we'll be eating."

"As long as I can cut it with a knife and fork, I won't complain," she promised.

"Hungry?"

"Yes." Looking around to be sure they wouldn't be overheard, she hesitated, then leaned across the table. "What happens if you are caught?" she dared to ask him.

"I'll go back, stand trial, and hang."

"Oh. Well, then I can see why you don't want to be caught."

"Yeah."

"Was it your fault?"

"If it was, do you think I'd tell you?" he countered.

"I don't know. I'd like to think so, anyway."

"I never met a guilty man who didn't claim to be innocent, Rena."

"No, I don't suppose anyone wants to hang."

"No."

Suddenly, he didn't want her to think the worst of him. "But for what it's worth, whether you believe me of not, it was self-defense. So, now that that's behind us, I'd like to spend your last night in San Antone talking about something else."

The yellow flame glowed steadily in the lantern's chimney, casting a long shadow over Matt McCready's face, giving him a sinister appearance. But maybe because she wanted it to be so, she reached across the table to clasp his warm fingers in hers.

"There are a lot of things wrong with you, Matt McCready, but being a murderer isn't one of them."

Before Matt could respond, the server returned with a bottle of burgundy wine and two silver goblets. "For the *señora*—for the *señor*," he murmured, pouring the dark red wine. Smiling broadly, he waited for them to taste it. Verena eyed hers with misgiving, but Matthew took a goodly swallow.

"It's good. You ought to try it."

"That's what you said at Brassfield's," she reminded him. "And that's what you said last night, too."

"Yeah, but you're eating with it. You probably drank the other down too fast. You want to digest it slowly right along with the food, then it doesn't hit you so hard."

"If I get sick, I won't catch the stage tomorrow, and then I'll miss the mail wagon. If that happens, I'll have to wait another three days for the next one."

"Yeah, I guess that's right."

She stared in fascination as he drained his goblet, then refilled it. "Doesn't it ever bother you?"

"Not anymore. I guess I'm used to it."

She looked at the dark liquid for a long moment, then sighed. "Well, I don't suppose a little would hurt, would it?"

"No."

As she lifted the cup, she looked over the rim, and her blood turned to ice. Gulping down a large swallow, she kicked McCready under the table with the toe of her shoe. "Look," she whispered, "over there."

"Over where?"

"Shhh. Over there—behind you." As she spoke, she slid down in her chair, trying to shrink into the shadows. When he didn't move, she kept her voice low and even. "We saw him at Sheriff Goode's."

Matt nodded. "I'll take a look in a minute."

He didn't have to. The tall blond man walked past him to sit at a nearby table. As he passed Verena, he lifted his hat slightly in acknowledgment. She sat up, knowing that it didn't make any difference now. He'd already seen her.

"It's probably a coincidence," Matt murmured.

But the man sat there, staring at Verena. "I don't think so." Needing courage, she took another gulp.

"Whoa now. You'd better wait for food before you finish that off." Leaning forward until his head was but inches from hers, Matt asked, "Are you sure you can't place him?"

"Just at Goode's."

"Look, maybe it's the dress. Maybe he can't take his eyes off the dress."

"I don't think so."

"You want to go back to the hotel?"

"And be followed? No. I want to outwait him."

"He's a handsome fellow," he allowed.

Another thought occurred to her. "What if he's after you instead of me?"

"Then he'd be a ranger, and he looks pretty clean to be one, as near as I can tell. Rangers usually look worse than the outlaws they're chasing."

As abruptly as he'd arrived, the tall, blond fellow stood up, came over to their table, tipped his hat again, and then walked slowly out the door. Verena sat as still as if she'd turned to stone until he was gone.

"Now there's a man who doesn't like to wait for his dinner," Matt said lightly.

The food, when it came, was excellent, the best she'd eaten since she left home. The meat could be cut with a fork, the peas were actually green, the potatoes were parsleyed with butter, and the bread was still warm from the oven. The only thing that told her she was in Texas was the ubiquitous rice with chopped peppers. As the meal wore on, she found herself having a second glass of wine.

As the tension passed, Matt leaned back, watching her. The gold embroidery on her dress sparkled as she moved, and the lamplight seemed to reflect off the gold specks in her hazel eyes. After the last bite of her steak, she wiped her mouth daintily, then looked across at him.

"I expect you think I'm somewhat of a pig for eating all of it," she murmured.

"Pig doesn't even come close," he said softly. "I was thinking you are one fine-looking woman, Miss Verena."

The way he said it sent a shiver down her spine that

had nothing to do with fright or cold. She leaned forward and held her chin, watching him dreamily. He was, to her way of thinking, one fine-looking man.

"Well, at least I bought you one good meal," he said finally. Leaning forward, he picked up the wine bottle and divided what was left between the two goblets. Handing her one of them, he held up the other. "Here's to you, Verena—may all your dreams come true." As he said it, he clinked one silver rim against the other. "I hope you know I'm going to miss you," he added quietly.

It was as though a grand adventure was coming to an end. And suddenly, as she looked into those dark, almost black eyes, she knew she didn't want to go on without him. San Angelo was distant now, her father's farm almost unimportant when compared to the loss she was feeling. After all she'd gone through, after all she'd spent just to get there, it didn't make any sense anymore.

Her mother had been right, after all. He was every bit as dangerous as she'd first thought him, but for a different reason. He hadn't had to seduce her with lies and promises. No, in less than a week of knowing him, she'd fallen for a dark-haired, dark-eyed rogue, who'd made it plain that he was a long way from wanting to settle down. And she wasn't foolish enough to think she could change him. Even if she could, it wouldn't help anything. He'd still be an outlaw on the run. So no matter how hard she wished him to go with her, she knew it wouldn't happen.

Touching her goblet to his, she managed to tell him, "I'm going to miss you, too. Terribly."

The way she said it told him far more than the words. Before he could stop it, a wave of desire washed over him, threatening his resolve. “Look, Rena—” He reached across the table to cover her warm hand. For a moment, he struggled with himself, telling himself there was no way on earth he could have her. “Rena—”

“You don’t have to say it, Matt—I know. I just never planned on this, that’s all.” Keeping her eyes on the white linen cloth, she said in a low voice, “I just thought I’d come down here, sell the farm, and go home. All I really wanted was to understand why he left, you know. I thought if I had that, I could go on.”

“Yeah.” His fingers almost burned where they touched hers. Reluctantly, he drew his hand back. “Come on—you’ve got a long way to go tomorrow.”

She’d had her answer. Again. “Yes,” she agreed simply.

As they walked back to the Menger, the warm night air was filled with the fragrance of roses, and the sky above was clear, midnight blue, and filled with stars. In one corner of it, the still-rising quarter moon looked down, the man in the moon’s smile decidedly benign. It was beautiful out, and there was a sense of time suspended beneath all those stars.

Beside her, Matt McCready seemed so strong, so solid, so alive that it was hard to accept that he wouldn’t be there tomorrow, that this was the end. When she looked up, she realized he’d taken the long way, leading her almost to the river’s edge. And now the moonlight made the water shine like a ribbon of silver. Any other time, she would have seen something magical, even mystical in it, but not now.

"I guess I'll be getting up to see you off in the morning," he said, breaking the long silence.

"You don't have to."

"I want to make sure you get on that stage. I'll feel a whole lot better knowing you're on your way, that you'll be able to catch the mail wagon when it goes through tomorrow. It'll probably have an armed escort."

"You don't think they've given up, do you?"

He took a deep breath, then let it out before answering, "I don't know."

"Matt—"

"Don't, Rena—I can't go. I've got to find a place to hide, and there's not much in San Angelo. A man like me would stand out like a sore thumb there."

"I wasn't going to say that. I was going to say that I think I'll be all right," she lied. "But I am going to buy myself a gun as soon as I get there. And I'm not going out to look at Papa's farm without Mr. Hamer."

"Yeah." Bending down, he picked up a rock, then skipped it across the slow-moving water. "Come on."

"I don't know as I want to go in," she said, trying to prolong the moment.

"You have to. Morning's going to come early."

He walked quickly back toward the Menger, as if he couldn't wait to be rid of her now. She hurried beside him in silence, knowing there was nothing more to be said.

At her door, he paused. "You think the man in the restaurant was following us, don't you?"

"Yes. Don't you?"

"It could be me he's after," he said. "You said so yourself."

"I hope not." She felt awkward and self-conscious now. "But if it were you, wouldn't he just arrest you? If he were a Ranger, I mean."

"Maybe. Or maybe he wants to make sure I'm his man."

"Oh."

It was hard letting her go, harder than he'd ever expected. "Look," he said finally, "maybe we'd better switch rooms again. Maybe that way you'll sleep better. I know once you get on that mail wagon, nobody's going to give you any trouble," he said again, reassuring himself. "But you might as well have some peace of mind tonight."

"I think it's probably a good idea," she murmured. "Unless, of course, he's looking for you."

He shook his head. "He's waiting for something—maybe a warrant." Reaching into his pocket, he retrieved his key and unlocked his door. Holding it open for her, he offered, "I'll bring your things over."

"Wait—"

"What?"

Somehow she managed to look up into those dark eyes again. "Thank you for the lovely dress, Matt. I've never ever had anything as nice as this. And I doubt if I will again."

"I just thought it'd look good on you. And it does—it looks damned good on you, Rena. Sometime when you're wearing it, I hope you remember me."

"Schoolteachers don't get many chances to wear fancy taffetas." Unable to think of anything else, she blurted out, "It's been a grand adventure just knowing you, Matt. It truly has."

Her wet eyes sparkled in the semidarkness. "God, Rena—hey, you aren't crying, are you?"

"No, of course not," she whispered, looking away. As the burning tears threatened to overflow her brimming eyes, she felt his warm hands on her shoulders, turning her around.

"Oh, Matt!" she wailed.

His arms closed around her, holding her close, and his head bent to hers. As his hot breath caressed her cheek, she threw her arms around his neck, shamelessly inviting his kiss. And he did not disappoint her.

He kissed her thoroughly, possessing her mouth completely, and as she responded wholeheartedly, he forgot everything but the feel of her. His mouth left hers to nibble eagerly at her earlobes, and he could feel the shiver of her answering desire. With his last ounce of reason, he told himself to stop, that he couldn't face her hating him afterward.

"I've got to go, Rena—you don't want this."

"Stay with me tonight, Matt—please. Hold me tonight."

"Rena—"

"I don't want to die a spinster without ever knowing how it ought to be. Just for tonight, I want you to love me."

Her eyes were like great dark pools, drawing him in, threatening to drown him. With the fleeting image of quicksand darting through his mind, he kicked the door shut behind him and kissed her again, damning tomorrow. For whatever it was worth, he was going to put everything he had into one night of loving her.

His hands moved over her shoulders, her back, her

hips, pressing her body against his, as his mouth traced hot, eager kisses along her jaw, then lower to her throat, to the smooth, silky skin of her shoulders. The mantilla slid silently to the floor.

"Tell me what to do," she whispered. "I want to know how to love you."

For answer, he turned her away from him, and before she could protest, he nuzzled her hair, smelling the sweet fragrance of roses. "Just don't be sorry—that's all I ask," he said softly.

"I won't, but—"

"Shhhh."

His lips found the sensitive nape of her neck, and he could feel the tremor going through her body. Reaching around her, he drew her back against him, then began unhooking the bodice of her dress, loosening her corset laces, freeing her breasts. As his fingers brushed over her nipples, she gasped in shock.

"I want to feel all of you, Rena," he whispered against her bare shoulder. "I want to touch all of you."

Closing her eyes, she leaned back, giving herself over to the exquisite feel of his hands on her skin. Her breasts strained against his palms and her nipples tautened between his fingers. Never in her life could she have ever imagined anything like this. It was as if the center of her being lay beneath his hands.

As he worked on the corset, he could almost curse the way a woman caged herself in whalebone. When it finally gave way, it joined the mantilla at his feet. She was bare to the waist, and her skin felt hot, almost fevered.

"I want you to get out of the dress, Rena." Even as he

said it, he pushed the loose bodice down over her hips. "I want to see you."

She hesitated, suddenly afraid, and her hands caught his, holding them. "No—please."

"Do you want me to go?" he asked softly.

"No."

"It'll be good, but you've got to trust me." Kissing her nape again, he continued working the gown down.

The taffeta swished as her dress and petticoat slid over her drawers, then billowed out in a whoosh as they fell around her ankles. Closing her eyes to hide from him, she felt his hands slip beneath the elastic waist of her drawers.

"You're beautiful," he whispered. "You know that, don't you, Rena?"

She couldn't answer. All she could do was swallow as his hands moved over her skin, lightly touching her waist and her hips, then her flat belly. Her whole body felt like a bowstring about to break and yet she didn't want him to stop. Just when she thought she could stand no more, he stood back to remove his coat and boots. Then he knelt in front of her to unlace and pull off her shoes.

When he stood again, he said hoarsely, "Undo my shirt for me."

Her fingers touched his chest, finding the buttonholes, slipping them over the buttons. His chest rose and fell beneath her fingertips. She slid her hands under his shirt, loosening it, feeling the solid, forbidden warmth of his body.

She was naked except for her drawers, he except for his pants. Turning her around again, he nuzzled the back of her neck, her silken shoulder, and he could feel the waves of excitement course through her. His hands cupped her breasts, and his thumbs rubbed her nipples again.

A low moan began deep within her, rising as one of his hands slid under the waistband of her drawers, over the flat plane of her belly to her hot thighs, then to the soft thatch between, touching her, caressing her *there*. She stiffened momentarily as he found the wetness, then slipped inside. She arched her head, her whole body, leaning back into him, giving herself over to what he did to her.

Telling himself she was more than ready, he lifted her from behind, half turned her into his arms, then carried her to the bed. Laying her atop the coverlet, he quickly shed his pants, then followed her down into the cradling depths of the featherbed. As his manhood touched her belly, her eyes flew open, betraying a sudden panic.

Cursing himself for his eagerness, he smoothed her hair back from her temples with both hands and bent his head to brush her lips. "It's all right, Rena," he whispered. "We've got the whole night ahead of us."

Her lips parted to receive his teasing tongue, and her answering kiss ignited the fire anew, making him forget everything but the woman beneath him. His mouth left hers, this time to explore the hollow of her throat, the rounded mounds of her breasts, the taut nipples. When his hand found the wetness between her thighs again, they slackened, giving him access to her.

Her closed eyelids were a deep purple in the semidarkness, and her breathing was rapid, shallow as she writhed beneath him, asking for more. Her fingers opened and closed almost spasmodically as she caressed his thick hair.

She moaned her protest when his hand left her to guide himself into the wet depths; then her whole body went rigid as her maidenhead tore. A sharp gasp escaped as her flesh closed around his. Whispering almost incoherent words of love, he began to move within her, slowly at first. Then as her legs came up and she clasped his bare back, digging in her nails, he gave in to his own all-consuming desire.

Feeling the exquisite agony of what he did to her, she followed his lead, bucking and writhing beneath him, straining for some distant ecstasy, while her hands urged him on. There was no yesterday, no tomorrow, nothing but what he was doing to her. Just as she thought she could take no more, he grasped her hips, and riding hard, cried out loudly. She felt the flood of warmth just before he collapsed over her.

Satiated, he floated back to earth, then lay there, his head on her breast, catching his breath. The thought crossed his mind that if heaven had a name, it'd be this. Gradually, he became aware that she lay quietly, her heart beating hard beneath his ear. The reality of what he'd done washed over him, making him almost afraid to look at her. He'd taken her maidenhead, and nothing he could do would give it back to her.

She looked on his dark, rumpled hair, on his bare skin gleaming almost white in the faint moonlight, and she wondered if he thought her no better than a cheap harlot now. If he did, she wouldn't be seeing him again after this, anyway, she told herself. And as the reality of that set in, she wanted to cry.

Finally, he got enough courage to raise up on his elbows and look into her eyes. They glistened wetly, making him feel like the greatest cad on earth. There were no words to make amends for what he'd done to her, and yet he had to try.

"Rena, I'm sorry—I lost my head—"

That was almost more than she could bear. "No, I threw myself at you," she managed, mortified.

"I didn't even give you a good time, did I?"

"Yes." Forcing a small smile, she dared to meet his gaze. "And as sinful as it sounds, I'm not sorry. For a few moments, you let me pretend that somebody loved me. That's something, isn't it?"

"God, Rena, you could have anybody you looked at."

"But I didn't want any of them," she said simply. "I don't know why, but you're the only one I ever thought of like this. I just didn't want it to end, that's all."

"I should've waited for you, but I sort of lost my head," he admitted. "I wanted it to be good for you."

"You mean you could've waited?"

"It's supposed to happen to both of us—it's better that way. But I got greedy too fast." Looking down on her tangled hair spilling over his pillow, on those wide, luminous eyes, he felt a surge of renewed desire. And he knew that this time it'd take him long enough to make it good for her. "Rena—"

She could see the heat return to his eyes, and it sent a fresh shiver of anticipation down her spine. And this time she knew exactly where he meant to lead her. This time when she twined her arms around his neck, pulling his head down for her kiss, she was more than ready for everything he'd do to her.

"You promised me the whole night, didn't you?" she whispered.

As his lips touched hers, some distant conscience warned him he could be giving her more than either of them bargained for, but somewhere between the smell of roses and the warmth of her embrace, he forced it from his mind.

He ought to be feeling pretty damned good, but he wasn't. No, he was feeling just about as low now as anytime he could remember, almost as low as those awful days after he'd lost his brothers. Sitting there, he swirled the amber liquid in his glass, looking into the depths, thinking he was a damned fool. But that wasn't the worst of it—no, he was a pretty worthless fellow.

"You're drinkin' mighty hard for ten o'clock in the morning," the man behind the bar said.

"Yeah."

"Guess if I'd put that purty little lady on the stage, maybe I'd be drownin' myself in the stuff, too."

"Maybe."

"She'll be back—I'd bet on it," the fellow offered.

"No."

"Why, the way she was lookin' at you, I'd—"

"No, you wouldn't," Matt cut in curtly. He didn't want to talk. Hell, he didn't want to face anybody. Lurching to his feet, he grabbed the nearly full bottle and his brand-new rifle, then headed for the door.

"Didn't mean to run you off, mister," the bartender called out after him.

He didn't want to go back to the hotel either. Instead, he found himself walking down by the river, taking idle swigs from the bottle, wondering how in hell he'd gotten himself to this pass. Every time he closed his eyes, he could still see her lying in that featherbed, her hair spilling over that pillow, her eyes inviting him to love her. Either that, or she was stepping up into that stagecoach, turning back for one last look at him. And like a fool, he'd stood there watching until the damned thing was out of sight, wishing he could go after her.

But it would have been wrong. Even more wrong than what had happened between them last night. He might be what she wanted right now, but he sure as hell wasn't what she needed, and someday she'd be almost certain to find that out. This way she could sell that farm and head home to Pennsylvania where she belonged. She could find somebody decent, marry, and raise some nice, well-scrubbed kids. That's what a woman like Verena Howard really deserved. Not somebody like him, somebody who was wanted for murder. Somebody she might see hang for it.

So instead, he'd made her go on, leaving him with nothing but fond memories and a fading black eye. In another two days or so, it'd only be the memories.

As he sat down on the riverbank, he caught a glimpse of a rider on horseback approaching him. Looking up, he saw it was the blond man they'd encountered at the Goode ranch and in the restaurant last night. That at least gave him a brief measure of relief. He wasn't after Verena. His relief faded with the realization that the damned fellow was probably playing cat and mouse with him. Fixing a bland expression on his face, he nodded a greeting.

"Howdy," the man said, dismounting. Walking over to where Matt sat, he dropped to his haunches beside him. Close up, the most striking thing about him were his eyes. They were ice blue and utterly cold. "You're drinking early."

"When a man drinks is his business," Matt muttered.

"Where's the Howard woman?" the fellow asked abruptly.

The question took Matt aback, and he started to deny knowing her. Instead, he answered softly, "Now that, my friend, is none of your business."

"Name's Ryder—Ben Ryder, Texas Ranger."

Figuring he was in the bluff of his life, Matt didn't react. "Ryder," he repeated as if it meant nothing.

"Look, I don't aim to beat the bush for answers."

"So far you haven't asked much," Matt murmured.

"I don't much cotton to sass either," the ranger warned him. "I want to know straight out where she is."

"She left town this morning."

"But she was with you all the way from Galveston."

"Yeah."

The ranger hesitated, digesting that, then asked curtly, "How well do you know her?"

"Where I come from, it's not a crime to know a lady."

"You were traveling as man and wife, then as brother and sister. Why?"

Matt shrugged again. "I was trying to help out a little. She had two, maybe three, hardcases after her, and she was afraid to travel alone. That's all there was to it. It was just to give the appearance that she wasn't alone. Before that, I didn't know her from Adam." Taking another pull from the bottle, Matt met the other man's gaze squarely. "What difference does it make, anyway?"

"She's in trouble—big trouble. You're damned lucky she went on without you. Otherwise, I'd be hauling you in as an accessory."

"Accessory to what?"

"Possession of stolen property, for one thing." The ranger looked out across the water, squinting in the morning sun. "She ever tell you about her old man?"

Matt's first thought was that she'd duped him, but he didn't want to believe it. No, he wouldn't believe it. "No," he lied, "why?"

"He stole a whole lot of money, then went into hiding."

"What's that got to do with her?"

"He's dead, McCready—or is it Herrick?" he asked, his voice deceptively soft. "Which one are you?"

As Ryder turned those cold eyes on him, Matthew knew he needed to be careful how he answered. He wasn't home free until he got across that Mexican border. "What difference does it make?" he countered again. "You don't have a warrant under either name, do you?"

"No, but I'd guess I could wire Austin and get one. Funny thing about having an alias—it usually means a man's wanted."

"If an alias was a crime, there wouldn't be enough jails in Texas to hold everybody."

"So which is it—McCready or Herrick? I don't aim to waste all day with you."

"McCready." Seeing that the man's eyes narrowed, he added, "Matthew James McCready."

"Got a reason for calling yourself Herrick?"

"No. Nothing that you'd care about, anyway. I got to gambling, got in too deep, and ran when I couldn't pay up. I thought I saw somebody I knew from Nashville at Columbus, so I registered as Herrick, that's all."

"You're from Tennessee?"

"Yeah."

"You're a helluva long way from home. Take a lot to make a man run that far, I'd say."

"I made a few enemies," Matt admitted. "I figured if they caught up with me, I'd be trying to swim the Cumberland with lead in my boots." Gambling that Ryder would buy it, he added, "They aren't the sort to bother with swearing out warrants. They kinda like to take care of the business themselves, and they want everybody to know it."

"Yeah, I've met some like that," the ranger allowed. "So she left town this morning?" he asked, returning to the matter at hand.

"Yeah. I figure she was going home—she said she'd had enough of Texas."

"Home? The hell she did!" For the briefest of moments, the ranger's face darkened, then he recovered. "If that's so, she must know we want to talk to her. I reckon that'd be flight to avoid arrest." Changing tactics again, Ryder stared hard. "And you've been with her since Galveston?"

"Before that. We came across the Gulf of Mexico on the steamer together. And it'd surprise the hell out of me if she knows anything about any money. In fact, I've got a hundred dollars that says she doesn't."

"Yeah?"

"She was about broke. I had to lend her some money in Columbus." Taking another swig of whiskey, Matt wiped his mouth on his sleeve. "If you've got a warrant out on her, why didn't you take her in? You've been following her since Goode's, haven't you?"

"I was waiting for her to lead me to the gold."

"I thought you said it was money."

"Gold bars. Howard stole them during the war."

"Oh?"

"Yeah. He was with a patrol of Union soldiers when they ambushed a Confederate shipment of gold. They kept it for themselves. The whole lot of 'em deserted." Ryder squinted at the sun, then exhaled heavi-ly. "And now I aim to find that gold and turn it in."

"The Confederacy's dead. I know—I was there for the funeral."

"The state of Texas wants that gold, McCready. I was closing in on Howard when he died. Now all we've got to go on is the girl."

"Then I'd say you're out."

"How do you figure that?"

"She didn't even know him. She was a kid when he went off to war, and she never heard anything from him until she got word he died. As far as she knows, all he left her was a rundown farm."

"You know a lot for somebody who didn't talk to her about him."

"She didn't say much except he never came back. I pretty much gathered she didn't have any use for him."

"He never wrote?"

"I guess not." Forcing the cork back into the bottle, Matt reached for a low-hanging branch and pulled himself up. Towering over the ranger, he turned the tables. "You know if it was me looking for that Confederate gold, I'd be hunting for the men who disappeared with Howard. It doesn't make much sense to chase after a girl he abandoned years ago."

"Most of 'em are dead. Murdered. Way I've got it figured, there's only about three of 'em left, and they could be anywhere by now."

"Yeah."

"You know, if they find the girl before I do, they'll get that gold out of her, and she won't be very damned pretty when they're done with her." He paused, letting that sink in, then went on. "They're desperate men, McCready. They've taken to killing their own kind for that gold." Heaving his body up, he faced Matt. "I'm not buying the business about going home, not for a minute. There's more than fifty thousand dollars hidden out there, just waiting for her—she's sure as hell not going to turn her back on that."

"No, I suppose not."

"She's headed for San Angelo, not back to Galveston. How about it?"

"If you know, why bother asking me?"

"You know, I don't like you, McCready—I don't like you at all. And you know what else? I'm going over to the stagecoach office and find out if she bought a ticket, and then I'm going to telegraph Austin. If there isn't a warrant out on you, I'm going to ask for one. I figure if you're not talking, you're aiding and abetting.

Either that, or you're damned stupid. Which is it, McCready?"

"You're calling it, not me."

"I don't think you're stupid. I think you stayed here to throw me off. I think you're going to join her in San Angelo after she gets the money."

"No. I'm headed for Austin myself. A man's got to ply his trade where he can, so I'm figuring on getting into a game or two with some rich Texas politicians. So if you'll excuse me, I'm going to do some serious drinking." Flashing his most engaging smile, Matt leaned over to pick up the Henry. "Fine-looking rifle, isn't it?"

"New?"

"Yeah." Tucking the bottle under his arm, he started to leave the ranger standing there.

"Hamer won't be meeting her. He's dead. Murdered."

Matt could almost feel his skin crawl. "I don't know any Hamer."

"The lawyer handling Jack Howard's estate for her. Somebody tied him up, then blew his head off. Probably with a double-barrel shotgun."

"I don't know why you're telling me."

"Whoever did it wouldn't think twice about hurting the girl." Apparently giving up the notion of getting anything more out of Matthew, the ranger heaved his body up, then walked to his dun-colored horse. He swung back into the saddle, then flicked the reins against the animal's shoulder. "If I were you, McCready," he advised, "I wouldn't bother with Austin—no siree, I wouldn't. I'd just head for that Mexican border."

"Maybe I will."

As Matt stared after him, he could feel a shiver coursing down his spine. He'd only caught a glimpse of the man's saddlebags, and it had taken a moment for it to register that the tooled initials didn't fit any Ben Ryder. They were GH—G as in Gib.

Instead of turning back toward town, the stranger wheeled his horse and headed for the same road the stagecoach had taken earlier, the west road. Toward San Angelo. At the same instant as that hit him, Matt dropped the whiskey bottle and broke into a dead run for the livery stable.

The interior of the stagecoach was crowded, the air hot and stagnant with the smells of garlic and sweat. And across from Verena, a fat, toothless woman named Ida Pickens gummed a tough crust of bread left over from her breakfast, while maintaining a steady stream of conversation with the little boy beside her. Little Jimmy, in turn, demonstrated his boredom with a constant, almost rhythmic kicking of the board beneath his seat. On the other side of the woman, a lunch hamper whimpered and whined, betraying its smuggled canine occupant. From time to time, she rapped the lid sharply, admonishing the unhappy creature with, "Blackie, be still! You'll be a-gettin' us throwed off this here stage!"

Next to Verena, Mr. Turner, a thin-faced man in a badly wrinkled suit lost his temper. "Why don't you just get the nasty little whelp out and be done with it?" he asked sarcastically.

"They don't let no critters ride, mister."

"Well, if it don't cease that howlin', I'm shooting

it!" Across from him, the little boy puckered up and started to cry.

"Now just look what you done!" the woman snapped.

"If he starts caterwaulin', I'll shoot him, too," the man declared. "Ain't no way a body can sleep with that racket. Ain't that so?" he asked, jabbing Verena with his elbow.

"I don't know," she responded tiredly.

"You don't know! Where in tarnation you been that you ain't been hearin' 'em?" he all but shouted at her. "Place's a damned menagerie!"

"It ain't no such thing!" the woman protested loudly. "It ain't nuthin' but m'boy's pup!"

"It's not bothering me—really," Verena told her.

Turning back to the window, she retreated again into her own painful thoughts. Aside from her father's desertion, losing Matthew McCready was the lowest point of her life, and it was going to take her a long time to get over it. If ever.

Closing her eyes, she could relive every sinful moment of a night spent in his arms. And now she realized she'd been a sham all along. She wasn't really a prim schoolteacher, and neither was she prepared to spend her life as a spinster. She was a flesh-and-blood woman who'd discovered what she wanted, only to learn she couldn't have it. Not forever. Not the way it was supposed to be, anyway.

But she'd had one night with him, and oh, what a night it had been. In those hours before dawn, she'd learned more about her body than she would have ever expected. And she'd learned a lot about his. Just thinking about it brought forth an aching yearning.

By the time she'd crept down the Menger's stairs with her carpetbag in hand this morning, she felt as if her lips were swollen from his kisses. Even now, when she dared to open her eyes, she wondered if Mrs. Pickens could tell by looking at her what she'd done last night. And how she would react if she knew.

But it didn't matter. If she had to spend the rest of her life atoning for it, it would still have been worth the cost. Only it was over and done with, she reminded herself. Without the intervention of some divine providence, she wouldn't be seeing him again. Ever.

A shot rang out, jarring her from her introspection, and the stagecoach picked up speed with a suddenness that threw her against the thin man, waking him again. "Sorry," she mumbled, righting herself.

"Mercy!" Mrs. Pickens gasped, grabbing for the hamper. Before she could catch it, the lid flew open, and a medium-sized, big-footed pup escaped. Almost immediately it hiked its leg on Turner's pantleg, leaving a wet streak that ended in a puddle on the floor. "Blackie!" the woman screeched.

Turner lunged for the animal with both hands, but came up empty as the little boy snatched it away. "Gimme that beast!" the man snarled. "I'm throwing it out the damned window!" Just as he said it, a bullet tore through the wood within inches of his head. Heedless of the puddle, he dived to the floor, where he sat, cowering against Verena's leg.

Alarmed now, she frantically tore into her carpetbag for McCready's revolver. Trying to remember what he'd shown her about it, she rotated the cylinders, making sure all five bullets were in it. When she looked up,

Mrs. Pickens had her arms around the little boy, and the child was holding on to the puppy for dear life. The woman's eyes were on the gun.

Two more shots hit the coach, and amid shouts of, "Halt, or I'll plug you!" answered by, "Don't shoot!" the team slowed, then stopped.

"He ain't a-gettin' my weddin' ring!" Mrs. Pickens declared, popping it into her mouth. With an effort, she swallowed it. Picking up her purse, she exposed a white fleshy leg as she stuffed the bag up under her skirt. "If he wants my money, he'll have to go atter it!" she said triumphantly.

The boy peered outside eagerly, then announced, "Robbers! They's two of 'em, Mama—two of 'em! And they got bandanas a-coverin' their noses!"

The man on the floor got a decidedly improper grip on Verena's knee. "He'll take my gold watch!" he wailed. "I gave five dollars for it!"

"Give it here," the Pickens woman told him. "I'll hide it in m'drawers."

Her own hands shaking, Verena pulled back the hammer, cocking it, then eased the heavy Colt down between her and the coach wall, where she held it out of view. When she looked down, her own purse was gone, too.

"Ain't to worry, dearie," Mrs. Pickens assured her. "I got it real safe for you."

"If she don't stand up," the man on the floor muttered.

"I oughter throw yer watch at 'em," the fat woman shot back.

Above their heads, the driver called down from the

box, "You got the wrong run! We ain't carryin' no payroll!"

"Shut up, old man! We ain't wantin' the money—it's the girl!"

Verena's stomach sank like a rock as she recognized the voice. Her finger tightened on the Colt's trigger. The fat woman and Turner stared at her, while the boy said excitedly, "They's comin' this way, Mama!"

"Well, I never!" Mrs. Pickens gasped when she found her voice. "What on earth would they want with you?"

Looking out the window, Verena could see a man in a blue coat dismount and start toward the coach. She sat very still, waiting.

"What d'you think you're doin'?" the fat woman demanded.

"When I count to three, you'd better hit the floor," Verena told her. "All of you."

"You'll get the lot of us shot!" But to be on the safe side, she ordered, "Jimmy, get down there—now!" Then she pushed him onto Mr. Turner.

Alarmed by the implication, the man insisted, "There ain't no room down here!"

A masked man wrenched open the door, then flailed wildly, trying to fend off the yipping puppy. "Dammit, Charley—get this thing off me!"

Verena leveled the gun on the open door. "Hold it right there, mister."

"Huh?"

"Mama, Blackie's loose!" the boy screamed. "He's out!" Scrambling over Turner, he tried to go after the animal.

Outside, the dog danced and barked, nipping at the robbers' horses. The mounted rider raised his pistol to shoot it just as Verena pulled the trigger. Within the small confines of the coach, the report was deafening, and the acrid smell of burned gunpowder set Mrs. Pickens to choking. When she heard Verena cock the gun again, she cried out, "Mercy! I ain't gettin' no breath!"

Taking advantage of the confusion, the driver managed to get his hands on his shotgun. "Awright, get 'em up!" he called out. "I got yuh covered!"

The man on the ground shot at him, hitting the barrel of the shotgun, and the impact knocked it out of the driver's hand. It discharged as it hit the ground, sending a spray of buckshot into the air. At the same time, the dog jumped, sank its teeth into a fleshier part of the horse's leg. The frightened animal took off with Blackie hanging on, and the rider trying to kick him loose.

"Mama, ain't it grand!" Tommy yelled, bouncing on Turner's head.

"Shut up," she told him.

The would-be assailant on foot picked himself up off the ground and tried again. Waving his gun, he yelled, "Ever'body out! We ain't aiming to hurt nobody—all's we want is the girl!"

The horse, rider, and dog made another pass past them, with the rider taking aim on Blackie. He missed, but his horse reared, unseating him. His gun fired as he fell. Then when he hit the dust, the excited dog was all over him, nipping and yipping.

"Lee! Get 'im off me!"

"You do that again, and I don't care if you're Jack's

girl or not," the other man warned Verena. "I ain't above wingin' you."

"She shoots that thing, and you ain't above nuthin', mister," Mrs. Pickens told him. "The buzzards'll have you picked plumb clean afore sundown."

Verena had both hands on the pistol, one finger on the trigger. "Get away from that door, or I'll shoot," she said loudly. *"Now."*

"Looks like you got yourself a Mexican standoff," the fat woman declared. "If'n you shoot, you get each other."

The man on the ground managed to knock the dog away and stumble to his feet. His coat was half off and above the dirty bandana, his face was red with dust. He drew his gun and lined the dog in the gunsight.

"No!" Jimmy cried, plunging past the startled man in the door. "You ain't shootin' Blackie!"

As the child tried to shelter the little animal, the fellow grabbed him. "I got the kid!" he called out. "Either the girl comes out, or I kill 'im! And the dog, too!"

At Verena's knees, Turner said, "You can have my watch if you do."

While she watched in horror, the boy's captor put the pistol to his head and cocked it. "Send the girl out, and you can have him back!"

Seeing that she wavered, Turner insisted, "Let 'im have the brat. There's no tellin' what they'll do to you."

"They got my boy!" Mrs. Pickens shouted at him.

"I ain't countin' but to ten! Lee, tell 'im I ain't countin' but to ten!"

"I reckon they heard!" Lee called back.

"Probably all the further he can count," Turner muttered under his breath.

"One. Two. Three. I ain't bluffin'—it's the kid or the girl!"

"Four."

As Matthew crested the hill, he saw the coach at the side of the road. Reining in, he took quick stock of the situation. All he could see was the man holding a gun to the head of what looked to be a child. The stagecoach door was open, hiding whatever was going on inside, but a man's legs were visible beneath it, indicating someone stood there. They were so absorbed in the drama of the situation that they hadn't even heard him.

He dismounted and reached for the Henry. It had been a long time, nearly eight years since he'd picked off anybody like this. Carrying the repeater, he crept closer for a better look. It was still a long shot.

"Five!" the man holding the boy shouted. "You hear me? I said 'Five!' "

"He's gonna kill my boy!" Mrs. Pickens cried. "For the love of God, he's gonna kill my boy!"

"We ain't gonna hurt you, I swear it," the man at the door told Verena. "We don't want anything that we ain't got comin'."

"Six!"

"You wouldn't kill a child," she said desperately.

"We been waitin' a long time for that gold."

"But I don't know what you're talking about! I don't have any gold! All I've got is a little over a hundred dollars to my name."

"A hunnert dollars!" Mrs. Pickens gasped, momentarily diverted. "With you?"

"You can have all of it if you turn the boy loose," Verena promised him. "Everything's in my purse."

"Seven!"

Matt raised the rifle, sighting his shot. Just as he hesitated, afraid he'd hit the kid, the boy twisted loose. And when the man lunged for him, Matt squeezed the trigger. The impact of the bullet spun the fellow around. Then he fell, clutching his shoulder as he hit the ground.

"I been shot, Lee!" he screamed.

"It's gotta be Gib!" The one who'd been holding his pistol on Verena went white as he turned around to look, and in that moment Mrs. Pickens's foot shot out, landing a solid kick to the middle of his back. He pitched forward, then hit the dirt face first. The full fury of a mother took over, and the woman jumped from the door of the coach to land on Verena's would-be abductor, knocking the wind out of him.

"Is it over?" Turner asked cautiously, putting his elbows on the vacated seat. "Is it safe to get out?"

"I don't know," Verena answered truthfully. "There was only one shot, and I don't know where it came from."

Coming down from the box, the driver beat her to the wounded man. Bending over him, he pried bloody fingers off the shoulder, then observed, "Bone might be broke, but if it don't get infected, he'll live." Lifting the fellow up by his hair, he demanded, "Just who the hell are you, anyway? And where the hell did that shot come from?"

"I don't know—mebbe Gib. Name's Pierce. Charles Pierce." Closing his eyes, he clenched his teeth. "Hurts like hell." He took several deep breaths before he looked up at Verena. "I wasn't—wouldn't have—shot the boy. Just want my share—that's all."

"But I don't have anything—nothing anybody would want, anyway," she insisted.

"Jack—"

"Jack Howard?"

"Yeah."

"He was my father, but—"

"Double-crossed. Shoulder hurts too damned bad to talk. Must be Gib after us—can't trust him."

"But I don't know any Gib," she declared positively.

"He killed Bob. Don't know how many others. Hamer even."

"Hamer? Mr. Hamer is in on this, too?" she asked incredulously. "I don't believe it. But *why*?"

"No. Gib got him." He twisted his head. "Where's Lee? Lee, you all right?"

"My back's broke, Charley!"

The black puppy gingerly edged his way to Pierce's side, then began licking his face. "Heathen hound," the man muttered. "Nearly kilt me."

The driver picked up his shotgun, then came back. "I'd say you both just bought yourselves one-way tickets to Huntsville."

Verena looked up. "Huntsville?"

"State prison. Attemptin' to rob a stagecoach. Attemptin' to abduct a female. Attemptin' to kill a kid. That judge and jury ain't never lettin' 'em outta jail."

As Mrs. Pickens stood up, Lee Jackson rolled over onto his side. "It wasn't none of those things—we was just wantin' to talk to her. We was wantin' to know what Jack did with it. We was wantin' our share, that's all. We was tryin' to get to her afore Gib did. He gets her, he kills her."

"But who is he?" she asked again.

"Bad fellow. Dangerous." With an effort, Pierce sat up. "We was all together when it started—the major, Lee, Bob, Frank, and the others—even Gib. Now only me and Charlie and Gib are left."

"But who *is* he?"

"The lieutenant. Gilbert Hannah." He took another deep breath, then held it, trying to lessen the red-hot pain. "Everybody called him Gib. He turned bad on us." His gaze strayed to the driver. "Who shot me?"

"Came from those hills."

"Gotta watch out—he's a killer, I'm telling you."

"I don't know who it was, but it looks like he's coming," the driver announced, pointing.

"It's Gib," Lee Jackson said glumly. "I knowed we couldn't beat 'im."

Verena stood up and shaded her eyes with her hand, trying to make out the rider, and her breath caught painfully in her chest. There had to some mistake. It was Matthew McCready—or was it?

No, he couldn't be Gib, not after . . . not after what had happened between them. The McCready she knew wouldn't do anything like this.

You guessed right in the beginning. . . . I'm a wanted man, Rena. . . . His words echoed in her mind.

"Gib was going to find you, do a little courtin', then when he got where the gold was from you, he was going to kill you," Lee Jackson said behind her. "Just like he killed everybody."

She could see him plainly now. "Is—is that Mr. Hannah?" she managed to ask.

Jackson followed her gaze, then shook his head. "Gib? Naw—that's your husband, ain't he?"

Relief flooded over her, pouring from every pore, as scalding tears burned her eyes. "Not exactly," she managed.

"Well, now either he is, or he ain't," Mrs. Pickens declared, raising her eyebrows. "I'd say that was something a body'd be mighty exact about." Her brow furrowed, drawing her eyebrows together. "Less'n you was a Catholic, and you wasn't married by no priest. Then—"

But Verena wasn't listening. "Yes!" she shouted, gathering her skirt and petticoat above her high-top shoes, and taking off at an unladylike run. "Yes! Matt! Matt! Over here!"

The fat woman stared after her, then shook her head. "Bein' a Baptist, I guess I don't understand 'em." Then another thought occurred to give her pause. "Hope there ain't no rattlers out there, 'cuz she's trippin' over them rocks like the devil was atter her."

Matt couldn't remember ever seeing anything prettier than Verena Howard right then. He spurred his tired horse, closing the gap between them. She was so out of breath when she reached him that she couldn't speak. She just caught his leg and held on, looking up at him through streaming eyes, trying to smile despite her quivering chin.

Disengaging her hands, he slid from the horse to gather her close. "God, Rena—I was afraid I was too late," he whispered into her soft hair.

"You came after me," she said foolishly.

"Yeah. I figured I could go to Austin—" Hell, there wasn't any sense in lying to her anymore. "I figured I could get across the border later," he admitted. "I decided I'd better make sure you made it to San Angelo before I took off."

Laying her head against his solid chest, she slid her hands around his waist and held on. He was here, and for now that was all that mattered. All she wanted to do was rub her cheek against his shirt and tell herself that somehow, some way, she could make him stay.

She didn't know how long she stood there locked tightly in his embrace. It wasn't until she heard the stagecoach driver shouting at her that she turned loose of him and stepped back. Wiping her wet eyes with her sleeve, she looked up at him.

"I know what they want now—it's gold, Matt."

"Yeah, I know."

Her hazel eyes widened. "You know? How?"

"I met Gib."

"Where?"

"This morning in San Antonio. He was claiming to be a Texas Ranger when he told me about it. You want to ride or walk back to the coach?"

"Walk."

"Same here. My backside's sore from the hardest ride of my life. I was afraid Gib was going to get to you first. Come on—you can tell me what happened on the way."

The street dust of San Angelo clung to her shoes, her petticoat, her skirt, and almost everything else. But at least she was there. At least she'd finally made it. Now she could get her business over and go home, and that was what she wanted, she told herself resolutely.

But it wasn't. After years of hardening her heart, after years of truly believing she wanted the inner safety of being a spinster, she'd come to the conclusion that her happiness lay in a rambling gambler named McCready. And to make it even more unfathomable, she'd set her heart on a man wanted for murder.

He'd been in the little adobe building that passed for the sheriff's office and jail a long time now, and that made her nervous. He was supposed to be talking to Charley Pierce and Lee Jackson, but surely they'd already told him everything they knew. When it came right down to it, they didn't seem to know much more than they'd told her after their botched-up attempt to take her off the stage. Oh, they had the names of her father's coconspirators, but what good did that do? As near as she could tell, the rest were all dead.

Except for Gib Hannah. He was still out there, lying in wait somewhere, like a rattlesnake coiled to strike. But unlike Pierce and Jackson, he wanted more than his share. If they could be believed, he wanted all of this gold fortune she was supposed to have. But at least now she knew she could recognize him, and she knew what he was looking for.

At least Matt hadn't left her. Not yet. He'd promised to stay until after the probate was over. And if Gib Hannah hadn't shown his face by then, he'd stay until she sold the place, and then he'd take her back to Columbus and put her on the train. But after that, she'd be on her own again.

What could possibly be taking him so long? She'd already met with the county recorder for a description of the farm and gotten rudimentary directions to it while he'd been in there. If he didn't come out pretty soon, she was going in after him. She would now, but she felt too sorry for Pierce and Jackson. Maybe they'd been Hannah's bumbling tools, but at least they hadn't wanted to kill her. They'd wanted to share the gold.

She found herself wishing there *was* gold out there, that she and McCready would discover it, and then maybe he'd want to stay. No, that was fanciful thinking, and she wouldn't want a man who loved her for her money.

"Ready?"

"Well, it's about time. What were you doing in there, anyway? Trying to obtain squatter's rights to the place?"

"Taking care of business." Taking her elbow, he guided her across the street to a rickety buckboard. "Compliments of the sheriff," he murmured handing her up to the seat. "Nice fellow, but he says the mules tend to be contrary." Swinging up beside her, he reached for the reins. "I told him we'd have it back before sunset."

"Can you drive this?"

"Yeah. Wait a minute—I forgot something." Jumping down, he went back into the building. When he came out again, he was carrying two long guns. He shoved them under the seat before he climbed up again. "What's the matter?" he asked when she frowned.

"You're expecting trouble, aren't you?"

"I'm ready for it, anyway."

"I'll say."

"It's just the Henry, and he loaned me his Whitney. Sometimes a man needs a rifle, sometimes a shotgun. Right now, we've got both. We're pretty much loaded for anything."

"And there's the revolver."

"And the revolver," he agreed. "After I gave it to you yesterday, I felt downright naked. I went out and bought the Henry so I'd have something to carry around." Patting his holster, he added, "To tell the truth, I'm damned glad to have it back. I've had it a long time. One of these days, maybe I'll get myself a new model." Changing the subject, he asked, "How was it with the recorder? You going to have clear deed to the place?"

"It was fine. He said everything was in order." She hesitated, then frowned. "He said Papa came down here a long time ago, right after the war—only then he called himself Bill Harper. He didn't change the name on the deed to John Howard until last year, and then he did it quietly."

"Yeah, that's what the sheriff said. Everybody else down here knew him as Harper until he died. I guess he kept pretty much to himself."

"Yes. But he—the recorder—told me Papa spoke of sending a package to a bank in San Antonio. When he asked him why he didn't just put his money over at the fort, he said it wasn't money—it was papers. Makes you wonder what they were, doesn't it? Mr. Hamer never mentioned anything about there being anything like that."

"Maybe he didn't know. Maybe it was a map to the gold."

"I don't know. I'd hate to go all the way back to San Antonio to find out. Anyway," she said, smoothing her skirt, "I got directions to the place."

"We're going in the back way." Pulling out a piece of paper, he handed it to her. "I had the sheriff draw me a map."

"So that's what took so long."

"More or less."

"I feel sorry for those men, Matt."

"Yeah, so do I."

"It wasn't as if they weren't entitled to it," she went on.

"They weren't. It's Confederate gold, Rena. They stole it when it might have done some good."

"It wouldn't have changed the outcome, Matt. The South was beaten by more than money."

"It still wasn't theirs—and it wasn't your father's either. They stole it."

"I guess it corrupted them—they deserted, then they turned against one another."

"Seems like that's what happened, doesn't it?"

Straightening his shoulders, he slapped the reins against a lazy mule's back. "Looks like he's taking 'em back to San Antonio for arraignment. I told him if you had to, I'd see you got there to testify. If that happens, you can pick up those papers."

"Isn't that dangerous? To you, I mean."

"I don't know. Probably." Half turning to her, he managed a smile. "You'd come to visit me in jail, wouldn't you?"

"You know I would, but—"

"But you don't want to see me hang," he cut in, finishing the thought for her.

"No. I couldn't stand that. I just wish things were different, that's all," she said wistfully.

The sun made her hazel eyes almost golden. "Rena—"

"What?"

No, he was a fool to even think it. "Nothing. I don't know what I was going to say," he lied. "Anyway, it slipped my mind before I got it out."

"Do you think there's any gold left, or do you think Papa spent it?" she asked suddenly.

"I'd say it'd be hard to spend that much without somebody noticing it. I'd say it's more likely he stashed it somewhere. But if Hannah and the others couldn't find it, I wouldn't bank on ever seeing any of it. Unless your father left some clue, you could spend a lifetime looking."

"I don't know if I'd want it," she murmured. "It's already cost too many lives."

"Yeah."

"But if we found it, maybe we—"

"Rena, you can't pin your dreams on me," he said,

cutting her off. "I probably won't be around once you get everything settled."

"Well, I didn't mean . . ." But she did, and it was hard to hide how much she wanted him to stay. "You know, something's not right with you today, Matt," she said instead.

"I'm all right. I'm just saying I may not be around, that's all. You've got to think of yourself, Rena."

Studying his closed face, she *knew*. "You're planning to turn yourself in—that's it, isn't it?"

"Maybe."

"Matt, you cannot! You could be hanged!"

"It's not much of a life running all the time."

"How do you know? You haven't even tried it! Matt, don't do it—listen to me! If you want, I'll even go with you!" She caught herself too late. It was out there now, just like wearing her heart on her sleeve. She closed her eyes, hoping she could at least hide a little of it from him. "Please," she managed, swallowing.

"You'd do that for me, Rena?" she heard him ask softly. "You'd give up your home, your reputation, and your way of life for me?"

"Yes," she whispered. "If we found the gold, we could go someplace where they'd never catch you. If that's what it took, I'd go to the ends of the earth for you."

"God, Rena." Reaching out, he touched a few straggling chestnut hairs with the back of his hand, caressing them against her temples. "No, I wouldn't ask you to. You don't want to hide in some hole in Mexico."

"It doesn't have to be Mexico, does it?" she managed to get out before her voice broke. "There's a whole world beyond Texas, isn't there? There's the territories—there's South America—Europe—"

"You deserve better than that. You deserve better than me, Rena."

She'd thrown down her cloak of pride, and he walked right across it. It had all been her throwing herself at him, not the other way around. She'd even been the one to offer herself to him. And now she was learning that her mother hadn't been entirely wrong. He was exactly what her mother called a dangerous man. And unless she wanted to make an even greater fool of herself, she'd have to let him go.

"Rena—"

She could feel his breath against her cheek, his lips brushing against hers. But she couldn't give in to the flash flood of desire that washed over her. She sat as still as if she'd turned into Lot's pillar of salt.

"I'm sorry," he said, moving back. "I guess we'd better get on out there."

"How far is it the back way?"

"About six miles."

It proved to be the longest six miles of her life. Beyond an occasional exchange about the heat and the dust, she couldn't think of anything neutral to say, and apparently neither could he. Finally, after what seemed like an interminable silence, he reined in again.

"There it is."

Her eyes scanned a flat expanse of land, finally finding a small clapboard house with a barn behind it. From a distance, there didn't seem to be all that much to it. Certainly it didn't look like anyplace a man with more than fifty thousand dollars in gold would live.

"It doesn't look like much, does it?"

"Actually, I was thinking it didn't look bad. I guess the difference is that you never lived on a farm. Believe me, where I come from, the place is a palace. When I was growing up, all we had were bare boards, and we had to put rags between 'em in the winter to keep from freezing."

"You must be exaggerating."

He turned to look at her again. "You think I came into the world like you see me, don't you? Listen, I learned to read with my head stuck almost into the fireplace—and I didn't have Lincoln's mother on my side, either. When I was little, we had to cover the milk with our hands in the summertime to keep the dirt from blowing into it, and we were inside the house. We were poorer than the Brassfields, Rena. I didn't get my first pair of shoes until I was ten years old. The first new shirt I got, I bought myself. I used to hate my pa for making us live that way just so he could plow his own land."

"You must be proud of yourself now, Matt," she said softly.

"For what? All I've got is more money, Rena. I still go to bed at night thinking I'm going to wake up poor. Being poor never leaves you, Rena. You just cover it up, plaster over it, and whitewash it. And in good times you pretend it isn't there."

"We didn't have that much either, you know. After Papa left, Mama had to sell almost everything we had. But I guess we were different—she always said the most important thing was who we were, not what we had. As bitter as she was about him, she still showed me how to be a lady. That was everything to her—being a lady, I mean."

"Did it make you happy?"

"I don't know. I didn't know I could live any other way, so how could I tell? Before I met you, I never did one daring thing in my whole life."

"What about the coal bucket on that fellow's head?"

"That was self-preservation. And the same with the hat pin and the tart tongue." Looking up at him, she found herself smiling. "When you told me to jump off that train, I thought you were a lunatic—that you'd lost your mind."

"And when you saw the Brassfields, you were sure of it."

"Until I got to know them. By the time we left, I actually liked both of them—and the boys, too. I can't say I ever became very fond of the pig, but they were obviously attached to it."

"When we were in San Antonio, you said it had been a grand adventure."

"Yes." His black hair shone like satin beneath the hot Texas sun, and as a concession to the weather, he'd unbuttoned the neck of his collarless shirt. The effect was both boyish and decidedly sensual at the same time. "I just wish it wasn't over. I wish it was just beginning," she managed painfully, looking away.

"Sometimes today is all we get, Rena. I learned that when my brothers didn't make it to the end of the war." Slackening the reins, he flicked one end over the nearest mule. "Well, let's go take a closer look at the place."

As they came up the wagon tracks into the yard, the farmhouse and barn took on an almost eerie aspect—as though they were devoid of all life. A sense of complete emptiness pervaded the atmosphere. The barn doors were wide open, betraying a cavernous emptiness, and the front door to the house was ajar, as if it had been left that way by some departing spirit. The silence that greeted them was overwhelming.

"It looks dead, doesn't it?" she said finally.

"It's the bare boards—a little whitewash would make a difference." Pulling up, he jumped down to loop the reins over a rough-hewn hitching post. Coming back, he reached up for her. "Let's see what it's like inside."

As his hands caught her waist, she looked into his face, and for a moment, she held her breath, and time stood still. Then the intense longing she felt gave way to the heat of blood pounding through her body, fueling desire. And what she saw in his eyes told her he felt it, too. He lifted her, lowering her body the length of his. The air seemed to crackle between them.

Right then, he would have given everything he had to keep her, but some small voice of reason told him he couldn't. He didn't have the right to ask her to live a lie with him. Not when he couldn't even give her his own name. He had to force himself to release her, to step back, to break the spell.

"I'll go first," he said. "There's no telling what's inside."

As she followed him up the two steps, she looked down, seeing a dark brown stain on the bare boards. "I—uh—guess Papa died here," she managed to tell him.

"According to what I was told, they found the body out in the yard. It looks like he was shot in the doorway, and he staggered down the steps before he died."

"He didn't even have a chance to put up a fight, did he?"

"His shotgun was in the house. I guess that goes along with what Jackson and Pierce are saying."

"That Gib Hannah killed him?"

"Yeah. But they weren't there to see it, so I don't guess anybody could say for sure. The sheriff thought he was answering the door when he was shot. Said it looked like he was just sitting down to supper."

"Mr. Hamer didn't write any of that, you know. He didn't even tell me how Papa died."

"Yeah."

"I guess if he stole the gold, he paid for it in the end, didn't he?"

"Yeah." Pushing the door open with his boot, he heard a dry buzz. "Watch out!" he shouted, jumping back to draw his gun.

"What on earth—?"

At close range, the revolver's report shattered the air, and something shot across the dim, dusty interior. Jamming the Colt back into his holster, Matt slammed the door back against its hinges. A thick, patterned rope lay bleeding on the floor, its head about three feet away.

"Rattlesnake," he said tersely.

"In the house?"

"They don't like the hot sun any better than we do."

"I don't know if I want to look in there or not," she said, hanging back.

"Tell you what—I'll go in and open it all up so you can see, then I'll come back for you."

"I don't know as I want to stay out here by myself, either," she admitted nervously. "It might have a mate somewhere."

"It probably does." Stepping into the front room, he

waited until his eyes adjusted to the dimness, then he walked across to a window and pulled back a dusty curtain. "Looks like somebody got here before us."

She followed him, unprepared for the devastation she saw.

"Ransacked," was all he said.

It was as if someone had gone on a rampage, turning things over, opening a cabinet, tearing everything out of the drawers, cutting open and pulling the stuffing out of the faded settee. A worn carpet had been flung back, a hole cut in the floorboards, showing the dirt below.

His hand on the butt of his gun, Matt walked into another room, finding more of the same. In the bedroom, the featherbed had been ripped lengthwise and shaken out, the feathers covering the floor like a carpet of wispy white. The slats had been removed from the bedstead, and an axe leaned against the headboard, directly above another hole in the floor. Even the walls hadn't been spared. Whoever'd been there had vented his rage by chopping holes in the horsehair plaster, baring the laths beneath in a number of places.

"By the time he got in here, I'd say he was damned mad."

"He couldn't have thought he was going to find gold bars in the walls."

"Maybe he thought Howard had converted some of it to money."

"If my father had gone into a bank with gold bars, there would have been a lot of talk, I'd think."

"He could've done it in Mexico, brought back pesos, then traded 'em for dollars."

"If he did, he didn't spend much of it here," she decided. "He couldn't have spent more than fifty dollars on every stick of furniture in here."

"Yeah, he didn't live like he had a lot of money," Matt agreed.

Moving to the kitchen, he stared at the broken door on the cupboard, at the shards of broken dishes scattered over the floor. "About all that's left is the tinware, a coffee pot, and some cooking pans."

Turning up a ladderback chair, she sat down. "I can't sell it like this—nobody in his right mind would buy this."

"You'd have to fix it up some."

"I don't even have the money to hire anybody. I mean—look at it! There's nothing worth anything left!"

"The land's worth something," he consoled her. "Looks like he had a cornfield going, and there's a vegetable garden out back—with a little tending, there's probably some things out there that can be saved."

"I've never raised any food in my life. We lived a block and a half from a greengrocer."

"I have. A little hoeing, a little watering, and the stuff just grows. You pick it, eat what you can, and put the rest up for the winter. It's a selling point, Rena. The garden's already in."

"If it doesn't sell right away, I guess I can learn," she said, straightening her shoulders.

"You can do a lot of things when you have to. Right now I'm going out to look at the barn—I'll be back."

"Not without me." Glancing to where the dead snake still lay in the doorway, she hurried after him. "You're seeing a lot more here than I am—you know that, don't you?"

"I've got a notion of what can be fixed, that's all."

The dirt floor of the barn was pockmarked with holes dug like a checkerboard from front to back, and the few hay bales had been dragged out and hacked open. Walking around it, he noted, "Roof's good, and so are the walls."

"If a horse fell into one of those holes, it'd have to be destroyed," she declared, unimpressed.

"Yeah, but they can be filled pretty easy." Grabbing a rung of the ladder, he swung up into the loft. "It's dry."

"It probably hasn't rained in months."

"The barn could be made habitable until the house is finished," he decided.

"There isn't any livestock left," she pointed out wearily.

"Fixed up, it's worth more."

"It couldn't be worth less."

He dropped down and dusted his pants with his hands. "If you'd seen my old homeplace, you'd know better. If it was me, I'd fix it up. A few weeks, and you'd have something decent to sell. But you're going to need a few things to tide you over—you can't be running into town for milk and eggs."

"If I spent my money on it, and then it doesn't sell, I can't go home. I don't see it—I just don't."

"It'd be a gamble, all right," he conceded. Walking to the open doors, he held a palm up to the light and tried to pick out a splinter. He turned back to her, his expression sober. "You'd have to work damned hard, Rena. It's a different life."

She made a full turn around, looking upward, then she met his gaze. Sighing heavily, she nodded. "I don't really have a choice, do I?"

"I guess you could go back to Philadelphia."

"With nothing. I'd planned on getting a little some thing out of this, but—"

"Yeah, you couldn't do it alone—you'd have to have a partner. It'd be like an investment against the sale."

"Nobody in his right mind would pour money into this, Matt. I mean, look around you."

"I would." As the words came out, he couldn't believe he was saying them. "Yeah, I could help out for a while."

"But you hate farming!"

"I'm not talking about farming. I'm talking about investing for a little profit. It'll be a cold day in hell before I walk behind a plow, Rena."

"You want to invest in this?" she asked incredulously.

He shrugged. "Might as well. For a few weeks, it'd be about as good a hiding place as any, I guess."

"It'd be like pouring money down a rathole, and—" She caught herself before she actually talked sense into him. If he worked on it, he'd be staying. Hiding the surge of elation she felt, she told him, "But I guess it's worth a gamble, isn't it?"

"Yeah."

"Do you think we'll find the gold?"

"If it was buried around here, somebody would've already found it."

"I'd share it with you."

"That's not why I'd be staying, Rena."

"No, of course not, but—"

"I figure it won't be long before Hannah shows up, and I aim to be waiting here for him. I'm not leaving you alone to face him."

Stopping to wipe his dripping forehead with his shirt, Matt leaned on the axe handle, resting his aching muscles. It had been a long time since he'd chopped wood, but Verena couldn't cook without it. And when he was done with this, he still had a full day's work left filling the holes in the barn. But he had to keep working. He had to be too damned tired to think of Verena when he turned in tonight.

Last night had been rough, downright awkward, when he'd taken her back to town. The place was so damned little—just an odd assortment of adobe buildings, sod and picket huts, and a few ramshackle shanties on the north bank of the North Concho, right across the river from the fort—that he didn't feel she was safe. After he finally persuaded her to stay with the sheriff and his Mexican wife, he'd spent the night outside on lookout for Gilbert Hannah.

In the early hours of morning, she'd crept out to keep him company, saying she couldn't sleep either. With the bright stars and three-quarter moon overhead and a warm, oleander-filled breeze, it had been hard to keep his head. But he had to—then, now, and tomorrow—until he had the right to love her. He'd promised himself after that night at the Menger that he wouldn't run the risk again of leaving her with a fatherless child. So he'd sat out there, talking about anything, everything, with her, denying himself what both of them wanted.

He was so damned tired he couldn't see straight, and the sun was just now at its zenith, giving him another eight or nine hours of daylight. And yet he knew he was going to have to drive himself harder just to get through the night. There wouldn't be anybody to play duenna tonight.

Picking up an armload of wood, he carried it over to the woodpile he'd made beneath a tree and stacked it. Staring at his progress, he thought of Drew and Wayne, wondering what they'd be doing now if they had lived. Farming. On cold winter nights, they'd piled between those old featherbeds together and lain awake talking about how things were going to be when they were on their own. For Drew, it had been the dream of buying himself a big piece of land somewhere along the Cumberland, someplace where the dirt was rich and black, where things would grow easy, where he wouldn't be coaxing thin stalks out of hard clay. For Wayne, it was the animals. He liked 'em all. Nothing came onto the place that he didn't name, including the chickens. And he had a way with all of them. Old Flora, the loose-skinned cow, gave more milk for Wayne than for anyone. But what he'd always wanted was sheep. Lots of them. He was going to buy himself the biggest flock in the state of Tennessee, he always said.

Those dreams had died with them. All they'd gotten was a little plot of Tennessee clay, just big enough to be buried in. And he, the last surviving son, had moved on, yearning for someplace clean, someplace where he wouldn't get dirt under his fingernails, someplace where he wouldn't have to break his back pushing a damned plow. Looking down at his dirty hands now, he wasn't missing the irony.

In some ways, Verena reminded him of Wayne. When he'd gotten back into San Angelo last night, he'd decided maybe a dog wouldn't be a bad idea, that maybe it would sound a warning if Hannah tried to sneak up on them. So he'd picked up the meanest stray dog he could find, brought it home with them this morning, and fed it a couple of fresh rabbits to make it stick around. The damned thing had a bark loud enough to wake the dead and a snarl that sent coyotes running, but Verena, with a true sense of the ridiculous, had named it Laddie. And within an hour, it was following her around, forgetting who'd fed it. But he guessed that was good. If he left, she'd at least have the dog for protection.

He had a splinter, the kind that turned nasty and festered, buried in the palm of his hand. Using his teeth, he tried to pull it out, but he couldn't get a hold on it. By night, it was going to be sore.

Out of the corner of his eye, he saw Verena carrying out a big bucket of wet laundry, the dog loping behind her. He turned around, calling out, "Did you get any salve at Veck's store last night?"

"No, but there's some inside—I found a tin under the bed!" she yelled back. Setting down the bucket, she darted for the house before he could tell her he'd get it.

Within the minute, she was heading for him, tin in hand. "Is it a blister?"

"A splinter."

"Which hand?"

"Left."

Taking hold of it, she took a closer look. "That's a bad one—you need a needle before you salve it." She looked up, and the sun caught the gold flecks in her eyes, taking his breath away. And there was no mistaking the naked desire in his face. "Uh—I'll get the needle."

"No." His hand closed around hers. "Rena—"

Behind him, the dog starting barking, then it circled them, whining. As Matt drew Verena into his arms, the animal seemed to go wild, making a furious racket. "Damned beast's jealous," he murmured against her lips. "God, Rena," he whispered, "I can't stand this."

"Neither can I," she said softly, reaching her arms around his neck.

As her body pressed against his, he heard the shot. The bullet hit a branch, knocking off leaves inches above his head. Pulling away, he gave her a push, yelling, "Get down behind the wood!"

As she scrambled for cover, the second bullet kicked up dirt next to the dog, barely missing the animal. Across the yard, the Henry lay on the ground beside the axe. Drawing the Colt, Matt crouched low, trying to catch sight of the gunman. All he could see was the small hill some seventy to eighty yards away. Too far to make the shot with the revolver.

The sun flashed off metal as the third bullet buzzed past Matt's ear. As Matt made a run for his rifle, the dog took off for the hill. Behind them, Verena raced for the house.

Diving to the ground, Matt rolled through the wood chips, grabbed the Henry, and came up shooting. The man on the hill raised up to take a shot at the dog just as Verena came out of the house, shotgun in hand.

"No!" she screamed. "He'll kill Laddie!"

The damned dog was in Matt's line of fire, headed for attack, when it yelped, dropped, and rolled. Matt squeezed the trigger, but the gunman had taken cover. Her eyes streaming, Verena racked the shotgun.

"Don't—it's too far!" Matt yelled. "You'll waste the shot!"

But she was running, yelling over her shoulder, "He won't kill me—he thinks I know where it is!"

"Don't be a fool!"

"He killed my dog!"

But Laddie struggled up, snarling again. The dog leaped into the air, then landed amid a lot of cursing and growling. Matt saw a fellow flailing at the animal, using his rifle for a club. The dog yelped again and fell. Nearly up the hill herself, Verena took aim and pulled the trigger. The recoil knocked her backward, and she hit the ground as the gunman's rifle shot went wide. Going after her, Matt got off several shots to distract him. Then the man behind the hill made a fatal mistake. He rose up to take aim, and a bullet from the Henry spun him around. He pitched forward, then tried to crawl for cover. This time, the wounded dog got him.

Matt stood up, and keeping the rifle trained on his assailant, he walked the rest of the way up the hill. "Laddie!" he shouted.

Still snarling and growling, the dog backed off to stand over the blond-haired man. Waving Verena back, Matt moved in for a closer look. It wasn't a sight for the fainthearted. Gib Hannah had taken a measure of buckshot in his face, but it was the bullet in his left shoulder that had gotten him.

As Matt leaned over him, Hannah tried to talk over the blood foaming from his mouth. "Cheated," he gasped. "He took . . . my share . . . of . . . the . . . gold. Got him . . . for it."

"What about the others?"

"Got . . . them. All . . . except—"

"Pierce and Jackson?"

"Fools . . . escaped . . . and Mac—"

Hannah's hand brushed at his mouth, trying to clear the foam away, then he coughed spasmodically, and his eyes rolled. He fell back, staring blankly into the sun.

Matt stepped back as Verena came up. "Don't look—it's not pretty." Turning around, he enveloped her in his arms, savoring the very feel of her. "He's done, so I guess it's over. I guess that's all of them." As his hands rubbed the ridges of her spine, he said, "That was a fool thing to do, Rena—I thought you'd be dead before I could get the shot off."

"I didn't think he'd kill me, not until he got the gold. I thought I'd be the only one he wouldn't shoot. And when I saw him hit Laddie—"

The dog edged its way to Verena, where it lay its bloody head on her shoe. Afraid to look down, she held on to Matt. "He's going to die, isn't he? I couldn't save him."

Loosening his hold on her, he stepped back, then

knelt beside the animal. "Well, he's peppered with buckshot," he murmured, feeling over it. "And there's a piece of his ear blown off, but I don't find any big holes in him." Rubbing along the dog's bony nose, he comforted it. "Come on, big boy," he said softly, "let's go home." Looking up at Verena, he added, "If you can get both guns, I'll carry him in." Lifting Laddie, he muttered, "If I'd known how this was going to play out, I'd have found a smaller cur, I can tell you that. Half-starved, he must weigh seventy or eighty pounds."

About halfway down the hill, Laddie apparently decided he'd had enough. Wriggling free, he jumped from Matt's aching arms and trotted the rest of the way on his own power.

"I'd say he's going to live," Verena murmured.

"Looks like it, anyway."

"Well, I don't guess we'll have to worry anymore about the gold now," she said, sighing. "I guess it's just gone forever."

"Would you be real disappointed if you never found it?"

She looked up, taking in his tousled black hair, dark eyes, and the strong, manly set of his shoulders. And she knew now that it was over, it was only a matter of time until he left her. "No," she managed, "it's already brought about far too much misery. And I never thought my happiness lay in gold or money, anyway. If I'd found it, I was going to use it to engage the best lawyer money could get me, just in case you decided to go back to stand trial. But I was still hoping against hope you wouldn't."

"I want clear title to my own name, Rena. I don't

want to live in Matthew McCready's shadow the rest of my life."

"I don't understand."

"When I give it away, I want it to be the right one. I want it to be Morgan."

"Morgan," she repeated.

"Yeah. Matthew James Morgan. But for what it's worth, that's the biggest lie I told you. Everything else was more or less the truth."

"Everything about being from Tennessee?"

"Yeah. So," he said, smiling, "how would you feel about spending another night at the Menger?" Before she could answer, he added, "I figured on cleaning up the dog and taking a good soaking bath myself. Then I was going to head back to San Antone."

She felt numb all over. "I see."

"I've got business there—and you do, too." Seeing that she just stood there, he reminded her gently, "This is why you came down here, wasn't it? You said you needed to know why he left, didn't you?"

"Yes, but—but what about you?"

"I need a few answers myself. And while I'm there, I aim to play some high-stakes poker. Right now, I feel pretty damned lucky. So, what do you say?"

"I don't know what to say."

"I'll buy you the biggest steak in San Antone," he promised her. "And I'm damned sure going to get another bottle of that wine. We'll get us the nicest room in the place. And if I'm lucky, we'll have one helluva celebration."

As she looked into the warm depths of his dark eyes, he was smiling at her with a boyish eagerness, and suddenly nothing else mattered. While her mother had warned her about dangerous men, she'd also always said half a loaf was better than none. He might leave her day after tomorrow, or the week after that, but until it happened, she was going to love him with heart, body, and soul.

A slow smile curved her mouth and warmed her own eyes. "I don't have much to pack, Matt. I can clean up, fix enough food to hold the dog for a few days, and put out a bucket of water. And I can be ready within the hour."

With Matthew Morgan at her side, Verena waited nervously while the bank teller disappeared behind the thick-paned glass door. It seemed an eternity before he came out, announcing, "Mr. Pointer will see you now."

The room was darker than the rest of the bank, probably because of the dark oak paneling on the wall, and the smell of oily polish permeated the air. A big man rose from behind the large desk to extend his hand.

"Miss Howard, is it?"

"Yes." Half turning to Matthew, she smiled. "And this is my friend, Mr. Morgan."

"Morgan." Gesturing to two heavy oak chairs, the banker said, "Go ahead—sit down." Retaking his own seat, he cleared his throat. "Your note said John Howard is dead," he began, going straight to business.

"Yes." Reaching into her purse, she drew out Mr. Hamer's letter. "I was informed by this," she said, handing it across the desk. "He was my father's lawyer."

"Poor Hamer," he murmured, shaking his head. "I knew him fairly well. It was a bad end to a good man."

"I never met him," she admitted. "I guess he didn't feel the need to notify you directly."

"I doubt he knew anything about the business. When your father put this into the bank's safekeeping, he asked for—and got, mind you—absolute privacy in the matter." As he spoke, he reached into a lower desk drawer and took out a large brown envelope. "As you can see, it is still sealed, just as he entrusted it to us. I just retrieved it from the vault when I received your note this morning."

"Thank you." Her hand shook as she took it from him. "I don't suppose he told you what's in this, did he?"

"No. Family papers, I believe he said—nothing more." Moving a few envelopes on his desk, he produced a piece of paper. "I do need a receipt, however, if you intend to take them with you."

"Of course."

"If you wish privacy, I'd be happy to step out for a few moments," he offered.

"No. I—uh—I should like to take them back to my hotel room before I look them over." Taking the pen he held out, she quickly wrote "Verena Mary Howard" on the paper. "Thank you," she managed, pushing it back to him.

"My pleasure. But I daresay we'll see you back here before you leave." Seeing that she rose, he stood also. "You have my complete sympathy, Miss Howard. John was a good man."

Once they were out in the warmth of the sun again, Matt's hand slipped from her elbow to her fingers. "If you don't want me there when you open that, I'll understand."

"No, of course not." Forcing a smile, she looked up at him. "You won't mind a good cry, will you?"

"No." He hesitated for a moment, then decided, "I'd like to stop over at the telegraph office while we're out, if you don't mind. I want to see if my wire's been answered yet."

"I didn't know you'd wired anybody."

"Higgins did—when he brought the prisoners over yesterday. It's probably early, but I'd just like to check on it. If it's bad news, I guess we can cry together."

She waited outside while he went in. When he came out, his expression was sober. "Nothing yet," he said, taking her arm.

On the way back to the Menger, he seemed preoccupied, almost distant. Then at the front door, he stopped abruptly. "I didn't want it like this, Rena—I wanted to do it right."

"What?"

"I don't want to know what's in that envelope. If he's left you fifty thousand dollars in gold, you're set for life, and you don't need me."

"And if it isn't?"

"I don't know yet." His hands slid up her arms to hold her shoulders. "I want you to go on up by yourself. Open that up when you get into the room and read it."

"Where are you going?"

"Down the street a ways."

At a loss, she fought to understand. "Why?"

"I just have to do some thinking, that's all."

"You got the telegram, and it was bad news, wasn't it?" she dared to ask him.

"No. I just think if you're a rich woman, you ought to think about what you want."

"But I know what I want."

"You're thinking like Verena Howard, that spinst schoolteacher from Pennsylvania. You might think dif ferently if you were the wealthy Miss Howard."

"No."

"Listen, I'll be back in a couple of hours, three at the most."

"But—"

"You brought the green dress, didn't you?"

"Yes."

"I want you to wear it tonight." Leaning closer, he brushed her lips lightly, then he stood back. "Trust me," he said.

As he walked away, she couldn't help wondering if he meant to disappear, if he thought she would be all right on her own. Turning around, she looked down at the envelope, dreading what she might find inside. And a sense of foreboding stole over her. She didn't want the money if it was going to cost her Matt McCready. No, Matt Morgan, she corrected herself. Morgan. It was hard to think of his real name, when she'd been calling him McCready ever since she'd met him.

She climbed the carpeted stairs slowly, then let herself into the room they would be sharing. If he came back. He had to come back. She'd promised herself this night with him. Her eyes took in the room that the desk clerk had assured him was the nicest in the house. A bouquet of pink roses was arranged in a large vase on an oak table.

Moving to the small desk, she sat down, staring at the handwriting on the envelope. All it said was "Verena Howard," but she recognized the script. She'd seen those words written just like that before—on the inside of the

Bible her father had given her for her seventh birthday. Back when he at least claimed to have religion.

Taking a deep breath, she slid her fingernail under the seal, then tore the envelope open. The first sheet was a letter. Holding it with trembling hands, she began to read.

My dearest Rena,

This is perhaps the hardest thing I have ever tried to write. How you must have come to hate me by now. For what the knowledge is worth to you, your opinion of me cannot be lower than mine of myself. I won't even attempt to make you understand how a decent man can be corrupted by his own greed.

She started to tear it up, thinking it was perhaps the most maudlin, self-serving letter she'd ever read. But she had it in her hand, so she continued on.

No, I am not asking for forgiveness, Rena. A few words cannot make up for years of neglect, and I don't expect them to do so. But you are all I have left in this world, and as my past sins are now haunting me, telling me I have little hope of continuing in this life, I am entrusting you with everything I am leaving behind.

The farm is yours to keep or sell. Everything else I have is in the care of Pointer at the bank where you received this. I pray you will not judge me too harshly for what I am telling you now, but I feel the need to explain how Devil Greed has brought me to this pass.

In late 1864, while on patrol, I and my men overran and captured a Confederate wagon containing a shipment of gold. Between us it was decided to keep it, and

I was to take care of it after we disappeared. But money corrupts, dear Rena, and with none around to dispute it, I decided to keep the whole to myself by taking it into Mexico and converting it into money. After the war, I came to Texas, where I encountered one of my men, a fellow by the name of McCormick, and I gave him half to keep him quiet. I haven't seen him since.

It was my plan to buy the farm, hide the money, and lay low for years before I spent much of it. But the past is coming back to haunt me, and I realize my days on this earth are numbered now in weeks, not years. I have instructed Pointer, my banker, to put the remaining twenty thousand dollars into railroad stock. You can either keep the stock and let it grow or cash it out. I just thought certificates would be the easiest to hide.

So, dearest Rena, I pray this inheritance will bring you more happiness than I have had out of it. Always your Papa, even in disgrace.

She had twenty thousand dollars in railroad stock. And there were the certificates to prove it. She reread the last line of his letter. He'd had twenty thousand dollars and he'd lived simply on a small farm. He'd had all that money, and he hadn't dared to use it. Well, she'd use it, all right. If McCready—if *Morgan* would let her, she'd spend it to defend him.

Slipping the papers back into the envelope, she hurried back to the bank, where she discussed how to sell the stock. At Mr. Pointer's urging, she decided to think on it until the end of the month. He assured her he was willing to do whatever she wanted, that it was simply a matter of her choice. As she came out of the bank, she kept telling herself she was a rich woman, but snc couldn't say she really felt all that much different

Now she had to find Matt, to tell him it was partly true. It wasn't fifty thousand, but it was still a lot of money. As she walked back across the street, her euphoria evaporated as reality set in. It was stolen money, and she had no right to it, none at all.

"Ma'am!" The desk clerk was waving her over. "Message for Mr. McCready, ma'am."

"Yes, thank you."

It was folded over, but it was on yellow telegraph paper. Whatever it said, it had to be Matt's answer, and he wasn't there to get it. She hesitated a moment, then put it into her purse.

"Where's the nearest gaming establishment?" she asked quickly. "Within walking distance, I mean."

Armed with a list, she set out to look for him. He might not like it, but she wasn't going to wait hours to find out what he'd been waiting for. And she didn't have to go far, either. As a big man in a black suit opened the first door, she could see Matt at a back table.

"No ladies," the fellow insisted.

"I'm not a lady," she told him grimly, "I'm an heiress."

"Huh?"

While he was digesting that, she made her way through choking cigar smoke to where Matthew Morgan sat, piles of chips in front of him. "Are you about done?"

"He can't leave now, lady," one of the players protested. "I'm into him for two hundred dollars."

"Cash me in, George," he told an attendant.

"Now see here—"

"Family emergency," he murmured, taking Verena's elbow. "How bad is it, my dear?"

Seeing the irate looks on the rest of them, she told him solemnly, "It's terrible. It doesn't look like she'll last the night."

"Well, you heard her—it's a deathbed vigil." Stopping just long enough for George to count out more than six hundred dollars, he hurried her outside.

Behind them, she could hear murmurs of discontent, but she didn't care. On the steps, she stopped to hand him the telegram. "This is what I really came for. I—uh—I hope it says what you want it to."

The expression on his face was as sober as she'd ever seen it as he unfolded the paper and read it. She could feel her heart pound painfully against her ribs when he said nothing. All he did was stick it in his pocket, then start walking. Turning her around a corner, he stepped into an alleyway and handed her the money he'd won.

She looked at it, then up at him. "What's that for?"

"You wanted to sell the farm, didn't you?"

"Yes, but—"

"If that's not enough, count it as a down payment."

"What?"

"You got bad news, didn't you? There's no gold."

"No, but—"

"Look, I know you're disappointed, but it makes it a whole lot easier on me. I wanted you to know I love you for more than the chance you're going to get some money. In fact, I'd like to think that it was my place to take care of you."

"You don't even like to farm," she said faintly. Then it sank in. "What did you say?"

"Which part did you miss?" he countered, flashing that broad boyish grin.

Relief washed over her. Whatever it was, it couldn't have been that awful. "I don't know—why don't you just repeat all of it?" she said, returning his smile.

"I don't even know where to start." Sobering somewhat, he slid his hand down her arm, sending a shiver the other way. "I'd wanted to do this with a little more style," he murmured, looking into her gold-flecked eyes. Holding both her hands now, he took a deep breath. "Rena, I never thought I'd ever want to settle down, but I do." As tears welled in her eyes, he nodded. "Verena Mary Howard, do you think you could stand to change your name to Morgan? It's free and clear now—and it's mine."

Her chin quivered, then she broke free to throw herself into his arms. "I thought you'd never ask," she whispered into his chest. "Yes—oh, *yes*!

He stood there, his arms wrapped around her, his cheek resting against her soft hair, thinking he had to be the luckiest man on earth. "My brother Wayne always wanted to raise sheep," he murmured. "What do you think of that?"

"I never met an animal I didn't like." Sniffing back tears, she managed to look up at him. "What on earth was in that telegram, anyway?"

"There's no record of any warrant for my arrest in Louisiana or Mississippi. I don't guess I'm a wanted man, after all."

Heedless of the stares of passersby, she pulled his head to hers and kissed him eagerly. "Oh, yes, you are," she whispered. "And if you don't believe it, I'll show you."

Early spring, 1875

Verena could see the field from her kitchen window, and for a moment she just stood there, watching Matt finish the last furrow. At the end of the row, he raised the plow and started the team of horses toward the barn. Quickly moving away before he caught sight of her, Verena removed her apron and hurried into the bedroom to finish pinning up her hair.

Outside, Matt unhitched the team, turned the horses into the stalls, then pitched fresh hay and filled the feed buckets with oats. Coming in from the barn, he stopped in the yard and looked toward the house.

Life was good, better than he could have ever imagined, Matt decided as his eyes took in the fresh coat of whitewash, the ruffled curtains at the windows. He hesitated, then decided to wash up at the pump. No need to track his dirt into the house, not when she kept it spotless inside.

She'd made a real home out of the old farmhouse, giving it all those touches that showed a woman's love, filling it with quilts, china, and a host of other pretty things. As soon as he got the corn in and finished the garden, he was going to start building that other room she wanted. A bright, sunny sewing room on the south side of the house.

Before long, he'd be having to hire help to manage the burgeoning flock of sheep. Nearly a hundred head now, at least double that next year. The way Laddie guarded them with an almost lupine ferocity, only two lambs had been lost to predators during the winter.

Yeah, life was good, all right. So much so that he seldom even spared a thought to the fancy New Orleans salons, or to those Mississippi riverboats. Oh, he still gambled some, sitting down to a game every now and then in San Angelo or over at the Fort, but it wasn't his ruling passion anymore. Verena was. After more than eight months of marriage, he could still say she was the best thing to have ever happened to him. After eight months of marriage, she could still make his pulse race with one tantalizing smile.

She'd left him a clean towel and a chunk of homemade soap by the pump, he noticed as he stripped down to his pants. Working the iron handle, he got a good stream going, then stuck his head under the spigot, sudsing the sweat from his hair. Invigorated by the cold water, he soaped his torso, then rinsed the whole. Throwing the towel around his shoulders, he picked up his boots and his dirty clothes and headed for the back porch. Reaching inside the door, he found the clean shirt and put it on.

The inviting aroma of fried chicken wafted through the air, making his mouth water, No, life wasn't any better than this. But as he looked through the open doorway, his mouth went dry, and he forgot all about any food. The very beauty of the woman elicited the now familiar ache within him.

She was bending over the table, lighting candles instead of the kerosene lamp. And when she looked up, her green-and-gold eyes warm, his breath caught beneath his breastbone. Her chestnut hair was knotted at the nape of her slender neck, and her pale shoulders were like ivory above the low-cut neck of her green dress. She walked slowly toward him, the taffeta skirt rustling seductively. She held out a fragile glass.

"It's elderberry wine," she said softly.

His mind raced with his pulse. "It's a special occasion," he decided.

"Yes."

"It's not your birthday—I know that much."

"No."

"It's too late for Valentine's Day."

"Yes."

He gulped the wine and set the glass aside. She was so close he could smell the clean scent of the lavender toilet water she wore. Her flecked eyes were warm as she reached up to twine her arms around his neck. "You can keep guessing, if you want," she murmured, pressing her body into his.

"Do I get a hint?"

"It looks like a cold day in hell," she said, her voice husky. "And—" she added mysteriously.

"Huh?"

"Well, for one thing, you plowed the field."

Sliding his arms around her, he nuzzled her soft hair. "And the other?"

"I don't really need a sewing room," she whispered. Her tongue darted along the sensitive part of his ear, tickling, as her warm breath sent a shiver down his spine. "Do you want to guess why?"

"Maybe later," he murmured, taking the pins from her hair, loosening the cascade of chestnut silk down her back. "Right now, I've got something else on my mind." Turning her around, he slid his hands under her arms, pulling her back against him as he loosened the hooks on her bodice. "No corset—I like that," he whispered, finding her breasts. As his thumbs rubbed over her tautening nipples, he could feel the tremor within her, the sharp intake of her breath. "You're the best thing that ever happened to me, Rena."

"Am I?"

"Absolutely."

"Last week you said you never wanted anything to change."

"I've got everything I'll ever want right here."

She leaned back, savoring what he was doing to her. "Do you think the room can be ready by August?"

"Maybe. But you just said you didn't want it."

Turning around within the circle of his embrace, she looked up through unshed tears, and her smile twisted. "It's not for me, Matt. Something's going to change."

He stood stock-still as it sank in, and then his arms tightened protectively around her, and he smoothed her hair with his hand. There were no adequate words to express the tenderness he felt for her. "You know,

Rena, if I live to be a hundred, I'll never be any happier than I am right now," he managed finally.

"Until August, anyway," she whispered. "But right now, we have the whole house to ourselves," she added softly.

COMING IN OCTOBER

For one moment Parsifal *was* astonished—and elated that she had guessed he was the Cavalier. But she had obviously dismissed the notion as soon as it had come upon her. Of course she could not think it, and she had felt silly even entertaining the idea.

"You needn't have felt *silly* thinking it, Miss Smith," he could not help saying, and smiled wryly.

She looked at him, startled, then remorse showed clearly in her eyes. "Oh, I didn't mean—I am so sorry! After you have been so kind to me and to my mother! No, I am sure you would be brave, should the occasion arise. And certainly you are strong—that is to say, it *looked* as if you would be, the way your mus— Oh, heavens!" Her face turned pink, and Parsifal knew she was thinking of the way he looked without his shirt. He felt heat creep into his face as well, knowing that he had embarrassed her.

But she looked unhappy, and he was certain it was because she felt she had hurt him. She was a kind and dutiful young lady, and of course it would distress her if she thought his feelings had been hurt. He put on a smile and shook his head.

"Never mind, Miss Smith. I know I am not at all dashing. And let us forget you saw me working in the garden, and pretend it was only a rough farmer you saw in passing."

She cast an apologetic and grateful glance at him. "Thank you, Mr. Wentworth, you are very kind." She impulsively took his hand and pressed it. "And a good friend. I would be pleased if you would call me Annabella if . . . if you do not mind."

He was certain she offered this familiarity to him to make up for her faux pas, and his hurt pride made him inclined to refuse it. But he knew she would be just as hurt at his refusal and he could not bear that. He smiled and brought her hand to his lips. "I am honored—Miss Annabella," he said. "You may call me by my Christian name as well . . . although I never did care for it much. But it will sound better to me when *you* say it."

She looked up at him, and he received his reward: her eyes were full of warm gratitude, her soft lips parted in a hesitant smile. She was so close to him that the scent of her perfume—lilacs—came to him and lured him to move closer to her. He stared at her, overwhelmed by the sudden urge to kiss her and hold her close in his arms.

Silence fell between them, and the only sound in the garden was that of the breeze through the trees. She did not move away, but stared at him in return, and her expression changed to an odd, puzzled wonder.

"Ohhh . . . I did not think . . . ," she whispered.

The sound of her voice broke the silence, and broke the trance that had come over him. He released her hand, and tried to gather his thoughts together.

"And—and why did you think it might not be the Duke of Stratton?" he said abruptly.

Annabella looked startled, and a little dazed, as if she had just wakened from a deep sleep.

"What?—oh! Oh, well, he is too tall, though he does bear a very slight resemblance to your family. Then, too, I recognized him easily, for he only wore a mask and domino. His character is wholly different from the Cavalier's, I am certain. While I am sure the Cavalier is a man of honor, he is clearly impetuous, and the Duke of Stratton is not impetuous. Indeed, there is no other man I know with such a spotless reputation for correct behavior as the duke." The tone of her voice became flat at the end, and Parsifal looked at her questioningly.

"Then why did it occur to you that he might be the Cavalier?"

Annabella looked away from him, and her shoulders raised a little, as if resisting some burden laid upon them. "He has asked for my hand in marriage. Perhaps he wished to impress me in some manner—I do not know. But I am sure it is not he; he would never wreck a country dance to be at my side." She smiled briefly. "No, he would never do anything so improper as that."

Marriage. The duke had asked her to marry him. A wave of despair overcame Parsifal—how could he compete with the Duke of Stratton? He swallowed his despair and took in a deep breath.

"My felicitations, Miss Smith." He was glad his voice sounded steady, even congratulatory.

Annabella looked at him, her expression startled.

"Felicita—? Oh, goodness, no, we are not betrothed! Not yet, at any rate. I . . . I could not give him an answer. But my parents expect me to . . . to . . ." She sat down on the stone bench again, her hands coming up to cover her mouth. "What am I to do?" Her hands fell to her lap, and she clutched her skirts tightly in her fists.

"Do you not wish to marry him?" Parsifal said the

words carefully, struggling against the hope that rose in him.

"No— I do not know." She gazed at him, her eyes miserable. "I should, for it is what my parents want—they have told me that I cannot wish for a more virtuous and well-situated man than the duke. I know they are right. But though I have felt a fondness for a few gentlemen in the past, I cannot feel it for the duke! Indeed"—and here she gave a short, despairing laugh, and gazed at him pleadingly—"I think I may have fallen in love with—with someone else, someone of whom they may not approve." She laid a hand on his arm, an imploring gesture. "Do you think my parents are right, and my feelings will change if the duke and I married?"

He wanted to tell her to ignore her parents' advice, to refuse the duke's proposal of marriage. He wanted to tell her that she would be unhappy with the duke, that he would be a monster to her and treat her badly and that she should run from him. But he knew no such thing of the Duke of Stratton, and to tell her to disobey her parents in this case would be dishonorable in the extreme. Indeed, if the Duke of Stratton loved her as much as he, Parsifal, did, then it'd be best if she married the duke, for the duke could give her so much more than himself, the second son of an earl. No, surely no one could love Annabella as much—it was an impossibility, for he hurt with it, thinking of her possible marriage to someone else.

It was no use thinking of it. Even if he advised her to refuse the duke, she had still fallen in love with another man. She would choose between the duke and that other man; if she considered him, Parsifal, at all, it would certainly be as her last choice.

"I am afraid I do not know if your feelings will change," he replied honestly. "I only know that my love—that is, were I deeply in love with someone—would not change." He paused, firmly tamping down the sadness that came to him as he said these words. "That is all anyone can say of emotions—what they, themselves, would feel. It is very difficult to say what course another person's love will take." He took her hand in his, and rubbed the palm of her hand with his thumb, wanting to comfort her, and allowing himself some comfort in the sensation of the warmth of her hand in his.

"But perhaps because the duke is a virtuous man, I should come to love him eventually?" She did not take her hand from his, but leaned closer to him instead. She seemed not to mind that he sat close to her, and he was glad. He had that, at least.

Parsifal gave her a wry smile. "Virtue does not necessarily attract love, I am afraid. My brother is not virtuous at all, but it does not stop ladies from falling in love with him. I suppose a good man might have someone love him . . . someday."

"But what should I do? I have gone about with the duke for a month now, and my feelings have not become any warmer toward him. But I should not refuse yet another gentleman's offer of marriage—my parents have been lenient with me so many times already. They only wish the best for me—and see what has happened to my mother because of my selfishness! How can I refuse?"

"You could not know—"

"If I had agreed to wed one of my suitors, Sir Quentin would not have tried to compromise me or hurt my mother. You cannot deny that."

Parsifal looked at how she pressed her lips together tightly, with a stubborn tilt to her chin, and felt it would be useless to argue the point.

"Has the—the other gentleman not spoken to your parents?"

Annabella looked down at her lap. "I do not think he has thought of me as a prospective wife. I do not know what he thinks of me."

Then he is a fool, thought Parsifal, *and does not deserve you.* He clenched his teeth, wondering who the gentleman might be, and wanting to smash the man's nose if he ever saw him. "He has not tried anything . . . untoward has he?" It was a blunt, awkward question, but he could not help himself.

Annabella's gaze rose to his, her eyes opened wide. "Oh, no! He has always been very gentlemanly, and so kind to me! But I am certain he is always so to everyone, and there is nothing remarkable in his attentions."

Worse and worse. Parsifal almost groaned. The man was gentlemanly and good also, and hardly someone against whom he could advise, much less from whom he could protect Annabella.

"Perhaps he will come to know you better, Miss—Annabella," was all he could say. "Then surely he will come to care for you as you deserve, and will make his affection known."

"Do you truly think so . . . Parsifal?"

Her voice was sweet and gentle, her blue eyes wide

and beautiful. His mouth felt dry, and he swallowed. He did not know how it could be, but the sound of his name on her lips did not grate on his ear as it did when he heard it from everyone else. He wanted to seize her, *now,* and kiss her lips to see if they tasted as sweet as they looked.

He could not. She was a guest in his house, and she was alone with him, and his duty was to protect her from Sir Quentin, not use her for his own pleasure, especially since she was as good as betrothed to the Duke of Stratton.

"Of course he would," Parsifal said, his voice abrupt and harsh, even to his own ears. He rose from the bench. "Any man would. He'd be a fool, else." He almost stepped away from her, wanting desperately to be away from Annabella and the despairing thoughts that came to him now that he knew about the duke's proposal of marriage, and her parents' plans for her. But he remembered that she wanted to see the gardens, and that his true duty in being with her was to protect her. He turned and held out his hand to her. "Would you like to see the rest of the gardens?"

She looked at him gravely for a moment, in silence. Then she smiled a smile of warm sweetness, and took his hand.

"Yes," she said. "I would like that very much."

Annabella sat at the window seat of her room, looking out at the walled gardens beyond the stables. She could not see over the top of the walls from where she was, for the gardens were upon a little rise and their walls were too high, even from her vantage point. She wondered if Parsifal was in one of them, working. She clutched at the skirts of her dress, wrinkling them badly, but she did not care. Wrinkles were trivial things compared to her confused and troubled feelings.

It had come upon her gradually, then burst upon her like the sun coming from behind the clouds on a rainy day. She had known it there in the garden with Mr. Parsifal Wentworth, as she looked into his hazel eyes that held such warmth and kindness, as he held her hands with such strength and comfort in his own.

She had fallen quite deeply in love with him.

It was clear, now, when it had all started. She had formed a liking for him at the Bowerlands' card party, for he was comely in his somewhat shabby and weather-worn way, and he had smiled at her with a sweetness she had never seen in a man before. Then he had squeezed her hand slightly when they entered the drawing room again, as if aware of her reluctance to encounter company again, and her heart had warmed to him for his understanding. But his kindness and generosity the night of her mother's attack had strengthened her feelings, for he had been a solid, comforting presence, and the thought had come to her more than once that she would have liked to have laid her head upon his chest and felt his arms around her—just for the comfort she would feel when she was so frightened, she had thought at the time, and had dismissed the images from her mind.

But the aura of solidity and subtle strength that came from him kept luring her to think of him, time and time again. He was never vain or arrogant, as many of the men in London were. Indeed, he was overly modest, never putting himself forward in an attempt to be seen at an advantage. It was why she had thought the growing warmth she had been feeling for him was a sisterly one, the warmth of a friend for a friend.

But then she had seen him without his shirt on . . . and while she had not been as shocked as she should be—she was honest enough about that at least—she found she could not think of Parsifal in a brotherly way at all after that.

And then he had offered the exchange of his Christian name in return for hers, and had said it as if it had been a vow from his heart. She had looked into his eyes, and had seen a deep hunger in him, as if he desired her and wanted to kiss her . . . and it had not frightened her, as it had when she had seen this from other men. Indeed, when he had held her hand in the garden, gently stroking her hand to give her comfort, she *had* felt comforted . . . and oddly breathless. She had wanted him to kiss her quite desperately, and she blushed to think of it, even now.

WE NEED YOUR HELP

To continue to bring you quality romance
that meets your personal expectations,
we at TOPAZ books want to hear from you.
Help us by filling out this questionnaire, and in exchange
we will give you a **free gift** as a token of our gratitude.

- Is this the first TOPAZ book you've purchased? (circle one)

  YES NO

  The title and author of this book is: ______________________

- If this was not the first TOPAZ book you've purchased, how many have you bought in the past year?

  a: 0 - 5 b 6 - 10 c: more than 10 d: more than 20

- How many romances in total did you buy in the past year?

  a: 0 - 5 b: 6 - 10 c: more than 10 d: more than 20 ____

- How would you rate your overall satisfaction with this book?

  a: Excellent b: Good c: Fair d: Poor

- What was the main reason you bought this book?

  a: It is a TOPAZ novel, and I know that TOPAZ stands for quality romance fiction
  b: I liked the cover
  c: The story-line intrigued me
  d: I love this author
  e: I really liked the setting
  f: I love the cover models
  g: Other: ______________________

- Where did you buy this TOPAZ novel?

  a: Bookstore b: Airport c: Warehouse Club
  d: Department Store e: Supermarket f: Drugstore
  g: Other: ______________________

- Did you pay the full cover price for this TOPAZ novel? (circle one)

  YES NO
  If you did not, what price did you pay? ______________________

- Who are your favorite TOPAZ authors? (Please list)

- How did you first hear about TOPAZ books?

  a: I saw the books in a bookstore
  b: I saw the TOPAZ Man on TV or at a signing
  c: A friend told me about TOPAZ
  d: I saw an advertisement in______________________magazine
  e: Other: ______________________

- What type of romance do you generally prefer?

  a: Historical b: Contemporary
  c: Romantic Suspense d: Paranormal (time travel, futuristic, vampires, ghosts, warlocks, etc.)
  d: Regency e: Other: ______________________

- What historical settings do you prefer?

  a: England b: Regency England c: Scotland
  e: Ireland f: America g: Western Americana
  h: American Indian i: Other: ______________________

- What type of story do you prefer?
  - a: Very sexy
  - b: Sweet, less explicit
  - c: Light and humorous
  - d: More emotionally intense
  - e: Dealing with darker issues
  - f: Other

- What kind of covers do you prefer?
  - a: Illustrating both hero and heroine
  - b: Hero alone
  - c: No people (art only)
  - d: Other____________

- What other genres do you like to read (circle all that apply)
  - Mystery
  - Medical Thrillers
  - Science Fiction
  - Suspense
  - Fantasy
  - Self-help
  - Classics
  - General Fiction
  - Legal Thrillers
  - Historical Fiction

- Who is your favorite author, and why?____________________________

  ____

- What magazines do you like to read? (circle all that apply)
  - a: *People*
  - b: *Time/Newsweek*
  - c: *Entertainment Weekly*
  - d: *Romantic Times*
  - e: *Star*
  - f: *National Enquirer*
  - g: *Cosmopolitan*
  - h: *Woman's Day*
  - i: *Ladies' Home Journal*
  - j: *Redbook*
  - k: Other:____________________________

- In which region of the United States do you reside?
  - a: Northeast
  - b: Midatlantic
  - c: South
  - d: Midwest
  - e: Mountain
  - f: Southwest
  - g: Pacific Coast

- What is your age group/sex? a: Female b: Male
  - a: under 18
  - b: 19-25
  - c: 26-30
  - d: 31-35
  - e: 36-40
  - f: 41-45
  - g: 46-50
  - h: 51-55
  - i: 56-60
  - j: Over 60

- What is your marital status?
  - a: Married
  - b: Single
  - c: No longer married

- What is your current level of education?
  - a: High school
  - b: College Degree
  - c: Graduate Degree
  - d: Other: ____________

- Do you receive the TOPAZ *Romantic Liaisons* newsletter, a quarterly newsletter with the latest information on Topaz books and authors?

  YES NO

  If not, would you like to? YES NO

Fill in the address where you would like your free gift to be sent:

Name:____________________________

Address: ____________________________

City:____________________Zip Code: __________

You should receive your free gift in 6 to 8 weeks.
Please send the completed survey to:

Penguin USA•Mass Market
Dept. TS
375 Hudson St.
New York, NY 10014